D1585570

THE
WAYWARD
GIRLS

Amanda Mason was born and brought up in Whitby, North Yorkshire. She studied Theatre at Dartington College of Arts, where she began writing by devising and directing plays. After a few years earning a very irregular living in lots of odd jobs, and performing in a comedy street magic act, she became a teacher, and has worked in the UK, Italy, Spain and Germany. She now lives in North Yorkshire and has given up teaching for writing.

Her short stories have been published in several anthologies, including collections from *Parthian Books*, *Unthank Books* and *The Fiction Desk*. *The Wayward Girls* is her debut novel.

THE
WAYWARD
GIRLS

AMANDA MASON

ZAFFRE

First published in Great Britain in 2019
This edition published in 2021 by
ZAFFRE
An imprint of Bonnier Books UK
80–81 Wimpole St, London W1G 9RE
Owned by Bonnier Books
Sveavägen 56, Stockholm, Sweden

Copyright © Amanda Mason, 2019

All rights reserved.
No part of this publication may be reproduced,
stored or transmitted in any form or by any means, electronic,
mechanical, photocopying or otherwise, without the
prior written permission of the publisher.

The right of Amanda Mason to be identified as Author of this
work has been asserted by her in accordance with the
Copyright, Designs and Patents Act, 1988.

This is a work of fiction. Names, places, events and
incidents are either the products of the author's
imagination or used fictitiously. Any resemblance to
actual persons, living or dead, or actual
events is purely coincidental.

A CIP catalogue record for this book is
available from the British Library.

Paperback ISBN: 978–1–78576–706–7

Also available as an ebook and an audiobook

1 3 5 7 9 10 8 6 4 2

Typeset by Palimpsest Book Production Ltd, Falkirk, Stirlingshire
Printed and bound in Great Britain by Clays Ltd, Elcograf S.p.A.

Zaffre is an imprint of Bonnier Books UK
www.bonnierbooks.co.uk

For Jim Mayer
07.10.46 – 16.08.16

1976

'Stand still.' Bee tugged at Loo's petticoat, trying to straighten it.

'I don't like it,' said Loo. The cotton was soft and cool but it smelt funny, as if it had been left out in the rain. It made her skin crawl.

'Oh, shut up.' Bee stood back, concentrating. Her own petticoat had a frill around the skirt and the top she wore – the camisole – had lace edging at the neck; she looked different, not pretty exactly, but more grown-up. She stood with her hands on her hips, her head tilted to one side, scowling, her long dark hair flopping into her eyes.

'It's too long.' Loo kicked at the skirt. 'I can't walk in it.'

'Well, we'll pin it up, then,' Bee said, as if her sister was either very small or very stupid. 'God, Loo, it's not – stay here, and don't let Cathy see you.' She opened the door, then turned back, her expression stern. 'Don't move a muscle,' she said, before ducking out of the room and running lightly across the landing, disappearing into their parents' bedroom.

They had found the box in the pantry, shoved out of sight under the shelves, and had brought it up to their room while their mother, Cathy, was busy in the garden with everyone else. The cardboard was speckled with damp and there was bold blue print running along one side: GOLDEN WONDER. It was old, but not as old as the clothes they'd found inside.

1

Cathy wouldn't be pleased. She might even take it away; it wasn't really theirs, after all. She might want the clothes – for that was all the box held, petticoats and nightgowns and camisoles, a lot of them, too much for one person, surely – she might insist they hand them over to their rightful owner, whoever that might be.

Bee was taking ages. Loo ran her hands across the fabric, trying to smooth out the deep creases that criss-crossed the skirt, some of them a faint brown. The fabric was paper-thin and she wondered if it might tear if she pulled it hard enough. What Bee would say if she did.

It was stuffy in their bedroom. She went to the window and, pushing it as far open as she could, she leant out.

They were still there, all the grown-ups and Flor and the baby, sitting on the grass under the apple tree at the far end of the garden, not doing much, any of them; it was too hot.

Simon was sitting next to Issy, and they were talking to each other. Loo wondered what they might be saying. Issy raised her hand to her face to shade her eyes whenever she spoke and Simon leant in close, as if he was whispering secrets in her ear.

Odd words drifted up to the open window, but nothing that made much sense. Issy laughed once or twice and Loo suddenly wished they would look up, one of them, see her, smile. She leant further out, bracing her hands on the window ledge, on the warm, blistered paint, letting the sun bake her arms.

There was a shift in the air as the door swung open. She felt Bee cross the room and stand behind her, looking at the same view, at Simon. She leant in closer. Her breath was stale, her hip nudged Loo, one arm draping around her shoulders and her weight settling on her, skin on skin, edging Loo off balance. It was too much, too hot; besides, they never hugged. Loo tried

2

to pull away and felt an answering pressure across her shoulders as her sister refused to budge, her fingers digging into the soft skin at the top of Loo's arm.

'I told you not to move.' Loo jumped back from the window, startled. Bee was standing by the door, well out of reach, her mother's pin cushion in one hand, needle, thread and scissors in the other. Loo felt dizzy, the room seemed to shimmer briefly, then everything came back into focus, sharp, solid. Bee was giving her a funny look.

'You're bloody useless, you are.' Bee dragged her in front of the mirror again. She grabbed the waistband of the skirt and pinched it, pulling it tight, pinning it into place before she knelt and began to work on the hem. 'You can sew it yourself, though,' she said. 'You needn't think I'm going to do it.' She worked quickly, so quickly Loo was sure the hem would turn out lopsided.

'Bee?'

'What?'

'Will Joe come back soon?'

Joe, not Dad. Cathy, not Mum. Loo wasn't sure when they'd started using their parents' proper names, or even whose idea it had been in the first place, but they all did it now, except for Anto, who was too little to say anything.

Bee stopped what she was doing and looked up. She didn't look angry, exactly, but still Loo wished she hadn't said anything. 'Suppose so,' she said, turning her attention back to the hem. She sounded as if she didn't care at all, but it was hard to tell. Bee was such a bloody liar, that's what Joe used to say whenever he caught her out. He thought it was funny, most of the time, and Loo had often wondered if she did it for that exact reason, to make him laugh.

'Bee—'

3

'Shut up, Loo.'

There was no point in asking anything else.

'There,' Bee said as she got to her feet. 'That's better.'

Bee's outfit didn't need altering. Her skirt didn't sag down onto the floor, and the camisole she wore was a little bit too tight, if anything. As if the girl they once belonged to fitted between the two of them, between Bee and Loo.

She should say something, about the window, about the . . .

'It looks stupid with this.' Loo plucked at her T-shirt, which had once been bright blue, and she could see that Bee was torn. 'I don't mind,' she said, 'you can have it all.'

And she didn't mind – the clothes in the box, she didn't like them. She tugged at the skirt again. It felt – wrong.

'Well, that won't work, will it?' said Bee. 'We have to match.' She rifled through the clothes on her bed, pulling out a little vest, greyish white and studded with tiny bone buttons. 'Here. Try this.'

Loo didn't move.

'Bloody hell, Loo. You're not shy, are you?' Bee chucked the vest at her. 'I won't look,' she said, turning back to her bed and making a show of sorting through the remaining clothes.

Loo turned her back on her sister and the mirror too, peeling off the T-shirt and letting it fall to the floor, shaking out the camisole and pulling it over her head as quickly as she could, her skin puckering despite the heat as the musty cloth settled into place.

It was too big. She didn't need to look in the mirror to see that, but she looked anyway. It was almost comical, the way the top sort of slithered off her shoulder, as if she had begun to shrink, leaving the clothes behind. She might have laughed, if it hadn't felt so . . .

Bee grabbed her and swung her round. 'We'll have to fix this too,' she said, pulling the camisole back into place and digging the pins through the double layers of cotton.

'Ow.' Loo flinched as Bee scraped a pin across her collar bone.

'Oh, give over. I didn't hurt you.' Bee swung her around again and began to gather the fabric at Loo's back. 'Now, stay still.'

Loo did as she was told. It was always easier to do as she'd been told, in the end. Anyway, the sooner Bee finished, the sooner she could have her own clothes back.

'Right.' Bee stood back. 'That should do.'

Loo looked in the mirror, straightening the camisole, trying to get used to herself. Bee stood next to her, admiring the effect, how alike they looked now. She posed with one hand on her hip. 'Say thank you, Lucia,' she said. She'd been in a funny mood ever since they'd found the box: loud, giddy, frantic.

Loo didn't say anything; she went back to the window.

The scene in the garden had changed. Michael was helping Cathy to her feet, and Flor was jigging around next to her, Simon and Issy were drifting towards the house. No one seemed to be missing them, the girls, at all. They were saying their goodbyes, getting ready to go. One day, soon, Michael and Simon would be gone for good. And then perhaps Joe would come back.

Loo placed her hands on the window ledge again and leant as far forward as she dared. As she watched everyone, it seemed to her that she could feel something underneath the paint, inside the wood, a sort of humming, and the more she concentrated on that, the clearer it became. Just like it had before. There was something scratching, something trying – she thought – to get in. Then she felt it, a sharp pinch, sharp enough to make her catch her breath.

She stretched out her arm, but all she could see was a little

5

brown smudge. She licked her thumb, and rubbed at it, then watched as more marks appeared, not much more than shadows at first. They darkened, blooming under her skin, resolving gradually into a series of purplish bruises, each one the size of a thumb print.

1

Now

The haunting began quietly once the Corvino family had settled into their new home; the girls heard it first, the knocking inside the walls.

A Haunting at Iron Sike Farm by Simon Leigh

'There.' Nina spots it first. 'That's it.'

The solitary redbrick house is set back from the grass verge. There's an overgrown path between two patches of lawn and the front door, a dull dark blue, is secured with a heavy padlock.

'Are you sure?' says Lewis. 'Shouldn't it be further along?'

'Of course I'm sure,' she says. 'And it's exactly where it should be.'

Hal parks high up on the grass verge in front of the gate and underneath the rusting metal sign; the name of the house has almost been lost, reduced to a faint tangle of letters, barely discernible, but this is the place all right. Nina is first out of the car. 'Can you make a start?' she says, before striding up the path and disappearing round the back of the building.

'Sure,' says Lewis.

They get everything stacked on the front step, Hal's cameras in their scuffed black holdalls, the boxes of AnSoc stuff on loan from the university, sleeping bags and rucksacks, laptops, spare

7

bulbs, cables, fuses, carrier bags stuffed with food. When they're done there's still no sign of Nina.

'Do you want to go and look for her, or shall I?' says Hal.

'You can if you like,' says Lewis, who is not inclined to go wandering around the overgrown garden. He's heard that there are snakes in this part of the world, adders, and besides, he'd rather keep an eye on their stuff; he doesn't know Hal all that well.

'Fine.'

She's standing in the back garden, underneath a tree, gazing up at the house.

'Nina, have you got the keys?'

'Sorry,' she says, rummaging in her bag, a large leather satchel crammed with notebooks and folders. 'I just wanted to get a sense of it, you know?'

Hal doesn't know. The house, Victorian from the front, but with a large and rickety-looking lean-to kitchen added at the back, looks distinctly unappealing to him: cramped, grubby and sad. 'Yeah,' he says.

'Here.' Nina leads the way to the kitchen door and once she's found the right key – the lock is relatively new, he notices – she lets them in.

'Hang on,' she says and he stands back by the doorway as she steps into the darkened kitchen – most of the windows at the back of the house have been replaced by hardboard – and flicks the light switch. There's a split second where Hal hopes it won't come on. No electricity, no field investigation, he thinks; but it does.

Most of the fixtures and fittings have been ripped out; only a small and greasy electric oven remains. The floor is a patchwork of faded outlines: here a dresser stood, there the fridge, and the walls bear the ghostly shadows of shelves and cupboards long dismantled. In a corner there's a cheap pine table and a couple of chairs and over the sink one of the taps drips steadily.

'Nice,' Hal says.

'Yeah. Sorry. It was a holiday cottage for a while, then it was on the market for two or three years, and the new owner hasn't got around to renovating yet.'

'Someone's going to move in? Actually live here?'

'I suppose so.'

'And they're not, you know . . .'

Worried.

'We didn't really talk about that,' says Nina.

'What did you talk about?'

'Practical stuff, picking up keys and—'

The knocking makes them both jump. It's heavy and insistent. The sound shudders through the house, echoing through the empty rooms.

'The knocking inside the walls,' says Nina in a mock-serious voice, and she sounds as though she might be quoting from a book, probably the book she and Lewis keep going on about.

'Once for yes . . .' Hal says.

'Don't,' Nina says as the knocking continues. 'I shouldn't have – we shouldn't joke about it, you know? It's not – respectful.'

She opens the kitchen door, revealing an uncarpeted hallway that runs through the centre of the house. At the other end the front door rattles on its hinges.

Once for yes. Twice for—

Lewis's voice is muffled, but they can still hear him.

'Let. Me. In.'

Hal follows Nina down the hall. She squats and pulls the letter box open.

9

'Lew? Lewis? I don't have a key for the padlock. Sorry. You'll have to bring the stuff round the back.' She smiles as Lewis swears under his breath. 'We'll be right out,' she says.

'It was a proper farm, then?' says Hal, once they've got everything in and he's standing on the kitchen step looking at the scrubby and neglected garden. Beyond the dry stone wall, fields stretch up to meet the moors, muddy grey and brown, and a little way off there's a solid-looking barn.

'Once upon a time, yes,' says Lewis.

'The original house was pulled down in the late 1800s. This one was built slightly nearer the road,' Nina says.

'We're not sure why, possibly it was an attempt to gentrify the place a bit, put some distance between the house and the barn,' adds Lewis.

It must have cost money, to tear down one perfectly good house and replace it with this. Hal is still staring at the garden, trying to picture what the vanished building might have looked like, when Nina taps his hand lightly.

'Come on,' she says, 'I'll give you the tour.' He follows her inside. 'The kitchen was added in the sixties. There's a room here that's a sort of scullery.' She pulls at a white painted door, set in the corner of the kitchen; it leads into a small dark room with a sink in a far corner. Cheap wooden shelves set on metal brackets run down both walls. 'This might have been the original kitchen,' she says.

'Right,' says Hal.

'But we won't be running any obs there.' She closes the door and squeezes past him. She smells of lemon and something sweet, honeysuckle, perhaps, and he's reminded of the first time they met, her fingers brushing over the back of his hand as she explained why she thought he might be able to help her out with a problem she had. It had been noisy in the bar and she'd had to lean in close, her breath warm on his skin.

She leads the way down the hall, past the staircase, and stops between two doors, one the mirror image of the other and both firmly closed. 'The dining room and the living room,' she says.

'Right. I give in. Which is which?' says Hal.

Nina smiles. 'Here,' she says, opening the door to her left, 'the living room.'

There's actually a sofa. And a chair. There's carpet too, faded green, spotted, thinning and stained in parts. But there are no curtains, and the exposed window looks out over the front garden, the valley, and the inky October sky. The fireplace, not original, but another 1960s improvement, is tiled and coated with dust. The grate is blackened and empty. It's cold.

'But we're going to set up in here,' says Lewis, opening the other door. The dining room is smaller, presumably to accommodate the scullery behind it. There's an empty bookcase pushed up against the wall and a dining table, the kind with leaves that fold down, underneath the window. Several wooden chairs, mismatched and one lacking a seat, are stacked in the corner. The floorboards are bare and the fireplace in this room has been boarded up.

'It's perfect,' says Nina.

Once they've got everything into the dining room – the various monitors for logging temperature changes and carbon monoxide readings, the voice recorders, and the stacks of spare batteries and chargers, and the cables, the metres of cables all this gear seems to need – then they need to think about sleeping arrangements. It's Lewis who's considerate enough to offer Nina the option of a little privacy.

11

'You could always sleep upstairs, you know,' he says. 'Or we could.'

'There's no need,' says Nina. 'Not if we're going to sleep in shifts anyway.'

'You want to work all night?' No one had mentioned this to Hal, not Lewis with his endless forms and questionnaires, not Nina when she'd first approached him in the pub with her open smile, her problem, and her proposition.

'No. Well, we won't be running obs in the rooms,' says Lewis.

'But since we've got the gear, we thought we could leave it all recording overnight,' says Nina. She looks up at Hal, pushing a lock of hair behind her ear. 'That won't be a problem, will it?'

'No,' says Hal, 'not really. But we'll still need to retrieve the SD cards, at some point, import the rushes.'

'How often?'

'Well, it depends on the camera: with two slots, say every five hours or so. But a DSLR will only film up to thirty minutes at a time and then you're looking at changing the cards every ninety minutes, importing the files to the laptop. It's a lot of hassle.'

'But it's possible?'

'Sure.'

'Right, well, sleeping bags in this room then. Yes?' She doesn't really seem to be expecting an answer from either of them. 'You said we could monitor one of the cameras?'

'On my iPad, yes, that's not a problem.'

'OK. Well, if we use that for the girls' room – Lew, is that OK with you?'

'Fine.' Lewis opens one of the AnSoc boxes and starts to make notes on some sort of checklist.

'I'll show you what we need, then,' says Nina.

*

12

They start in the kitchen. Hal works quickly, setting up a small boxy camera facing the blocked-in window and the back door. He considers the dimensions of the room for a moment before selecting a lens and fitting it to the camera body. Nina watches in silence.

'You happy with that?' Hal adjusts the tripod and stands back so she can look at the image in the viewfinder. Nina bends down to look, suddenly self-conscious.

'That's great, thanks.'

'OK. Two cameras upstairs?'

'Yeah, I'll show you.'

Nina leads the way. It's not so bad, Hal thinks, the house. It's smaller, more mundane than he'd been expecting. It's on the chilly side though. Maybe it's just as well they want to work through the night; he can't imagine sleeping here. He can't imagine that at all.

A couple of steps ahead of him Nina stops, her fingers resting lightly on the banister. 'That's it,' she says, 'the girls' room.' The door is closed, the white gloss paint dingy, the brass doorknob tarnished and dull. Hal pauses, not sure if he should give her time to tune in, sense the atmosphere, or whatever it is she needs to do.

She waits a minute or so before stepping up onto the landing, then turns to smile at him. 'Thanks for doing this,' she says.

'It's no problem.'

'Really,' she says, 'it's great.'

Someone has torn up the carpet here; dusty floorboards give under their weight. Hal finds himself wondering about Health and Safety, about dry rot and collapsing beams. The air is stale, still. 'It's just us then?' he says.

'Sorry?'

'From the – from the AnSoc?'

'Oh. Yes. We're just going to focus on the most active area and next time, well, we'll see what we come up with this weekend before we worry about that.'

'Active?'

'Yes. You know, the room where – where stuff happens.'

Anomalous activity, that was one of the phrases she'd used in the bar, downplaying the whole thing really, trying to sound serious, responsible. He'd noticed her around, once or twice, but they'd never spoken before. He was in the final year of his Film and Media Production course, and she and Lewis were in their second year of Psychology. Someone must have recommended him, he supposed. It had seemed like a laugh at the time, and he knew he'd be able to scrounge up some extra gear as well as bringing along his own cameras. 'Right,' he says, 'so, you want something here?'

'Please. And if we could get the bedroom door in frame, that would be brilliant. And then the last camera in the bedroom itself. If that's OK,' she says.

'Sure. Whatever you want.'

Nina moves out of the way as Hal squats and sets to work, pulling a different type of camera from the padded bag and assembling another tripod.

They have all filled in the usual forms prior to this trip, following established AnSoc procedure, questionnaires dealing with personal beliefs and experiences, opinions on the supernatural and anomalous phenomena, the purpose of which is to fix each team member in place on the percipient scale.

Have you experienced paranormal activity?

Have you ever consulted a medium?

Do you believe in the survival of the human soul after death?

14

Both Nina and Lewis have read through the results. Hal's responses were depressingly absolute.

No.

No.

No.

She and Lewis are both inclined to believe, and they are both aware that investigation protocols are there to prevent misinterpretation or, worse, fraud. This visit, their first, is purely to collect baseline information and readings, and she knows she shouldn't be jumping to conclusions, yet something about this part of the house bothers her, and she wonders if Hal feels it too. She could ask, but that would be against the rules.

He assembles the tripod and attaches a small microphone to the top of the Sony, flipping out the viewfinder and making various adjustments to the lens until Nina has the coverage she wants.

'OK,' says Hal, picking up a holdall and heading towards the girls' room. 'In here?'

The room is at the back of the house and there's a single window, boarded up, a remnant of net curtain hanging underneath the window sill. Someone has tried to strip the wallpaper in this room, but only one wall is fully exposed. The others are a palimpsest of half-revealed patterns, a plain blue over a Regency stripe, over a psychedelic swirl, over a pale floral print. There's a wardrobe, with one door missing, and a mattress, with an armful of blankets piled up at one end. It smells, that damp paper and wallpaper paste smell, and it's dark.

Nina flicks on the light switch. 'Shit.'

No bulb.

'Bring one up from downstairs?' Hal says.

'Best not. I don't want to – you know – start messing around

15

with the rooms we're observing. We should work with what we have. You can cope with this? The low light?'

'Sure, I can fix a light on the camera, but if you want to work all night it's something else to keep an eye on.'

'OK. Well, we'll do that. Facing the window again, I think.'

Hal kneels down and starts unpacking his bag. The floorboards are dusty and spotted with candle wax and Nina treads carefully, as if she might disturb someone, something. She stands with her back to the boarded-up window, trying to imagine the room as it once was, the bunk beds against the wall, the dressing table to her left. The sensation she'd had before, as they were walking up the stairs, that faint fluttering anxiety, has turned to something else – anticipation, perhaps.

'So, do you want to tell me what went on here?' Hal says.

'You know I'm not supposed to.'

'Not even a bit of a clue?'

'Not a word, not from me.'

They'd agreed, the three of them, that they'd let Hal experience the house with no preconceptions, that his experience that weekend wouldn't be coloured by any expectations.

'You know,' he'd pointed out, 'both of you know what's supposed to be going on here.'

'But that's the point,' Lewis had said. 'It's brilliant for us, really. We can measure our experiences against yours – you'd be a sort of test case, a control group of one.'

'You'll keep us honest,' said Nina. 'We'll be able to look for similarities in our responses, all three of us, and blind spots too – with you, if you don't know what to expect, there'll be no danger of you, you know, playing along? We'll just have your first reactions to the farm, and to any – incidents.'

It hadn't made much sense to him, not really. But neither had it seemed like a big deal. Only now they're actually here,

16

inside the house, he finds that he'd like to know more after all. 'Go on,' he says. 'Just a hint. Just so I know what to keep an eye on.'

She leans back against the wall, smiling, pretending to consider his argument. 'There was this family,' she says, 'and they were – troubled, I suppose; dysfunctional. There was a whole bunch of kids, and the two oldest girls, Bee and Loo, shared this room.'

Lewis takes his time unpacking. Sound recorders in each room, despite the fact they're using cameras, because he's happier relying on equipment he's familiar with and, besides, it never hurts to double up. He sets up the temperature monitors and carbon monoxide loggers too, and checks over the electromagnetic field meters: all of this gear from the uni's AnSoc, all of it temporarily his responsibility.

Back in the dining room he pauses to take stock, going over his notes. They'd borrowed every bit of gear they could lay their hands on, but what had seemed far too much stuff when crammed into Hal's car now seems barely adequate, and he tries to ignore the creeping sensation that maybe they're not quite so well prepared after all. He's still standing there, lost in thought, when they come down the stairs, the two of them, and he can hear Nina's voice drifting along the hall.

'Not a re-creation,' she's saying, 'there'd be no point in that at all. But because they never came back, they weren't able to reproduce their results. The lead investigator, Michael Warren, he died.'

'Here?'

'God, no,' Nina says. 'No. Back in London, it was a road accident – nothing to do with . . . But what that meant was that everything just stopped.'

Lewis reaches the doorway in a couple of strides. 'Hey,' he says, 'we agreed. No spoilers.'

'Sorry.' Nina leans over the banister, smiling. 'See?' she says to Hal. 'He's on to us.'

They have timetabled their evening. They spend the first hour in the dining room, gathered around the table, leaves extended, working on their laptops, or patrolling the rooms monitoring their readings and making notes. Then they run the first series of percipient observations for an hour with Nina and Lewis in separate rooms, making notes. Nothing happens, at least nothing out of the ordinary. The house settles into itself for the night and the three of them, Nina, Lewis, and Hal, work quietly.

At about nine o'clock they decide to run a second set of observations. Nina is in the bedroom and she chooses to sit opposite the camera underneath the boarded-up window. Lewis is in the kitchen, lit by a single light bulb, and he sits on a wooden chair in the far left-hand corner of the room, where he can see the door and the window. He spends the first thirty minutes doing a crossword in today's paper, occasionally looking up, deep in thought, or possibly listening. Nina reads, going through one of the files she's brought along, her bag propped against the wall beside her.

Hal is left alone in the dining room, and he spends some time looking at the rushes from the kitchen, scanning idly through the static image of the door and window, and the speeded-up motion of himself approaching the camera, of Lewis and Nina as they enter the room to check their monitors. He doesn't think about the house.

He checks his watch. Half an hour exactly.

He knows that for Nina and Lewis their thirty minutes engaged in unrelated activity, simply being present in the room, are over; for the next thirty minutes they must be active, open, concentrating on the space, making notes and observations, recording the subjective impressions which can later be read against the data their monitors and meters have gathered. They explained that to him at the start of the evening.

One participant in the control room, the room with no history of phenomena, and one in the live room, the place that's experienced problems. Those are the rules. The protocols state the observers go in blind, unaware which room they've been given, but obviously, given they both know the history of the farm, that's not been possible here, although Hal has no idea which room is which.

Nina had insisted she go upstairs the second time round.

Hal has come to the conclusion that he definitely doesn't like the house; it may only have been empty for a couple of years but he can't shake the feeling that it has been abandoned for much longer than that. He wonders if that observation is the sort of thing Nina and Lewis are after, if this vague sensation – not unease exactly, but certainly of discomfort – is part of his role as the control observer.

He yawns, he's getting cold, colder, and he resists the temptation to check the time. They'll be done soon and then maybe he can persuade Nina to take a walk down to the pub, somewhere warm and bright and noisy. It's just an old house, he reminds himself, empty and unloved.

He picks up his iPad and taps the icon that allows him to monitor the camera in the upstairs bedroom, the girls' room. Nina is sitting in the far left corner, next to the boarded-up window, very quiet, very still. He can't quite make out what's going on in the opposite corner though; the shadows are darker there, thicker.

It's possible for him to control the camera via this device, he'd explained that to both Nina and Lewis, and they'd decided that this time round they were going to work with static shots. But still, there is definitely something about the shadows in that part of the bedroom that's bothering him.

He taps on the pad, adjusting the image on-screen, zooming in, just a little, not wanting to lose sight of Nina altogether, not wanting to leave her alone.

At first, he thinks he can see a person, someone lying on their side, facing the wall, hunched up, cold perhaps, or sulking. He zooms in closer.

Blankets, that's all. Idiot.

Nina is still in position, unaware that he's been operating the camera, and he indulges himself for a moment, letting her face fill the screen, silent, serene, before trying to move the camera back to its original position. He taps the pad again but nothing happens. His hand cramps and he finds himself struggling, his fingers moving clumsily, cold and unwilling.

He's still looking at Nina's face, puzzled by this sudden loss of control, when it begins.

The sudden pressure in his ears is almost unbearable as the room, the air around him, fills with a buzzing, hissing white noise, enraged and alive, and the light above, a single glass bulb, seems to burn brighter, dazzling him. He's vaguely aware that he's dropped the pad, that he's trying to stand.

It's all too bright. Too close. Too much.

It lasts for hours, minutes, seconds, he can't tell.

The air crackles, and the light fades, gradually, until it's no more than a faint blue spark.

He can't look away.

The spark vanishes and he's alone in the dark.

The silence that follows is broken by a slow, deliberate knocking.

One.

Two.

Three.

It's coming from upstairs.

2

Now

When the phone rings she is dreaming about the farm. She does that sometimes. In her dreams they are all back living there again because they still have the keys and the new owners don't care for the place and never visit. Dream logic.

She understands that they shouldn't be there, that someone is bound to come and find them, and one day they will have to leave all over again, but for now this is a distant possibility. They run through the rooms, Bee and Loo, and they find all their things, furniture, carpets, books, have been miraculously restored. Cathy is there and Joe has come back too. He moves silently through the house, across the first-floor landing, down the stairs and into the kitchen, standing by the sink, blocking out the bright light that streams in through the open window. Everything is exactly as it was, but it's not right, Lucy knows that much; they shouldn't be there.

In her dream she's running along the path in the heavy summer heat. Bee is leading the way, and they have to get round to the front gate before

before

before

She grabs her phone, struggling to unlock the screen. It's 6.03 a.m., and it's her mother, Cathy.

'Lucia?'

'Mum. Yes. What's wrong?' She sits up in bed. The central heating hasn't kicked in yet; she's cold and she's wide awake.

'Where are you?' Her mother sounds irritated, as if Lucy has wandered off without permission.

'I'm at home. Mum, what's wrong? Is something wrong?'

For a moment or two all she can hear is her mother's breathing, slightly laboured. When Cathy replies her voice is too loud and too close. 'I can't find her. She was here a moment ago, and I came straight down and now I can't find her.'

'Who?'

'She should put some shoes on, she'll catch her death.'

'Mum?'

'Bianca?'

'No, Mum, it's me, Lucy.'

'I came down to let her in, but now I can't find her.'

'Down where?'

'The garden. I was looking out of the window—'

'You're outside?'

It's still dark, and it's freezing. It's October, for God's sake.

'I put a coat on.'

'Mum, go back in. Go back into the house, right now.' Lucy gets out of bed and pulls back the curtains. The street below is empty, the pavement streaked with rain.

'Will you come and help me? Lucia?' Her mother's voice is closer now. 'I don't know where she is.'

Lucy rests her head against the window and briefly closes her eyes. She can't cope with this, not now. 'Mum, this is ridiculous. You need to go back inside—'

'She was here and then she was gone.'

'Yes. You said.'

'I tried to call you, but you never answer.'

'You can leave a message. I check my messages every day.'

24

'I don't like those things. I can't—'

'Can we discuss this later?' says Lucy. 'Once you're back inside.'

'Well, there's no point now, is there?'

'Mum?'

A minute ticks past, then another.

'It would be better if you came and helped,' says Cathy, sounding much more like her old self, much more decisive, 'don't you think?'

Lucy can't possibly leave work, not even for a couple of days. 'You know that's not possible,' she says. 'I've got too much on. Just go back to the house, please, and I'll see if I can visit sometime next week. Maybe Sunday. OK?'

'No,' says her mother, 'I can't find her.' She's slightly out of breath. 'But I'm sure she's here. Somewhere.'

'Who? What are you doing?'

'I'll just go – I can . . .' Cathy stops speaking. She seems to have come to a halt. She must have lowered her phone; when she next speaks her voice is distant, muffled, even though she appears to be calling out. 'Wait – just – please wait,' she says. It's as if she's has forgotten Lucy is on the line.

Silence. Then Lucy hears her mother start to walk again.

'Mum?'

'Where are you?' Cathy says. 'What do you want?'

There's a curious muffled sound, followed by a dull thud. Then, nothing.

'Mum. Can you hear me?' Lucy checks her phone. The contact icon is still glowing gently on the dark screen, but there's no response.

'Mum.' She doesn't know what to do. 'Cathy,' she says, flinching as the only response is a loud burst of crackling, a thick buzzing that seems to fill her head.

'Jesus. Mum?'

She's still looking at her phone as somehow the connection is finally broken.

The house is set on a gentle slope with a sea view. It looks for all the world like an expensive hotel, a polite Victorian building, with polite Victorian gardens: the brickwork is neatly pointed and the woodwork is glossy and fresh. In the summer it's charming; today an October mist is obscuring the coast, the line between the land and the sea hazy and ill-defined. Blue Jacket House, Cathy's home. Cathy's care home.

Lucy pulls her suitcase behind her, bumping it up the steps. The entrance hall serves as the reception area and one of the care assistants – Megan? Melissa? – is sitting at a desk and, not for the first time today, Lucy feels uneasy. Maybe she should prepare herself to find Cathy altered in some way, diminished. She tries not to think about what could have happened this morning, about the panicked minutes as she tried to ring the home, to rouse someone, anyone, to go and find her mother. Cathy's fine, she reminds herself as her heart lurches, replaying the final few moments of their conversation. She's fine.

The girl looks up as she walks in, and Lucy could swear that her smile is genuine.

'Mrs Frankland, how lovely to see you.'

Divorced and the only childless child, it has gradually fallen to Lucy to keep an eye on Cathy. And it makes sense, she knows that – the home is only a few hours away from London, and she can visit whenever she's needed. Her mother is still independent and, given the circumstances, is generally in excellent health.

'Where are you? What do you want?'

She thinks that's what Cathy said before she fell, before her phone disconnected.

It's not fair, the thought, the perennial complaint of child-hood, surfaces suddenly, taking her by surprise, but she doesn't pursue it. She straightens her back and smiles at the young woman.

Leaving her case at the front desk, Lucy goes up to her mother's room, the home still reassuringly familiar although it must be two months, three, since her last visit. She taps lightly on the door before she goes in, not really wanting to disturb Cathy, expecting to find the hushed atmosphere of a sickroom.

'There you are,' says the small figure sitting by the window, neatly dressed in black, her fine grey hair cropped close to her skull. 'We thought you'd got lost.' She's playing Scrabble with a young girl dressed in pale blue nurse's scrubs.

'I had to organise things at work.' Lucy crosses the room to kiss her mother's cheek.

'This is my daughter, Lucia,' says Cathy to the girl, who is lifting the card table to one side, neat and competent and discreet, 'and this is . . .'

'Sarah,' says the girl, holding out her hand. 'Nice to meet you.' She finishes tidying the game away and – to Lucy's surprise – she puts Cathy's laptop in its place. It had been a Christmas gift two years ago and, as far as Lucy knows, her mother barely uses it. 'Would you like me to fetch you some tea, Mrs Corvino?'

'Thank you, Sarah,' says Cathy, settling back in her chair and looking at her daughter, inspecting her, 'that would be lovely.'

Cathy pours the tea herself, left-handed. Her right wrist is strapped up, the flesh-tone edge of the support bandages peeping out from underneath her sleeve. They'd thought it was broken at first. They'd suspected concussion.

She adds milk, stirs it, then lifts the cup to her lips, blowing

27

across it gently. Lucy is reminded for some reason of being a little girl, four or five years old; she's in the kitchen, and Cathy is bending over the table and adding a swirl of milk to a bowl of tomato soup.

'How are you feeling?' she asks.

'I'm . . .' For a moment Cathy looks hesitant, as if the right words are eluding her, but then she recovers herself. 'I'm fine.' She glances down at her wrist. 'Everyone made such a fuss,' she says.

It could have been worse, Lucy reminds herself again, much worse. 'You sounded worried on the phone. Before you fell.'

Cathy puts her cup and saucer on the table and looks out of the window. Her room is at the back of the house, giving her a view of the large and well-kept garden. There's a bruise blooming over her right eye and a long scratch running down her cheek towards her chin. There had been a suggestion that she should stay in hospital, under observation, but Cathy had refused. 'Well, I was worried,' she says.

A little over a year ago Cathy had been diagnosed with vascular dementia, but it had been caught relatively early and while there was no cure, no real possibility of halting her inevitable decline, she had still been well enough to choose which home she'd like to move to, and to make a plan for her own care.

'And maybe . . .' Lucy's not sure how to go on. 'A bit confused?'

Moving in with any of her children hadn't been an option; Cathy wasn't a fool. Nor had she wanted to move across the country to be nearer any of them. She'd chosen a care home in the same seaside town she'd lived in for the past twenty years and she'd seemed to settle in perfectly well. She was still staring out of the window; the garden was empty.

'Mum?'

'Not confused, no.'

'You said you saw someone.'

'Yes. I thought I – are you going to stay?' Cathy asks, picking up her tea again.

'I can stay over tonight, if you like,' says Lucy.

'Good.'

Lucy sips her tea and looks around the room. It's different from the last time she was here, busier, more cluttered, and at the foot of the bed there's a canvas bag, stuffed with pads and pencils and broken pastels. It's worn and battered. It used to belong to her father.

'I didn't know you still had that. Have you been drawing? Can I see?'

'A bit. Now and then. It keeps them away from me.'

'Sorry?'

'The trouble with a place like this is they can't stand to see you sitting about. They think you're brooding or, worse, drooling.'

'Oh,' says Lucy.

'Crafting classes,' says Cathy. 'Music appreciation. But if I take that with me every time I want to go outside, they leave me alone.'

'Right. I see.' Lucy is tempted to suggest that her mother might enjoy crafting classes, whatever that might involve, but she thinks better of it. They sit in silence for a while, and through the open window – Cathy is still a believer in the power of fresh air – someone's music drifts in. It's an old song, vaguely familiar, something to do with Romeo and Juliet, one of the songs Dan used to play on his stereo. A few notes circle round and round each other, 'Don't fear the—' The radio is switched off suddenly, a door is slammed shut.

'I had a card from your sister,' says Cathy. Always your sister, your brother, as if it was Lucy's fault these people existed at all.

'Really?'

'She's still with him, you know.' Her husband. 'That . . .' Cathy's mouth hovers around the insult. 'That's why she never comes, you know. He won't let her.'

'It's too far, Mum. You know it is. She'd come if she could.'

'Yes. Well.'

Her sister lives in San Francisco, she's married, and her life is relayed to Lucy by intermittent emails and occasional phone calls. She has the impression this distance suits them both. 'What did she say? In her card.' They haven't spoken for months, and now Lucy thinks about it she suspects she's missed her nephew's birthday. But Cathy doesn't answer. She leans forward, frowning.

'I tried to call you,' she says, 'but you never answer.'

'You could leave a message,' says Lucy. She's checked her phone on the long journey north, and has discovered three missed calls from Cathy in the last week alone; she can't imagine how that's happened. 'Even if it's just to ask me to ring you back.'

'I shouldn't have to ask, Lucia.'

Work. The gallery. It's not much of an excuse, but it's all she has.

'I looked out of the window and there she was, so I went down,' Cathy says, 'but I couldn't find her.'

'Who?'

'I told you – there was a girl, she was outside, all on her own.'

Alone in the dark. Lucy pushes the thought away. 'Maybe it was one of the staff, Mum, one of the auxiliaries.'

Cathy falls back in her chair, irritated. 'The trouble is,' she says, 'that once people know you're . . .' She taps the side of her head in frustration. 'They stop listening.'

'That's not true.'

'Oh, you wait.'

Lucy looks across the lawn. It's empty except for a scattering of orange and brown leaves, and the ornamental fountain, switched off now for the winter. 'Anyway,' she says, 'I'm here now.'

'Yes.' Cathy seems to come to some sort of decision. She leans forward and picks up the laptop. 'Yes . . .' but before she can get any further there's a knock at the door; it's Sarah.

'I'm sorry to interrupt,' she says, 'but Mrs Wyn Jones is free now, Mrs Frankland, if you'd like a word with her. She's waiting at reception.'

'Ah,' says Cathy, her expression a combination of irritation and guilt, 'Jean. You'd better go. And if the pair of you could manage to not discuss me as if I were a naughty child, I'd be very grateful.'

'That's not fair,' says Lucy. 'Jean was very worried about you. So was I.'

'I know, and I'm – I didn't mean to – I saw – I thought I saw someone, but – there was no one there. I got outside and there was no one there. That's all.' Cathy opens the laptop. 'You can go now,' she says. 'Tell her that. Just – tell her I made a mistake.'

'Are you sure?' asks Lucy. 'I mean – is there anything else?'

Cathy looks up, holding her gaze for a long moment. 'No,' she says. 'The rest will keep. Tell her I'm sorry; it won't happen again.'

Jean is waiting for her by the front desk. 'Lucy, I'm so, so sorry, we have no idea how this happened,' she says, pulling her into an embrace as if they are old friends. 'But we're working on finding out what went wrong.'

Cathy had once told Lucy that she'd settled on Blue Jacket House because she liked the atmosphere, very positive, she'd

31

insisted, very healing, and Lucy had often wondered if her mother was making fun of her, or, possibly, of Jean Wyn Jones, the owner and manager. Maybe she had meant it; her mother had been one of nature's huggers too, once upon a time.

'This isn't good enough, you know.' Lucy stands back; she's had the time to think about this on the train, to come up with a strategy, but already she's struggling to maintain some sort of distance. She likes Jean, warm and friendly Jean who runs Blue Jacket House single-handed. The residents like her and Lucy trusts her, too.

Had trusted her.

'Yes, of course, and we're reviewing our procedures.'

'She fell. If she hadn't had her phone—'

'Please.' Jean takes hold of Lucy's hands and squeezes them gently. 'We'll go into the dining room, if you don't mind? It's easier just to show you what we know so far.'

'So. You're aware we have emergency buttons in the rooms here?' says Jean, leading the way through the empty tables, neatly arranged for dinner, and towards the French windows.

'In case anyone is taken ill, yes.'

'Yes. Well, just after five thirty in the morning, your mother pressed her button and when Carol Baxter, who was the supervisor on duty last night, got to her room, she'd gone. At first Carol thought she was in the bathroom, but when she couldn't find her there, she had to search the rest of the house.'

'On her own?'

'No, she had a couple of our auxiliaries with her.'

'I see.'

'At this point she thought that Cathy must be somewhere indoors, and to be honest, she wasn't that concerned. Your mother is in good health, she's mostly lucid, she's not in need of meds. She thought Cathy had got tired of waiting for a response and decided to get whatever it was she needed, for herself.'

'Right.'

'I must stress that we don't think she was outside for very long. She'd put her coat on. She was quite composed, really, quite rational.'

'How did she get outside?'

'Our residents aren't prisoners, Lucy.'

'But they are in your care.'

'Yes.' A fine blush begins to creep over the other woman's face. 'Well, when she looked in here Carol found both these doors open.'

Lucy looks up at the French windows, fitted out she can now see as fire doors, easy enough to open from the inside, no key required.

'The issue for us is why she didn't trip the alarm when she went out and, believe me, we are currently having both the fire and burglar alarms thoroughly checked. I'll also be interviewing everyone later today. Someone clearly made a mistake and that's not acceptable.' Jean looks so severe, Lucy almost feels sorry for the staff. 'Carol found Cathy quickly enough, she was round towards the staff car park at the back, and got an ambulance and paramedics out here straightaway.'

'It was Carol I spoke to?' It had taken forever, waiting for someone to pick up the home's landline.

'Yes. She rang me and I arrived just as the ambulance did. I followed it to the hospital.'

'And now?'

'Cathy's fine. A little tired, perhaps. She cut across the grass instead of sticking to the path, it was dark, the ground is uneven there and fairly steep, she says herself she was rushing. Cuts

33

and bumps and bruises, a sprained wrist. But very much her old self.'

She'd got off lightly and both women knew it.

'Could I speak to Carol?'

'She's on nights,' says Jean. 'She'll be at home, asleep.'

'Oh. Yes.' Lucy hadn't thought of that. 'How has Cathy – Mum – been generally?'

'Fine. I've heard no concerns from staff.'

'It's just that, at one point, she seemed – she called me by my sister's name.'

'Ah.' Jean takes a seat at one of the tables and Lucy sits opposite her. 'Well, your mother does have some memory issues; we've known that for some time. Some occasional confusion is to be expected, especially if she's under any kind of stress.'

'I know. But it was odd. And she seemed quite convinced that there was someone in the garden.'

Jean looks out of the window. 'Yes. Carol told me,' she says. 'There wasn't, by the way. Both sets of gates were closed; there's no way anyone could get in. She's not still worried about that, is she?'

'No. She says not.'

Tell her I made a mistake.

'Well, I think Cathy woke from a very vivid dream and, as you said, she was confused for a while. It does happen, you know. To all of us.'

'Yes,' Lucy says. A fragment of this morning's dream comes back to her: the farm, the house.

Running along the path, before

before

'Yes. I suppose so,' she says.

'I'm so sorry that you had to come up at such short notice. I know you're very busy.'

Now it's Lucy's turn to blush; she sees Cathy three or four times a year, if that. 'No, that's – it's fine. It's good to see her.'

'And I'm sure she's happy to see you.'

'Yes,' Lucy says. She could pursue it, of course, be difficult about the situation, but it was Cathy herself who'd caused all this trouble, all this fuss. And there's no real harm done, after all. Her wrist will heal. 'I'm sorry, Jean. I'll – have a word with her. I'll make sure this doesn't happen again.'

'Thank you,' says Jean, clearly relieved, 'for being so very understanding. And if you could speak to Cathy – well, I'd appreciate that. I'll let you know about the alarm, and if we need to reassess any of our procedures.'

'OK.'

'And if you've any other questions, any concerns at all, you know where to find me.'

'Sure.'

Jean places a hand gently on Lucy's shoulder. 'I know this has been a bit – difficult, but try not to worry,' she says.

I tried to call but you never answer.

'I'll do my best,' Lucy says.

She waits until Jean has left the room before she pulls her phone from her pocket. Dan answers on the first ring.

'Loo?'

'She's all right.'

There's a silence as her brother composes himself. She'd told him not to worry, she'd told them all not to worry, sending each one a version of the same text, promising a phone call, keeping everyone in the loop. She loves her brother; she wishes she saw him more often.

'You're sure?'

'Yeah. She got herself into a bit of a state, that's all. I think she woke up and was – confused, I suppose. She's back from the hospital with her arm strapped up and whatever it was that set her off has been forgotten. She's back to her normal self. More or less.'

'She gave you a fright, though.'

'Yeah, well. There's no harm done.'

'I could still come over,' says Dan. He and his wife have retired to the south of France and his two daughters live and work in Paris. He last visited five, six years ago.

'There's no need,' she says. 'I can manage.'

'Really?'

'Really. I'll stay over tonight, take her out for lunch tomorrow then catch an afternoon train home. I'll try to get back up again next month.'

'And you'll ring me if, if you need me, if you change your mind?'

She tries to ignore the relief she can hear in his voice. 'Yes,' she says.

The rest of the conversation is brief; he asks about her work, about the current exhibition, and promises to get over to the gallery with the girls next summer.

'Well, thanks, Loo, for all of it, for ringing, for being there with her.' He sounds brighter now Lucy has reassured him that Cathy is fine.

'Yeah, well.'

What else did he expect her to do?

'Dan?'

'Yes?'

'Has she rung you recently?'

'Cathy? God, no, not since Julie's birthday. Why?'

'No reason – just something she said.'

Cathy hardly ever rang. Birthdays and Christmas, but that was it.

'Could you do me a favour and let everyone know?' Lucy says. 'That she's OK? I just can't quite face it. You know, telling the same story over and over.'

'Poor old Loo,' he says, and she can feel him smiling. 'No problem, I'll do that for you.'

When she gets back to her mother, Sarah has tidied away the tea things and Cathy is still sitting by the window, her open laptop on her knees. 'Are you and Jean all done?' she asks.

'Pretty much.' Lucy takes the seat opposite her mother. 'I said I'd talk to you.'

'Really? What about?'

'Mum.'

'I'm sorry, Lucia.'

'You need to take care of yourself, you need to – I don't know what you were thinking.'

'It was a mistake,' says Cathy. 'It won't happen again.'

Lucy leans forward and tries to soften her voice. She hasn't had much time to think this through, but if she doesn't try now who knows when she and her mother will next have the chance to speak, face to face? 'Is there anything else, well – bothering you?'

Cathy looks down at the computer screen and begins to type.

'Only – three phone calls, Mum. In a week.'

'I know. I should have left a message.' Her hands moving carefully across the keyboard. 'But I wasn't sure how to tell you. I kept putting it off.'

'About the girl in the garden? But I thought—'

'No. Not her. That was – I told you, I made a mistake.' Cathy looks up. 'Maybe I shouldn't—'

'Shouldn't what?'

But Cathy doesn't answer.

'Come on, Mum. What is it?'

'I'm sorry, Lucia,' says Cathy, 'to bring you all this way. Here.' She lifts the laptop and, not without effort, hands it to Lucy.

She has logged into her email account. There isn't much in the inbox: newsletters from a couple of arts organisations, a bank statement, some emails from Dan, the most recent having arrived a month ago, nothing from any of the others. One from someone called N. L. Marshall, dated the previous Friday, with the subject line Re: Field investigation, is pinned to the top of the list.

'What's this?' Lucy asks, trying to ignore it, the growing sensation she has that something is wrong. The phone call and the fall, they were bad enough, but this is – wrong.

'The top one,' says Cathy, 'read that.'

Dear Mrs Corvino,

I'm writing to let you know that the field trip to Iron Sike Farm I mentioned will be going ahead tonight. I'm so sorry you feel you won't be able to accompany us, but I do look forward to being able to share our findings with you. As you can imagine, the whole team is delighted to have been granted access.

I was wondering if you'd given any further thought to forwarding our correspondence to your children. I would very much like to be able to interview them, particularly Lucia. But perhaps we can discuss on Monday? We are all so looking forward to meeting you – hopefully, we'll have some interesting material to share!

Kind regards

'Who's Nina Marshall?' Lucy asks.

'A researcher.'

'A paranormal researcher?'

'Oh, they call it something else these days, something much more respectable. There's a folder, marked "Farm".'

Lucy clicks on the icon and the history of their correspondence is laid out in front of her. The first email has some photos attached.

'Lucia?'

Lucy flicks through the images – recent colour photographs. 'She's been there,' she says, looking up from the screen.

'Yes.' Her mother's expression is unreadable.

'And she wants you to go back.'

'Yes.'

'Jesus.'

'Lucia.' The rebuke is mild. Automatic after all these years.

Nina Marshall hasn't been inside; all the shots are exteriors featuring peeling paintwork and cracked and grimy windows. The buildings in the pictures are obviously abandoned and the garden, never properly tended in their time, is completely overgrown now. Lucy's head aches, she can't focus. 'You should have said. You should have told me.'

'It's too quick,' Cathy says, 'that's the trouble. You press a button and you can't call it back, you get – caught up. I'm sorry, Lucia.'

'And what's this about a meeting?' Lucy looks down at the screen once more; she can't believe Cathy would get mixed up with these people, whoever they are.

'They want to talk to me,' says Cathy. 'And I want to talk to them.'

THANK YOU FOR USING
NORFOLK LIBRARIES
You can renew items online
by Spydus Mobile Phone App
or by phone at 0344 800 8020
Ask staff about email alerts
before books become overdue

Self Service Receipt for Check In

Title: Let's hope for the best

Item: 30129084953885

Title: The rapture

Item: 30129085823806

Title: Entry Island

Item: 30129085752757

Total Check In: 3
30/09/2021 10:25:30

Norfolk Library and Information Service
Please keep your receipt

3

Then

Loo was always awake before Bee. At first, she used to get up, but no matter how hard she tried to be quiet she'd bump into something, the end of the bed, the chair by the window, and Bee would rise up in a towering fury, yelling and throwing anything to hand, pillows, clothes, even books, at her sister.

So now she'd got into the habit of retrieving one of her own books from under her bed, and reading for an hour or so. It was always light enough, despite the drawn curtains; in the winter she'd have to think again. They had used up half a dozen bulbs in this room the first week they'd moved in, until Cathy decided she'd had enough and told Joe he needed to sort out the wiring upstairs. He hadn't got around to it yet though. They used candles in the evenings, sticking them onto cracked and chipped saucers and placing them on the window ledge and the dressing table, but that would be no good if she wanted to stay in bed and read. Maybe she should buy a torch.

Bee had the top bunk, Loo the bottom. It was just like having a four-poster bed, she'd told Bee – only that wasn't strictly true. She didn't like the way the mattress above her sagged underneath her sister's weight. The way Bee would make the cheap wooden frame shake when she rolled over. The way she was always there, pressing down.

Above her, Bee snored softly, lying on her side, no doubt,

her nose to the wall and her back to the room, protesting, even in her sleep, against the unfairness of having to share. Loo heard her father get up first, then Dan. She closed her book and concentrated for a while on the comforting rumble of their voices in the kitchen until the slamming of the back door indicated they'd both had the sense to get out of the way. Then the house fell silent again and she read a little more.

When they'd first got here, their mother had said they were going to live in tune with nature, but really, if anything, what they lived in tune with was the baby, and another half hour passed before the familiar yowling issued from the big bedroom overlooking the front garden, prompting Bee to swear and roll over, and marking the start of another day.

Despite Loo being the first out of bed, Bee had beaten her to breakfast again.

'There's no bread left,' said Cathy, wrestling the baby, Anto, into a scratched and faded high chair. Florian, the child between Loo and Anto, six years old and only half dressed, was sitting in front of the cold Aga playing with two of his cars while at the table Bee was spreading a generous helping of cherry jam onto a thick piece of toast.

'Florian, leave that be and come and eat your breakfast,' said Cathy.

'Bee's got bread,' said Loo.

'Bianca got out of bed first.'

No she hadn't, she just never bothered to brush her teeth or wash her face.

'What is there, then?'

'Can I have Frosties?' asked Flor.

'No. No more Frosties, Florian, we agreed,' Cathy said. 'There's porridge.'

'Mmm. Porridge. Yum,' said Bee, grinning obscenely, her mouth speckled with gobbets of brown bread and scarlet jam.

'Mum. Tell her.'

'Bianca.'

'Sorry,' said Bee, swinging her chair onto its back legs. Behind her, on top of the gas stove, the oven they actually cooked with, there was a small pan of porridge. From the smell of it, it was starting to catch.

'Florian, come and eat.' Their mother had settled the baby in the chair and was trying to tempt her with a spoonful of something grey and milky.

'I don't want to.' Flor hadn't quite got over not being the youngest any more.

Fetching a bowl from the sink, Loo wondered if a bit of cherry jam would improve her mother's porridge. Since they had moved to the farm all ready-made foods had been banned. As well as no more Frosties there were no more biscuits, no more sweets and no more chocolate. They had all got into the habit of stealing the occasional spoonful of jam or honey from the kitchen, but this had only prompted Cathy to find increasingly devious hiding places for the jars; if you wanted to sweeten your food, you had to ask for permission. Loo took her porridge to the table, but as she sat down, Cathy whisked the jam away.

'Lessons this morning,' she said as she came back in to the kitchen. Bee's chair hit the kitchen floor with a thump.

'I don't feel well,' she said. 'I feel . . . wheezy.' The doctor in Leeds had diagnosed asthma, and two inhalers, one blue and one brown, lay abandoned on the dressing table upstairs.

'You look well enough to me.'

'Dan doesn't have lessons,' said Bee.

'Your brother Dante,' said their mother, insisting as she always

43

did on her children's full names, 'is old enough to leave school. He's excused lessons.'

Actually, Dan was fifteen, and only just fifteen at that.

'It's not fair.'

'Dante has chores.'

'So do we,' said Loo.

'And have you done them? Either of you?'

'We haven't had time,' said Bee, pushing her chair back and standing. 'We'll go and do them now.'

Her mother put Anto's spoon and bowl down again and turned to face her oldest daughter.

'Bianca,' she said.

Bee lifted up her chin. 'Cathy.'

Loo always hated this bit, the bit where it was just Cathy and Bee, each one determined to win. The silence was broken by Anto making a grab for the bowl and knocking it to the floor. Bee waited until Cathy was at the sink wringing out a cloth, her back turned.

'Let's go for a walk, Loo,' she said.

It was warm outside. The farmhouse, unlovely red brick, ugly and awkward, might have been gloomy, but at least it was cool. The thick air wrapped itself round the girls on this, the first properly hot day of the summer. Bee set off towards the field at the back of the house, Loo trailing behind her. She could feel it coming off Bee in waves, not anger exactly, although she was definitely cross, but something more like electricity, something unreliable, dangerous. She thought it might be to do with Cathy and Joe, with raised voices late at night, and the farm and the heat.

'Fuck!' Halfway up Bee turned and looked out over the valley, stopping so abruptly, Loo almost bumped into her.

'What?'

And then just like that, the fire seemed to go out of her and she dropped into a heap on the dry grass.

'It's so dull here. Look at it. So fucking empty.'

Loo winced. Cathy had promised to wash their mouths out with soap if she ever caught them swearing.

'It's not that bad.'

'There's nothing here, Loo. Nothing.' Bee threw herself back on the ground, almost as if she were Anto's age, ready to throw a tantrum. 'I fucking hate it.'

'Bee—'

'Fuck. Fuck. Fuck. Fuck.' Her voice rose up into the air and floated across the valley. Loo sat down beside her sister and tentatively reached for her hand. Usually, Bee discouraged physical contact – 'Get off, don't be such a bloody baby' – but today she clutched so fiercely at her sister's fingers it almost hurt.

'I can't stand it, Loo. I can't breathe.'

Loo sat still for a moment, looking back at the farmhouse and the old barn. Joe's studio. They weren't supposed to bother him, and if they did dare to they were never quite sure how he would react, throwing down his brush to join in a lunatic chasing game, swinging them in turn over his shoulder and spinning them round, provoking both girls into hysterical shrieking, or swearing at them in the sort of language Cathy had banned in the house, telling them to sod off, and worse. Not that either of them cared; Joe's smile and his attention – however fleeting – were always worth the risk. 'Shall we play a game?' Loo said.

The barn had come with the house. It was pretty much empty; the remains of an ancient tractor were covered by a tarpaulin and a few rusting tools – a saw, a scythe, a mallet – lay abandoned in a corner. Someone had knocked the animal stalls apart at one time or another, trying to clear space for some long-forgotten project. There was a hayloft too, although the ladder was unsteady. Joe suspected woodworm, and the kids had already been banned from going up there. In fact, the kids were banned from the barn, full stop. This was his studio.

Joe had cleared himself a decent enough workspace, Cathy had been right about that, at least, and now in the summer with the double doors propped open, there was light enough to work by. They were running low on money though and he'd have to start looking about for some paid work soon, something to tide them over. He had no idea about farming, and he'd never pick up anything in the village; he'd need to see if there was anything going back in Leeds, something temporary, casual.

The farm had been Cathy's idea. She didn't like the city, she'd said the last house was damp, it was unhealthy – why else did he think Bee had got asthma? – and she'd spent months going on at him about the move. She'd got her way in the end, and here they were in their new home. He and Cath and – Christ – five kids.

Joe didn't feel old enough to be a dad, not old enough to be married at all to tell the truth, and yet here they were, still together after sixteen years.

When it came to the kids, Cath had the final say on most things, bedtimes and bathtimes and what they should eat. She managed the house and the money too. So when she'd said let's be done with it all and move to the country and home-school them, well, he'd thought, in the end, why not? Moving might be the answer, it might make it go away, the itch he felt, the restlessness, the sense that time was slipping away from him.

He wasn't so sure now, though. It was all right in the summer, this place, but he couldn't imagine passing the winter here. He'd need to fix up some sort of heating system for one thing, and for another . . .

It was proving hard to focus, to stay focused.

He couldn't say why.

He got up early, most days, and fixed himself his breakfast. Then he made a cup of tea, strong and sweet, and took it across to the barn, rolled a cigarette and sat down in the studio. Just sat, looking at whatever it was he was working on, feeling his way back in. The trouble was, it seemed to take longer every day, and nothing he finished ever seemed – enough.

No kids. I don't want them anywhere near, he'd told Cathy, right at the start, and if I want something I'll come and get it. Just leave me be. And Cathy, her own artistic ambitions fulfilled these days by baking bread and changing nappies, went along with it. So off he went to the barn, the studio, every day and tried, tried to make it all come together.

He had been working for a couple of hours or so when he first noticed it.

A scratching, low down somewhere.

Rats.

He was working on a big canvas, sky, mainly – a dull heavy sky rolling up over the valley – coming along quite nicely, for a change, making him think that he might settle here after all and then . . .

Not scratching.

Tapping.

A tree branch, then. Except of course there were no trees.

Tap tap tap.

Silence.

Then a slithering sound.

He used to listen to music when he worked, not for pleasure, more to shut the world out. But that was back in Leeds and the batteries in the radio had long since packed up. He'd asked Cathy to get some more but she kept forgetting.

Tap tap tap.

Behind him.

Tap tap tap.

To the left now.

He put his brush down, wiped his hands on his jeans.

'Who's there?'

Silence.

Outside, down the hill, a car swept past the farm.

'Cath?'

Tap tap tap to his left.

Tap tap tap to the right.

Silence.

Then a scrabbling sound, something treading on dried earth and pebbles.

Moving around the side of the building towards him.

'Is there anybody there?' said the traveller. 'One knock for yes. Two knocks for no.'

His voice bounced off the walls, swirled around the rafters.

Silence.

Tap. Tap.

No.

Right.

'Is that you, Bee? 'Cos if it is, you should piss off now. Piss right off or I'll come out there and when I catch hold of you, you'll feel the back of my hand.'

Cathy didn't believe in hitting the kids, but that wasn't to say they hadn't all had a passing slap from her now and again.

No answer; just something that might have been a sneeze, or a giggle, or a sigh.

Silence.

The interruption dealt with, Joe picked up his brushes and went back to his painting. But the mood had been broken: the strokes didn't look right now, the colours lay flat against the canvas, clumsy and uncertain.

Eventually, hunger won out and Bee and Loo returned to the farmhouse, a little after one o'clock.

'Cathy?'

The front room was empty, although someone had left the stereo playing, one of Dan's records, doomy stuff that Loo didn't really like.

Bee led the way into the kitchen, which was also empty, but at least there was evidence of domestic activity: the kitchen table was covered with a fine layer of flour and something had been left in the oven. Bee opened the door and peered in.

'It's a pie, I think.'

'Is it done?'

'No.' She slammed the door shut and inspected the two mixing bowls, both cracked, that Cathy had left on the kitchen dresser, covered with grubby tea towels. Loo's stomach growled. She wished she'd stayed and finished her porridge.

'She's making bread,' said Bee, sticking her fingers, not much cleaner than the tea towels, into one of the bowls and pulling out a large clump of pale speckled dough.

'You can't eat that,' said Loo.

'Why not?' Bee shoved the dough into her mouth and began to chew.

'You'll get stomach ache, or something.'

Maybe the dough will rise inside her sister, fill her gut, bubbling and stretching and distending her belly. Maybe Bee will die in agony. Or maybe not; Bee never got ill, apart from her asthma, and Dan reckoned she made that up half the time.

She hardly bothered to carry her inhaler these days, now there was no school to get out of, and anyway their mother's bread never rose that much.

'Bianca! Lucia!' Cathy's voice drifted in from the back garden. 'Are you back? It's time for your lessons.'

Anto was fast asleep in her pushchair and Flor was sitting on the eiderdown Cathy had spread on the ground. It was something they'd found when they moved in, abandoned among a pile of junk in the attic, a satiny smooth fabric, pale gold, torn and stained. Next to Cathy was a broken wicker basket, the handle no use to anyone now, crammed with a selection of books of varying quality and age. As the girls came out of the house Flor wriggled free of his mother, who had been looking at a picture book with him, and picked up a plastic bucket and spade lying in the overgrown grass.

'Can I go now?' he asked and without waiting for an answer he took himself off to the vegetable patch Dan claimed to be in the middle of digging over.

'Where have you two been?'

'For a walk,' said Bee.

'Up on the rigg,' said Loo. 'Is that a pie in the oven?'

'Can we take Joe some?'

'Can I get a drink?'

It was hot in the garden, sheltered as it was by three dry stone walls and lying in the lee of the hill. The air was still and the tree, an apple tree, was small and sparse and provided little shade.

'Use the beakers,' Cathy said, 'and bring your drinks out here.'

It was Maths first and Loo hated Maths. Lessons consisted of her mother drilling her in her times tables and Bee jumping in with the right answer. Clever Bee, who had never stumbled with numbers back in Leeds and who took delight in mocking her younger sister and never mind that this was primary school stuff and she should be thinking of 'O' level options and maybe shutting up once in a while.

By the time her mother moved on to Maths for Bee herself – referring to a tattered algebra book Dan had failed to return to his last school and leaving her younger daughter to struggle on alone through a page of long division sums – Loo could have wept with frustration. She felt hot and confused and stupid. All she really wanted was to have lessons with her mother on her own, the way Flor did. The hour passed slowly, the heat building up as Flor sat in the vegetable patch hunting for worms.

'Right,' Cathy said eventually, getting to her feet and shaking out her skirt, 'reading time while I go and make lunch. And after lunch, chores.' She bent over and rummaged in the basket. 'Here.' *Wuthering Heights* for Bee and *Jane Eyre* for Loo. 'Two chapters each or there's no lunch for either of you, and remember I'm only in the kitchen, I can hear what you're up to.'

Bee waited until her mother had gone inside, before she threw her book to one side and lay back on the eiderdown.

'You first, Loo. Slowly.'

As Loo began to read aloud, Bee closed her eyes.

4

Now

Lucy has tried to talk her out of it. First when she and Cathy went through all the emails, and later through a stilted and difficult dinner. She has done her best to mask her irritation with her mother and with these strangers poking around the farm, and Cathy has refused to be persuaded out of meeting them.

It's all arranged, Lucia.

As if plans couldn't be cancelled.

After dinner they spend the rest of the evening in Cathy's bedroom. They listen to the radio and play a game of Scrabble. It's dark outside, but neither of them has bothered to draw the curtains. When they finish their game they sit for a while in silence, following the news headlines, with Lucy gazing idly at their reflections. She catches her mother yawning.

'Tired?' she says.

'Not really.'

'You've had a difficult day, you know, you're allowed to be—'

'I'm fine.' The news ends and a low voice announces the start of an arts programme. 'You can go up, if you want.'

Jean has already offered the use of one of the home's spare rooms, nothing more than an attic really, too small and inaccessible to be occupied by the frail or unsteady. Cathy stifles another yawn.

'Mum, this is ridiculous. You should be in bed.'

'I don't want . . .'

'Do you need some help getting undressed?' Lucy asks, before she's had the chance to consider what this offer might mean.

'Now you're being silly,' says her mother. 'Don't fuss. You know I can't stand fussing.'

'I could read to you, if you like, if you don't want to go to sleep just yet.'

Her mother doesn't bother to answer. She stands and, not without some effort, she begins to tidy her belongings away, switching off the radio, gathering up a pile of books and placing them on her desk.

Lucy makes an excuse about needing the bathroom. She takes her time washing her hands and tidying her hair, undoing it, running her fingers through it, and plaiting it again. She'll have to ring Dan again – God knows what she'll say to him this time.

When she goes back into the bedroom Cathy has changed and is sitting on the bed, her old-fashioned men's paisley pyjamas buttoned up to her neck. She takes her turn in the bathroom without comment. After a few minutes she returns and clambers into bed; propped against the pillows Cathy looks smaller than ever, frail and childlike. She has dabbed some ointment, arnica, probably, on the damage to her face.

'Right,' Lucy says, turning to the bookcase, as if they've actually come to an agreement about something, 'what would you like me to read?'

'I don't know. I don't want anything gloomy.'

The shelves are in disarray, with books and papers pushed in lengthways on top of the vertical volumes – there are New Age magazines, stuff on stone circles and spiritual development, as well as more respectable art periodicals. Lifting some of these, old editions of *Tate Etc.* and *RA Magazine*, Lucy dislodges the whole pile and they slide lazily onto the floor.

Gathering the magazines together, Lucy tries to put them back in place, and that's when she sees a sketchpad, wedged at the back of the shelf. She pulls it out and starts flicking through the pages. It's full of drawings: light, views of the house, the garden. The work is vigorous and confident. There are swift pencil portraits of the staff, a girl – half-finished, familiar, somehow, Sarah perhaps, her long hair tumbling loose – standing by the fountain.

'That's private,' says her mother.

Lucy closes the pad, but keeps hold of it. There are more, she notices, stacked between the bookcase and her mother's desk. 'I'm sorry. I just – sorry. I didn't realise – you've been busy,' she says.

'Well, what else is there to do?' Cathy's tone is mild.

'I mean – I thought you were . . .' Dabbling. A hobbyist passing the long hours of her retirement. She can't remember her mother sketching or painting when they were kids, for all her talk of the joys of creativity, although she knows her parents met at art school. She's ashamed, suddenly, of her easy accept-ance of her mother's dismissal of her abilities that afternoon. Not for the first time, she has underestimated her. 'I'd really like to take a look, a proper look,' she says.

Cathy fiddles with the top button of her pyjama jacket. 'I'm surprised you can be bothered, what with having a whole art gallery to play with.' She still doesn't look up. 'They're nothing special.'

'But they are. This is your work. If nothing else, it's special to me.'

'What would you do with it, Lucia? Pick one out to take home? Stick it on the fridge?'

'Mother.'

'Oh, put it away, for goodness' sake. I didn't draw them for you or for anyone else. I told you – they're scribbles to keep me occupied and the vultures at bay, and they certainly wouldn't fit in with your – your – "Women of the Landscape", or whatever it is.'

She knows the title perfectly well, of course. Lucy can see the invitation to the exhibition, the exhibition she is currently curating, tucked among the letters on her mother's desk: 'Women in the Landscape – A Retrospective' – not that Cathy has bothered to reply.

'Just put it away, please.'

'Fine,' says Lucy, dropping the pad on top of the magazines and turning back to the bookcase. She makes an effort to concentrate on the titles in front of her. Tomorrow, she decides, when her mother's in a better mood, she will choose a sketch to take home. She'll hang it next to her father's painting, the only piece of his she's been able to find, unfinished and far from his best; but it's his, all the same, and someone even got him to sign it, a single word in jagged black paint: Corvino. It's all she has left. There are no photos, no letters, and Cathy rarely speaks of him. She likes the idea of their work hanging side by side.

She glances at Cathy, who is still fussing over her jacket collar. Her mother has never visited the flat. She probably never will.

Lucy settles at last on *Frenchman's Creek*, one of Cathy's favourites, and after switching the radio off and dimming the lights, she begins to read.

She wakes with a start.

She sits up and the book slides off her lap, hitting the floor with a muffled thump. She swears softly, but Cathy doesn't stir and Lucy picks up the book, placing it gently on the table before switching off the bedside lamp. She walks slowly to the door, taking one last look around the darkened room, her mother now little more than a tumble of bedding, still and silent. Lucy's not afraid of the dark, she never has been. They used to play a game, she and her sister, lying in bed at night.

What can you hear?

She stands still and listens.

The traffic passing by outside, the ticking of the alarm clock, the gentle rasp of her mother's breathing, which is almost, but not quite, a snore.

She tries again.

The traffic, the ticking . . .

The faintest sigh of the floorboards under the thick carpet as someone crosses the room.

'Mum?'

Cathy hasn't moved.

Lucy waits.

The traffic, the ticking . . .

Silence.

There.

The skin on the back of her neck prickles; there's someone there in the shadows, just out of reach, pacing softly across the carpet, back and forth, back and forth. She's sure of it.

She can feel it.

She places one hand on the light switch by the door, her heart thudding. She doesn't want to look, doesn't want to see, and yet she can't help herself. She presses the switch.

When she sees her standing in front of the window her heart leaps. It's the girl, she thinks, she's there, before she realises it's her own reflection, pale, wide-eyed and still; it's not a girl at all.

Idiot.

Cathy sighs and stirs and Lucy switches off the light, then crosses the room and closes the curtains. She waits for five minutes, maybe more, alone in the dark, listening, before she can finally bring herself to leave.

Next time she wakes in the guest room. The bed is narrow and sometime in the night she's kicked away the duvet. Her back and knees are stiff, the mattress is so hard she's surprised she slept at all. She checks her watch. It's almost seven o'clock, still too early to bother her mother, but there's the kitchen downstairs and all she really wants is a cup of tea and a cigarette.

She hasn't smoked for years.

Tea, then. She dresses quickly, brushes her teeth and washes her face at the little sink in the corner. On her way out, she grabs her phone; she'll need to let Dan know about this business at the farm.

'Bloody hell, Loo,' he says. 'After all this time? What do they want?'

'I don't know. As far as I can tell, they have some idea of carrying on where Michael left off. You know, finishing the investigation.'

'There's got to be more to it than that – some sort of . . . financial angle.'

'I don't think so. Not now, surely.'

'And Cathy's OK with this?'

'Apparently. More than OK. She's agreed to meet them.'

'Why?'

'God, I don't know. Curiosity?' The kitchen is empty, spotless and ruthlessly organised. Lucy fills the kettle, then switches it on.

'Well, it's out of the question. You'll have to stop her.' Dan, the oldest, the boss.

'Well, obviously.'

'Tell her you'll take legal action. We all will.'

'Mum?'

'This Nina person.'

'I don't think that will work.'

'I should definitely come over.'

Lucy can hear a voice in the background. Julie, telling her husband to calm down.

'No,' she says. 'By the time you get here they'll be long gone.'

'You think?'

'Yeah.'

There's a silence as Dan takes this in. 'Ah, Loo,' he says, 'you're stuck with this all on your own, aren't you? I'm sorry.'

'It's all right.'

It's not fair.

'I'll talk to her again,' says Lucy. 'Try to stop things getting out of hand. I can stay over another night, make sure that she puts them off.'

It will mean cutting things fine with work, but it's probably doable if there's an early train.

'OK,' says Dan. 'Ring me later, though. Let me know what she says.'

They say their goodbyes and Lucy slips her phone back into her pocket. She's not really sure there is anything she can do in the long run, but the sound of her brother's voice has been a comfort, for a few minutes, at least. The older he gets, the more like their father he sounds, or so she likes to think.

Behind her the door opens and a young woman walks in, shedding her hat and scarf. It's the girl from yesterday, Sarah.

59

Lucy has the distinct feeling she's been caught out of bounds. 'I was just hoping I could get a cup of tea,' she says, standing up. 'Sorry, I didn't want to get in anyone's way.'

Sarah takes off her coat. 'That's all right,' she says. 'I can do you a bit of toast too, if you like. I don't really need to get started until quarter to.'

'I don't want to trouble you.'

'It's no trouble,' says Sarah. 'I usually make myself some anyway.' She opens one of the cupboards. 'You won't tell, will you?'

'Sorry?'

'Well, Mrs Wyn Jones doesn't really like us making ourselves breakfast; she thinks it's unprofessional. Only I have to get an early bus and, you know . . .'

'No,' says Lucy, 'I won't tell.'

The tea comes in what is clearly a staff mug and they sit at the table, a plate piled high with buttered toast between them.

'How's Mrs Corvino this morning?' asks Sarah.

'I haven't checked yet. I thought I'd let her lie in for a bit.'

'Oh, right. She'd got herself into a bit of a state, hadn't she?'

'I suppose so.'

'But looking back, she'd been off-colour for a couple of days.'

'Really?'

'Oh, nothing serious,' says Sarah, looking stricken. 'It's not like she was ill, or anything. We'd let you know if there was something really wrong.'

She's very young, a student perhaps, working long hours to get herself through university.

'Yes, I know that. She's very happy here, we're all very . . .'

Happy.

Cathy's children all contribute to the cost of her care, but they rarely visit. Lucy wipes buttery crumbs from her fingers. 'Off-colour how, though?'

'She just seemed a bit teary, I suppose. A bit low. I put it down to, I dunno, nostalgia. She'd been talking about your sister a bit.'

'She said she'd had a card.'

'Yes. She showed me,' says Sarah. 'Maybe that sort of started her off, she was talking a lot about the farm you used to have, it sounds amazing.'

'That's one way to describe it.'

'And she showed me some photos.'

'Really? I didn't think she had any.' Lucy can remember the great purge when they finally left, the huge bonfire of books and papers and paintings; she's pretty sure this had included the photos they'd collected over that summer.

'She was showing me on her laptop, she wanted to know how to find them online. She has quite a few.'

'Oh. Of course.'

Sarah puts her mug down and sits forward. She seems to have made some sort of decision. 'But I don't think . . .' she says. 'The thing is . . .'

Lucy's phone buzzes angrily on the table top. She picks it up.

Flor.

Sarah's not tired, or not just tired; she's worried. But as Lucy unlocks the phone's screen, this thought flutters away. 'Sorry,' she says, 'it's my brother. I'd better answer this.'

When she's finished speaking with Florian, who seems only to be ringing to have everything Dan has already told him confirmed, with no intention of making the long journey north, or of cooperating with any investigation at the farm, Jean has arrived and she and Sarah have made a start on organising breakfast.

'Lucy,' Jean says, 'is everything all right?'

'Fine,' says Lucy. 'I woke up early and I thought I'd make myself some toast. I hope you don't mind.' The kitchen table has been cleared, their mugs and plates have vanished, Flor has said his piece and she has promised to keep him informed.

'Of course not, but you're welcome to eat with Cathy in the dining room.'

'Actually, I thought I might take her a tray up. If that's allowed.'

'I'm sure we can manage that, can't we, Sarah?'

'Yes, Mrs Wyn Jones,' says Sarah, conspicuously busy at the sink, 'I can sort that out for you.'

Cathy disapproves of breakfast in bed. 'Is that for me?' she says, struggling to sit up. 'I'm not an invalid, you know, not yet.'

Lucy stands in the doorway. 'Well, I'll take it back downstairs, then, shall I?'

Cathy pulls herself upright and looks at her daughter waiting.

'Here,' says Lucy, placing the tray carefully on her mother's lap.

'Thank you.'

Lucy draws the curtains and ties them back. The garden below is empty and lightly dusted with frost. 'Did you sleep all right?' she asks. 'How's your wrist?'

'Sore. But I'll live.' Her mother lifts her hand, flexes it gently; she looks well enough this morning, despite the darkening bruises on her face.

'I spoke to Dan,' Lucy says. 'He sends his love. Flor too.'

Her mother nods. 'The last time Dante wrote he suggested we talk on – the sky, well, not the sky but—'

'Skype.'

'Yes, that's it.'

'Do you have an account?'

'I think so. Sarah helped me set something up, so I can talk to the girls.' Dan's daughters, Helen and Marianne. 'But I haven't used it yet.'

'That was kind of her.'

'I suppose so,' says Cathy, 'but I think I'd rather write. Proper letters, you know, emails are too – quick. There's no time to think.'

Lucy sits in one of the armchairs.

'I was talking to Sarah. She said you'd told her about the farm. That you'd been showing her some photographs.'

Cathy looks down, stirring the milk around her cereal bowl. 'Yes,' she says. 'I had to get her to help me. I can manage most of the time but, looking for things, you know—'

'Using a search engine.'

'Yes. So many answers and most of them no help at all.'

'You have to think about the terms of the search.'

'So she said.'

'Only – I was thinking. Do you think that might be it? What happened when you went outside? Maybe you were looking at old photographs and . . .'

You forgot where you were.

Cathy doesn't reply and Lucy blunders on. 'Because – well . . . I wouldn't like to see you getting . . . upset.'

'I wasn't upset.'

'I think you were. When you rang me, when you went wandering off.'

'I told you. I made a mistake.'

'We were worried. Me, Dan, Flor—'

'I didn't mean to frighten anyone.'

'Anything could have happened.'

'But nothing did.'

'You can't do that, Mum. You can't just leave the house in the middle of the night chasing . . .'

She can't bring herself to say it.

'It wasn't the middle of the night.'

'There was no one there.'

'Then there's nothing to worry about.'

'You could have been hurt. Seriously hurt.'

'I'm fine, Lucia.'

'But even so. It's not a good idea, raking over the past like that. People shouldn't be bothering you with questions about the farm. Look where it's got us.' She doesn't want to think about it. She will not cry; she will not.

As her mother dresses, Lucy goes through the emails again; they've been corresponding for weeks. She makes a mental note of the group Nina Marshall keeps referring to, the Society for the Study of Anomalous Phenomena. She's never heard of them.

She rereads the most recent message. They'll be there now, at the farm, and Cathy still won't be put off meeting with them.

She has to do something.

Lucy closes the laptop and when she looks up, her mother is sitting on the bed, coat on, hat and scarf in hand. She looks like a schoolgirl expecting a treat. 'Let's go out,' Cathy says. 'We could go down to the harbour.'

They walk along the sea front, past the shuttered amusement arcades and the row of cafes still stubbornly open for business, plastic skeletons and pumpkins lighting up windows which face out onto the flat grey sea. 'We used to make turnip lanterns,'

Cathy says, as they pass one window, 'do you remember? We used to cut a face into them and put a candle inside.'

'I remember you doing it,' says Lucy. 'I think I remember trying, but it was hard to cut the flesh out with a blunt knife. I must have been what, five or six?'

'We did them every year.'

'When we were still living in Leeds.'

'Yes.'

Leeds before the farm, Ipswich after.

Home-educated and running wild on the moors one minute, secondary school, uniforms and 'O' level options the next. It had been a relief, in the end, trying to fit in, to go unnoticed. No longer one of a pair, just herself alone. Lucy had erased her accent within a month of starting school, beginning the long journey away from Iron Sike Farm and the summer they spent there. 'Tired yet?' she asks, as they cross the road that runs along the sea front and leads to the little harbour and the pier.

'I'm fine,' says Cathy, her hands shoved into her coat pockets. 'Shall we walk along to the Lifeboat House?'

'If you like.'

Ipswich had meant staying with their grandparents: regular bedtimes, proper table manners and pocket money. Lucy had ended up attending Cathy's old school – a comprehensive doing its best to pretend it was still a grammar. By the time they'd moved out to a place of their own, Lucy had caught up with her classmates, and was starting to outstrip them. Good marks were predictable, safe, and she began to treasure them.

The sky was doing its best to hold back the rain, but Lucy could practically smell it in the air. Clouds hung low over the sea. Fishing boats, cobles for the most part, were tied up in neat rows alongside the pier, jostling gently against each other in the lazy swell. At the far end of the sea front the Lifeboat House loomed, Victorian redbrick, damp and solid.

As soon as the last of her children had left home Cathy had moved back north, to be close to the farm.

They reach the Lifeboat House. Beyond it on the pier a fisherman sits, wearing waterproofs and wellington boots, solitary and silent. Lucy isn't really dressed for walking along the beach, but still she follows her mother down the slipway and onto the sand.

'It's not as if we can stop them, you know,' Cathy says as they walk down towards the bay, following the curve of the high-water mark. 'And it's not as if any of you would want to speak with them, is it? Or have I got that wrong?'

'No, of course not.' Lucy tries to ignore the flutter of panic this idea provokes. 'But I'd still like to know what they're looking for.'

'You read the letters,' says her mother. 'They call it something different now . . .' But she hesitates, struggling with the unfamiliar phrase she can't call to mind.

'Anomalous phenomena,' says Lucy carefully.

'Yes. That. She sent me a letter,' Cathy says. 'I don't know how she found me, but it's an unusual name, isn't it? So I expect that helped. And she told me what they were going to do; that they were going to go back. And I wasn't going to answer, not at first. I thought she'd get tired in the end, maybe she'd write me off as a dotty old lady and leave me alone. I meant to tell her to . . . But then I saw . . . I didn't expect . . .' She stops and looks out to sea, where in the distance a container ship makes its slow way along the horizon, blocks of grey and brown and white stamped against the pale grey sky. 'She asked me about you.'

'Yes.'

'And Bianca too.'

'Oh, Mum.' Lucy takes her mother's hand. 'I'm going to talk to them. I'll make sure they don't bother you any more. I think it's for the best—'

'No. Absolutely not.' Cathy pulls away.

'They can't do this. It's our lives. Don't they understand that they might . . . upset us?'

That they might confuse an ailing old lady and send her out of the house in the middle of the night, looking for a girl, a girl who couldn't possibly be there.

'I said no,' says Cathy. 'I want to talk to them.'

A sharp breeze cuts through Lucy's coat, and she can feel icy seawater leaking through the expensive suede of her boots. 'Can we just – go get a coffee or something?' she says. 'I'm freezing.'

'You used to beg me to bring you to the seaside. Both of you.'

'Yes, well. That was then.'

'You told me once that if I brought you here, you'd never ask for anything else, not ever.'

'What a delightful child I was.'

'You used to follow Bee around like a little shadow.'

'Mum. Don't.' This is the last thing Lucy wants, and exactly what she fears. Her mother reminiscing, wallowing in the past; it won't do any of them any good.

She looks at the footprints they have left along the beach and tries to ignore the chill prickling at her spine, the feeling she has that someone is following them, just out of sight.

5

Then

Isobel lit a cigarette and inhaled deeply. She'd had to park on the grass verge, still within sight of the village school, so she was hardly setting a good example to the little darlings, but she was gasping for a smoke. Primary schools, or maybe it was just the kids, seemed to bring out the worst in her. She could have driven back down into Longdale, but it was another clear, blazing hot day and the car was like a bloody oven. She'd left the driver's door as far open as she could get it and then she'd hoisted herself up onto the dry stone wall and kicked off her sandals. Five minutes, then she'd make a move. The school was right on the edge of the village and the road was quiet; she didn't have to be anywhere. Five minutes' peace. She closed her eyes. She was still sitting there when she heard the car pull up.

'All right, love?'

Isobel sighed and opened her eyes. It had been nice while it lasted.

Across the road, the police officer had wound his window down, his hand resting on the door frame. Carefully, she stubbed her cigarette out on the wall before getting down and putting her shoes back on.

'Martin. Your turn for the toy car today, I see.'

'Oi, less of your lip, or I might have to get the cuffs out.'

Oh, please. Martin was nice enough, but he was the village bobby.
Born and bred here and likely to die here too.

'You coming or going?' he asked.

'Going. Rehearsals for the end of term concert.'

'You get some nice snaps?'

'Nice enough.'

'I'll look out for them on Friday, then. Front page, is it?'

She was used to the heavy-handed teasing that seemed to be part and parcel of her job and mostly she ignored it. So she only worked for a local paper? That didn't mean she wasn't ambitious, or that she didn't have a plan. Not that Martin was particularly interested in her career prospects, she was sure. She crossed over the road and bent down to look in the car.

'Am I keeping you from something, PC Thorpe? A bank robbery? Drugs raid? A nice juicy murder?'

'I've always got time for you, sweetheart, you know that.'

She couldn't be sure, but she thought he might be looking down her shirt. She stood up again. 'Right. OK. I'll see you, then,' she said, turning away.

'No. Hang on.' He was flushed and sweaty, and no wonder, in his stupid uniform in this heat.

'Well?'

'Do you fancy a pint tonight?' He'd asked before, and he'd probably ask again.

'What, here?'

'Well, I can't drive anywhere, can I? Not if I want a beer. And I'm on early tomorrow.'

'What about me? How am I supposed to get back home?'

'We'll think of something.' He smiled up at her hopefully.

She could almost admire his nerve. 'I don't think so, Martin. You're not the only one with work in the morning.'

70

'Oh, go on. Just a quick half. Two at the most. I'll make it worth your while.'

Isobel smiled, despite herself. 'And how are you going to do that? Have you got a big story on sheep rustling?'

'Better than that, Issy. Go on. Seven at the Lion.'

There was a beer garden at the Red Lion, and it might be nice, just for half an hour, to see what Martin Thorpe thought passed for news round here. She could get over to the office in Whitby and then drive back when she'd done the contact sheets.

'Go on then,' she said. 'Eight o'clock though, and I'm not hanging around all night, so don't be late.'

The beer garden was full by eight o'clock so they'd had to settle for a table in the public bar, squashed in next to the huge fireplace. Martin had bought her a drink, and they'd chatted for a bit – he was all right really, Isobel supposed, if only he could work out that he really wasn't her type – and when she'd laughed at enough of his jokes he'd insisted on a second round, refusing to let her pay. She'd given in, in the end, knowing full well that was the only thing he'd be getting his way on. A few visitors, hikers most likely, were squeezed around one of the tables by the door and Isobel watched as one of them, a pretty blonde girl, walked across the room to the jukebox and leant over it and the lads close by raised their voices, hoping she might turn and favour them with a smile.

'So, what's this big story then?' she said, fanning herself with a damp beer mat as Martin put their drinks on the table: beer for him, orange juice for her.

'Bloody hell, I thought we were having a good time.' He pushed her glass across the table. 'It doesn't all have to be business, does it?'

The ice in her drink clattered as she picked it up and she

71

resisted the temptation to press the beaded glass to her neck to feel its comforting chill. 'You're the one who said he had a story. You wouldn't have got me here under false pretences, would you? 'Cos that's not nice, Martin. Not very nice at all. Not when I could be home with my feet up and a good book.'

Martin looked at her. 'OK,' he said, 'OK, have it your own way.' He took a long swallow of his pint, put his glass on the table and then glanced over to the bar. 'But you didn't hear this from me, right?'

'Right.'

'It's not really a police matter, there's no charges going to be made or anything . . .' He fell silent for a moment, tapping his fingers against his glass. 'You're not going to laugh, are you?' he said eventually.

'Well, I don't know, do I?' She could feel the sweat trickling down between her shoulder blades, and the backs of her legs were sticking to the fake leather bench. All she really wanted now was for Martin to get on with it so she could go home.

'Do you know Iron Sike Farm?' asked Martin.

'No.'

'Well,' he trailed a finger through a beer puddle on the table, 'the road goes through the village, right? Slices it in half, goes out past the school, out past where I saw you today, then over towards Whitby?'

'Yes.'

'And a couple of miles past the school, there's a turning on the left and that goes past Iron Sike Farm and then up onto the moors.'

Why did men have to do this? Reduce everything to bloody road maps?

'OK.'

'The farm – the land and the animals – that belongs to Peter Eglon, right? Alongside everything at Low Moor Farm, so the house there – at Iron Sike – that's no use to him and so he rents it out.' He stopped and took another drink of beer.

'And?'

'He's rented it out to this bloke, reckons he's an artist, and his wife and their kids.'

Across the room, the jukebox kicked into life and Martin hunched over the table, his voice so low Isobel had to lean across to hear him.

'I got called out there the other night.' Martin picked up his pint and finished it in one swallow. 'They've not been there that long, OK? They moved in back in April and they're – I don't know, hippies. There's a handful of kids but none of them go to school. He paints, she – well, I don't know what she does, the house is a bloody tip . . .'

He fell silent again.

'So why did you go?'

'Hmm?'

'Who called you out to the farm?'

'She did. And she was bloody terrified.'

She must have been. In Isobel's experience, the kind of people Martin was describing didn't generally want to have anything to do with the police.

'What had he done to her?'

'Who?'

'Him. The husband.' Isobel had the vague idea she might have seen him once, here in the pub, a tall, dark man with raggedy hair and a handful of silver rings. Good-looking, she supposed, with no one to talk to but the barmaid, not that he'd seemed to mind that.

'Nothing. He wasn't there. He's away, working somewhere.'

73

'So what was it then?'

'This is private, right? Just between us.'

It had been knocking first. Apparently.

The girls, who shared a room, had gone up to bed and after a bit the knocking had started. Quite gently at first, they'd said. As if someone was sending them a message.

'Is there anybody there?' one of them had asked, as a joke, really.

One tap for yes. Two taps for no.

Then it had gone quiet. The oldest had got out of bed, put her ear to the wall. 'Is there anybody there?' For a laugh. The youngest was in her bed, giggling.

'Is there—'

The knocking, so loud they thought the wall would crack, nearly deafened the girl. It practically threw her across the room, booming over and over again.

'Kids,' said Isobel, 'messing around.'

'Maybe,' said Martin. 'But eventually, the noise gets so bad that the mother – Cathy – goes upstairs. When she gets there, the room's in a hell of a state and the girls are huddled in their beds, howling with fear, near enough.'

Pushing his pint to one side, Martin ran his hand through his hair. 'So she's standing there, the mother, trying to calm the youngest girl down, or so she said, when . . . She's standing there, and out of nowhere someone throws a marble at her, hard.'

Isobel wished she'd asked for a proper drink. As far as she could tell, Martin's big story wasn't going to be worth two glasses of orange juice and the possibility of an unpleasant tussle when he walked her to her car.

'And she's about to really let them have it, tell them off for messing her about, when there's loads of them, heavy glass marbles, falling out of nowhere, smacking down onto the beds, the carpet, the dressing table, her, and the girls. It was like a hailstorm, she said. She had bruises.'

'You're not telling me—'

'I'm telling you what she told me. There was this . . . hail-storm—'

'Of marbles.'

'And then?'

'She got them out of there, didn't she? Got them both down-stairs.'

'And then rang the police?'

'Not straightaway. She checked on the other kids – the little ones were sleeping through all the commotion, or so she reckoned – then she got the eldest boy to look around outside, but yeah, in the end she rang the station and I was nearby anyway—'

Isobel had heard more than a few tall tales in her time; perhaps it was something to do with her being young, being a woman. It was definitely to do with having the nerve to come from Cambridge, with sounding posh every time she opened her mouth. And God knows she'd been sent out to take pictures of some very iffy news items because someone – usually a bitter old fart who'd got nothing to look forward to except the pleasure of knowing one day his own obituary would be there in the paper instead of his by-line – had decided she needed bringing down a peg or two. So she knew the signs to look for: the smirk, the smug you-didn't-fall-for-that-you-silly-cow-did-you look that they all got in the end.

Only Martin didn't look smug. He looked uneasy.

'Why did she call the police?' Isobel asked.

'I don't know. The husband was away. She said on the phone she thought there was someone outside, an intruder. But when I got there . . . She said it was upstairs, in the bedroom.'

'It?'

'Yeah.'

'Did you go upstairs, then?'

'Yeah. There was nothing there – the room was a mess, bedding everywhere, drawers open and clothes scattered about.'

'Marbles?'

'They were there too. Just, you know, kids' toys.' Martin took another sip of his beer. There was something else, Isobel could tell.

'What happened next?' she said.

'I thought she was worried that there was a burglar or some-thing. So I had a look around, the kids' rooms, the main bedroom, the bathroom. And then I went downstairs. They were in the living room, the youngest girl clinging on to her sister, her eyes the size of saucers, and I was trying to reassure her – the mother, Cathy. I told her there was no one in the house that shouldn't be, and that the girls should get back to bed. Then the girls sort of looked behind me and pointed. "Look at that," one of them said, "look there," and before I could answer . . . There was an armchair in front of the fireplace.' He looked at Isobel, then shook his head as if he couldn't quite believe what he was going to say next. 'It moved, Issy. Swear to God. There was no one near it and the bloody thing moved.'

'Right,' said Isobel.

'Only you can't tell anyone, right?'

'Tell me,' said Isobel, reaching for her glass, 'tell me everything again.'

*

The house looked empty and Isobel took a couple of shots as she leant against the car. They wouldn't be much use though, she knew that; what she really needed were some pictures of the family, of the girls. If she could get inside, win them over. As a rule, she was given her assignments by Trevor Weatherill, the paper's senior photographer, and of course she never interviewed anyone; her job was to take the pictures.

'Make sure you get everyone in, and make sure you get all their names right.' Trevor's voice ringing in her head, day in, day out, reminding her that she wasn't actually a journalist.

But as she'd got Martin to go over everything again, at some point in the retelling she'd known, just known, that this was going to be her story. So instead of going to work at the *Gazette* offices in town as usual, she'd got up early and driven back to Longdale. And here she was, squinting up at the redbrick house, wondering how to begin. Trying to summon up the nerve. She was still leaning against the car when a figure appeared from the back of the house and walked down the garden path.

'All right?' he said as he opened the gate.

One of the kids. Sixteen or seventeen. Long, raggedy hair, like his father. He looked her up and down, and she waited for the inevitable comment, something obvious about red hair and a hot temper, but he surprised her by walking past her down the lane towards the village.

'Excuse me.'

'Yeah?' He turned and stood still, the shadows cast by the low morning sun making it hard to read his expression.

'Isobel Bradshaw,' she said, swinging her camera bag onto her shoulder and extending a hand.

He waited just a second too long before taking it. 'Dan Corvino.'

'I'm in the right place then,' said Issy.

'Sorry?'

'This is Iron Sike Farm.'

'That's what it says on the sign.'

'I work for the *Gazette*. I'm here about the business with the girls,' she said. He looked away, almost but not quite hiding a half-smile.

'Right, well, I don't think Cathy will want to talk to the papers, to be honest. Sorry,' he said.

'Cathy?'

'My mother.'

'Yes. Right. Well, could I have a quick word with you?'

'I'm on my way to work.' His accent was different to the one she was used to hearing around here, a bit like Martin's, but Dan's vowels were fuller, stretching out his words.

'Just for a minute, and if you're worried about being late I can give you a lift.'

'I wasn't there, you know. I wasn't actually in the room.'

'Just a couple of questions.'

'All right then,' he said, moving out of the road, further into the shade, and leaning against the dry stone wall. 'Ask away.'

'Oh, OK.' She moved into the shadows too, the tall grass cool against her legs. 'So, where were you when it happened? I mean, you were in the house, right?' She should have thought to get her notebook out.

'I was upstairs. In my bedroom.'

'Did you hear anything?'

'Not really. I was listening to music.'

She should have thought out her questions too.

'The first I knew about it was when Loo came and got me. She came running up the stairs going on about the furniture flying around and it hitting a policeman. She was making a hell of a racket and that set Flor off.'

'Flor?'

'My brother. Florian. One of Cathy's stupider ideas.'

The brother or the name?

'I see.'

'So we went downstairs and they were in the kitchen, Cathy and Bee and this copper. He was as white as a sheet.'

'What were they doing?'

'Nothing. Just standing there.' Dan pulled out a packet of cigarettes from his shirt pocket and offered Issy one.

'No thanks,' she said. 'Did you notice anything else?'

'Not really. They told me what had happened and I went and had a look. The room was a mess and they were all – look, I've got to get on, you know?' He retrieved some matches from his pocket, stood up straighter. He was done and she'd barely started.

'Oh, right. Thanks. Do you need a lift?'

She could ask more questions in the car.

'No, ta. I'll be all right.' He smiled at her. He was a good-looking boy, dark and tanned and confident. She could imagine him breaking a few hearts with that lazy smile.

'Do you believe in all that stuff then?' he asked, lighting his cigarette.

'What stuff?'

'Ghosts and ghouls. Things that go bump in the night.'

'I don't know. Do you?'

'I didn't use to,' he said, exhaling, smoke swirling between them.

Issy stood back, her eyes smarting.

'Look,' said Dan, 'if you want to talk to Cathy it's no use knocking on the front door, she won't bother answering. Go round the back to the kitchen.'

'I'll do that. Thanks.'

'Right. Well. Bye, Isobel.' He pushed himself off the wall and walked away.

'Goodbye.'

She got as far as the front gate before she realised she should have asked if there'd been any other disturbances in the house, stuff Martin hadn't witnessed, stuff that had happened since. She'd let him get away far too easily. Irritated, she glanced back down the lane. Dan was still there. He was standing in the middle of the road, motionless, watching her. A dark shadow sketched into the pale green landscape. He raised a hand in farewell, and she pushed down on the gate's iron latch.

The woman who answered the door looked tired. Her hair, a mousy brown, fell in a rough plait over one shoulder and she clearly wasn't the type to bother much with makeup. She had a large and drowsy child balanced on one hip, and behind her, a little boy, maybe five years old, barefoot in dusty blue shorts and a grubby T-shirt, stared at Isobel with blank dark eyes. Florian, she supposed. The kitchen smelt of burnt toast and wet nappies.

Issy smiled broadly and extended a hand. 'Cathy? Hi, I'm Isobel. I'm from the *Gazette*.'

The woman didn't move. She just stood with one hand on the door, the other cradling her child. Braced. Waiting.

'What do you want?' Her tone wasn't aggressive, exactly, but she was wary.

'I wanted to talk to you about – well, the events you've been experiencing. You and your family.'

'I see.' The woman's voice was soft, but firm. 'I don't think so.' She began to close the door.

'Only, I was talking to Dan, you see, and he suggested I have a word with you.'

Which was perfectly truthful, as far as it went.

'And actually, I was wondering if there was anything I could do to help?'

The woman hesitated. The baby sighed and slumped against her. It looked heavy. 'Help how?'

'Well, I'm not sure.'

The sun beat down on them both. Behind Cathy the house was gloomy and still. The little boy edged closer to his mother.

'But we could just talk for a bit, if you like. It can't be much fun for you, coping with all of this on your own.'

Cathy lifted the child, trying to bump it gently into a more comfortable position.

'The *Gazette*? Would there be a story? Pictures?'

'Well, yes, possibly.' She could feel the camera bag hanging from her shoulder, damning her. She should have thought to hide it. 'It's interesting, you see. At least, I think it is.'

'Interesting.' The woman almost smiled at this. 'That's one word for it.'

'But it is. People can be so – narrow-minded, can't they? And then something like this happens and it's a chance to – I don't know – to think again, to look at people's preconceptions, to make a difference.'

She was pushing too hard, saying too much. Shut up, she thought, shut up.

'You're not from round here, are you?' said Cathy.

'No, I'm not.'

'Neither are we.'

'I know,' said Issy. 'I mean – I heard that.' The baby, a chubby thing with thick dark curls plastered against its head, began to stir in its mother's arms. Issy wondered if she should say something pleasant about it, or at least ask its name.

'They never let you forget it, do they?'

'No,' said Isobel, 'no, they don't.' Certainly no one at the office did, and neither did the people she'd spent the past three years photographing. Issy had the feeling she could spend the rest of her life turning up at football matches and prize-givings, village shows and the Whitby Regatta, taking pictures of locals and their little triumphs, and no matter what she did, she'd always be a visitor, an outsider. She doubted things were any easier for the Corvino family here in Longdale where families had been sticking together for generations.

'Do you like it here?' asked Cathy.

'It's all right,' said Issy. 'It's – quiet, I suppose.'

'And you're a journalist?'

'Yes. Well. A photographer.'

Cathy looked at the camera again, assessing it, and Issy, recalling Martin's assertion that the father, Joe, was an artist of some sort, decided to take a gamble. 'It's a Canon F-1,' she said. 'This one's seen better days, but I like it.'

'It's a good camera.'

'Yeah, I think so. So, you do a bit, then? Photography, I mean.'

'Not really. I did some at college, as part of my degree. But I haven't done anything in ages – you know.' Cathy jiggled the baby gently. 'I used to do my own developing, though. I used to like that.'

'Really?'

'Yeah, it was – satisfying, you know? Completing the process myself.'

'Yes,' said Issy, 'I know what you mean.'

The conversation died away. Never leave, one of the reporters at the *Gazette* had once told her over a beer after work, when he'd been trying to impress her with tales of his time on one of the tabloids. Never leave until they tell you to go.

It was already ridiculously hot, and she wondered if she should ask for a glass of water.

'All right,' Cathy said, stepping back, 'come in. Don't bother to close the door. It's too dark in here anyway.'

Once they got inside Cathy settled the baby on the rag rug in front of the Aga and made them some tea. Isobel watched her moving around the room, slow and careful, in the manner of someone who was unwell, or recuperating from an illness, perhaps. She kept glancing anxiously at the baby – maybe that was it, maybe the child had been ill or was teething; it held a wooden brick in its pudgy hand and gnawed at one corner, dribbling.

Issy took a seat at the table and watched Florian trail around the kitchen after his mother. 'Hello,' she said.

'Say hello, Florian,' said Cathy. The little boy mumbled something, then scooped up a handful of toy cars from the floor.

'I'm going out to play,' he said.

'Stay where I can see you, then,' said Cathy.

The kitchen was on the small side, a later addition to the Victorian house. An open door revealed a dark and shadowy passage: on both sides wooden shelves ran the length of it, at waist height, as far as the front door, and Issy could see these were crammed with books. The walls had paintings on them, although she couldn't make out the details. Joe's work, she supposed. Rectangular canvases, no frames – landscapes, perhaps. She tried not to stare and wondered how she might get to see the rest of the house. She rummaged in her bag for her notebook and pen, which she placed neatly on the table, and then picked up her camera, flicking off the lens cap and checking the settings. It was dim in the kitchen, but she could make do.

Two pots of tea later, Cathy saw her off at the front gate, with Florian hanging on to her skirts as she wrapped Isobel in a clumsy embrace.

'I'll be back tomorrow,' Issy said, trying not to breathe in the scent of food and baby and sweat, warm skin and olive oil soap.

'Great.' Cathy stood on the step watching as Isobel walked down the lane, got into her car and drove up onto the moors road. Prompted by his mother, the little boy waved as she passed the house and Issy waved back, smiling.

Cold spots in the house.

Knocking and banging in the walls.

Things: spoons, pens, bits of jewellery, anything put down for a second or two, going missing.

Furniture moving.

She had pages of it.

Pages.

She'd got a couple of shots of Cathy too, backlit softly by the kitchen door, the baby grizzling gently on her knee. A modern-day Madonna. As far as she could tell, most of the events, the paranormal activity, centred on the two girls, Lucia, eleven, and Bianca, fourteen.

'Can I speak to them too?' she'd asked.

'I don't . . .'

On the rug the baby dropped a toy and, reaching for it, fell over and began to howl.

'Sorry,' said Cathy, standing and picking it up, crooning softly and walking up and down the room. Behind them in the hallway, a floorboard squeaked and something pattered swiftly up the stairs. Camera in hand, Issy went to the doorway and looked into the hall.

'Hello?'

It was darker in this part of the house. The paintings ranged along the walls were just a little too big for the space, crammed in together awkwardly. She'd been right, they were landscapes: the moors, mostly, purple and black swirls of land pressed down by sullen skies. Impressionistic, bold. She wondered if he managed to sell any.

Glancing back into the kitchen she wandered down the hall, hoping to look as though she was absorbed in Joe's work.

She got as far as the bottom of the stairs as behind her the baby's cries grew more insistent, more enraged, and Cathy continued to pace up and down the kitchen.

'Hello?' She lifted her camera. It was cold here, the skin on her neck and arms puckered into goose bumps. Through the lens the staircase came into focus; at the top of the stairs, on the landing, something in the shadows seemed to move.

Three quick thuds, inside the walls, or maybe above her head. She stepped back, almost colliding with Cathy who was still holding her fretful child, and with Florian who had evidently abandoned his game in the garden.

'Sorry,' said Issy. 'I thought – did you hear that?'

'Yes.' Cathy looked almost apologetic.

'Is that it? Is it like that all the time?'

'Sometimes it's louder. Sometimes . . .' Cathy's voice drifted away. She smoothed the baby's hair back from its red and puffy face. 'It's hard to describe,' she said.

'So, if I could speak to the girls, then?'

'I don't think so. Not today. I'll need to check with their father. Can you come back tomorrow?'

'Is he not back yet, then? Your husband?'

'No. He can't get away – I'll speak with him later.'

'Where is he?'

The question seemed to take Cathy by surprise. 'Glasgow,' she said. 'He was asked to teach – just for a few weeks, in an art college, it was all a bit last-minute. There's no one who can cover for him.'

'It would be really helpful if—'

'No. Not right now.' The baby struggled in Cathy's arms, drew breath for another onslaught. 'They have their lessons and I want to keep things – normal.'

'OK. Well, tomorrow it is, then.'

'Good. That would be – good.'

And that's where they'd left it.

Isobel drove through the village and up onto the moors road. She was late for work and she desperately needed to pee – after seeing the state of Cathy's kitchen, she hadn't wanted to risk the bathroom – but none of that mattered. There was more going on in that house than met the eye, she was sure of it; she had felt it, the chill, the sense of expectation. She got to the top of the moor and turned onto the road towards the coast. It was another glorious day and finally she had her story.

6

Then

'Do you mind?' said Professor Warren, as he leant forward and switched off the radio. 'I have a headache.'

'Of course not,' said Simon, who did mind. It was his car after all, but Michael Warren was the senior researcher on this trip, and Simon still couldn't quite escape an upbringing that had demanded polite acquiescence to the wishes of one's elders and betters at all times. The car filled with silence.

They'd left the motorway behind an hour or so ago and were edging their way carefully along the valley from one village to the next, each one smaller than the last, each one baking under an endless blue sky. They'd wound down the windows but every time they had to slow for a tractor, or worse, a sturdy and belligerent sheep, the breeze this afforded them vanished. It might have been Simon's imagination, but these stops seemed to be occurring more and more frequently. He began to worry that the car, second-hand, and a gift from his parents, might not be up to the job.

'Do you know this part of the world?' asked the professor.

'No, I don't. Do you?'

'The coast, a little; holidays when I was a boy, that sort of thing, but I don't know the moors at all.'

To their right empty fields, pale and sun-bleached green, stretched down to the river. To their left, there was a steep incline, rough and undomesticated, but still marked out as someone's property by the dark grey dry stone walls that rose and fell and clung to the earth. Up beyond the final boundary lay the black and gold and budding purple of the moors.

Simon didn't like it.

It was too . . . bare.

He'd been pressed into service by the Society at the very last minute. There'd been some sort of falling out between Roland Miskin, another senior researcher, and the professor – he wasn't sure what and he certainly wasn't in a position to ask – and Simon had suddenly been presented with the chance to take part in his first field investigation. He still couldn't quite believe his luck and had spent much of the journey north wondering why the professor had decided to single him out. It was a remarkable opportunity for one so inexperienced, and certainly worth the inconvenience of giving up his weekend.

Simon had first attended a Society lecture at the beginning of the summer, 'Towards an Understanding of Mediumship', given by Professor Michael Warren. He'd been nearing the end of his second year studying Psychology and wasn't really convinced that he was going back for a third. He'd been at a loose end one evening and curious, that was all, slightly amused that anyone might take the study of psychics and fortune tellers seriously. But the lecture – hosted by a student group calling itself the Paranormal Society – and the man who gave it had taken him by surprise. Professor Warren had a far more formal approach to his subject than Simon had expected; he was clearly a thoughtful, disciplined thinker who stood in stark contrast to the lecturers on Simon's Psychology course – some of whom were barely older than he was, and all of whom insisted on first names and a shambling informality in lectures. The professor's attitude to the cases under discussion, which might have seemed lurid in other hands, had been rational, calm and above all scientific. Simon had been impressed.

Unwilling to admit to anyone that he'd been feeling lost, untethered somehow as the long summer vacation stretched out in front of him, Simon had attended several more lectures – a couple more on the campus, then at the Society's head-quarters in Kensington – and had gradually got to know a few members of the group. He'd begun to help out behind the scenes too, taking the minutes at meetings, volunteering in the archives, answering the phone. Unable to explain to anyone, not even himself, what had stirred this sudden interest in the para-normal, he'd kept his involvement hidden from his university friends, most of whom had fled London anyway, the moment term had ended.

The call, when it had come yesterday evening, had been a complete surprise.

'It's very good of you, you know,' said the professor.

'Sorry?'

'To give up your summer at such short notice.'

'I thought this was just a preliminary visit?' Just the weekend, he'd been told, over the phone, not by the professor, but by a woman – his secretary, Simon supposed. She'd sounded distant, disapproving and almost disappointed too when he'd confirmed he did have a car and was indeed free this weekend.

'True,' said Professor Warren, opening the file he'd been studying on and off since they'd got into the car that morning, 'but there's something about this case, the location, the circum-stances of the family – one gets a feeling for these things, you know.'

'Right,' said Simon. 'I see.'

He'd been given the bare bones of the story over the phone, about the farm and the two little girls who heard bumps in the night, and he'd been trying to play it cool, to prepare himself for a weekend spent hovering in the background as yet another case was proven to be a dead end; he was well aware that generally most field investigations led to the uncovering of minor and very unimaginative hoaxes. That the Society's most senior researcher, a man who dealt only with the most difficult and demanding phenomena, was already thinking of a long-term investigation, was, however, pretty exciting. He wondered, for a moment, if he might suggest taking a break from driving, swapping seats with the professor, and reading through the file himself.

'So, you think this might be the real thing?' he asked, hoping to hear more details, to be asked perhaps for his opinion. But Professor Warren was busy reading his notes again, and Simon didn't quite have the nerve to repeat the question.

They'd booked rooms at the village pub. Simon had been expecting quaint oak timbers and whitewashed walls, but the interior of the eighteenth-century building had turned out to be hastily modernised, no different to the city centre bars at home. Upstairs, the two box rooms available were plain and cramped; he took the smaller one, naturally.

He opened his bedroom window. The catch, painted over more than once in its lifetime, was stiff but he got it to move in the end, and leant out. The view was of the back of the pub. There were a few trestle tables set up in a scrubby beer garden. The garden wall was covered with a tangle of bushes and brambles and beyond that the land rose steeply, the moor seeming to loom over the pub, too high, too close, almost blocking out the sky; he couldn't imagine that many tourists would choose to stay for more than one night. He left the window on the latch and went downstairs.

They were in the bar, the professor and the young woman, chatting by the fireplace. He in his linen trousers and fading checked shirt, a battered briefcase in one hand, looking exactly like one's idea of a friendly academic, a good sort of chap who likes his beer and cricket. She was pretty enough, Simon thought as he walked towards them, younger than he'd expected, attractive in a pale sort of way.

'Here he is,' said the professor. 'Simon Leigh, this is Isobel Bradshaw. She's very kindly agreed to help us out for a few days.'

'I've agreed to think about it,' said the girl. She shook his hand firmly, looked him full in the face. Her smile was welcoming, but Simon had the distinct feeling that he was being sized up.

'Nice to meet you,' he said.

They took their drinks into the beer garden. The moor cast its long shadow over them as the midges circled their table. The professor pulled a manila folder from his briefcase and produced some newspaper cuttings. The first, from the *Whitby Gazette*, had a picture of two girls, more or less the same age, staring solemn and wide-eyed at the camera as they sat on the edge of a sofa, holding hands. The headline read *Unexplained Events at Local Farm*.

The second article was from a national paper. It carried the same photo but above the headline screamed Is THIS HOUSE HAUNTED? HORROR AT IRON SIKE FARM.

'You're familiar with these, I take it?'

'Yes.' Isobel picked up the first piece of paper. 'I went up to the farm on my own at first, but once I'd got the beginnings of the story the paper sent Liam Carthy, one of the reporters. I wanted to follow things up myself, but I was – overruled.'

'It's your photo, though,' says Simon. Her name ran beneath the image in small black letters.

'Yes. They decided they could trust me with that.' She kept her voice steady. 'Cathy and I get on all right, you see. Though I did have to explain to her that I don't get to write the headlines, particularly in the nationals.'

'Have there been further incidents since you became involved?' asked the professor.

'Apparently.' Isobel put the news cutting on the table, smoothing it with her fingertips. 'Usually at night and usually in the girls' room. Unexplained knocking, furniture being tipped over, toys, marbles, Lego bricks flying through the air. The usual sort of thing,' she said.

'Usual?'

Issy took a sip of her orange juice. 'I read up on a couple of cases,' she said. 'Research.'

'And the girls?' asked the professor. 'What do you think of them? How are they coping?'

'I don't know. They're – quite clever, I think. Lively. The sort of children who don't fear adults.'

The professor looked confused. 'Fear them?'

'You know – they use your first name, they ask questions, contradict you. They're not – biddable.'

'Do you like them?' asked Simon.

'I suppose so. I feel . . . sorry for them, more than anything else.'

'Because of the phenomena?'

'I suppose so, yes. Cathy is doing her best, but she's out of her depth.'

'And the father?'

'Joe? Apparently he won't be able to get away from work for another week or so. It's just Cathy and the kids for now.'

'He's been gone how long?'

'I'm not sure. A few weeks, I think.'

Professor Warren picked up the second paper. 'And did you witness the events in this account? The taps turning themselves on, the cold spots in the house, the girls being pinched and bruised by unseen hands?'

'I didn't witness any events. I mean – not the things they're talking about.'

'But something?'

She hesitated. 'Not really. Nothing I'd swear to in court. I heard – I thought I heard something upstairs – someone knocking. It doesn't sound like much, but it was – odd.'

'And you were the one who contacted the papers?'

'Yes.' Her tone hardened, as if she'd had this argument before and was weary of it.

'And they ran your photographs?'

'Yes.'

'There are others?'

'Contact sheets, yes.'

'May we see them?'

'I suppose so.'

'And the local paper, the *Gazette*, is it continuing to follow events?'

'No, they think . . . well, they've printed the one story, they think that's enough.'

'Do you?'

Isobel put her glass down. 'I think there's more to it,' she said. 'As far as I can tell, things are as bad as ever up there.'

'And that might be good for you,' said Michael, 'professionally speaking.'

'You too,' said Issy.

Michael consulted his notes again. 'The name of the farm, Iron Sike, is that significant?'

'I doubt it; sike is just another name for a beck, a stream. There must be one on the land somewhere.'

'I see.' If he was embarrassed, he hid it well. 'Is he reliable, this policeman friend of yours, the one who came to you with the story in the first place?'

'I think so. He seemed . . . unnerved by what had happened.'

'Will he talk to us, do you think?'

'I doubt it; he's barely talking to me now. Coppers who see spooks don't get taken very seriously, you see, and I'd promised not to tell.'

'Really?' The professor managed to hide his disapproval, most of it, and Issy took a sip of her drink, flushing a little. 'It seemed the right thing to do, at the time,' she said.

They ate inside, the only customers in the tiny and poorly lit dining room.

'Do you believe them?' Simon asked.

'Sorry?' Isobel hadn't eaten much, he noticed, and he couldn't blame her: the salad leaves on her plate looked warm and wilted. His food, gammon and chips, might best be described as filling.

'You didn't say whether or not you believe them.'

'That's not really relevant, is it? Martin – PC Thorpe – passed on a story, I took some pictures, you saw the papers and here we are.' She ran her fork around her plate, scraping a path through her food; she had short nails, practical hands.

'Are you a sceptic, my dear?' asked the professor.

'I have an open mind,' said Isobel.

'And you're ambitious.'

Isobel smiled. 'Well, you have to admit it makes a change from Lifeboat Day and golden wedding celebrations.'

She was his age, more or less, Simon thought, maybe a bit older, which he didn't mind. He wondered what she'd look like with her hair, a pale coppery gold, let loose. He wondered if she had a boyfriend.

'What about you?' Isobel asked, turning her attention to Simon. 'Do you believe what you've read?'

'I – I haven't had a chance to look at all the case notes yet.'

No one at the Society had thought to send him any copies.

'Well, generally speaking, then. You're a paranormal investigator, so that means you're predisposed to believe these girls, doesn't it?'

'It means I'm interested in the possibility of . . . something else. Something beyond our knowledge.'

'Our current knowledge,' said the professor.

'So, what do you want, exactly?' asked Isobel, pushing her plate away and leaning back in her chair.

'To evaluate the evidence, to record the girls' accounts, to consider alternative explanations for the phenomena experienced so far.' The professor could have been quoting from a Society monograph. He probably was.

'Such as fraud?'

'Sometimes people can become . . . caught up in the atmosphere of a place, shall we say. A significant proportion of supernatural occurrences can be explained as perfectly natural activity, poorly observed. A smaller but no less significant proportion is – yes, you're quite correct, fraudulent.'

'You seem to be in a disappointing line of work, Professor.' Her smile took a little of the sting out of her words.

'Ah, but you see, Isobel, there is a fraction, a tiny fraction, of

95

unexplained phenomena that remains exactly that – unexplained. And there, there is where our true calling lies.'

'Do you believe them?' Isobel asked. 'Do you think there's something here worth investigating?'

The professor hesitated for a moment, weighing his answer.

'I should like to see for myself,' he said, 'I should like to find . . . proof.'

'Have you been in touch with Cathy?'

'Not yet. I wondered if you would arrange an introduction, an interview, perhaps.'

'If I agree to get involved with your project.'

'You're already involved, surely? And it would be helpful, I think, to have a reliable witness, someone willing to document the investigation.'

Isobel picked up her drink and smiled. 'Like I said, I'll think about it.'

Michael left Simon and Isobel downstairs in the public bar and made his way up to his room. He wasn't tired, far from it. But he wanted to go over the notes he'd made once more before turning in and anyway, he assumed the two of them, the two young people, would rather get to know each other without him there, playing gooseberry. He was fairly certain Isobel was going to agree to speak to Cathy Corvino, that she might even be persuaded to photograph the investigation, to become part of the team, despite her evident scepticism.

He made his way down the carpeted hallway, the noise from the bar muffled now and rather comforting, in its way. He let himself into his room and dropped his briefcase on the bed two lamps, one on the bedside table, one on the small writing desk under the window, gave the room a pale golden glow. The windows were open, of course, and the night air was still.

It hadn't taken him long to unpack. He prided himself on that: he wasn't like so many men, so many widowers – the word unfamiliar, awkward, even after all this time – helpless when it came to domestic matters. The only personal touch he'd added to the room was a photograph set in a simple silver frame – himself, his wife Judith, and their daughter Carol. It was an old picture, nothing more than a blurred snapshot really, but it had always been one of his favourites, taken one sunny afternoon in their garden, a commonplace keepsake. He never travelled without it.

He picked it up and smiled as he always did, certain that Judith was there beside him somehow, the same warm and steady presence he had known throughout their marriage, guiding him, supporting him.

She'd be disappointed about the business with Miskin. He could have handled that better, should have handled it better. But he still had hopes that he could persuade Roland to come up to the farm at a later date, in a week or so perhaps, once he'd been able to generate some reliable evidence. Until then Simon could probably be counted on.

He replaced the photo and settled himself at his desk. This case interested him not so much because of the girls' situation, dramatic as it was, but because of the research opportunities it might afford. He had to plan accordingly. He's become aware recently that the rules and regulations of the Society had begun to chafe. What had begun for him as an experiment in radical thought had become safe, over-reliant on procedure and protocols. How, after all, could one begin to classify the unknown? This, he felt, was an opportunity to experiment with a new approach. He wondered if he might not give a lecture on this, once they were back in London, and began to idly plan his rebuttals to the inevitable objections of some of his more conservative colleagues.

After a while he picked up his notebook and pen and turned his attention to the farm and to the two girls, Bee and Loo: there was work to be done and he needed to be prepared.

Apart from a courting couple who had taken the shadiest spot, Simon and Isobel found that they had the beer garden to themselves. They chose a table at the far end, as far away from the pub as possible; neither of them really wanted to be overheard. Isobel lit a cigarette and the two sat in silence for a few minutes.

'Have you worked with Michael for long?' she asked.

'No, I – not long.'

'I looked him up; he's quite famous in his way, isn't he?'

'He's very highly regarded, as a researcher. He's worked on some very important cases.' Simon wished he could say something that didn't sound so formal. He looked up at the night sky, blue-black now and filled with stars. Some of the constellations looked familiar, but the more he looked the more he saw, until he felt quite dazzled and his head began to swim.

'Would it be hard to fool him, then?' Her voice was low; he had to lean forward to hear her.

'People have tried,' he said, thinking of the crowded shelves in the Society's archives, yellowing paper clippings with terse notes attached: 'No further action required.'

'And if it was faked, he'd say so?'

'Of course.'

'And he'll . . . watch out for them, will he?'

The other couple had stopped talking; Simon could see them, just in the corner of his eye, wrapped around each other. 'I suppose so,' he said.

'They're not well liked around here, the Corvinos,' said Isobel.

'Really? Why not?'

She drew on her cigarette. 'Some people think that living in the country will be simpler, healthier – but it isn't easy. You have to make an effort and . . . They don't fit in, you know? And the piece in the *Gazette* didn't help. They need someone who's going to be on their side.'

'What happened there?' asked Simon. 'With you at the newspaper?'

'Nothing. I do the pictures, that's all. They needed to send in someone better qualified, more experienced. I should have known they would.' She stubbed out the cigarette in the cheap tin ashtray and stood up. Her thin dress was creased and she tried to smooth it down.

'It's not fair though, is it?' said Simon. 'The way they took the story away from you.'

She looked across the garden towards the pub, its lights blazing, music from the jukebox leaking out into the warm night air. 'No,' she said. 'No, it bloody isn't.' She turned her gaze onto the couple for a moment or two, regarding them quietly, without embarrassment, as if they were no more than an interesting composition.

'But what if, what if it is, you know – a fraud of some sort?' asked Simon.

'It's still a story, isn't it?' she said. 'Better for me than you, perhaps. But I'd be . . . all right, I suppose.' She picked up her bag, wrapping the leather strap around her fingers, gently testing the weight of it, deciding. 'I'll go and see Cathy in the morning, see what she thinks,' she said. 'I'll see if she wants to meet you, if she's happy for you to interview the girls.'

'And you'll stick around? This weekend, I mean. Photos would be useful.'

'I suppose so. If she goes for it.'

'OK.' Simon scrambled to his feet. He thought he might

suggest she stay for another drink now that they were allies, but Isobel hoisted the bag onto her shoulder.

'Right. I'll see you tomorrow,' she said. 'At about eleven.'

'OK,' said Simon. 'I'm looking forward to it.'

But she was already walking back towards the pub and if she heard him she didn't bother to reply.

7

Now

Nina doesn't really like to sleep late, but at some point, in the early hours of Sunday morning, after two broken nights and a day of reviewing footage and writing up notes, her body had simply given in. She had last taken the readings from all the monitors at about five. Hal had dealt with the cameras and the SD cards, importing the rushes onto his laptop, and she'd decided to take a look at that. She'd carried the computer to the sofa and begun the long and tiresome process of watching the empty rooms.

She wakes now, covered with one of the sleeping bags and the laptop nowhere in sight.

'Jesus.' Her back aches and her mouth is dry. Hal is sitting at the table with his back to her.

'Morning,' he says, without looking round.

A second sleeping bag lies abandoned on the floor. 'Where's Lewis?'

'Bathroom. The pair of you went out like lights.'

She sits up slowly, stretching out the muscles in her neck. 'What about you?' she asks.

'Couldn't sleep,' says Hal, 'so I thought I'd get on.'

'Thanks,' she says. It doesn't seem enough. 'I really do appreciate you stepping in like this, you know. We both do. It means a lot to us,' she adds. 'To me.'

Hal turns round to look at her, resting his arm along the top of the chair. He looks pale, anxious, but at least he's smiling. 'You're welcome,' he says. 'Has it been worth it?'

'Of course it has.'

The silence that follows is filled by Lewis clattering down the stairs. 'I'm hungry,' he says, picking up a rucksack and shaking it experimentally.

'You're always hungry,' says Nina. She gets up and opens one of the carrier bags that litter the floor. 'Here.' She hands him a bottle of orange juice and an energy bar. 'Breakfast.' Lewis doesn't look pleased, but he takes a seat and begins to tear at the biscuit wrapper.

'We're up to date on the temperature readings,' he says, 'if you want to take a look at the EMF monitors.'

'It's been brilliant,' Nina says to Hal as she walks behind his chair. 'Worth every sleepless minute.'

'Right. Well. If you say so.'

Nina uses the loo and brushes her teeth. Once she's done she can't resist going into the girls' room one more time. She makes a show of checking the camera as well as the monitors before taking a careful circuit of the room, just in case they've missed anything significant. It's just as it was the last time she checked, of course, and the time before that.

She can hear the guys in the dining room. Lewis is lecturing Hal on some poltergeist study or other and Hal appears to be tolerating him. They hadn't managed to duplicate their findings, which has been, yes, a bit disappointing, but still they have it, on audio and video.

The girls heard it first: the knocking in the walls.

It's more than she had dared hope for.

*

102

'How's it going?' Lewis gestures towards the laptop screen with his cereal bar.

'Fine. I mean, nothing unusual, you know. Just you guys moving around, and the rooms. Just – fine . . .'

There has been nothing else since that first extraordinary evening – and if they hadn't got the film and the audio, Hal might have been able to persuade himself that he'd imagined it all.

He's reviewed the rushes a couple of times: Nina is standing motionless in the centre of the room, then he and Lewis both run into shot, rules and protocols abandoned, and the knocking in the walls – whatever it was – suddenly stops.

All their other evidence is, as far as Hal can tell, entirely subjective. Lewis insists there's a cold spot on the staircase, although given the lack of heating in the house, how he can isolate just one example is beyond Hal. Nina has been writing in her notebook fairly frequently, referring back to the notes in her folders, but she hasn't shared her feelings with the team.

Hal has got through the weekend by concentrating on the cameras and the images on his screen; he hasn't mentioned the power surge that messed around with the light that first evening, before the knocking in the walls began, although they have all replaced bulbs in various rooms, bulbs that blow with alarming regularity.

Still, Nina and Lewis are pleased with the way the weekend has gone, which is the important thing, Hal supposes. He still doesn't like the house, perhaps because it's cold and dark, perhaps because he can't quite shake the feeling that there might be something there in the dark. Something watching them.

Or maybe he's just seen too many horror films.

He turns back to the laptop and continues fast-forwarding through the footage from the camera on the upstairs landing.

Even at five times normal speed, this is going to take hours. Aware of Lewis sitting by the window, eating his breakfast and not really paying attention, Hal nudges the speed up and up again. The image flickers slightly.

Thirty times normal, and there it is, on the landing.

'Fuck.'

Lewis is on his feet and across the room in seconds. 'What?'

'Hang on, hang on.' Hal hits stop and goes back, pauses again and presses play. The hallway is empty.

He's gone back too far, or not far enough.

Hal tries again, and presses play. Nothing.

'What?' says Lewis again, standing over the table. Too close. Too impatient.

'Just wait.' Hal speeds up the video and by the time Nina comes back, they've found it.

'What's that?' She leans in close to the screen.

'We're not sure.'

It looks like it could be a fault on the screen, a smudge, a smear, a stain, in the corner of the landing, almost but not quite out of frame. A trick of the light, perhaps.

'Play it again.'

Hal presses play, slows the image down to half normal speed.

It's still there.

Back upstairs, after lunch by the harbour and the slow walk home up the hill, Cathy puts away her coat and bag, and Lucy watches her pace around the room, picking up magazines and stacking them on her desk, pulling out books from the shelves and pushing them back into place. Fussing, fretting, unable to settle down. Lucy knows better than to suggest a nap and she can't bring herself to mention Nina Marshall or the farm again.

'I think I'll read for a while; you don't mind, do you?' She doesn't bother waiting for an answer, she simply picks up a book at random, a collection of short stories, and sits in the chair by the window. She doesn't look up as her mother kicks off her shoes, nor does she acknowledge the tell-tale creak of bedsprings as Cathy sits on the bed, sighing softly as she swings her legs up and leans back on her pillows. It doesn't take her long to fall asleep.

Lucy stares at the open book on her lap as she listens to her mother breathing and counts slowly to one hundred. Only then does she risk turning her head. Cathy lies on her side on top of the bed, her knees drawn up to her body, her hands curled over her face. Lucy stands, putting her book to one side. She is on her way to the door when behind her Cathy's laptop pings softly. She has a new email.

Lucy doesn't think twice. She reads the note quickly, conscious of the sleeping figure across the room.

extraordinary results
really remarkable footage
so looking forward to sharing with you

She glances at her mother and finds herself considering deleting the message, imagining for a moment that with a tap on the mouse pad she can make it all go away. On impulse, she takes a shot of the email on her phone and she's still bent over the laptop when there's a discreet knock at the door and it opens. It's Sarah, a pile of fresh bedding in her arms.

'Oh. Sorry.' She begins to back out of the room and Lucy closes the computer, glad she no longer has to make a decision.

'Hang on,' she says, 'I'll come with you.'

*

105

She closes the door softly and walks down the corridor with Sarah, the younger woman still apologetic. 'I didn't mean to disturb you,' she says. 'Usually I'd do the beds in the morning, but we're a bit short-handed today.'

'That's fine; I think my mother just needs to catch up on her sleep. We've been for a walk.'

Sarah places Cathy's bedding on a laundry trolley at the end of the corridor, and begins sorting through a pile of sheets. 'Right. I'll do her room later, then.'

Lucy should really go upstairs and check her own emails. She's sure there'll be stuff from Eloise to deal with and some calls to make. She can't just abandon everyone at the gallery, and she needs to think about this girl, Nina, about that last email, about what she should do next. 'I'll let you get on,' she says.

'Actually . . . Since you're here – I just wanted to say – she's all right, you know, your mother.' Sarah has found what she was looking for and hugs the sheets, snowy white and edged in lace, close to her chest. 'She's usually very active, very – I mean she's not—'

'I know,' says Lucy. 'But she did get a bit confused. She thought she saw someone in the garden.'

'Yes.'

'And she's not completely well, you know – she doesn't always remember things.'

'But that's just names and stuff, new words. She's forgetful now and then but she's not – I wouldn't like you to think she was . . .' Sarah is starting to look uncomfortable. 'The thing is, I've worked with dementia patients before. We all have. What she said, what she did – that doesn't fit, you know. That's not how – well, it's not how her disease progresses.'

'Sarah, have you finished?' Jean's voice floats up the stairwell, uncomfortably close, and Sarah flushes.

'Nearly,' she says, raising her voice, clutching the sheets so hard she's creasing them. 'When I'm done, I'll take my break, if that's all right?'

'Yes. That's fine.'

The two women stand motionless until they hear a distant door close.

'In the garden,' Sarah says. 'I need to finish this, but I usually take my coffee out into the garden.'

There's a bench set back against the house just a little way along from the kitchen door and Lucy finds Sarah sitting there, clutching a mug. It's not exactly getting dark, but nor is it fully light; the days are growing palpably shorter and the air is cold and damp. Lucy pulls her coat around her and sits down on the bench.

'We don't get long,' says Sarah, 'only quarter of an hour.' She takes a sip of coffee. 'But still, it's a nice place to work, you know? Mrs Wyn Jones wants it all done right, but that's only because it's important, caring for people. She always says if you don't care there's no place for you here. She's really mortified about your mother. She'd never forgive herself if—' She stops, takes another sip of coffee. 'That's why we're short-staffed today. She had to sack Jo Lawrence – because of her not setting the alarms. It wasn't to get back at her, it was because Mrs Wyn Jones has to trust us, all of us, to look after the residents.'

'I know,' says Lucy. She can feel the girl's panic rising: see it in the thin hands gripping fiercely onto the cup.

'And we all get on. We like each other, we have a laugh.'

'That's nice.'

Sarah nods absently. 'It's hard sometimes though, especially when a resident,' her eyes flicker anxiously towards Lucy and then she looks down again, 'you know, dies.'

'Well, it's like you said, you care.'

'And it's an old house,' says Sarah. 'It's a bit . . . spooky.'

'I suppose it is.'

'Sometimes, sometimes you can think you might have . . . seen something.'

'Really?' Lucy tries to keep her tone even. 'Has that ever happened to you?'

'Yes.' The girl's voice is barely audible. She sounds almost guilty.

'Where?'

Sarah hesitates. 'There.' She points to the far wall, shaded by a beech tree and some low, scrubby bushes. 'She was there, looking up at the house.'

'Right,' says Lucy. 'Do you want to tell me?'

Sarah looks into the mug, gently swirling the contents around. 'It was morning and Mrs Leeman, she has the room next to your mum, she was down at breakfast and I'd been doing her bed, because she . . . Well. I did her bed and tidied round a bit and I was tying back her curtains, and I looked out of the window and . . .' She clears her throat. 'We're not supposed to talk about it, only I don't want you to think Mrs Corvino's, well, making it up, or anything. Because she's not. And it's not – you know – it's not her illness.' Sarah is pale, she has dark shadows under her eyes; she must work long hours, caring for those who have no one else to tend them. She wears a ring on her left hand, a bright blue stone surrounded by tiny diamond chips that spark and catch the light. Lucy is surprised – she's far too young to be thinking of marriage, surely.

'I saw a girl,' Sarah says. 'A girl that shouldn't have been there. I thought it was a reflection at first. Because we were all busy inside, with breakfast and that, and she wasn't wearing a coat or anything. But then I moved and she didn't, and the

108

angles were all wrong anyway, and then I could see she was wearing a long dress. She was tall and pale with long blonde hair, she was standing perfectly still and she was looking up at me. Like she could see me. Like she could see into me.' Sarah shivers, looking across the garden. 'She must have been cold, because she was barefoot, just like everyone says.'

'They've let their imaginations run away with them, that's all.' Jean's office is warm, and the lamps on the desk and over the fireplace cast a comforting amber glow. The room smells of beeswax polish and freesias. There are snapshots and family portraits scattered about, and the effect is comforting, intimate. It's hardly the place for a confrontation.

'They call her the barefoot girl,' says Lucy.

'They've given it a name?' For the first time, Jean's confident expression seems to fade, and something in her sags, gives in a little.

'It?'

'It's not real, surely you can see that. It's just . . .'

'They've all seen her,' says Lucy, relentless now the obvious explanation has presented itself. She's relieved too, now that her mother's ghost is no more than a rumour, a story circulated by bored and impressionable young women. The emails from Nina Marshall, well, they can't have helped much, but that's something else, something private, she can deal with that later.

'Some of the staff claim they've seen . . . someone,' says Jean. 'But you're not suggesting anything—'

Supernatural.

'Of course not,' says Lucy.

'And we do have quite a few young women working here, you know. Any one of them could be outside, be seen through a window, and be back at work a few minutes later.'

109

It's a perfectly reasonable explanation.

'Well, that's not the problem, is it?' says Lucy. 'I don't care what any of the staff here think they might have seen. I care that these ridiculous rumours are getting back to my mother.'

'They're not . . .' Jean leans back in her chair and her tone softens. 'The thing is, when you work with older people, the frail, the ill. Well, you build up a little collection of experiences, the odd things that happen that you hear or sense when you're on your own on a night shift – you know the sort of thing I mean.'

'Ghost stories.'

One of them has to say it.

'I suppose so. And you tell those stories, don't you? You pass them on to the people you work with, you share it, that odd feeling you had late one night, the prickle on the back of your neck. It helps you cope sometimes, with fear and loss. And – they're so young, some of them – they enjoy scaring themselves.'

Sarah hadn't looked like she was enjoying it.

'And the barefoot girl?' Lucy asks.

'I first heard about her a month or so ago. Which means they were talking about her for a little while before that, I suppose.'

'She's just a figure in the garden?'

'Yes. A pale figure dressed in black, with long fair hair, looking up at the house, only if you go outside to find her, she's vanished.' Jean pauses, looking embarrassed, and more than a little guilty. 'It's nonsense, of course. There's no reason for her to be there, no story about a girl connected to the house. It's just kids being silly, scaring each other.'

Lucy remembers the girl she'd seen in the window in her

mother's room, the relief she'd felt when she realised it was her own reflection.

'Someone must have mentioned it to Cathy,' says Jean. 'Planted the idea somehow. I've spoken to them all about it and I'll speak to them again. I'm so sorry, Lucy, truly I am.' She lifts her chin. 'I'll quite understand if you feel you need to make other arrangements for your mother,' she says, 'but I hope you won't. I've spoken with the staff concerned, and there'll be no repetition of the oversight with the alarms.'

The possibility of taking Cathy away hadn't even occurred to Lucy and her irritation is replaced by a sudden rush of guilt. 'Yes. I know. I don't think – Mum's perfectly happy here. We don't need to upset her over this,' she says. 'Moving her would be – well, we'd have to discuss it as a family.' She can just imagine the emails and phone calls that would provoke. 'We'd have to think about that.'

'I see,' says Jean. 'Well, maybe you should do that. Have a chat with Cathy. Let me know how you all feel. We'd be very sorry to see her go.'

Lucy goes up to her attic room and sits on the bed. All this turmoil, all this fuss because of a few emails and a foolish rumour. It makes her head ache.

She weighs her phone in the palm of her hand. Maybe she should call Dan first, let him know she's solved the mystery. That there has been nothing to worry about after all. Someone has told Cathy the tale of the barefoot girl, and the rest is just—

Tell her I made a mistake.

She finds the screenshot and reads the message again.

so looking forward to sharing with you

111

She can't imagine why Cathy's become involved with these people, these strangers. Look where it's got them. She can't have her upset like this, she won't.

There's a phone number at the top of the email and Lucy comes to a decision: enough is enough.

8

Now

They'd arranged to meet that evening in a bar just down the road and Lucy shoves her hands in her pockets as she walks briskly along the cliff top, welcoming the stinging cold and the chance to get away from the house, her mother, for a while.

She won't be able to put them off their investigations, she's fairly sure of that, and there'll be nothing she can do if the girl wants to write an article or another book about the farm, but that doesn't matter. She can write as much as she pleases. Cathy and her children have all survived far worse. But she'll have to do it without their help, she'll make that perfectly clear and if she can put them off their meeting with Cathy, maybe that will minimise the damage. With no new interviews, no new material from the Corvino family, the best Nina Marshall will be able to manage is a rerun of the original story and Lucy can't imagine anyone will really be interested in that.

It's not perfect, and her mother won't be pleased, but she can't think of anything else.

The bar is on the ground floor of a large hotel which stands on the cliff top overlooking the bay. In the summer the views must be spectacular, but tonight the building feels remote, almost forbidding, built on a scale a little too large for comfort. It's not busy – there are maybe half a dozen customers, mainly couples, and the long room is all discreet polished wood and gleaming mirrors, nautical brass instruments and sepia prints, someone's idea of a luxury yacht, perhaps.

The three of them are easy enough to spot: young, slightly dishevelled, a little out of place. They've taken a table by the window. The two men look up as she walks in, and one, the fair one in glasses, says something to a young woman with her back to the door.

Lucy undoes her coat and unwinds her scarf as she walks towards them, trying to catch her breath; she's still running through it all in her head, what she needs to say, how best to make a start. The young woman turns to look, as the man next to her carries on speaking, whispering in her ear.

And everything falls apart.

'Hello. I'm Nina,' the girl says, standing. 'Nina Marshall. It's so good of you to agree to meet us. We were just going to get another drink.' They shake hands and the girl keeps on talking, bright, friendly, confident. 'What would you like?'

Lucy can see herself reflected in the windows and the polished brass table top; the girl is there too – she shimmers. It occurs to Lucy that she should have picked somewhere else, somewhere busy, one of the big cheap pubs along the sea front, somewhere less . . . exposed. She feels dizzy.

'Beer?' Nina is asking. 'Or wine?'

'White wine. Something dry, please,' Lucy says, and she takes off her coat as Nina goes to the bar. Her hands are actually trembling; she can't believe they haven't noticed. Maybe they're all too polite to comment.

'Lewis Wellburn,' says the blond boy, offering his hand, 'and this is Hal Fletcher.' The other one, darker, older perhaps, slumps back in his seat. He nods but doesn't speak.

114

'Lucy Frankland.'

'Yes.' Lewis is smiling, beaming. 'We know.'

Lucy takes a seat and again turns her attention to the girl standing at the bar. The resemblance is quite clear, unmistakable. She's tall and slender and her long hair is streaked with blonde highlights.

'Thank you for calling,' says Lewis. 'We really appreciate it.'

'Well,' Lucy says, 'I thought we needed to talk.' She takes a deep breath, trying to compose herself.

'Oh, it's brilliant,' says Lewis. 'I can't tell you – this is just fantastic.'

Lucy doesn't know what to say. She hadn't expected such enthusiasm. She pulls her phone from her coat pocket and pretends to check it. She puts it on the table, face down.

Nina places their drinks on the table, wine for Lucy, beer for the rest of them. She sits and Lucy is certain: she has the same eyes, the same nose, the same smile. He's there, right in front of her.

Simon.

'This is so great, really,' Nina says. 'I have so many questions, we all do.'

'Questions?'

'Well,' says Lewis, 'we were hoping to get a bit of background from you, some sort of context for the events at the farm, now you're able to – well, now you have some . . . perspective.'

'I'm sorry.' Lucy tries to focus. 'I think you've misunderstood. I rang because I wanted to talk to you about my mother. Not because . . . I'm not interested in your project and I can't help. I thought I'd made that clear.'

'Well, I suppose we hoped you might change your mind,' says Nina, looking at the others, drawing them in. 'We have some amazing material, if you'd just take a look.'

'We can show you here?' says Lewis.

'No. I don't want to see.' Lucy's voice is just loud enough to merit a more than casual glance from the barman; she picks up her glass, tries to regain some sort of control, to still the tremor in her hands. 'I don't need to see what you've been doing. My mother – Cathy – has explained to me what's going on, and really,' she puts the glass down, hides her hands under the table, 'you need to understand that we, that my family has no interest in your project and we can offer you no help.'

There. Formal, clear, final.

'That's not the impression I have from Cathy,' says Nina.

'Yes. Well, I'm afraid my mother is . . . unwell. She has vascular dementia and she . . .' Lucy finds that the details of her mother's condition escape her. 'I can't have her upset, or disturbed,' she says. 'Surely you can see that?'

'Oh,' says Lewis, in the awkward silence that follows. 'I'm so sorry.'

'Thank you.' Lucy finally allows herself a sip of wine.

'I'm sure that's very worrying for you,' says Nina, 'but Cathy's emails all seem – well, quite clear. She's been very helpful, she obviously remembers life at the farm in great detail, the inves-tigation and everything that came after.' Her words are mild, but there's an underlying tone, not a threat exactly, more an insistence that she is not going to back down easily.

'Well, she has good days and bad days,' Lucy says. 'And you talking with her about . . . that summer, my sister . . . surely you can see that's going to be difficult for her, even at the best of times.'

'Has she said something?' Lewis asks. 'We really didn't mean to upset her.'

'I'm sure you didn't. But – she's old, she's . . . ill. She's had a fall, actually – that's why I'm here. It was quite serious and to

116

be honest, I'd prefer that you didn't contact her again. You must see that any questions you have might be distressing.'

Lewis, at least, seems to be listening. He's starting to look worried.

'I didn't know your mother was ill. None of us did,' Nina says, swiftly. 'We never meant to . . . But don't you think that talking to us might help?'

'No. I think that's rather naive, if you want my honest opinion.'

'But it can't be healthy, keeping things bottled up.'

'Nina.' Hal's voice is soft.

'Healthy? I'm sorry, but I don't think you have the—' Lucy leans forward. 'It's not as if you're doing this for our benefit, is it? You don't actually believe this will help my mother, or any of us, for that matter.'

'I want to complete the investigation at the farm. By any definition that's closure?'

'Nina,' Hal says. 'Maybe you – we should all just slow down for a minute.'

'Closure?' Lucy's voice rises. 'Closure for who, exactly? Closure for my mother? Me? Or for you, and your father?'

'Hal's right,' says Lewis. 'If we could just—'

'I mean,' Lucy's not sure how to go on, 'I'm not wrong, am I?'

For once Nina seems lost for words.

'Because the thing is – you are very like him. Simon.'

'Sorry, what?' Hal says.

Lewis sits back and picks up his glass.

'And Cathy would have told me, if she knew. But she doesn't know, does she? And that's – that's inexcusable.' Hal looks confused, turning first to Lewis, then to Nina for some sort of explanation.

At least the girl has the grace to look embarrassed. 'I was going to tell her,' she says.

'Really? When? Why wait?'

'Because I thought if she knew, then she might not – she wouldn't want to see me. I thought it would be better to present the project more – formally.'

'So you lied. You didn't even use your real name.'

'I didn't lie.' Nina's words travel the length of the room and once again, the barman pauses and looks over at them.

She lowers her voice. 'Mum and Dad never married. My name is Nina Marshall. Leigh is my middle name. I was going to tell her, but once we got in touch, after she answered the first letter, I didn't know how to – how to bring it up. And then we started emailing a bit and I thought it would be better to do it face to face.'

'Who do you work for anyway?' Lucy asks. 'Don't you have rules about this sort of thing?'

'The Society for the Study of Anomalous Phenomena,' says Lewis.

'AnSoc,' says the other one, Hal.

'It's a voluntary thing,' says Nina.

'A student organisation,' says Hal, ignoring the sharp look of disapproval that crosses Nina's face.

'Students?' Lucy can barely keep the relief out of her voice, and suddenly they're no longer a team, they're just a bunch of kids, playing at research. If the worst comes to the worst, she can always contact the university and make a complaint, a thought which is satisfying as well as comforting. 'Well,' she says, 'as I've made clear, we can't possibly get involved, and really, it's not as if you need us. You can still speak to Simon, can't you? He probably remembers it better than I do.'

She falls silent, and as Lewis looks at Nina, his expression oddly tender, Lucy realises she knows what's coming next.

'The thing is – I'm sorry – he died,' says Nina. She leans forward across the table. 'My dad. Simon. He died about six months ago.'

Lucy can't meet her eyes.

'It was a heart attack. It was very – sudden.'

Nina opens the bag she's propped up against the table, her words tumbling out now. 'After the funeral we had to sort all his stuff out, his files and, well, you know . . . Everything was pretty well organised, the research for his books, and the TV shows, the documentaries . . . Here.' Nina has found what she's looking for: a manila folder, worn and tattered at the edges. Lucy remembers those folders, in his leather satchel, inside the tent. 'The only material not filed away, that was on his desk and laptop, was this, well, lots of these, actually. I thought it must be a current investigation at first. The TV programmes had sort of dried up a while ago, but he still took on new cases, wrote articles, lectured at the Society. But it wasn't a new case; it was an old one, the first one, the one they never finished, and I could see that he'd started making revisions, and I thought – I suppose I thought we could finish it for him.'

'Your university group?'

'Not exactly,' says Nina. 'But, you know – some of us.'

Lucy can't help herself. She opens the file and there they are, her and Bee looking up at the camera. She can feel the dusty fabric of the old red sofa, with half its springs gone, she can smell the joss sticks her mother had been so very fond of and she can remember how crowded the room had seemed. There was Michael, serious, slightly formal, and Isobel and her cameras, and Simon sitting cross-legged on the floor, smiling reassuringly at them both, as the tape recorder wheels went round and round; and now, astonishingly, Lucy does cry.

Lewis and Nina go to the bar for more drinks while Lucy tries to pull herself together, rubbing at her face with a tissue as Hal finishes his drink and finds an excuse to check his phone.

119

You're so fucking wet, Loo.

'Sorry,' she says.

Nina and Lewis are talking at the bar. Lewis can't help glancing back at their table and although neither of them looks happy, Lewis in particular seems disappointed.

'That's OK,' Hal says, glancing up, 'it's obviously all a bit . . . difficult.'

Nina leads the way back to the table, Lewis following in her wake, and Hal puts his phone away, murmuring a thank you as Lewis places his beer on the table. Lucy scrunches up her tissue. 'I haven't thought about Simon, about his book, about any of it, for years,' she says, which is almost true.

'Neither had Dad, I think. But he'd obviously been going through all his notes and recordings, and . . .' Nina hesitates. 'He was planning a new edition, I think,' she says. 'I've been trying to work out what it is he wanted to include, but there's so much . . . He was going to go back to Iron Sike Farm, though, I found the correspondence with the new owners and . . . well, I went there, you know, a couple of times, to look around, just to get a sense of the place.'

'I know,' says Lucy. 'I saw the photographs.'

'On your own?' says Lewis. 'You went to the farm on your own?'

'Yes.'

'You never said.'

'Don't, Lew, please.'

'Why didn't you say?'

'The thing is, it's what he wanted,' says Nina, 'and this weekend has been amazing. We've been able to gather new data, findings that support Dad's book, and with your account of what happened—'

'You've already got my account,' says Lucy.

'Yes, but you were just a child; now you can make your own case.'

'We don't need to make a case.'

'We?'

'My mother and I.'

'That's not what she said in her emails. She seems very . . . interested.'

'She's ill. My mother is ill, I told you that. She fell. She fell because you'd managed to confuse her so much she went wandering around the garden, chasing – and she—' Lucy's on her feet now, reaching for her coat, but Nina doesn't notice, she's rooting through her bag again.

'If you'd just take a look,' she says.

Lucy shouldn't have called, she shouldn't have come. 'Stay away from us,' she says, determined not to cry again, 'and stay away from the farm. Stay away from my mother and stay away from me.' She knocks against the table, spilling their drinks as she pushes past, and then she's gone.

'Well,' says Lewis, 'that went well.'

Nina gathers her documents together, ordering the photographs, using the activity to regain control, to calm herself, to think. 'If she'd just listen,' she says. 'If she'd just give us a chance.'

'You should have told me,' says Lewis. 'I'd have gone with you. To the farm.'

Lucy Frankland. It had occurred to her that she'd have married, of course it had, but not that she'd have changed her first name, too. Nina wonders if all the children have followed suit; she hasn't asked Cathy too much about this, she hadn't wanted to scare her off. She wonders if Lucy is still married. She hadn't noticed a ring. She picks up a photo of Loo, the little girl her father knew. She's sitting in the garden holding a book in her lap; her smile is sweet, if a little uncertain. There's no sign of this child in the woman she just spoke with. The tangled dark hair is now held back in a neat plait, her clothes are casual but sober, discreet. Loo has vanished.

Nina puts the photo on the table. Lewis is frowning as he stares out of the window and Hal just looks plain pissed off. 'Shit,' she says, 'shit, shit, shit.'

Lucy is halfway along the street when the phone in her pocket buzzes. Blue Jacket House. It's Jean. 'Lucy, I'm sorry to disturb you, but your mother is asking for you.'

'What's happened?' That little jerk of anxiety making her breathless, her pulse thudding in her throat.

'Nothing. Sorry. It's nothing, really. She's – she's a little distressed and she'd like to see you.'

'Distressed?'

Jean lowers her voice. 'That's right. If you could come back to the house?' She must be worried about being overheard.

'Of course. I'm not far away. I'll be as quick as I can.'

Lucy puts her phone in her pocket and glances back towards the pub. At least they've had the good sense not to follow. There's unfinished business there though; she's not at all sure Nina was listening to her or that she's managed to put her off. She should have been firmer, clearer, but there's nothing else she can do tonight. She turns and walks quickly up the hill. The town is quiet, a fog has rolled in from the sea, smothering the wind, and the night air is damp, cold. She keeps her head down, her hands shoved deep in her pockets, replaying the conversation from the bar in her head. Simon, she thinks. Dead.

The main gates to the care home are locked and she has to stop and think for a moment before she can remember the code for the smaller entrance set slightly to one side. She punches in the numbers, slips through the gate, and makes her way up the gravel drive.

All that time the two of them used to spend, watching him.

She's just out of sight of the road and not quite in view of the house when she realises that she's not alone; there's someone behind her, following her. She stops and turns. She hadn't noticed anyone in the street, certainly there had been no one close enough to slip in through the gate, so there's nothing to fear; whoever it is must surely have good reason to be there.

'Hello?' She sees it, thinks she sees someone – something fluttering in the dark, a dress, perhaps, or a nightgown.

She'll catch her death.

There one moment, gone the next; a shadow folding in on itself.

It will be one of the auxiliaries taking a break, or someone arriving for the night shift, perhaps. Someone who knows the code to the gate. She has a vague memory of the staff car park being situated to the rear of the house, and there's a back road they all use, isn't there? There's another gate there, with another code. So she's perfectly safe.

She stands still, waiting. Apart from the dull, distant wash of the sea, the night is silent. But any moment now, someone will come into focus, and they'll carry on towards the house together.

She can't hear anyone, not exactly, but she can—

'Who's there?'

—feel it.

Of course, there's no reason someone arriving at the back of the house would be suddenly walking up the front drive – that wouldn't make sense at all. Anyway, it's not that important and she needs to get back to Cathy.

But Lucy finds that she is oddly reluctant to turn her back

on whoever might be following her. The house is just around the corner, she reminds herself as she peers into the darkness, the trees and bushes shadows against the night, and the bare-foot girl just a story the staff tell each other to pass the time. She's not real.

Maybe they did follow her back from the pub after all – not all of them, three people couldn't keep so quiet, so steady in the dark.

'Hello?'

Nina might follow all on her own, though. She didn't look as if she was done with any of this yet.

'You don't scare me,' Lucy says, turning, trying to keep her voice conversational, reasonable, 'so you may as well show your-self.'

She waits, the skin on the back of her neck rising, puckering into tiny goose bumps. Maybe someone is late for work, maybe they've sneaked out for a cigarette, maybe someone is as scared of her as she is of—

'I don't have time for this,' Lucy says, forcing herself to turn towards the house. She walks briskly, refusing to give them the satisfaction of looking back, resisting the temptation to run.

Jean meets her at the front door.

'What happened?' asks Lucy.

'I don't know. She rang her buzzer about an hour ago and I went up myself. She was very agitated, she wanted you – but of course you'd gone out.'

Jean hesitates; Lucy can see her trying to find the right words. 'She said she had to speak to you, straightaway, and when I suggested that she ring you, she said that wasn't good enough – that she needed to show you.'

'What?'

'I don't know. She'd been going through her things. She became very agitated, I'm afraid. I had to call for help.'

'Help?'

'To get her back into bed.'

Above them, on the first floor, there's a muffled thump and a door slams.

'Right,' says Lucy. 'I suppose I'd better go up.'

Her mother is asleep. The room is illuminated by the bedside lamp and long shadows lie against the walls. The curtains are open, the darkened window panes beaded with mist. Cathy's breath is soft, but even.

Did they sedate her?

Surely not.

Lucy walks carefully to the bed. The room isn't exactly untidy, but someone has knocked over the contents of the dressing table and a pile of magazines on the bedside cabinet has fallen askew. Some books have been taken from their shelves and stacked in unsteady piles on the floor. Propped up against them are a selection of used sketchbooks, a dozen or more.

Lucy crosses the room and pulls the heavy curtains together. She won't look down into the garden; you can't see anything anyway, not unless you lean in close.

Cathy sleeps on peacefully, but Lucy can't bring herself to leave.

She won't look, she tells herself, as she picks up a book from one of the shelves and takes it to the armchair. There's nothing there.

Nina can't possibly sleep. She can't believe it – she'd got so close, face to face with Lucia Corvino, and still she'd managed to blow it. The long walk from the pub to the B and B has done

125

little to improve her mood. She sits on her bed, surrounded by her father's files, replaying the conversation again and again, trying to see where she'd gone wrong.

The tapping at the door makes her jump, even though she's half-expecting it. She's going through a folder of photographs, Isobel Bradshaw's work; stuff that hadn't made its way into the book.

'Come in,' she says.

Hal. He closes the door and leans against it. He looks weary; out of the three, he's had the most to drink, insisting they stay in the pub long after Lucy Frankland had walked out on them.

'Hi,' he says.

'Hi.'

'Do you want to tell me?' he says. 'About your dad?'

'It's a bit complicated, Hal.'

'Yeah.' He's still leaning against the door, just out of reach. He does that, she's noticed: he always puts some distance between them, choosing always to sit opposite her, never close by; placing her in frame, fixing her in place. She wonders, from time to time, how he really sees her. 'It would be,' he says. 'But you were going to mention him at some point, I take it?'

'Don't be like that,' she says. 'Come here and take a look at this. Tell me what you think.' She holds out a sheet of photos, proofs, black and white thumbnail images.

He doesn't move. 'Is there any point in being angry with you?' he asks.

'Not much,' she says. 'Come on, give me your professional opinion.'

He gives in then, sitting at the foot of the bed and taking the photos from her. 'They're a bit overexposed,' he says, tilting the paper towards the light. There are two figures, young girls, behind them a large door opens on to – it's hard to tell, a bright

126

sky, perhaps. As he glances through the images he can see another, third figure appear in the scene, blurred as if it's moving too quickly for the exposure. 'What am I looking for?' he says.

'I'm not sure,' says Nina. 'It's something my dad left behind, a classic case of too much information.'

'Is that her, then? Lucy?'

'She was the younger one, but yeah, that's her.' She leans forward, gently taking the paper from his grasp.

'So what's the deal there? No. Hang on. Complicated, right?'

'Yeah.'

'She looked like she'd seen a ghost earlier.'

'Not funny, Hal.'

'I need to know what's going on,' he says. 'If we're going to carry on with this,' and it hangs between them for a moment, the possibility of confiding in him.

'Come here,' she says, putting the contact sheet back in its folder and placing it carefully on the bedside table. 'Come here and I'll tell you in the morning.'

They hadn't turned the lamp off and as Nina lies snoring softly, one arm flung over his chest and her face obscured by a tangle of hair, Hal stares up at the ceiling, looking for patterns in the shadows. His head aches. He's spent the past two nights monitoring cameras and scanning through hours of unchanging footage until he can barely focus. Over the weekend his sleep, what little he's managed, has been fractured by the routine of exchanging and formatting SD cards and punctuated by uneasy, half-forgotten dreams. But still he can't quite let go, he can't bring himself to close his eyes.

Instead he finds himself replaying the scene in the bar. Lucy Frankland, whoever she was, hadn't been expecting Nina to be, well, Nina. And of course, neither Lewis nor Nina would have bothered to tell him what was going on, because he had agreed to be their test subject as well as their tech guy. They'd needed his cameras – but his ignorance about the farm, about what had gone on there, that had been a bonus. So they had worked at keeping him in the dark. They hadn't even bothered to tell him it was Nina's dad who'd written the book they kept going on about.

He's still more than a bit pissed off about that. But there's something else bothering him.

A couple of nights in a haunted house. A bit of a laugh, really.

Only now he can't sleep and the vague, queasy feeling that he'd had when he'd first arrived in the house hasn't let up. He has the sense of being . . . infected with something.

Stupid.

The bed, a single, is too small for them really, that's all it is; he's never going to sleep if he stays and he should probably go back to his own room anyway. He edges out of the bed and dresses quickly, as Nina sighs and sleeps on. Next to the lamp she's left a pile of books and folders, some half open, spilling out photocopied notes and photographs. Her dad's research.

He looks at the bed. Nina doesn't move. He picks up the top folder and finds the contact sheets again, black and white shots of children, two girls standing in a field, side by side, then the same girls playing in a large sunlit room. The image is highly contrasted: the girls are little more than silhouettes and he can't make out their features. He's about to take a closer look when he notices the book, lying half hidden under a pile of notes.

A Haunting at Iron Sike Farm by Simon Leigh.

It's the same two girls, staring out from the front cover, and what is indistinct on the contact sheet is clearer now; they are barefoot and wearing flowing white dresses. Both have long dark hair, loose and curling wildly, and both are looking solemnly at the camera, almost, but not quite holding hands. Hal looks at Nina one last time and then quietly slips the book out from under the pile. He'll tell her in the morning.

9

Then

The girls were in the back garden when they arrived. Anto was dozing in the pushchair and Loo and Bee were sitting on the eiderdown, drawing. They liked their art lessons: their mother always allowed them lots of time and as long as they didn't argue too much over pencils and pastels, or complain about the tasks she set them, she would pretty much leave them to get on with things.

They heard a car pull up, that was the thing with it being so quiet. And they knew the men were coming, that Isobel was bringing them in her car; Cathy had told them so this morning after Issy had called in.

'They just want to talk to us,' she'd said, although really, she meant they wanted to talk to them, to Bee and Loo.

'Will we be in the papers again?' Bee had asked. 'Does Joe know?'

But Cathy hadn't answered, she'd only told them to go upstairs and tidy their room before lunch. She hadn't mentioned the visit since and now they were here, outside the house.

'That's them,' said Loo and she would have jumped up to go and see, only Bee grabbed her by the wrist and held her back.

'Hang on,' she said. There was a pause between the car doors slamming and someone knocking on the front door. Flor burst into tears in the kitchen.

'Wait – wait for me—' The girls could hear him as he followed their mother out of the kitchen, down the hall and to the front door, his furious sobbing drowning out the distant adult voices.

'We should go in,' said Loo.

'No, we shouldn't,' said Bee. 'They have to come to us.'

There was a lot of fussing about in the kitchen, or so it seemed to Loo. She could hear them all in there. Grown-ups introducing themselves and Flor getting in the way and the baby whimpering every so often. She could hear the door on their rickety little fridge being opened, the taps being turned on and off, and another woman's voice, Issy's, and they all went on and on in that way that adults did.

Beside her on the ground, Bee was staring fixedly at her sketchpad, but like Loo, her entire attention was fixed on the kitchen and the people in it. Her knuckles were white where she was gripping her pencil.

'Bee,' Loo said softly.

But Bee just shook her head. 'They have to come to us.'

Loo looked down at her own paper. She'd been drawing the garden wall with its broken stones and wallflowers. She'd added a butterfly, which she was quite pleased with, and before the car had pulled up, she'd been considering adding more.

She looked over at Bee's paper. It was a view of the same bit of garden, but Bee's picture couldn't have been more different: wild lines chased each other across the page, shadows had been cross-hatched with such force she'd almost torn the paper, and beyond the wall Bee had sketched in the suggestion of the moor that overlooked the house. She probably wouldn't do any more to it. Bee abandoned her drawings on a regular basis, leaving them in the garden, the kitchen, their bedroom; pages torn roughly from their pads and left to gather dust or to be swept away in one of their mother's periodic tidying fits.

Loo had seen her father looking at one, once. She hadn't been able to work out what he thought about it, but he'd looked at it for a long time before putting it carefully on the kitchen table. The picture had vanished by supper time. It wasn't even one of Bee's good ones, but Loo wished Joe would look at her own work like that, once in a while, just really . . . look, even if he decided he didn't like it. He was supposed to be back by now, back from Scotland, and Loo wondered what he might make of their visitors and all the fuss that was going on.

She was starting to need the toilet, but she didn't think Bee would let her go. She shifted around a bit. Maybe if she offered to get them both a drink of water . . .

'Hello.' The man was standing in the doorway, a leather satchel over one shoulder and a glass in his hand. She felt Bee stiffen beside her. She could almost hear her sister counting in her head, one, two, three . . . all the way to ten, before she looked up at him and smiled.

'Hello,' she said.

'Do you mind if I join you?' he asked, and he actually waited for an answer.

'If you like,' said Bee, pushing her hair off her face and looking up at the man.

'Thanks.' He walked across the garden to where they sat, unlooping his bag from his shoulder and dropping it onto the grass, somehow managing to sit by crossing his feet at his ankles and dropping down onto the bed cover, arriving at eye level with them both in one easy movement, and without spilling his drink.

'I'm Simon,' he said, as the sun caught the water droplets in his glass and bounced tiny mirrors onto his white cotton shirt. He took a sip and waited.

'I'm Bee and this is Loo.' Bee put her pad down. Loo closed

133

her own sketchbook and placed it to one side. She drew her knees up close to her chest and rested her chin on them, her thick hair lying heavy against her neck, as she stared at the man. He was young, older than Dan, but younger than Joe. They'd had a student teacher once, in school, back when Loo still went to school, and this man, Simon, reminded her of him.

'This is nice,' he said, looking around the garden. The grass on the little lawn was overgrown, and the vegetable patch was dry and crumbly. Against the far wall, runner beans were tangling themselves around some sagging and splintered stakes. Above them in the tree, hard little apples were forming on the branches. They weren't ripe yet. Bee and Loo had tried one and, finding it sour, had fed it to Flor. But it was pleasantly shady there, and Loo liked the patterns the gently shifting leaves made on the sun-bleached eiderdown.

'It's all right,' said Bee. 'We had a bigger garden at our last house.'

'Do you know why we're here?'

Loo pressed her lips together.

'Yes,' said Bee.

The man took another sip of his drink – not water, Loo realised, but her mother's home-made lemon barley water, cloudy and with little bits floating in it. It was sour stuff too, like the little apples. No one ever asked for more. Because he was looking at Bee, she felt all right about looking at him, as if she might put him into her picture if she felt like it. He wore jeans and a shirt, they were faded but clean, and he had light brown hair, quite long and with blond streaks in it. He has browny-green eyes, she thought, before looking away, hugging her knees closer.

'Can you tell me a bit about what's been going on?' he said.

But before either of the girls could answer, another voice interrupted them.

134

'Hello.' Isobel, from the newspaper, in the doorway, holding a glass of water.

'Did you bring our photos?' said Bee, standing up, as if the man didn't matter at all.

They decided to interview the girls in the front room. Bee and Loo sat on the sofa, and Michael, the professor, took the armchair by the fireplace. He was a tall man, serious, with thinning grey hair and clothes that looked expensive but old: summer clothes, soft and worn in.

Simon sat cross-legged on the floor next to him. He looked up at Loo and smiled. She wriggled into the back of the sofa, hugging her knees close. She didn't smile back.

Simon propped his satchel against the fireplace. It contained notepads and brown cardboard folders and a portable tape recorder, and it seemed to be his job to manage all these things.

'Can you say your names for me? For the tape?' he said. His voice was nice, friendly, posh: it made Loo think of old books and people off the telly. The girls looked at each other, then did as he asked, Bee first, then Loo.

The afternoon was bright and hot. That was all they talked about these days, the grown-ups, the weather, as if sunshine in July was unusual, and it was all they could find to discuss as they waited for Simon to get everything ready.

The professor asked the questions. He listened to their answers carefully, and made notes in a little black book. He seemed very nice, he seemed to accept every word they said, but Loo noticed that the same questions kept creeping into the conversation, circling their way back as if by accident. Questions about the noises they heard upstairs at night, about the way things, little things, pens and pencils, house keys and bits of change, kept vanishing. This was beginning to bother her. She had the feeling that maybe neither she nor Bee were getting the answers right, and a nervous, ticklish sensation started to nudge at her insides.

In the corner of the room Isobel was leaning against the sideboard, a camera in her hands. Loo couldn't see her without turning her head, but she could hear her, the stammering *click click click* of the shutter. The professor didn't seem to notice, but it was driving Bee mad, Loo could just tell.

Bee sat with her hands locked in her lap, her head down, peering up occasionally at the professor from under her fringe; if you hadn't known her, you might have thought she was shy. She was taking little glances at Simon too, as he bent over his tape recorder. From time to time she stretched out a long leg and rotated her foot thoughtfully as she answered a question. Simon didn't look up, though.

Cathy had stayed for the first bit. But she hadn't been much help. She'd kept interrupting, correcting the two of them, filling up the silences if either girl hesitated. The professor was very polite, but anyone could see that he wanted Cathy to shut up; that it was the girls, Bee and Loo, who were important.

After a while Bee said that she was getting tired and wasn't it too crowded in here anyway, and then, luckily, Flor had burst into tears and Cathy had to take him away. He'd been stung by a wasp, he'd said, refusing to let anyone look at his arm, which he kept clamped to his chest.

They had listened to him carrying on, inconsolable, as Cathy practically carried him all the way down the hall to the kitchen, and Loo had edged forward on the sofa, the better to see the little wheels spinning round in the tape recorder with their white plastic teeth. She wondered idly if Flor's sobs had been recorded, if they might rewind the tape and wipe it clean and restore some peace and quiet to the room.

It didn't seem to occur to the professor that they should stop and wait for Cathy to return. He just carried on with his questions, not minding if either girl stumbled or hesitated when they spoke, smiling pleasantly at every answer, in a distant sort of a way. Simon flipped over the little cassette once, then a while later he replaced it with a new one, making neat notes on the label with a blue Biro.

The clock on the mantelpiece ticked softly. Cathy didn't come back. She might be making tea, Loo supposed, maybe even opening a packet of biscuits as a special treat.

The professor, Michael, looked through his notes. 'Do you remember the night the policeman came to the house?' he asked.

'Yes,' said Bee.

'And something happened here, in this room, didn't it?'

'Yes.'

'Can you tell me what happened, Lucia?'

'We were standing there, by the door, and he – the policeman – was talking to Cathy,' said Loo.

'He was telling her not to be stupid,' said Bee. 'He didn't say it out loud but that was what he meant, anyone could see that.'

'She called him because of the noise and everything.'

'She made him go all around the house.'

'But he didn't believe us.'

'He thought it was a joke.'

'Then I said, look at that, look there,' said Loo, 'and he stopped talking and he looked.'

'And he sort of forgot what he was saying. He just stared. Cathy grabbed hold of his arm – she went really pale and grabbed hold of him.'

'The chair was moving,' said Loo.

137

'That chair,' said Bee, leaning forward and pointing at Michael's chair.

He was silent for a moment. 'Can you describe how it moved?' he asked.

'It—' Loo stopped.

'It was shaking,' said Bee, 'like it was going to burst or something.'

'Then it slid forward, as if someone had pushed it.'

'But there was no one there.'

'Really?'

The little wheels of the tape machine moved on.

'Do you think the chair might move again?' said Michael eventually. 'Do you think it might move now, for instance?' He placed each hand carefully on the chair's arms and braced his feet on the floor, looking at the girls. The atmosphere seemed to thicken, the warm air close against Loo's skin, and she half-expected the knocking to start up again, the thuds and bangs that had been rolling through the house at night. It had been fun at first, but sometimes now, she had to admit, it was a little bit scary.

She hoped they would stop soon. She was getting tired of talking. It was hard work, going over everything that had happened, and it made her head ache.

Bee flopped back into the sofa, grinning. 'It might,' she said. 'You never know, do you?'

'No, I don't suppose you do,' said Michael. He turned towards Simon, who was still sitting at his feet. 'I think that's enough for—'

He was cut short by a sharp crack which seemed to echo through the room, making everyone jump.

'What the hell?' Isobel still held her camera, but she had no idea where to point it. Everyone stayed perfectly still, as if moving might set it off again, whatever it might be.

'Are we still recording?' asked Michael.

Simon checked the little black box. 'Yes.'

The professor stood, slowly unfolding himself from the chair.

'Are you familiar with the term "apport", Simon?' he asked, speaking slowly, clearly, for the tape.

'The transference of small objects from one place to another.'

'Good. Very good.' As if they were in a classroom and Simon was the pupil. The professor examined the cold fireplace, running his hands over the pale mauve tiles surrounding the dusty grate.

'Look,' he said, 'here.' One tile was cracked, a spidery line running diagonally from corner to corner, and just below it, on the flattened rag rug, a marble lay. He picked it up, holding it gently between thumb and forefinger.

'How curious,' he said, 'it's warm.'

Isobel raised her camera and took a shot of him holding the clear glass ball with its bluish-greenish twist in the centre.

'I don't like it,' said Loo, although whether she meant the marble or the clammy sick feeling in her belly, she couldn't say.

'Where's Cathy?' said Bee, standing up. 'I want to stop now. We want to stop. Come on, Loo, let's go.'

But Loo couldn't move. Her headache had turned into an itching, a buzzing in her ears, like the noise the radio in the kitchen would make when it needed tuning in. The noise seemed to press down on her, to hold her in place.

'Loo.' Bee was standing over her now, both close and far away all at once, and Loo wondered if this was what it was like when people fainted. 'Come on,' said Bee.

But before she could move, Loo heard Issy gasp. The professor told Simon to stand back and to keep recording please, as more marbles began to fall out of nowhere: blue and green, red and

139

yellow, clear and speckled, shimmering briefly in the sunlight, before thudding softly onto the faded living-room carpet, and Issy lifted her camera and pressed the shutter release over and over again.

10

Now

'Hi.'

Cathy is still in bed, but she's awake, sitting up, a sketchbook propped open on her lap. She looks tired. The bruises on her face are worse today, purple and blue stains on her pale skin. 'Lucia.'

Lucy edges her way into the room. 'How are you feeling?'

'Don't fuss,' says Cathy, but her heart's not in it.

Lucy closes the door behind her, crosses the room and pulls back the curtains. The sky is a pale grey, the garden below, empty. 'I was worried,' she says, 'when Jean rang.'

'I didn't know where you were,' said Cathy.

'No. Sorry.' Lucy doesn't know where to start. She's spent half the night lying awake, rehearsing what she'll say to Cathy, and to Nina should she speak to her again.

Cathy is picking at the corner of a page, a still life composed of flowers in a stubby glass vase. 'I thought of something,' she says.

'You could have rung me. Texted.'

'You never answer.'

'That's not true. You know that's not true.'

'I remembered something,' Cathy says, 'and I needed to check. But I couldn't find it, at first. And then, when I did, they wouldn't listen, none of them would listen. I just wanted to

141

'show you.' She turns a page, then smooths it down. 'Here.' She hands the sketchbook to Lucy.

'The first time I saw her, I didn't realise she wasn't there, you see. I was sitting in the garden, working on a sketch of the kitchen, and there she was, by the door – she was there, and I was looking at the page, and the next time I looked up, she'd gone. I didn't think anything of it. I just – carried on. I put her in the drawing without thinking about it, and then I forgot – until last night. But I couldn't find it. Then I did, but you weren't here.'

Lucy takes the book to one of the armchairs and sits. The girl is half in shadow, captured in profile, a long braid of pale hair falling over one shoulder. She is unfinished, indistinct. She's standing by the kitchen door, looking across the garden.

'And this is her?' Lucy asks. 'This is the girl you saw?'

'Yes. I thought – well, if you showed this to Sarah—'

'Mum, no. They see her because they want to. They've made her up. She's not real.'

'I saw her.'

'Well, maybe you – I don't know – maybe you wanted to see her.'

Cathy leans back against her pillows. 'Where were you?' she says, and her tone is fretful. 'I wanted to talk to you, but you weren't here.'

She takes it better than Lucy had expected. The business about the book, about Simon's daughter, his death. 'Oh,' she says, 'the poor girl. What's she like?'

'Mum. No.'

'Please.'

'She's – I don't know. She's very like him. She's very young – determined, I think.'

'To complete his research?'

'That's what she said.'

'You had no right,' says Cathy mildly, 'to go behind my back.'

'You're not well.'

'I'm perfectly fine.' Cathy raises a hand, runs her fingers through her hair, her pyjama sleeve falling back to reveal the strapping around her wrist. She pushes back the bedclothes.

'I could fetch you a tray,' Lucy says.

'Don't be ridiculous.' Cathy slides her feet carefully into her slippers, then stands slowly, testing her balance.

'I told them not to come.' Lucy feels oddly guilty making this confession. 'I told them you wouldn't see them. I'm sorry.'

'Oh, Lucia, what were you thinking?'

'They're just kids, Mum. They have no idea what they're getting into, what they're dragging up.'

Cathy walks to the window and looks down into the garden. 'Did they mention her?' she asks. 'Bianca?'

'No. I didn't give them the chance.'

'And she has Simon's research? All those notes he took? All Isobel's photos?'

'Apparently.'

'You should go down and get something to eat,' says Cathy. 'Go on. I won't be long.'

The dining room is busy and Lucy stands in the doorway, unsure which table she should take. She suspects that the residents probably have their regular seats, and she's fairly sure her mother wouldn't want to sit with anyone else.

She can't decide and it's all too much, the polite clatter of the dining room, the smell of cooked breakfasts and milky

143

porridge. She makes her way to the French windows and slips outside, heading towards the bench by the fountain. She's not hungry anyway.

She sits and looks back at the house. It's a dull morning, with the promise of rain in the air. She'd like to think she's put her off, Nina, but she doubts it, and she couldn't possibly leave Cathy to deal with them alone.

Nina Marshall.

Simon's daughter.

He had tried to keep in touch for a while. He had certainly written to Cathy, once when he'd got back to London, and again six months later, to tell them about Michael, and the accident – such a shock to everyone – and a third time, announcing that he had been asked by the Society to complete the book Michael had begun, as a memorial to him and his life's work. Lucy doesn't know if Cathy ever wrote back.

She didn't allow them to talk about it, any of it. Not the investigation, not what happened afterwards.

By the time the book was published Lucy was in her teens, although she'd not been allowed to read the copy someone, Simon she supposed, had sent to her mother. That had gone straight into the bin.

She had waited for over a year for it to appear in the local library, and had read it that first time in secret, a few pages at a time, only risking taking it from its hiding place when she was sure her mother was out of the house altogether.

It had puzzled her at the time, the difference between what she remembered and what she read; she barely recognised any of the people in the book. Cathy seemed paler, less substantial, and they, the children, were artificial, flat and two-dimensional. No one sounded like themselves any more. It was like being in the newspapers, but worse, somehow. Permanent.

And there was nothing about Joe, just a blurry photograph and a paragraph or two which had made it seem that he didn't care about them at all. That had hurt, the way Simon had got rid of him, and Bee too. What had happened to her had been reduced to a footnote, and that seemed to be the worst thing of all.

remarkable footage

She can't go through that again. None of them can.

She won't think about it. She should call Eloise, she should check her emails, but she can't bring herself to move. She tilts her head back and closes her eyes. The farm is nothing to do with her, not any more, and she tries to focus on that. And whatever Cathy might think, the girl in her sketchbook has nothing to do with the farm either, nothing to do with Lucy, or with Bee.

Something hard catches her on the shoulder, making her gasp, and she opens her eyes. Her first instinct is to look up at the house, but all the windows are firmly closed, blank and dull in the damp morning air.

Lucy stands, scanning the ground, trying to ignore the faint, familiar crackling sensation in the air. It doesn't take long to spot it. Nestled in the slick, wet grass is a small glass marble with a blue-green twist at its centre.

After a long moment, she picks it up.

It's still warm.

11

Then

The weekend had turned into a week, then two. Michael had taken up permanent residence in the Red Lion, but Simon, unable to afford such luxury indefinitely, had been reduced to borrowing a tent from one of Isobel's friends. The two of them had pitched it a little way up the field behind the farm with much bad-tempered swearing and argument.

The girls had been delighted with this development. They seemed to regard the field, and therefore the tent, as an extension of their own home and thought nothing of bringing their school books and sketchpads to show Simon two or three times a day. If he'd gone off on an errand for the professor, they would set up camp, waiting for him to return. Sometimes they'd feed him too, carrying up thick cheese and tomato sandwiches and mugs of sweet lukewarm tea. There were times when Simon wasn't sure who was observing who.

He sat on a faded red cushion, a recent gift from Loo, outside his tent, reading over his notes. The incident with the marbles hadn't been repeated, much to the professor's disappointment, although they had managed to record several incidences of the inexplicable knocking in the walls.

All the usual reasons for the disturbances, which took place mostly at night, had been discounted. And over the past week or so everyone had been plagued by small items – pens, pencils, cigarette lighters – going missing. Sometimes these items would be found again, usually in the oddest of places – a Biro popping up in a mugful of toothbrushes, for instance, or a pencil in the cutlery drawer – but this wasn't always the case; a few days ago, Isobel had lost a small mirror that had yet to be returned.

According to the professor, they were dealing with a classic poltergeist manifestation and Simon knew he intended to stay on for another week or so to complete his observations, and to interview Joe when he got back. He'd been in touch with several members of the Society and had received a couple of lengthy letters from Roland Miskin, although he hadn't seen fit to share their contents. For a while now Simon had been half-expecting to be replaced by someone more senior, more experienced, and he wondered how he might feel when that happened.

He looked up from his notes and saw Isobel walking up the hill. He waved but made no move to go and meet her. He looked down at the professor's work again – his work. Their scribbled notes transformed by his careful transcribing into something formal, official, lasting.

'Hi.' Isobel flopped down on the grass next to him.

'Hi.' He put his papers to one side.

'What are we up to today, then?' she asked.

'I don't know.'

'Is Michael here?'

'I don't know.'

'You don't know much, do you?' Isobel lay back on the grass. As she stretched her arms above her head, the hem of her skirt lifted a little and her T-shirt rose, exposing a narrow slice of her pale white belly. Simon looked away.

'No,' he said.

'So, is he falling for it, Simon? Are they the real thing?' Isobel lay still with her eyes closed.

'What do you think?' he said.

'Oh no, I asked first,' she said. 'Besides, I don't have to believe, my opinion doesn't count.'

'It's not a matter of opinion, it's . . .'

Evidence.

'Poltergeist phenomena are often recorded around young girls,' he said.

'Really? So, what, this is all run-of-the-mill stuff, is it? Up there with acne and mood swings and puppy love.'

'That's not what I meant and you know it.'

There were books in the tent, borrowed from the Society, containing accounts of similar cases, of unquiet spirits drawn to adolescent girls. When he couldn't sleep, which was quite often, Simon read about them, these young women plagued by noise and chaos and confusion.

'Well, enlighten me.'

'Puberty is a time of change, of physical and emotional growth – it's turbulent, it's powerful. So the theory is that anyone experiencing it might well be more open to – well, to psychic phenomena.'

'And that's what we've got here, is it? Psychic phenomena.'

In the distance a bird called softly and Simon wished Issy would sit up, so he could see her face, read her expression.

'Yes,' he said. 'Yes, I think so.'

Bee and Loo were lying in the grass a little further up the hill, spying on Simon and Issy. Behind them the dry stone wall cast a deep band of shadow over the rough ground. Loo rested her head on her arms, flattening herself against the sharp and scratchy grass as Isobel's voice drifted over the field. Issy, she

149

had noticed, always sounded as though she was laughing at Simon, even when she was saying the most ordinary things. Simon's voice was harder to make out; it was lower and didn't seem to carry so well. Bee nudged her.

'Ow!'

'Ssh!'

'But it hurt.'

'Don't fall asleep.'

But Loo couldn't help it. It felt like months since she had last slept the whole night through with no noises to wake her, no hands tugging at her bedclothes, no pinching and nipping, no sudden shocks echoing through the house. And it was so hot. She closed her eyes and felt herself begin to drift again. Bee prodded her, her sharp fingernail digging between Loo's ribs.

'This is boring,' she said. 'They're boring. Let's go back to the house.'

Bee didn't usually find Simon boring. She was – Loo was fairly certain – as fascinated by him as she was, only Bee spent a lot of time pretending she wasn't: rolling her eyes and looking away as he spoke, walking past him out of the room, tossing her hair over her shoulder, producing one-word answers if he ever stopped to pass the time of day. Someone who didn't know her might think she didn't care much about Simon at all; Loo knew better, though. She saw the way her sister looked at him. It was – she didn't quite have the words for it – as if she was greedy for him.

It was Issy Bee couldn't stand to look at. 'Come on,' she said.

Loo didn't really want to go. It would be much nicer to stay and listen to Simon, to close her eyes and fall asleep to the sound of him. Not that she would ever dare tell Bee that.

Keeping as low as they could, the girls crawled down the

150

hill, hidden by the fall of the land as it dipped to meet a ditch which ran alongside the dry stone wall. Behind them, Issy and Simon's voices faded into the landscape. Even if they thought to look, neither would catch sight of them.

It didn't prove to be a satisfactory session. They started out in the living room, Michael in the armchair – his chair – and Simon sitting on the floor with the tape recorder. Cathy didn't stay, she had lunch to make and there were Flor's lessons to think of, but they left the door open and they could hear her moving around, talking to Flor and the baby in her singsong voice. Issy stood behind the sofa, out of sight of the girls, her camera clicking away – it was odd, Loo thought, how normal this all seemed these days, how everyone had so quickly got used to taking up the same position without any discussion.

'So,' Michael began, 'did you sleep well?'

'Not really.'

The same questions every time, and always it was Bee who answered first.

'Ah. What happened?'

'It was noisy,' said Bee. 'Again.'

'Lucia?'

'Yes,' Loo said. 'It was banging on the walls.'

'It?'

'Yes.'

'So it's one thing – not a person, but a – personality, perhaps?'

'It doesn't like us,' said Bee. 'It waits until we're asleep and then it pulls the bedclothes off us.'

'I don't like it,' said Loo.

'I'm sure you don't,' said the professor and Simon glanced up, smiling sympathetically at her.

'We don't like it,' said Bee.

151

'Who is it, do you think?' Michael had asked this before.

'We told you,' said Bee, 'we don't know.'

'But it doesn't like you? You said that.'

'Yes.'

'So perhaps,' said the professor, 'it knows you. Do you think that might be possible?'

'I suppose so,' Bee said, slowly, as if she suspected some sort of trick.

'It might even – be watching you?'

'It might be watching you.'

Bee's answer made Michael smile, although Loo didn't think it was so very funny. 'What will happen when Joe comes back?' he asked.

'I dunno.'

'Do you think everything will stop?'

'No,' said Bee.

'Yes,' said Loo.

'Why?' the professor asked.

Loo wished she hadn't said anything. She could feel Bee looking daggers at her. 'He won't like it,' she said. 'He'll get rid of it.'

'How?'

'I – I don't know. He just will.'

'Yes. Well,' the professor consulted his notes, 'I wondered if we might sit and wait quietly for a while this morning, just to see if our friend will make an appearance. Would that be all right?'

That wouldn't work; it hardly ever did. Their 'friend' mostly played tricks when their backs were turned, when everyone least expected it.

'If you like,' said Bee, settling back on the sofa.

Loo never really knew what to do in these long silences; it

seemed rude to stare at Michael or Simon, silly to close her eyes. Mostly, she settled for staring at the mantelpiece, watching the second hand on the clock tick round, trying not to fidget. It was nice, having their photos taken and everything, but this part was always boring.

Lunch that day turned out to be bread and cheese and tomatoes, and because there were so many of them, they decided to take everything out into the garden. Issy bagged a place under the tree and Simon made sure to sit next to her. The girls, sent to fetch cushions from the living room, arrived last, and had to sit in the full glare of the sun, Bee finishing her food first and lying back on the parched grass, spreading out her arms and legs.

The grown-ups talked about the weather and the drought and about when Michael and Simon would leave, and Isobel even let go of her camera as she ate.

'I'm thirsty,' Bee announced, eyes still shut, unmoving.

'Well, you know where the kitchen tap is,' said Cathy.

'I'll make some tea, shall I?' said Isobel.

'It's too hot for tea,' said Bee.

'I'd like some,' said Simon.

'Cathy?' Isobel was on her feet, brushing bits of grass from her legs.

'Yes please. You know where everything is.'

'I'll help.' Loo got up. 'Can we have biscuits?'

Issy filled the kettle and put it on to boil, then stood at the kitchen window, staring idly at everyone grouped under the tree. 'That,' she said, 'makes a pleasing composition, don't you think?'

Loo joined her and looked. 'Dunno,' she said.

Isobel rolled her eyes. 'And you the daughter of an artist.'

Loo looked again. 'It's all right, I suppose.'

'Do you miss him, your dad?'

Loo nodded, but she didn't much want to talk about Joe, not with Issy, anyway, because it was hard to explain. Missing him was only the half of it. Sometimes she wondered if he'd ever come back.

'When's he due home?'

'Dunno,' Loo said. 'Are you going to take a picture?'

Isobel glanced down at her hands. She seemed mildly surprised not to see her camera there. 'Can't,' she said.

'I'll fetch it for you, if you like.' Loo went to the door. Maybe Issy would let her have a go.

'Don't bother. By the time you get back one of them will have moved, or will have noticed us. The moment will be gone.' Issy smiled at her and appeared to be about to say something else when she stopped. She looked around the kitchen, frowning.

Loo could hear it too. A faint scratching. Nails perhaps, maybe even claws scrabbling, worrying at the scullery door. 'What's that?' she said. This was different, new.

Issy, paler than ever, took a step backwards and shook her head. 'I don't know.' She looked frightened, which might have been funny if Loo hadn't felt it too, a prickly feeling all over her skin. 'A cat,' she said, but she sounded uncertain.

It was still there, it sounded trapped.

'But how?'

'It could have wandered in,' said Issy. 'The kitchen door's been open all morning.'

The noise stopped, but that didn't make things better. The silence was heavy, cold, despite the bright sun outside.

'Shouldn't we let it out, then?' said Loo.

'I suppose so.' But neither of them moved. Outside in the

154

garden, the warm summer afternoon carried on. One of the men asked a question, and Cathy answered. Flor was playing, making his stupid engine sounds, and a bee buzzed hesitantly around the window before vanishing.

Loo waited for Isobel to move. She was the grown-up. But she didn't.

Loo licked her lips, wiped her hands on her skirt and crossed the room. She raised one hand to the old-fashioned iron latch, but instead of opening the scullery door, she laid her head gently against the wood and listened. She felt the sound this time, a deep thrumming that seemed to travel through the door and into her head, and if she concentrated, she thought, then maybe Issy would feel it too.

'Don't.' In one movement Issy had pulled her back and opened the door.

The scullery was empty.

'It likes to play tricks, that's what Michael says,' said Loo, walking the full length of the narrow room. 'There's nothing here.'

'Right.' Isobel hovered near the doorway.

'I can't reach the biscuits,' said Loo, looking at the top shelf. 'Will you get them down?'

Behind Isobel the kettle began to squeal.

'Well, there's nothing here now,' said Simon as he and Michael finished examining the scullery. Isobel had retrieved her camera and was blocking the doorway taking pictures as everyone else milled around the kitchen taking up too much room.

'A scratching sound, you said?' Michael was examining the back of the door.

'Yes.'

'We thought it was a cat,' said Loo, who knew Isobel had thought no such thing. 'We were going to let it out.'

155

Michael smiled down at her. 'How very kind of you.'

He led the way back into the kitchen and out again to the garden with Simon and the other grown-ups following. Bee and Loo hung back, Bee making a show of finding a glass and getting a drink of water until she was sure they'd all forgotten them. 'Well,' she said, putting the glass down on the kitchen table, and turning to the scullery, 'let's have a look.'

The shelves were stacked with food, bags of flour and rice, bread, sacks of onions and potatoes, some tinned stuff too, jars and bottles, and all of it well out of reach. At the back underneath the single window were piles of old newspapers – not the ones with their pictures in, just ordinary out-of-date ones – some logs and bundles of kindling. The lower shelves held spare pots and pans, boxes of candles, washing powder and old plastic bowls. It was all exactly the same as it had ever been and Bee stood still, taking it all in. 'Weird,' she said, rapping her knuckles on the back of the door.

'Don't,' said Loo.

'Are you scared?' Bee's grin was wicked.

'No. Course not.' Loo wondered if Bee could feel it too, the funny crackling sensation in the air. 'Can we go now?'

'In a minute.' Bee stepped back and craned her neck. 'I reckon she's got chocolate up there on the top shelf,' she said.

'So?' Loo was edging back towards the door.

'So they're all out there, aren't they? Busy.'

'Yeah.'

'Well, then.'

Cathy kept an old stool wedged underneath the bottom shelf; it was a little low thing like the ones they used to have in the kids' section of the library back in Leeds, and she needed it to reach the top shelf. Bee dragged it out and hopped onto it, then reached up to the top shelf and began feeling around. 'I can't,' she said, going up onto her tiptoes. 'Shit.' She shifted her weight and the stool wobbled furiously.

'Bee.'

'What?'

Loo wasn't sure what it was, the wobbly stool or the uneven flagstones, but one minute Bee was reaching up for chocolate, the next she'd crashed to the floor, the stool sent scuttling across the room.

'Ow. Shit.' Bee lay on her side, cradling her elbow against her body. 'That hurt.'

'Bee.' Loo gave up her post by the door and crouched down on the dusty flags. 'Are you OK?'

But Bee didn't answer. She was staring into the darkness under the shelf.

12

Now

They get to Blue Jacket House at around eleven.

Hal lets Nina and Lewis deal with the girl on the front desk as he looks around the entrance hall, trying to imagine he's the sort of person who could afford to have his parents live in a place like this. The meeting is still on, as far as Nina is concerned, anyway; he wonders what she will do if Cathy doesn't show up.

One open door leads to a dining room, tastefully set out as if it were a hotel, not an institution, and beyond that he can just make out a garden. Another door leads to a sort of living room – there's a TV and bookcases and pleasant but impersonal prints and paintings on the walls, landscapes, mostly. There are no family photos as far as he can see, no clutter.

'If you'd like to take a seat,' the girl leads the way into the living room, 'I'll let Mrs Corvino know you're here.'

They choose the two sofas by the fireplace, set facing each other across a long low coffee table. Nina sets up the laptop and Lewis goes over his notes. It's a dull day outside and someone has switched on the table lamps, which cast a pale yellow glow around the room.

'There,' Nina says, looking up as the door opens. She's nervous, Hal realises, in a way she hadn't been last night. His head aches, and every now and then he's seized with a dizzying nausea. He thought he could hold his drink better than this.

Lucy Frankland walks into the room. She looks dreadful, tired, ill, and there's something else, an underlying strain – she almost looks afraid. 'I asked you not to come,' she says.

'Yes. Well.' Nina looks to Lewis for some sort of support. 'We arranged this with Cathy and we couldn't just not turn up.'

'Is she still willing to see us?' Lewis asked. 'Only it is very important.'

'She's—' Lucy appears to lose her nerve momentarily. 'Yes. She's just getting ready. I needed to – I do need to insist on a couple of things,' she says.

'Such as?' Nina manages to keep her tone civil.

'My mother is not well. If she says she doesn't remember, or doesn't want to discuss something, then you will need to respect that.'

'Of course,' says Lewis.

'And any questions you may have – you're here to discuss the investigation, yes? You do not mention my sister. Anything that happened at the farm after Michael and Simon had gone, everything that happened afterwards – it was nothing to do with them and it's nothing to do with you.'

'But—' Nina begins.

'I mean it,' says Lucy. 'I will not have my mother upset.'

'Of course not,' says Lewis. 'We don't want that either.'

'Right, well. As long as that's understood.' She looks around the room, taking in the way they've set up the table, and then says something about fetching Cathy.

Cathy Corvino is not what Hal expected; everything about her seems to have been stripped away, pared back. He's not

160

read much of it, but the young mother in Simon Leigh's book had been a pretty thing, given to loose, flowing clothes and jangling jewellery. This woman – a slight figure dressed in black – looks sober, severe, by comparison. The bruising and grazes on her face stand out against the pallor of her skin and she moves carefully across the room. She's had a fall, Hal remembers, noting the strapping around her right wrist. Lucy hadn't said where or when, though. They should have asked.

'Hello,' says Cathy and she takes Nina's hands, both hands, looking up into the young woman's face. 'I had no idea,' she says. 'About your father. You should have told me. It would have saved so much . . . I'm sorry – I'm so sorry for your loss.' Lucy doesn't speak at all; she hangs back by the door.

'Thank you, that's very kind of you,' says Nina. 'Shall we sit down?'

Lewis and Nina arrange themselves either side of Cathy, facing the open laptops. Hal takes a seat on the sofa opposite and Lucy only joins him after a silent and pointed look from her mother.

'Would you like anything? Some tea, coffee?' asks Cathy.

'No, thank you,' says Nina. 'I just wanted to – we just wanted to . . . we really appreciate you seeing us. If we could talk a little about the farm, first? If that's OK?'

It seems to Lucy that the marble might burn a hole in her pocket. She can feel it pressing against her hip every time she leans forward or shifts in her seat. She is, on some level, still irritated that she can't change Cathy's mind about this meeting, that she can't make her mother see how reckless this is, but it's the marble that frightens her. At best it's a joke: one of them got in early somehow, was sneaking around, waited until she wasn't looking and just threw it at her. To frighten her, to knock her off balance.

At worst it's – she finds she can't follow that train of thought. She wishes she had the courage to pack up and go, to let them get on with it. She can barely stand to be in the same room as them all, but neither can she bring herself to leave.

'Yes,' Cathy says. 'That was taken by Isobel. You remember Issy, don't you, Lucia?' Lewis leans forward and helpfully spins the laptop round, adjusting the angle of the screen for her.

The children are standing in the front garden, squinting in the sunshine, and are arranged by age, oldest to youngest. Isobel had given them a copy of this photo, Lucy remembers. It had been taken before Michael and Simon had arrived. Cathy used to keep it propped up on the kitchen mantelpiece. 'Of course I do,' she says.

'Dante, Bianca, Lucia, Florian and Antonella,' Cathy counts them off, left to right.

All of them favouring their father, with his thick dark hair and olive skin. Florian holding the baby loosely in his arms, both of them scowling.

'Such lovely names,' says Nina.

'We spent a summer in Italy, before the kids were born. Joe still had some family there. A great-aunt and uncle, lots of cousins. We always thought we'd go back, take the children with us, but of course that never happened.' Cathy reaches out and brushes her fingertips across the screen. Bee stares fiercely into the camera, her hands on her hips. 'Look at them,' she says. 'That's the last photograph, the last one with them all together.' Cathy's hand is trembling. 'Bianca,' she says softly.

'Maybe we should come back another time,' says Hal.

'Oh, no,' says Cathy. 'It's quite all right.' She folds her hands in her lap. 'Lucia tells me you have your father's notes, from 1976.'

'Well, yes.' Nina looks embarrassed. 'He intended for everything to go to the Society, I think. And we'll do that, of course. But yes.'

'Do you have them with you?'

'Most of them. There's a lot to go through.'

'Things he left out of the book.'

'Yes. Transcriptions of the interviews with the girls, mostly, a sort of diary noting the events they witnessed, and Isobel's photographs. Michael Warren's archive all went to the Society after his death. I'm hoping we can get access to that at some point too.'

Lewis leans forward and begins to tap at his keyboard. 'We don't want to keep you too long,' he says. 'Maybe you'd like to see what we got this weekend?'

'Of course,' says Cathy.

Nina does most of the talking, explaining how they'd set the cameras up, how they'd had to look through most of the footage afterwards. 'Except the camera in the bedroom,' she says, leaning forward and clicking on a file icon, pretending not to notice the way Lucy flinches before adopting a determinedly neutral expression. 'We were able to monitor that from the dining room. It's easier if you see for yourself.' She presses play and sits back. The first clip shows the bedroom with Nina sitting on the floor. 'This was the second set of observations, at around nine thirty.'

'I see,' says Cathy, her eyes fixed on the screen.

The camera moves a little, shifting towards the far corner, zooming in.

'The sound's a bit rubbish here,' says Lewis.

'The sound is perfectly fine,' says Hal.

On-screen Nina is suddenly in full close-up.

'What happened there?' asks Cathy.

'Nothing,' says Hal. 'Technical issues.'

Nina looks up and she jerks back, vanishing momentarily from the screen.

'Did you see something?'

'No,' says Nina. 'Listen.' They can just about hear it, a faint thudding in the walls. The camera pulls back again, and the darkened room comes into focus.

'Who's there?' The Nina in the video stands and looks into the camera. 'Can you hear that?' she says as the two boys run into shot, Lewis first and a few paces behind him, Hal. The noise stops.

'That's it,' says Nina, pressing pause. 'But it was much louder in real life, fuller, somehow.'

'Does it remind you of anything?' asks Lewis.

Cathy nods, but she doesn't speak.

'Mum.' Lucy's voice is soft, almost pleading. 'Maybe that's enough for one day.'

'It's the same, isn't it?' Cathy turns to face her daughter. 'Lucia?'

'You can't say that, it's not – you can't tell, not from a few minutes of film. Anyone could be messing with the sound.' Lucy looks at them all, pale, stubborn, her arms folded, shrinking into herself. 'I'm sorry,' she says, 'but you could, any of you could, you must see that.'

Cathy turns to the screen, the three of them frozen there, in the girls' bedroom. 'It's the same,' she says again.

'There's something else,' says Nina, clicking on a different icon. 'We missed this at the time. Hal found it when he was going through the rushes.' They watch the clip she selects: a static image of the first-floor landing. A minute passes; two.

'How long does this go on for?' asks Lucy.

'Keep watching,' says Nina, leaning towards the screen, the empty hallway. 'There.' She hits pause and it seems to Lucy that one of the shadows in the corner of the screen has taken on a more distinct form, has elongated itself into a figure of some sort. The closer she looks, the more familiar it seems. 'Can you see? Her head here, her arm,' says Nina.

'No,' says Lucy. It's shapeless, a shadow, an illusion. There's a word for it, isn't there, the human need to give form to abstract patterns, to find faces in things? 'There's no one there.'

'It's not brilliant quality.'

'There's no one there,' Lucy says again. *There's no one there, because that would be impossible.*

'I'll play it again.'

'No.' Lucy stands. 'That's enough. I'd like you to go now.'

Cathy leans forward, frowning. 'Show me again,' she says.

Nina taps on the mouse pad and once more a figure, no more than a dark smudge on the camera lens, appears to step out of the shadows to turn towards the girls' bedroom door before fading away.

'Can you slow it down?'

Nina taps on the pad again, playing the clip at half speed, but she's out of focus, the figure, if she's there at all, and slowing her down only makes her less substantial, less present. 'Again,' Cathy says and the shot at normal speed, the girl stepping forward and they play vanishing in the blink of an eye. She leans back against the sofa cushions. 'Thank you,' she says.

'Mum . . .'

'I'm fine, Lucia.' But she's pale.

'Do you recognise her?' asks Nina.

'I . . .' Cathy looks puzzled, the way she does when she's

struggling to find the right word or to recall a once-familiar name. 'I think Lucia is right, that's enough for one day.'

'The girl in the video, is she—'

'Jesus, Nina.' Hal leans across the table, snapping the screen down. 'We should go,' he says. 'We've imposed for long enough.' He stands but neither Lewis nor Nina move.

'It would be so helpful,' Nina says, 'if we could persuade you to visit the farm again.'

Cathy raises a hand to her eyes. 'I'm sorry. I get so tired these days.'

'We wouldn't expect you to stay there. But perhaps you'd consider—'

'I'd like you to go now,' Lucy says. 'We both would.'

Lewis packs up the laptop. 'We're sorry,' he says. 'We didn't mean to upset you.'

'Oh, you didn't,' says Cathy, 'but it's – difficult, sometimes.' She gets slowly to her feet with a weary smile. 'We could talk again, though,' she says. 'You could bring along Simon's notes. I'd be happy to go through them with you.'

'Thanks,' says Nina. 'I'd – we'd like that. Thank you.'

Lucy walks them to the front door and sees them out of the house in silence.

13

Then

Simon was awake. It had been light since four and his sleeping bag and thin mat provided no real cushioning against the hard, unyielding earth. He wondered if Issy's friend would ever want his tent back or if he could just set fire to it when he was done. He lay on his back, staring at the orange nylon interior, trying to work out just how soon he'd be back in London; he was tired of sleeping rough, of the long hot summer. He missed the city, civilisation.

Still, they were done now, more or less. They were heading back tomorrow, taking their evidence with them. They'd stay in touch with Cathy and the kids, of course, Issy too, but he doubted he'd ever return to the farm. He couldn't say he was sorry about that.

He became aware that he'd drifted off only when he woke up again with a start. He was lying on top of the sleeping bag, naked; it was far too hot to attempt sleeping inside it, and the damp fabric was sticking to his bare skin. It must have been a bird call that woke him. But no, what was that?

'Issy?' he said. Not likely, of course, but she might be the person walking round outside, circling the tent. He could hear someone picking their way through the clumps of long grass, the dry swish of it. He could see too the way the light kept changing as a shadow fell across the tent and then slid away. She was close. Too close. 'Isobel?'

No reply. It was the girls then. Shit. He'd better cover himself up. He picked up his jeans and started to pull them on, the heavy fabric dragging against his clammy skin.

'Bee? Is that you?' Cautiously he raised himself up onto his knees, struggling to fasten his fly, keeping his eyes focused on the front of the tent as he tugged at the zip. His mouth was dry. He had a bottle of water somewhere, warm, no doubt. The figure stopped. And in the silence, despite the heat, his skin prickled.

'Loo?'

The hail of stones, most no bigger than his fist, fell all at once and from all sides, collapsing the tent on top of him.

'Fascinating.'

'Thanks.'

Simon and the professor were sitting at the kitchen table, drinking tea. Cathy was at the sink, washing up as Flor played in his usual spot on the rag rug in front of the Aga. The baby, Anto, was asleep in her pram outside, wedged up against the kitchen step.

'You had the sense the presence was female?'

'I thought it was Isobel, at first, then possibly Bee or Loo.'

The professor was making notes, and Simon watched him write, unsure how he should feel about this. He'd been hoping for sympathy or a rational explanation – some lads from the village making mischief, perhaps. He hadn't expected to become a footnote in his own investigation.

'Are you all right?' asked the professor. 'Not hurt?'

'No. I just felt . . .'

Foolish. Once the tent fell apart he'd felt ridiculous, but before that he'd felt, just for a moment, afraid. 'I'm fine,' he said.

'Have you cleared the tent up?'

'Not yet. I thought you'd want to see it first.'

'Good.'

'See what?'

Simon looked up and there by the kitchen door stood Bee and Loo. They looked different today, and it took him a moment to work out what it was. Instead of their usual shorts and T-shirts, each girl wore an old-fashioned petticoat, full-skirted, frilly, and some sort of chemise. They reminded him of—

'Where have those come from?' asked Cathy.

'The dressing-up box,' said Bee.

'We found them,' said Loo.

'Well, which is it?' asked Cathy.

Bee looked at Loo. 'We found them in the scullery, under the shelves, then we put them in the dressing-up box,' she said.

'So they're not yours,' said Cathy.

'They're not anyone's,' said Bee.

'See what?' said Loo, looking at Simon.

'Simon had a bit of an adventure this morning,' said the professor, closing his notebook and slipping it into his pocket.

'Really?' said Bee.

'Are you all right?' asked Loo.

Simon rubbed his head. 'A bit bruised,' he said. 'Nothing serious.'

Loo walked over to him and gazed into his face, her dark eyes serious, brimming with tears. 'Does it hurt?'

'No, Loo, I'm fine.'

'I'm sorry, Simon,' she said. 'Was it the poltergeist?'

'I thought they stayed in the house,' said Bee. 'Poltergeists.'

'Well, maybe this one doesn't,' said the professor. 'Maybe this one likes to get out.'

*

That night Michael, Simon and Isobel stayed for dinner. It was a special occasion, to say thank you, to say goodbye. Simon showed Loo how to bake apples: they sat at the kitchen table side by side preparing a tray of knobbly green Bramleys.

'Like this?' Her fingers, slick with juice, slipped and she narrowly missed gouging a hole in her finger.

'Nearly,' said Simon. 'Just put it down on the table and I'll help you core it.'

Bee was hovering close by. 'Do they take long to cook?' she asked.

'Half an hour or so.'

Behind them the kitchen window slammed shut.

'Bianca,' said Cathy automatically.

'I didn't touch it,' said Bee, slipping into Simon's seat as he stood and opened the window. She picked up an apple and bit into it.

'You can't eat that, it's sour,' said Loo.

'Watch me,' said Bee.

They sat in the kitchen, the four adults and the older children crammed around the table, eating ham salad as the oven belched out heat and the scent of sweet cinnamon. The little ones, Flor and Anto, sat on the rag rug, Anto chewing on a soggy crust of bread.

As they ate the grown-ups talked about art and books and music and Cathy began to relax. It was, Loo thought, like it used to be back in Leeds when Joe and Cathy would have their friends round. Simon fetched the apples from the oven and he and Loo served them in a variety of mismatched bowls, each scorched and sagging apple topped with a dollop of runny ice cream.

'Do you like it?' Loo asked, as she solemnly handed each

bowl out around the table, her hands sticky with vanilla and brown sugar.

'Delicious,' said Michael, scraping his spoon around the bowl.

After dinner, they went out into the garden. Bee and Loo and Cathy carried out blankets and old quilts and cushions and the adults sat quietly under the tree as the children, even Dan for a short while, lay down on the quilts and looked up into the darkening sky, waiting for the stars to come out.

'Look,' said Bee, pulling her skirt back to reveal a bruise, a dark purple ellipse on the inside of her knee.

'What have you done to yourself now?' said Cathy.

'I didn't do anything. I just woke up today and it was there.'

Loo shifted along the quilt, drawing up her legs, as if she was trying to get away from Bee, from all of them. She had bruises too, Simon noticed, tiny brown fingerprints scattered along her arms. He wondered if the professor had noticed. Maybe they should get Issy to take some pictures later.

'Why are you leaving?' asked Bee.

'Well, we have to leave at some point,' said Simon, who had grown used, over the weeks, to Bee's abrupt manner, her habit of ignoring the cues and prompts of polite conversation. He'd found it irritating at first, childish. Now he almost admired it.

'Why?'

'We have notes to go over, reports to write,' said Michael.

'About us?'

'Yes.'

'You could do that here. We could help,' said Loo.

The professor smiled and said that was a kind offer.

'We should leave you alone,' said Simon. 'Let you get back to normal. Joe will be back soon, won't he?'

'End of the month,' said Cathy.

'See?' said Simon. 'There'd be no room for us.'

'Will you come back?' asked Bee. 'Will you come and see us again?'

'Yes,' said Michael, 'if your mother and father don't mind.'

Dan went up after an hour or so. Even in the garden they could hear the distant *thump thump thump* of his music. Then Cathy stood and picked up Anto. 'Come on,' she said, holding her hand out to Flor, 'bedtime.'

'Don't want to.' Florian folded his arms and stuck out his lower lip, a parody of a sulky child.

'Florian.' Cathy waited a moment or two then he stood and took her hand. 'One more hour, you two,' she said as they walked towards the house.

'God,' said Bee, kicking her long legs up at the sky. Cathy had got very keen on bedtimes ever since Michael and Simon had arrived. As if she had something to prove.

It took Cathy longer than an hour to settle Flor and the baby. When she came back outside, she found Bee and Loo still sitting under the tree with Isobel. Bee was holding one of Issy's cameras and was looking through the lens.

'Can I take some photos?' she said, swinging around to face her mother.

'It's too dark,' said Isobel, reaching over and taking the camera back.

'Bedtime,' said Cathy.

'I'm too old for bedtime,' said Bee, looking at Loo who was already scrambling obediently to her feet.

'Both of you,' said her mother.

Bee sat down on the quilt, crossing her legs and her arms. She looked just like Florian. Cathy glanced over at Michael and Simon; both men were watching quietly.

'Bianca, please.'

'I don't want to. I don't want to go up there.' Somewhere inside the house a door banged and Bee turned to look at Simon. 'I'm frightened,' she said. He glanced at the professor, surprised at her tone of voice, that she should single him out to back her up.

'There's nothing to be afraid of,' he said.

'There is. It won't let us sleep.'

'Really?' Michael reached into his bag for his notebook. 'What makes you think that?'

'It won't leave us alone.'

'Bianca, stop making a fuss,' said Cathy. 'You're spoiling a perfectly pleasant evening.'

'It's not me! It's not my fault.' Bee's voice rose into the air, jagged, threatening. 'Tell them, Loo.'

Loo was edging closer to her mother, she looked as though she might burst into tears at any second. 'It's too noisy,' she said. 'We don't like it. We want it to stop.'

'Well, what if we stayed?' Michael said. 'What if we stayed until you both fell asleep?'

It took them another half hour to persuade Bee and Loo to go to bed. They agreed that Cathy would sleep with her door open, and Simon and Michael would sit on the landing with one of their machines, the EMF monitor, which measured changes in the air, and a tape recorder. Isobel would stay for a little while, she said, but she had to be at work in the morning. Satisfied with this arrangement, Bee followed her mother and sister through the kitchen and up the stairs, Michael, Simon and Issy trooping obediently behind.

They probably wouldn't have bothered washing their faces or brushing their teeth if Michael and Simon hadn't been there. Issy too, always hanging back, snapping her photos. But because they were, they did, squashing themselves into the little bathroom, taking turns to pee and to use the sink. Bee liked having her picture taken, Loo knew, but she didn't really like Isobel doing it. Something about Isobel made her angry.

'Are you two done?' Cathy rattled the door handle.

'Nearly,' said Bee, looking at her reflection in the mirror, pulling at the neckline of her fading cotton nightie.

The bedroom was quiet. For once everything had been left in place. The little bits of makeup Bee had managed to acquire were clumped together on the dressing table. Cathy had picked up the girls' clothes and hung them in the wardrobe. Someone had lit a candle and placed it on the window sill.

'Right.' Cathy bent down to kiss Loo. As she did, Bee hauled herself into the top bunk and rolled onto her side in one swift movement, facing the wall, out of reach. 'Goodnight, then.' Cathy looked around the room. It was dusty and a couple of Loo's posters were starting to come loose. It smelt of stale bedding and cheap perfume and it was hot despite the open window.

Loo picked up a book from a pile on the floor and got into bed. 'Goodnight,' she said.

Cathy closed the door behind her, shutting them in.

When the noises started, the first thing Michael did was make a note of the time and the position of everyone in the house.

He, Simon and Isobel were on the first-floor landing, the Corvino family were all in their respective bedrooms.

It was a random series of thuds and bangs at first, erratic and arrhythmic. Then one of the girls, possibly Bee, called out, sounding sleepy and bad-tempered.

'Shut up!'

Then silence. Michael stayed in position, sitting on the top stair, hunched over his notes.

Behind the door something heavy rumbled across the room and the banging in the walls started up again.

Dan's voice drifted down from the attic. 'Will you bloody well stop it?' He slammed his door shut. At the same time, Cathy came out onto the landing, barefoot and fastening her dressing gown, an old-fashioned, oversized man's one, pulling the collar close at her throat, as if she were cold.

'Cathy? Mum?' In his room Flor sounded uncertain, on the brink of crying, and Simon could see Cathy was torn; she couldn't decide which child she should go to first. Flor called out again, properly awake now, clearly frightened. 'Mum.'

'It's OK,' Simon said. 'Get Flor, we can manage here.'

Cathy brushed past him and went into Florian's room. Simon could hear her murmuring soft, comforting words as the faint orange light from his bedside lamp pooled out onto the dim landing.

Above them, Dan's door opened and he padded downstairs, barefoot, bad-tempered. 'I've got work in the morning,' he said. 'Aren't you going to do something about that?'

Michael stood up and went to the girls' door. The knocking was so loud he'd later swear he saw the wood in the frame bulge. Behind him Simon was holding their tape recorder and a microphone. Slightly to one side, Isobel stood with her camera ready. 'We should go in,' Issy said, 'shouldn't we?'

'Not yet.'

Inside the room the knocking was building in a rattling, shaking crescendo, as if something was pulling at the bunk beds and then smacking them against the wall, harder and harder, intent on shaking the girls awake, on waking the whole house. Simon could feel it, the energy pulsing through the walls – the air was live with it. It was – enraged.

Something landed heavily on the floor and Loo's voice cut through the sudden silence that followed, rising unsteadily, out of control. 'I don't like it. Stop it. Stop it. Stop it!'

Michael threw the door open and stepped into the room, Simon close behind him. Loo was curled up on the floor inside the overturned bunk beds, her arms wrapped around her head, crying softly.

'I don't like it, I don't like it.'

Bee lay on the floor underneath the window, in a tangle of sheets as if she'd been scooped out of her bed and dropped into place from on high. She was breathless, exhilarated, triumphant. She looked at Michael and Simon each in turn and then directly into Isobel's camera, daring her to look away. Feathers from a torn pillow drifted dreamily down onto the upturned mattresses and scattered bedding.

'Did you see that?' said Bee. 'It lifted me up. It lifted me right up and floated me across the room.'

Michael took another step closer. 'Who did? Bee, who lifted you up?' he asked.

Me.

The voice was low, hoarse, uncanny.

Me.

Me.

Me.

14

Now

Hal waits until they're approaching the outskirts of town before he speaks. 'I borrowed your book,' he says.

Nina is next to him in the passenger seat. Lewis is crammed in with their bags in the back.

'I was reading about them, about their investigation, Michael and your dad.'

'We agreed you didn't need to know too much background,' says Nina. 'You agreed.'

'Yeah, well. I've changed my mind.' The young mother in the book, so sad, so old now. The way Lucy seems so anxious, rattled. She can hardly bear to look at any of them. The whole situation bothers him in ways he can't fully express. It doesn't feel right. 'It's not just a story to them, it's not a case; it's their lives,' he says. And the farm, the house, he wants to say, that doesn't feel right either.

'Well, we know that,' Nina says. 'That's why we want them involved.'

'The trouble with the original investigation was that it was incomplete,' Lewis says. 'After Michael Warren died, after the family left the farm, they never had the chance to reproduce their results.'

'But we can,' says Nina. 'We are. This is an incredible opportunity.'

'Don't you think it's making life a bit . . . difficult for them?' says Hal.

'You heard Cathy, she's perfectly happy to help,' says Nina. 'It's Lucy who's being difficult.'

'Well, maybe if you slowed down a bit – maybe if you listened.'

Nina shifts around in her seat to look at him. 'Whose side are you on?' she asks.

'It's not a matter of sides,' Lewis says.

'I just think,' says Hal, 'that it wouldn't kill you to be a bit more sensitive.'

'Really?' Nina looks out of the window. 'Well, thanks for the feedback, Hal. I'll bear it in mind.'

They drive past the last few houses that look out over the bay, then turn inland towards the moors. 'And what was the deal about the sister?' Hal asks. 'What went on there?'

'You've got the book,' says Nina. 'Look it up.'

They drive on in silence for a while. The drizzle turns to rain and Hal switches on the windscreen wipers. 'I have a shoot this week,' he says.

'But you're free at the weekend?' says Lewis.

'I'm not sure. I'll have to see how things go. I've got other commitments, you know?'

'Sure,' says Nina, leaning back and closing her eyes. She's not about to give up now, even if she has to go back with no camera, no technical backup. 'Whatever.'

It's getting dark, it's been one of those gloomy October days that never seems to get light, and Cathy switches on her bedside lamp. They have been talking in circles for over an hour now.

She opens the sketchbook again, pressing the pages back,

frowning. 'But it's her, yes? It's the same girl, Lucia. The girl in their film is the girl I saw.'

'Only it can't be, can it?' says Lucy. 'That's just – it's ridiculous.' If only she could get her mother to slow down, to see that she's making connections where none exist, that she's creating a story from little more than wishful thinking.

'Why did I see her? The girl? Why did they see her?' Cathy's voice rises then breaks. Lucy hopes she won't cry; she couldn't bear that. 'How can she be there and here too?'

'She's not real.'

It's not the same girl, Lucy wants to say. *It can't be.*

And outside, the marble in the grass, the marble in her pocket, that's just . . . a coincidence.

'I want to go,' says Cathy. 'I want to see.'

'You can't go back, Mum. You said it yourself, you're not well.'

'I need to know, Lucia,' says Cathy, pale, agitated, determined. 'I need to understand what happened. Don't you?'

Lucy makes the phone call once she's sure Cathy is settled in her room, feet up with a book and a cup of tea.

'Look, I'll do what I can from here,' she says. 'I can stay on top of the paperwork and brief the team, but I can't leave my mother right now.'

'Oh, God, Lucy, I'm so sorry.' Eloise sounds genuinely upset and for a moment Lucy feels guilty. She's hinted that Cathy is ill, properly ill. But then, she thinks, what else was she supposed to say?

I think my mother is haunted.

She bites the inside of her mouth. The thought of returning to the farm makes her feel sick. She can't possibly do it, but she certainly can't let Cathy go either. Round and round she goes, convinced this is absolutely the wrong thing to do, but unable to find a way out.

'Do you know how long you'll be staying?' asks Eloise.

This is a big project, it's her project, a retrospective of the work of women artists the gallery has shown over the past half century. She's been working on this for two years on top of all her other responsibilities and she's about to hand it over to her assistant, her team. She feels tears pricking her eyes. If she lets this go now, she will never get it back. 'I'm not sure,' she says, pulling the marble from her pocket, rolling it between her thumb and forefinger, letting it catch the light. 'Certainly a week, possibly longer.'

The silence at the other end of the line says everything. Lucy can feel it falling away: everything she's worked for, the exhibition, the life she has so carefully constructed. 'I'll email you my diary and copy you in to all my correspondence from now on, OK?'

That night Lucy waits until her mother announces that she's tired, then she goes down to the kitchen, giving her some privacy as she heats up some milk and scavenges some biscuits. When she takes the tray back upstairs, she finds Cathy sitting up in bed, childlike, smelling of soap and skin lotion.

'You shouldn't have bothered,' she says as Lucy hands her a mug.

'It's no bother.'

Cathy blows across the top of the mug and then takes a cautious sip. Lucy takes her own drink and sits at the foot of the bed.

'I rang Eloise, at the gallery,' she says, 'to let her know I'm staying on for a while. I spoke to Dan too.'

That had been yet another circular conversation, with neither of them able to arrive at a satisfactory solution.

I'll deal with her, Loo. Leave her to me.

As if he could succeed where she had failed.

'Yes,' says Cathy. 'He sent me a message. I said I'd ring him tomorrow.'

'I'll speak to Nina in the morning,' Lucy says. 'Make some arrangements.'

'So, you'll go back?' asks Cathy. 'You'll go and see?'

'Yes,' says Lucy. 'Yes. If you want me to. Just me, though. You are going to stay here and look after yourself.'

'I'm not a—'

'I know. But please, Mum. Just finish your milk and go to sleep. Let me worry about everything else.'

And for once Cathy does as she's asked.

15

Now

Once the presence had made itself known, the investigation took on an urgent quality. After all, for it, her, to speak with the living after so many years, surely that meant there was a message to communicate; that this was literally, a matter of life and death.

    A Haunting at Iron Sike Farm, by Simon Leigh

Lewis tries to make polite conversation as Lucy turns the hire car off the main road and drives slowly through Longdale. He finds it hard to imagine this woman is the little girl he has read about: Loo, with her matted gypsy hair and her hand-me-down clothes. She is, he reckons, about the same age as his mum. Not that she looks or sounds like anyone's mum. Away from Cathy she's a lot more imposing and he's struck with a sudden need to impress her.

'Do you know what happened to the house after your family left?' he asks.

'No.' Lucy looks straight ahead, concentrating on the road. She hadn't made it back to London in the end; she'd stayed on at Blue Jacket House, entertaining her mother with walks and day trips along the coast. She'd tried to supervise the exhibition at the gallery from a distance, relying on Eloise and the team, communicating by email and Skype. If she's detected a chill in the more recent emails, a note of disapproval in the tone the Board of Directors are taking with her, she's found it increasingly hard to care.

She'd spent most evenings watching over her mother as she slept, keeping the bedroom curtains firmly closed and very definitely not looking into the garden. Waiting. Listening.

A week has passed since her mother first called her.

'Well,' Lewis leans forward, pulling a notebook from his bag, checking the details, 'the owner, Peter Eglon, tried to find some other tenants and when that proved . . . difficult, he put it on the market. It took a while but eventually he sold it to a family – the Trents – who sold it on within the year.'

'Right.'

'It's passed through several owners since then. And no one, no one else that we can find anyway, has ever managed to make a permanent home there.'

'Really?' A fine rain has started to fall and outside the car the landscape is fading to monochrome, the road taking on a greasy sheen.

'Yes,' he skims through his notes. 'It's passed from one owner to another fairly regularly, but always as a second home, occasionally as an investment. You know, a holiday let.'

'I see.'

'No one else claims to have experienced – well, what you experienced. But that might be because no one ever bothered to ask them, or it could be that the house remains inactive unless there's, well, a sort of conduit, I suppose. Someone sensitive who can make contact.'

'A medium.'

'Yes.'

'And now?' says Lucy. 'Who might have made contact now?'

'There are tests, you know, that measure psychic ability. Nina and I both score quite highly on them. Well, higher than average anyway. That might be it.'

'I see. What about Hal?'

'He wouldn't take the psi tests. He said there was no point.'

'Ah. Well, that's no help, is it?'

He can't tell if she's making fun of him, nor can he find the courage to ask if she has ever taken a psi test herself. They fall silent.

'Maybe they exorcised it, in the end,' she says after a mile or so. 'That was what they wanted, really, what Cathy wanted anyway. To get rid of it. It scared her.'

'It?'

'The voice. It was just a voice at first. Not a person. Michael asked the questions and the voice answered and the more they asked the more real it became.' She takes the turn without bothering to indicate, despite Nina and Hal following behind in Hal's car, and the house looms up suddenly, set in the fields that huddle underneath the moors. Iron Sike Farm. She parks the car high up on the grass verge, switches off the engine.

'But if they did get rid of it,' says Lewis, without thinking, 'does that mean we've brought it back?'

'I hope not,' says Lucy.

Behind them, Hal and Nina watch Lucy get out of her car and walk up the garden path, pulling her long dark coat close as her bright blue scarf, borrowed from Cathy, flutters in the damp breeze.

'Thank you,' says Nina, 'for doing this. I know you're . . . busy.'

'That's OK,' Hal says. 'I brought a couple more cameras, to give us better coverage this time.' It's the most they've said to each other for the whole journey.

185

Maybe it's that word, us, that wins him a brief smile from Nina. 'Thanks,' she says.

Lucy stops and looks up at the house. The windows are opaque, paint is peeling away from the front door and the chain that holds it shut is rusty. She turns and says something to Lewis, who shakes his head and points back towards Hal's car.

'Keys,' says Hal. 'She wants to get in.'

Nina unlocks the door and then stands back, watching closely as Lucy steps into the kitchen. She's very still for a moment, almost holding her breath. She switches on the light. 'There's nothing left,' she says.

Nina can't tell if she's saddened or relieved. She follows her inside. 'Do you want to take a look around?' she asks.

'Yes. Thanks.'

They walk down the hall. Nina follows Lucy up the stairs.

'Cathy and Joe were in there,' Lucy says, pausing on the landing.

The larger of the front bedrooms.

'And Florian in here?' asks Nina, pointing to the second front bedroom, as if she didn't already know.

'Yes. And we were at the back, next to the bathroom,' says Lucy. Nina wishes she'd brought a camera up, or even had the nerve to get her phone out, but that would likely scare Lucy off, close her down.

The door to her old room is shut. Lucy pushes it open. The windows here are boarded up, the room is dark and Lucy tries the light.

'The bulb's gone,' says Nina.

'We never used it anyway. We used to read by candlelight,

we liked that,' says Lucy. She walks into the middle of the room. 'We thought it was . . . romantic.'

'It must have been cold here in the winter.'

'I don't know,' says Lucy. 'We never got to find out.'

The floorboards, smeared and scuffed with a jumble of footprints, give slightly under their feet. Lucy looks around carefully, her hands jammed in her coat pockets. 'We should go down and help the others,' she says.

It doesn't take long to get everything inside. Nina and Lewis take their laptops into the dining room and start setting them up on the table.

Hal follows them, dropping a couple of camera bags onto the floor. 'Right,' he says, 'I've managed to borrow another EX1, which means we won't be messing about quite so much with SD cards tonight. And I thought we could use these too.'

He pulls out three cameras from a holdall, black and silver boxes, so small they might be children's toys, and Lucy is reminded of the little camera Issy used to have, the one with the name that used to amuse them so. A Trip.

'GoPros?' Lewis doesn't sound impressed.

'They're not brilliant in terms of battery life,' says Hal, 'but they're pretty much idiot-proof and you can either leave them in the other rooms or carry them on you.'

Nina picks one up, weighing it in the palm of her hand. 'Great,' she says. 'That's brilliant, thanks.'

'Yeah, well.' Hal picks up the larger of the two bags. 'I assume you want everything else set up as before?'

'Yes,' says Lewis.

'Thanks,' says Nina.

*

187

Hal starts in the kitchen. He doesn't really need any help, but Lucy goes with him anyway, listening politely as he explains about the cameras he's brought along, how they allow him to take extended shots of both the kitchen and the bedroom this time, and about the Wi-Fi system which allows him to monitor one of them.

'But there's no internet connection here, surely?' asks Lucy.

'The signal is transmitted by the camera itself,' says Hal. 'We don't need broadband. So I can keep an eye on you with my iPad when you're running your observations.'

'I see,' says Lucy. She supposes she ought to find that comforting. 'So, how does it work? The AnSoc?' she asks as Hal begins fitting a tripod together. 'Are there very many of you?'

'Sorry, you're asking the wrong person. Nina needed a camera-man – and cameras – so she asked me. A friend of a friend sort of thing. I'm in my final year and . . . It was a bit short notice, I suppose. We had a talk and a drink, I filled in all of Lewis's forms and that was that.'

'You're not a believer, then? Like the others?'

'I wasn't.'

'Until?'

'Until we got here.' He stops what he's doing altogether, there's something odd in his expression, anxiety coupled with distaste. 'This house is—' He shakes his head. 'I don't know. There was something, and I felt it. A sort of something that's not on film, I mean. Sorry, I don't really know – I didn't know what to make of it.'

'And now?'

'Now I have more cameras.'

'Ah.' Lucy lets him get on, making a slow circuit of the room, which seems smaller now, diminished by years of neglect. She can barely imagine the whole family in here, eating together, her mother at the sink, Florian playing with his cars. She runs her fingertips gently over the damp walls. It all seems so long ago.

'I wasn't going to come back,' Hal says, fitting a SD card into a slot and checking the viewfinder, 'not after last time. I thought they'd pissed me about a bit, to be honest.'

'In what way?'

'They didn't really tell me about what went on when you were a kid.' He looks embarrassed. 'I didn't know about your sister.'

'All that happened after they'd gone back to London, when it was just us again,' says Lucy, 'and I'd really prefer that you didn't bring it up with Cathy.'

'Yes. But still – I'm sorry.'

'Thank you,' she says, looking through the viewfinder. The kitchen seems bare and unremarkable, safe.

'What about you?' Hal asks. 'Why did you come back?'

She smiles at him sadly. 'Well, it was me or my mother, I'm afraid. And she really isn't up to it. This seemed like the lesser of two evils.' It seems like a reasonable answer: she hopes it sounds reasonable. 'And you? Surely you've got better things to do with your weekends.'

'Well, I suppose I thought I couldn't let Nina down,' he says.

'Oh. I didn't realise.'

'There's nothing to realise. Not really. We're sort of—' But he stops; a definition of their relationship is beyond him. Once he'd texted her to let her know he could come back this weekend after all, they hadn't been in touch again. She'd been busy, according to Lewis: research. And apart from that brief moment in the car, she'd barely spoken to him, barely even looked at him. 'We don't know each other very well.' He looks around

189

the room. 'Plus I had a very long email from Lewis on the importance of duplicating procedures and personnel on this sort of investigation,' he says, trying to smile.

'Right. But it's not the same personnel, is it? There's me,' says Lucy.

Hal's been thinking about that in the car on the way up. For all Lewis's talk of protocols and procedure, he's sure they are breaking the rules by bringing Lucy with them this time. And as far as he can work out, Nina and Lewis aren't so much interested in investigating the farm this weekend as they are in seeing what happens when they bring Lucy into the house. He wonders if she realises that.

'Can't start a fire without a spark,' says Lucy, softly.

'Sorry?'

He'd missed what she'd been saying, most of it anyway.

'Nothing,' she says. 'I was being flippant.'

He picks up a camera bag and leads the way out of the room, trying to ignore the faint buzzing sensation that has begun to crowd in on him once again.

Lewis has made it his business to check the monitoring gear, to organise the observation rotas and to collate the information they have gathered so far. He's aware that this makes him a figure of fun as far as Hal's concerned, but he tries not to care. Someone has to keep proper records, otherwise it will have all been a . . .

Vanity project.

That had been the verdict of the others at their last AnSoc meeting. Nina had given in, in the end, or at least she'd appeared to but she'd borrowed the gear anyway, just taken it, really, helping herself to the equipment Lewis looked after in his shared house, setting things in motion without worrying about the consequences and dragging him along in her wake. No one else at the AnSoc knows they were here last weekend, no one knows that they've come back – neither he nor Nina have said a word about the investigation. They both know they're on to something, and if the AnSoc don't want to get involved – well, it's their loss.

Hal knows there's something not quite right with the whole setup, he's not stupid, but he doesn't seem to care, and whatever happened to him last time – because Lewis is pretty sure Hal is hiding something – it was enough to ensure he came back this weekend, looking for answers. Just like Lewis, just like Nina. Just like Lucy.

He checks the list on his clipboard. They'll get the second round of observations done and then go back to the Society. Once they've seen their results, then he and Nina will get the resources, the manpower. They'll be able to set up a long-term project, if they can persuade the owners. They might even get to write their own book. The thought makes him smile.

When they're done here, they're going to have an immacu-late set of data, baselines and tests. He still can't believe they got Lucia Corvino – Lucy Frankland – to come back. He's not sure that Nina has explained everything to her, and he wonders if he should have gone into more detail in the car, done some groundwork. Talked a little more about the importance of the connection they need to make – about the work some investi-gators have done with mediums. He and Nina have discussed this, wondering what Lucy might say, how they should approach her.

'You all right?' Nina says as she walks into the room. She drops her bag on the sofa, and rummages in it before pulling out a notepad and pen.

'Fine.'

191

'Aren't you cold? We could put the heater on for a bit.'

'No. I'm fine. We're still going to monitor the camera in the bedroom? Hal knows that, right?'

'Yeah, he's setting that up.' Nina starts checking the EMF monitors and making notes as Lewis watches her, unable to stop himself wondering when exactly she and Hal have been discussing this weekend, what other plans they might have made.

She looks up from table, catches him staring and smiles. 'Lew?'

'Yes?'

'I've been thinking about the obs.'

They begin, as usual, with the distraction activity. Only this time, Lewis goes into the living room with his crossword. There had been an intense debate about this, well out of Lucy's earshot – stuff Hal could only half-follow about procedure and rules – and Lewis had been pretty annoyed, but Nina had got her way in the end.

They'd put observers in the bedroom and the living room this time, the active rooms, rooms where the girls had been the focus of paranormal activity, and there was little doubt in Hal's mind what Nina might be after there. They had left the camera running in the kitchen though, as a control, despite Nina's assertion it was a waste of time; Lewis had at least got his own way on that.

Hal has set up the spare DSLR on a chair in the corner, and Lewis sits on the sofa with a GoPro close to hand. He leaves the living-room door open.

Lucy goes upstairs with Nina. They each have a torch and a book, although it's apparent to Hal, who is watching them on his iPad, that neither is actually reading. They sit with their heads bowed, occasionally turning a page. Listening.

192

Hal remains in the dining room watching them on the monitor, observing the observers. The odd car passes by and a bird calls – it's probably an owl, he writes 'owl' in his notes anyway, as Lewis has asked if he too will keep a record of his observations this weekend. He checks the time as he writes: five o'clock, fully dark. He tries to resist the temptation to look around the room, tries to focus on the screen in front of him.

It's cold, cold and draughty. He stretches his fingers, then shoves his hands in his pockets. Hal very much hopes that nothing is going to happen in here, not while he's on his own, not again. He tries to ignore the faint buzzing of the light bulb above him. Maybe he should turn the lights off himself, that way he'll beat her to it.

Stupid.

It's just an empty house.

Lucy leans back against the wall, trying to find a comfortable position. She can't concentrate. Odd, that, after all the hours she must have spent in here when she was a girl, reading, shutting the world out. She sneaks a glance at Nina, Simon's girl, more at home here than any of them.

She's so like him, that's the trouble, and the last time Lucy had seen Simon – photos and television programmes aside – he'd have been more or less the same age. She starts to do the maths in her head. 'Are you an only child?' she asks and the question surprises both of them.

'Yes,' says Nina. 'I think they'd have liked more. My mum, she was a lot younger than my dad. But it never happened.'

'I see.' Lucy goes back to her book, the words blurring on the page.

'He was still at uni when you knew him, wasn't he?' says Nina.

'That's right.' Lucy's heart is thudding painfully. She can't tell if it's the house, or the girl. She shouldn't have asked, she shouldn't have said anything.

'He lived here for a while, didn't he?'

'In a tent in the back field.'

A bright patch of orange in the pale gold grass.

'What was he like, back then?'

'He was—' Lucy's mouth is dry, and she shakes her head. Tries to find the words, any word – something to get her through this endless moment and on to the next. 'Kind. He was very kind, patient – we were quite horrible kids, I think – sometimes, anyway. Michael Warren tried, but he seemed terribly grown-up, a bit – remote. Simon was more relaxed, we liked him best.'

The warm feeling she'd get when she saw him walking down the field, the sound of his voice in the kitchen. Simon sitting in the garden, smiling, the tiny reflections from his drink dancing about him.

It had been terrible though, once Bee had realised how Loo felt. She wouldn't let her alone, mocking not just her childish, half-formed crush, but the fact that she had any feelings at all. Laughter or tears, it didn't matter, as far as Bee was concerned; the only important feelings in the world were hers, and everyone else was fair game. Lucy has never understood accounts of sisters who tell each other everything, who are best friends as well as blood relatives; in her experience, sisterhood had been a battle.

'I've seen the pictures,' says Nina, 'obviously. But it's not the same as . . . hearing about it.'

'I suppose not,' says Lucy. Isobel standing in the doorway, her face in shadow, her camera held loosely in one hand. 'Did they stay in touch, your father and Isobel?' she asks.

'Yes, a bit, cards at Christmas, the odd phone call. She couldn't come to the funeral, but she wrote to my mum. She lives in Italy now, with her partner.'

Lucy had wondered now and then what had become of Isobel. She knew she'd written to Cathy a couple of times once they'd moved away, but gradually, inevitably, she'd vanished from their lives.

'I got in touch with her when I knew we'd be coming here,' says Nina. 'She sent me quite a long email, actually.'

It's definitely getting colder in the little bedroom. Lucy shifts position slightly, drawing up her legs, resting her chin on her knees. 'So, she knows you were planning to come back?' she says.

'Yes,' says Nina. 'She wasn't happy about it, but yes.'

Hal is really feeling the cold now. His legs and back are starting to ache. Nina had been talking to Lucy, but they seem to have fallen silent.

He hasn't asked Nina about the room upstairs, about what happened that first night before the knocking in the walls started up, although he has heard her audio.

Who's there? Can you hear that?

He stands and looks across the hall into the living room. Lewis is still working on his crossword.

A car passes along the lane outside. He watches Lewis make a note, goes back to the table to do the same himself. It's so cold in here he can barely use the pen. His fingers cramp and as he leans forward he sees his breath frosting in the air.

Not again.

He doesn't want this.

Why me? Why not Lewis? You'd make his day.

He should write this down. This feeling of . . .

195

The overhead light flickers. He thinks it does, and something edges past him, circling the room.

Something cold, deliberate.

She's here, behind him, just out of sight.

The light flickers again and dies.

'Shit.' It takes Lewis far too long to find his torch. Switching it on, he scans the room carefully. He checks his watch. 'The light's gone out at 5.28 p.m.,' he says for the benefit of the audio recording, hoping he doesn't sound unnerved but cool, professional.

What to do now? Find the fuse box or continue the observations? He sits for a moment or two, uncertain. He can't hear anyone else moving around.

'I'm not sure if it's the whole house or just this floor. I've got . . .' He checks his watch again. '. . . another thirty minutes to go.' He stands and goes to the open door, laying a tentative hand against the wood, sweeping the pale beam of light across the other room. He can hear Hal moving around clumsily in the dark, catching against a chair and scraping it across the thinning carpet, but he can't see him.

'Hal? You OK?'

There's no reply.

The fuse box. He needs to find the fuse box. Hal's the only team member not to have a torch. He gave his to Lucy when they began the observations, but he does have a lighter in his pocket. It doesn't help much. Shadows swoop and dance around him as he makes his way across the kitchen, trusting that Lewis and the others will follow. He should wait for them, perhaps, but he can't. The fuse box is on the wall in the corner by the sink. If he can't fix it he can always get outside. Get away.

196

The kitchen is still pitch dark, of course, because the windows are boarded up. A darkness that feels thick and soft and close. The flame from his lighter seems to shrivel a little, to flicker and fade, and Hal realises that he couldn't possibly stand it if he was to find himself alone here with no light. A wooden cupboard is set high up on the wall and as he fumbles with the handle he's sure he can hear someone walking into the kitchen behind him. But he won't look.

Lewis.

Not Lewis.

He will not look.

The cupboard door opens and he can see that something has indeed tripped the switches. All he has to do is reach up and reset the master switch. But the cupboard is a bodged job, set up that little bit too high, and as he reaches for it again he could swear there's someone behind him, someone close enough to slip an arm around him. He pulls down on the switch, dropping the lighter and moving quickly away. He can see the lights have come on in the living room, a sickly yellow bleeds into the hallway, but here in the kitchen it's still dark.

He can't see her.

But she's there.

'Lucy?'

The tapping is faint, and despite herself she looks across to the open door, half-expecting to see someone there.

'I heard it.' Lucy gets to her feet. Nina stands and lets her flashlight play slowly across the room.

The knocking, louder this time, seems to come from below, three sharp raps shaking the floorboards, then silence.

'Was that—'

197

But whatever Nina was going to say is lost as below them a door slams and someone, Lewis or Hal, cries out.

By the time they get downstairs, Lewis has switched on the kitchen light and he and Hal are standing by the sink. As Lucy walks in, Hal turns away, runs the tap and washes his hands, his head bowed.

'We tripped a fuse,' says Lewis.

'Oh,' says Nina, 'I see. We heard something upstairs. We'll need to check the tape.'

'Are you all right?' asks Lucy.

'I fell over,' says Hal. 'Can you see my lighter anywhere?' The naked bulb doesn't seem to cast enough light, and the boarded-up window seems to deaden sound.

Not active, Nina had insisted, when she and Lewis were arguing in lowered voices about the obs and the changes she wanted to make. There was no point in setting anything up in the kitchen, she'd said. It's really not worth bothering about. Just leave the camera running while we concentrate on the real stuff.

He should say something, but he can't. He can feel it again, the pressure building in his head, and Hal wonders if the others feel it too.

16

Then

'Do you want to tell me your name?'

'No.'

Hearing it on tape was definitely worse than hearing it in person. In daylight, in the front room, with the girls sitting on the sofa and the professor in his armchair quietly making conversation with . . . it, well, that was odd – those hoarse rasping tones issuing from that tiny frame – but not so very bad. But on tape, even in broad daylight on a sunny summer's day, the voice was, Simon had decided, uncanny. He'd tried listening to it in the tent once, late at night, with only a torch to see by, but had quickly switched the machine off.

'My name's Michael. Can you say that? Can you say Michael?'

There was a pause, just the sound of breathing on the tape. His own, he realised; he'd been sitting too close to the microphone.

'*Mmm . . . Mike . . . ill.*'

'Almost. Try again, say Michael.'

'*Mike . . . Mich-ael.*'

'Well done.'

The next pause was longer. Someone, one of the girls, cleared her throat. A door opened and closed.

'Where are you?' Michael asked.

'*Dark.*' Each word forced out painfully.

'Is Loo with you?'

'*No.*'

'Where's Loo?'

'*Ask.*'

'Ask who?'

'*Her.*'

'Where are you, Loo?'

'Here.' Her voice was quiet; he had to strain to hear this part. 'Sitting next to Bee.'

'Where's the voice coming from, Loo?'

'I don't know.'

'Are you there? Are you?'

But there was no reply.

Simon switched off the tape and looked at Isobel. They were sitting in the front garden on an old blanket, the machine on the ground between them.

'So, what do you think?'

'I don't know.'

'Well, that's a big help.'

'What can I say? If it was Bee,' Isobel said, 'if it was Bee, I'd say, no way, she's definitely pulling your leg. But . . .'

'It's Loo.' Quiet little Lucia.

'Yeah.'

Simon fiddled with the machine, rewinding the tape.

Isobel leant back, stretching her legs out in the sun, and yawned. When she wasn't working for the *Gazette*, covering village shows and cricket matches, she was at the farm with Simon and Michael, recording everything on film. She'd been working long hours for almost a month now, with no real time off.

'It's been a textbook case so far, you know,' Simon said. He lay down with his hands behind his head and closed his eyes.

200

Sometimes he found it easier to gather his thoughts if he could look away from Issy, shut her out. 'All quite in keeping with other recorded poltergeist activity.'

A noisy spirit.

Unquiet.

'We thought we'd been dealing with a force, an energy, I suppose. But now we're seeing evidence of – I don't know, a desire to communicate, a personality.' He opened his eyes and found that Isobel was leaning over him, her expression serious, hesitant.

'Simon, do you think—'

She was close; he could reach out and pull her closer, but Bee's voice broke the spell.

'There you are,' she said. 'We've been looking for you.'

Issy drew back, irritation clouding her face. Bee and Loo were standing in the doorway.

'It's time,' said Bee.

Issy scrambled to her feet. 'How are you this morning, Loo?'

'OK.'

'Michael wants to talk to the voice again,' says Bee. 'He thinks that's what been making a mess, chucking things around.'

'Nicking stuff,' said Loo.

'And levitating,' said Bee. 'I was the one it levitated.'

'What's it like, levitation?' asked Simon.

'I dunno.' Bee leant back against the door and considered this question. 'Like swimming,' she said, 'swimming in the air.'

'Could it do it again, do you think? If I got a camera and tried to film it? Could it lift you up again?'

'Dunno.'

'Does it hurt,' said Isobel, 'when you talk in that funny voice?'

Loo raised a hand to her throat. 'It . . .'

'Michael's waiting,' Bee said.

'I . . .'

'You can say, you know,' said Isobel. Inside the house, a door slammed and the baby started howling.

'It's not me,' said Loo. 'I'm not the one talking.'

Isobel found a place out of the way, by the living-room door, where neither Bee nor Loo could see her without turning their heads, and sat on the floor with her back against the wall, watching. Since the arrival of the voice, the other phenomena had become sporadic, with events – the familiar knocks and thumps, the upturned furniture – mostly confined to the girls' room at bedtime. But the voice itself seemed to be getting stronger with every passing day and according to the professor, a distinct personality was emerging. The investigation to all intents and purposes was now focused on this personality.

'We're close,' Michael had said, the other evening, as they all sat round the kitchen table, going over the day's findings. 'All we need is a name, a place to start.'

Simon nodded at Michael, who spoke briefly, stating the date and time and the names of those present, before turning to Loo.

'How are you feeling today, Loo?'

'All right.'

She fidgeted in her seat and looked at Bee and smiled. Bee bit her lip and tried to look serious.

'I thought we could have a little chat before we begin today. If you don't mind.'

'No. I don't mind.'

'Where do you think the voice comes from, Loo? The voice we've recorded.'

'I don't know.'

'Does it frighten you?'

'No.'

202

'Does it hurt?'

'No.' Again she risked a look at Bee, who looked away.

'Does it tell you what to say?'

'No. I can – it's like someone's whispering in my ear. But it's not me.'

'It's someone else?'

'Yes.'

'Who?'

Loo hesitated, and Isobel had the impression she wanted very much to ask Bee for something . . . support. Permission. Bee leant back on the sofa and crossed her legs and Isobel was struck, for the first time, by the age difference between the girls. Bee and Loo. She hardly ever saw the one without the other. She, Michael, Simon, everyone referred to them as 'the girls', as if they were inseparable, twinned.

Loo looked younger than her age, drowning in her oversized frock, her voice soft and hesitant. Bee, for all her petulance and her posturing, looked older; her dress was more revealing, if it had been through a wash recently it might even look fashionable. In repose, not clamouring for attention, not complaining, one long leg slung over the other, Bee almost looked like a young woman.

As quietly as she could, Isobel picked up her camera, and after wavering for a moment, focused on Bee. The click of the shutter made her look, of course, and she frowned before turning away and curling up on the sofa. Sulking.

'Is the voice here today, do you think?' asked Michael.

'I suppose so.'

'Can I speak to it?'

'If you like.'

Michael leant forward. 'Are you there?' he asked.

They waited.

'Yes.'

Loo's head had drooped forward.

'Do you remember my name?'

'Yes.'

'What's my name?'

'Mike. Michael.'

'That's very good. Where are you?'

'Farm.'

'This is Simon. Do you remember him?'

'Simon.'

'And Isobel over there.' Michael glanced across the room and smiled encouragingly at her.

'Issy.'

She was hot and her back was sticking to the wall. She wished he hadn't made it say her name.

Simon was sitting cross-legged on the floor by Michael's chair, reduced again to the status of technician. He tried to concentrate on either the tape or on Loo, uncomfortably aware of Bee's tanned legs and the way her dress had risen as she'd curled up on the sofa. He didn't look, even though he could feel her eyes on him.

'Where are you?' asked Michael.

'Here.'

'What year is it?'

'Now.'

'Do you live here?'

'No.'

'Did you use to live here?'

'Yes.'

'When?'

There was no answer and Loo's head fell further forward, her long dark hair obscuring her face.

'Do you live here now?'

'*Don't . . .*'

'Are you dead?'

'*. . . know.*' Her voice was so low, so forced, Simon had the urge to take her hand, to comfort her.

'Did you die here? Can you tell me? Are you—'

Loo began to shake her head slowly as if trying to clear it, as if trying to break free. Across the room Issy leant forward.

'Did you die here?'

'*Dark.*'

She clutched at her stomach.

'What's your name? Tell me your name.'

'*Can't.*'

'Why not? Why can't you tell me?'

'*Can't.*'

'What's your name? Tell me your name.'

'*I . . . I . . .*'

'Where are you?'

'*Dark.*'

'Can you see me?'

'*No.*'

'Can you see Loo?'

'*I . . .*'

'Lucia, can you hear me?'

'*Not. Loo.*'

'What do you want?'

'*My – my—*'

'What do you want?'

'*Mine.*'

'Who are you?'

'*I – I—*'

'Tell me. Who are you?'

Loo was almost completely doubled up now, on the verge of falling to the floor.

'Tell me your name,' said Michael. 'Tell me.'

'I—'

'Tell me.'

'Tib.'

'Who?'

I'm Tib. I'm Tib. I'm—

'Stop it.' Bee reached forward and grabbed her sister's wrist. 'Stop it. Leave her alone.'

'No.'

Loo tried to push her sister away.

'Stop it,' said Bee.

'Stop it, stop it, stop it.'

'Loo.' Bee pulled her sister close. 'Loo, stop it.'

The younger girl arched her back, but Bee was too strong for her and after a brief struggle Loo gave in, collapsing into her sister's embrace. Tib, whoever she was, had gone. There was only Bee wrapping her arms around Loo and the both of them rocking back and forth, trembling.

Isobel stood up, lifting her camera as she moved closer. Loo had fallen back, her eyes were closed and her face was wet with tears as she gasped for breath.

'I—' she began. 'Let me – I'm—' She tried to push her sister away, and looked up at Isobel. 'Issy,' she said.

Bee's arm swung out and knocked the camera out of Issy's hands.

'Shit!' It wasn't broken, but when Isobel picked it up, the back swung loose, exposing the film. The images would be lost.

Bee held Loo close once again, whispering in her ear.

Simon picked up the tape recorder and placed it on the sideboard. 'Are you all right?' he asked Loo.

206

'Leave her alone. Leave us alone.' Bee wouldn't look at him, at any of them.

'It's OK, it's fine,' said Simon.

'We'll stop there for now.' Michael stood and Isobel began to move away, snapping the back of the camera into place.

'It's too hot in here,' she said. She left the room, not bothering to close the door behind her. A moment later Simon heard the back door open and a gust of warm air blew into the house, shifting his notes and the professor's papers, unsettling them all.

'Simon, I'd like a word, if I may?' said Michael, gathering his notes up, placing them in a manila folder, his eyes bright.

'Sure.' Simon looked at the girls on the sofa. Loo had her face buried in Bee's shoulder, still trembling.

'It's all right,' said Bee. 'I'll look after her.'

They went outside to talk. Michael was doing his best to remain calm. He was the lead investigator here and he felt a certain duty of care to Simon and to Isobel. But this – today's session – was really quite . . .

'Extraordinary.' He even permitted himself a smile. 'We have a name, Simon.'

'Yes. I mean . . .' Simon looked back at the house. 'Has it been her along, then?' he asked.

'Loo?'

'No. This . . . Tib character. The knocking, the other disturbances, all her, do you think?'

'I suspect so, yes. Yes.'

There was a great deal to organise. The Society would need to be informed, obviously, Roland Miskin and the others, the press too, when the moment was right. Michael had already agreed to a TV interview, just the local independent station. It had taken quite a while to set it up, as a matter of fact, but that would definitely have to be postponed. The last thing he needed was the burden of media scrutiny, not in the face of such an extraordinary development. He needed to know who he was dealing with first, get some background information then once he was sure, an interview and a formal statement perhaps, with some carefully selected audio to back things up. He was almost certain he'd be able to get Cathy to agree to that. And there was more material here than could be outlined in an article or lecture series; he had enough here for a book, he was sure of it.

He walked down the garden path and into the lane, turning without thinking to the left, where the road began its lazy ascent to the top of the moor. 'This really is quite, quite remarkable, you know. One spends so much time hoping – a career, a – lifetime and here it is, at last.'

His voice drifted away. He stopped and looked out across the valley. She had lived here, died here too, he was sure of it. Tib. Beside him Simon waited.

'So, the next time we speak with her, with Tib, we'll need to elicit some details. Dates, family names, anything which will help us place her in the public record. That really is a priority. I'll put you on to that, if you don't mind, a little research project for you. And we'll need to get in touch with the Society again.'

'With Dr Miskin?' Simon asked, bracing himself for the kindly explanation that his services were no longer needed.

'As a matter of fact, no,' said the professor. 'I think the time has come for a more specialised perspective.'

He looked back towards the house, set a little way up from the road, silent and solid. There was so much to do, he barely knew where to begin.

'Damn.' Cathy put the receiver down with more force than was strictly necessary and leant back against the bookcase, looking up at the landscapes that crowded the wall opposite. It was her own fault, she supposed, for ignoring the red bills, but she hadn't thought they'd cut the phone off quite so quickly. They were stuck now if she needed to call anyone, or if anyone wanted to call them. She wondered again how she might go about selling a couple of Joe's paintings for a halfway decent price. They had no contacts here, that was the trouble. There was nothing like an art gallery in the village, so she'd have to get herself and the canvases, and God help her, the kids, out to the coast somehow. Issy would probably give her a lift but even then, she'd have to try and find somewhere that set its sights higher than the usual tourist tat. Maybe she'd be better off trying to sell them back in Leeds.

She sat down on the stairs, leaning her head against the wall. Glad to have five minutes to herself, to be honest. Michael and Simon had gone off somewhere, full of their latest development – it had a name, now, Tib. Sue wasn't sure how she felt about that. At least the house was quiet now, peaceful. They'd had such plans for this place when they'd moved in. They'd even made a start, on the garden at least.

But everything seemed to take longer without Joe. She'd always been the practical one: managing the house, the kids, dealing with buyers. She had thought that without Joe she'd get on much as she had before, better, but she'd been wrong.

It was starting to feel as if everything was slipping away, that it was all her fault. If only she could take it back, start over again. She needed him. She missed him. How was she supposed to manage without a phone?

The living-room door crashed open behind her and the girls came out, Bee first, then Loo.

'We're going for a walk,' said Bee.

'Where?' Cathy stood, pushing her hair out of her eyes.

'Don't know. See you later, Cathy.'

Loo followed her sister down the front path and out onto the lane. The sky was clear and the warm air was still. 'Where are we going?'

'Out. To the shop. Have you got any money?'

'No.' Loo stopped and took a precautionary step back, ready to dodge out of reach. 'You can go if you want. I don't want to.'

'Baby.'

Ignoring this taunt, Loo pulled herself up onto the wall and perched among the slabs of stone, wiggling her toes. 'I'm tired,' she said.

'We could go exploring.'

Loo recognised this for the bribe it was, but still, she was tempted. 'Can we go and see if Simon's in his tent?'

'Boring.'

'Where then?'

Bee hoisted up her dress and climbed over the wall. 'Come and see,' she said.

'We're not allowed,' said Loo, standing well back as if their father might suddenly appear. The barn was built of stone with black double doors at the front and ground-floor windows covered by wooden shutters. There were double doors up at the top of the building too, round the side. They were the entrance to the hayloft: that always seemed a bit wrong to Loo, two improbable doors opening out onto nowhere.

'No one's going to know, stupid.'

The two girls looked at the barn, solid in the summer heat, its stones set against them, the door locked.

'We don't have a key,' said Loo. Almost the first thing their father had done when they moved in was get hold of some chain and a padlock for his studio.

'We don't need one.' Bee walked around the back of the building, leaving Loo to decide for herself.

She could leave her to it. She could go back to the house. She could get her sunglasses and a book and maybe even some of the money she'd quietly managed to keep hidden away from her sister, and go off on her own for a bit. Maybe she'd do that and then Simon would find her sitting on her own by the War Memorial and he'd talk to her, just her, and that would be . . .

It was very quiet. Loo wondered if Bee had found a way in after all. They'd never been in the barn, none of them, not even Dan, and he wasn't scared of anything. Maybe she'd hurt herself. Maybe Bee had climbed up onto the roof or something and had fallen and was now lying unconscious somewhere. Bee was only ever quiet if she was asleep. Loo turned away and looked back across the field, pretending she wasn't going to tag along this time.

Bee had found a sturdy stick and was kneeling up on the stone window ledge, wedging it in between the shutters.

'You can't do that. He'll know someone's been in,' Loo whispered, even though no one else was around.

'So? He won't know who, will he?'

'Bee, we can't go in. Get down—' A shutter gave way with a sudden crack, and, throwing the stick away, Bee pulled at the flimsy wood now hanging lopsided on its hinges.

'See? Easy,' she said, as she squeezed herself through the window and dropped out of sight.

'Bee? Bee?' There was no answer. Maybe she really was hurt this time. Loo climbed up onto the ledge and stuck her head and shoulders through the gap. It was dark inside the barn, and

211

the air was still and cool. She couldn't really make much out at first, just gloomy shapes and the scent of paint and turps, and she couldn't see her sister at all.

'Where are you?' Loo leant further in. Maybe she'd have to go for help. If she got Dan, then they wouldn't get into trouble. Below her, her back pressed against the wall, Bee reached up and, grabbing hold of her arm, she pulled. Loo landed more or less on top of her, her right arm and leg scraped by the raw wood, the breath knocked out of her.

'That hurt,' she said, scrubbing at the marks on her leg, blinking back the tears.

'Oh, shut up,' Bee said, pushing her away and clambering to her feet.

It was a bit of a disappointment, at first. Joe had made a point of putting everything away before he left, so there was precious little to look at. A stack of unused canvases against one wall, a series of four landscapes in varying stages of completion leaning against each another. Dust motes dancing around the jars of pencils and brushes.

They had to pick through everything to find him: bits of paper and card, broken stubs of charcoal, discarded rags stiff with paint. Squashed and crumbling cigarette butts on the floor, and tea cups stained and toppled to one side. It felt as though he had been gone for a very long time.

'What are we looking for?' Loo asked.

'Clues,' said Bee, leafing through a sketchbook.

'What clues?'

'Look.' Bee held the book open and there she was, sitting on the kitchen step, scowling. It wasn't a proper portrait, not even a sketch – it was more like a cartoon, the Bee on the paper was thinner, more elastic than the real-life girl, but it was still her.

'Let me see,' said Loo. 'Did he do me too?'

They looked through the book together. The cartoons covered only a couple of pages and some of the figures were overdone and scribbled out, but they were all there, all Joe's children, even the baby: comic-book versions of themselves, grouped together in twos and threes. It seemed to Loo that Joe had drawn Bee the most, over and over, in bold clean lines, and with different expressions, as if he couldn't quite get her right.

'Are there more?' Loo asked. 'Can we keep them?'

'Cathy won't like it,' said Bee, snatching the book back and looking at herself again. If Loo had drawn her like that – with mad hair and a moody face on – she would have been furious, but because it was Joe . . . Bee almost looked sad.

'Why not?'

'She's gone off him,' said Bee. 'It's all her fault.'

'What is?'

'God, Loo, you are so thick sometimes.' Bee put the book carefully on the table and picked up another.

'I am not.'

But Bee had turned her attention to the loft. 'Let's try up there,' she said.

'No, we should go. When he comes back, he'll guess; he'll know.'

'Oh, bloody hell, Loo.' Bee looked exasperated, her hands on her hips, more like her mother now than she'd care to admit.

'What?'

Bee glanced at the sketchbook again. 'Nothing,' she said.

Cathy had told them their father would be back soon, and Loo wished he would hurry up. He'd never been away this long before. She wasn't even sure where he was – Edinburgh, Cathy had told them, but then Loo had heard her tell Issy he was in

213

Glasgow – and the house felt odd, odder, without him. Being in the barn, the studio, was the closest she'd felt to him for ages.

'Come on,' said Bee, 'let's go up top. And don't say no again.'

17

Now

Lewis works his way through his list. He'll let Hal deal with
the cameras, but he wants to check the audio as well as making
notes of times and readings. He works methodically, the front
bedroom first. He can hear the others downstairs in the dining
room, chatting quietly as they eat, although he's not convinced
that's a good idea. As far as he's concerned, any detail Lucy
provides about the past might influence the others' perceptions
of the house. Better by far, surely, to get through the rest of the
evening before asking Lucy for her version of events; before
moving on to the next phase.

Up here in the bedroom everything seems to be OK, although
of course there's no proper light here, just the one Hal fixed to
the Sony. He moves carefully, trying not to block the light from
the hallway. He's reluctant to turn his back to the door; he can't
escape the feeling that someone – he's not sure who – might
think it funny to slam it shut. To leave him there in the dark.
Although of course he has his torch and anyway—

He switches it on and directs the beam of light towards the
landing; there's no one there.

No one has followed him upstairs.

No one.

But still, he has the urge to speak, to communicate.

'Hello?' His voice is tentative, low. He makes a slow circle of the room. This was the girls' bedroom and the starting point for all the phenomena. He lets the light from the torch sweep lazily over the walls and their palimpsest of paper. The mattress in the corner bothers him: even though he knows it wasn't there in 1976, he could almost convince himself there's something in it, something very still, something waiting.

He's lost track of what he's doing; his list, his clipboard that he never really needs anyway, seems to have vanished. He brought it upstairs, he knows he did, but he must have put it down when he was checking the batteries in the camera and now the bloody thing has vanished and if he could just find it then he'd be able to get on, to restore some order, to regain control.

The yellow-white light dances over the floorboards and he can see footprints in the dust, so many now between the five of them that he couldn't retrace his footsteps if he tried. And then he remembers, not five, four.

A floorboard gives and he drops the torch.

'Can you tell us about Tib?' Nina glances up at the door, glad that Lewis is out of the way for a few minutes.

'There's not very much to tell.' Lucy's voice is even, not defensive, but not forthcoming either. Supper isn't much, shop-bought sandwiches and crisps and bottled water, but at least it's provided an excuse to sit down together. Nina wishes she could get rid of Hal too, she'd rather it was just her and Lucy; they'd been getting somewhere earlier, getting closer at least, and there were so many questions she wanted to ask.

'Was she here all along? Right from the beginning?' she asks.

Lucy is silent for a long time. Next to her, Hal clears his throat and shifts slightly. She can smell cigarette smoke on him, on his jacket and in his hair.

'I'm not sure,' says Lucy, eventually. 'I suppose so. That's what

216

everyone decided in the end, isn't it? That the disturbances were all her, Tib, trying to get through.'

'From where?'

Lucy tips her head back slightly and closes her eyes. 'Oh, I don't know.'

'Were you frightened?' asks Hal. 'I mean, the bit with the voice, it must have been . . . disturbing.'

'I don't remember,' says Lucy.

'But she spoke through you, surely—' Nina can't help herself; they haven't gone to all this trouble just for Lucy to fob them off like this.

'I was very young and for a long time I didn't want to remember,' says Lucy, opening her eyes now and sitting up straight. 'If you want to know what Tib had to say for herself, you have Simon's book. It's all in there. I can't tell you anything more.'

'I'm sorry,' says Hal. 'I didn't mean to upset you.' Although actually, it's Hal who looks upset, pale and slightly sickened. He stands. 'Sorry,' he says again, before leaving the room, heading upstairs.

In the bathroom, Hal flushes the loo and washes his hands.

It's not a sudden change, like last time. This time it's been gradual, a vague buzzing at the back of his head, something you could ignore really, just put to one side as you got on with things. Only left to its own devices the buzzing, the unease, has got worse and now it's just there, in the way, blocking everything.

He could leave, of course. No one is forcing him to stay. It doesn't seem to get to anyone else, this place, and it's worse after dark. So he could leave, let them all get on with it; he's set the cameras up for them and they could manage the rest.

The water gurgles and splutters in the sink and as he watches Hal tries to remember what it was he'd decided.

Something about the cameras.

Something about leaving.

Lewis still can't find the clipboard, although he's sure he brought it in with him. At the doorway he stops and checks one more time, the light from the torch cutting through the thick shadows in the corners of the room. He'll have to ask the others.

The light in the hall makes him blink, the bulb there seems very bright, he could swear he can hear it buzzing; the harsh yellow light almost fizzes. He stands at the top of the stairs, waiting for the bulb to pop. It would be a relief, a comfort. But it doesn't.

He finds Nina and Lucy in the living room.

'Everything's fine,' he says. 'If we give it another hour, take a quick look at the new footage, then we can switch rooms and do the second session.'

'Right,' says Lucy. She doesn't look afraid, not exactly – tense perhaps, uneasy. He hopes she's not about to change her mind about staying. 'Whatever you say.'

'Thanks,' says Nina and above them Hal crosses the landing, slamming a door behind him.

Hal has switched cameras so they can still monitor Lucy and Nina, who have swapped rooms with Lewis. They're just about to start when Lewis calls down the stairs.

'Nina? Hal? Problem.'

Lucy follows Hal and Nina up. Lewis is standing outside the bedroom, which is in total darkness.

'That's odd,' says Nina, flicking her torch around the room, making light trails on the walls and ceiling.

'Shine that over for me, would you?' says Hal, following her inside. 'Batteries,' he says, after a brief examination of the small light fitted onto the camera.

'It was fine earlier,' says Lewis.

'Well, it's fucked now.'

'Do we have any more?'

'They're charging.'

'Can we still film up here?' asks Nina.

'Sure,' says Hal, making some adjustments to the camera's settings. 'The quality of the image might be a bit grainy, but you should be OK. If Lewis can manage with just his torch for company.'

'Great,' says Lewis. 'Thanks.'

Nina takes the chair, which leaves Lucy the sofa, positioned in front of the fireplace, just as it had been all those years before. She sits and for a second she can hear the whir of the tape recorder, she can see Simon sitting by the chair, and her calm deserts her, because this can't possibly end well and she should tell someone quickly, before—

'Lucy? Are you OK?'

'Yes.' She leans back into the sofa, unwraps the scarf she's been wearing and places it on the empty seat next to her.

Bee's seat.

'Did you bring your book?' asks Nina.

Something to distract her, that would help, but she can't remember where she had it last. The kitchen, perhaps, or maybe upstairs in the bedroom.

'Sorry.'

It's disconcerting. A patch of the floral paper Lucy remembers so well has been uncovered on one wall, a great gash of it from ceiling to floor, and the fireplace with its cracked tile has remained untouched, but the furniture in the living room, a sofa, a chair, and an empty bookcase, is unfamiliar. Yet still it's there, the faintest sensation that she has come home. She could close her eyes, fill the room with her mother's books, Joe's work on the walls, Flor's toys scattered over the carpet.

The blue-green marble still tucked in her pocket.

'What was it like?' asked Nina.

'I'm sorry?' She hadn't been listening.

'When you moved here,' said Nina. 'What was it like?'

Lucy shifts position, trying to get comfortable on the sagging sofa, deciding how much to share. 'We didn't much like it,' she says in the end. 'Not really.'

'I always thought it sounded idyllic, like something out of a book.'

The Railway Children. Swallows and Amazons.

'Yes. Well. No one in the village liked us. They thought we were hippies, or gypsies, or both. And Cathy and Joe – they didn't care, you see. They didn't care what people thought, so they made no effort to get on. It was just us, too many of us, crammed in here. And we didn't have a clue about living in the countryside. We didn't fit in.'

Nina resists the temptation to fill the silence that follows.

'And we had to share, me and Bee. God, we hated that.'

'Weren't you close, then?' asks Nina.

She doesn't understand, of course. Only children never do.

Nina hesitates. 'Tell me some more about my dad.'

Lucy doesn't know where to start. She casts around for something, anything, to fill the silence. 'He used to sit there,' she says, nodding towards the fireplace. 'He would sit cross-legged on the floor, in charge of the tape recorder. Michael used to say he didn't know how to work it, but I'm sure he did. I think he just liked having Simon around, he liked having an assistant, an apprentice.'

'Did he mind that?'

'Simon? I don't think so. He thought they were doing important work. I think he really believed that they were going to reveal something amazing to the world, a great truth. I think that's why he wrote the book, why he carried on after Michael died.'

'Did you like him?'

'Yes.' Lucy doesn't have to think about that response. 'We both did. He was very . . .' She teeters on the edge of those feelings again, the breathlessness both girls would feel around him, the blushing shyness, the terrible need to be liked by him.

Deep in her coat pocket her phone buzzes. A text message. It can't be an emergency. If there was a problem with her mother, the home would ring, but even so she pulls it out and checks the screen. It's from Dan.

What's happening?

'Is everything OK?' asks Nina.

'Fine,' says Lucy, dropping the phone onto the sofa. Having it switched on is probably against Lewis's rules, but what can he do, send her home? 'Were you close?' she asks. 'You and Simon?'

'Yes. I think so. We didn't always get along, Mum says we're too – we were too similar for that, but yes. I have lot of happy memories.'

'He used to take us into the village, buy us sweets and ice cream. Cathy was going through a brown rice and carob phase at the time.'

'What about your father?'

'Joe?' Something changes in Lucy's expression. She looks sad, resigned.

I've lost her, Nina thinks. I've pressed too hard too soon. 'Sorry,' she says. 'I'm just – he's barely there, in the book, and I just—'

'We all learned fairly early on to leave him alone to paint,' says Lucy. 'That rule never changed. But sometimes he could be – just so much fun, you know? Larger than life, full of energy – the trouble was, you could never tell, or we couldn't anyway, maybe Cathy could. We never quite knew what sort of a mood he'd be in, so we'd spend all our time testing him, hoping for a smile, any sort of reaction, really.' She picks up the scarf, wraps it around her fingers, unwraps it and sets it down again. 'We thought he was wonderful, and everything was different without him,' she says softly. 'We just wanted him to come back.'

The light bulb above them flickers and there's a sound, a faint hissing. They both hear it, and Nina leans forward in her seat. 'What's that?' she says.

Then the knocking begins.

It seems to circle the room, around Nina and Lucy, before leading them upstairs – a quite distinct tapping, guiding the way as the two women follow, step by step, Nina barely able to contain her excitement, Lucy trying not to think about it too much at all.

This can't be happening again.

It stops on the landing, and Lewis comes out of the bedroom. 'Did you hear it?' Nina asks him, beaming. 'Did you?'

'Yes. I—' Lewis glances uncertainly back into the darkened bedroom. He looks half asleep.

'Lew?'

'You heard it too?' he asks.

There is wine in the kitchen. A couple of bottles of red among the bottles of water, the discarded disposable coffee cups and sandwich wrappings, the bag of oranges and the packets of cheap biscuits they have brought with them. Lucy made sure to add the wine to their shopping trolley when they stopped off on their way out of town. Lewis had been wise enough not to comment.

There are no glasses, of course, but this is not a problem.

Lucy stands by the back door looking out over the garden, car keys in one hand, bottle in the other. She could just go, leave them to get on with it. She can't decide.

In her pocket her mobile rings. She puts the bottle by the sink, checks her phone.

Dan, again.

Hal would like a cigarette, but that means going outside – Lewis has been very clear on that – and going out means going through the kitchen and he has the feeling Lucy would appreciate some time alone. He can hardly blame her; the knocking in the walls obviously bothers her as much as it does him. Sue's left them to it, Lewis and Nina, replaying the audio, the knocking. He wonders if Lucy might leave, and if she does whether that would change the atmosphere.

He sits down on the sofa and closes his eyes. Was it like this the last time? The sense he has that the house is aware of them, responding to them? He can't remember.

He closes his eyes and she's there by the window. She's pale and blurred somehow, a grainy black and white still. A girl looking through a rain-streaked window, her face pressed close against the glass, one hand, fingertips splayed, pressing against the pane, searching. Outside or inside? He can't tell.

But she wants to get . . . close.

'Jesus.' He opens his eyes and he's alone once more. He gets to his feet and – unwilling to look any more closely at the room, at his solitary reflection – he decides he will have that cigarette after all. He makes sure to shut the door behind him.

'What's it like?' Dan asks.

'Weird. The same and not the same,' says Lucy. 'Empty.' She leans against the sink, her back to the boarded-up window, sliding her key ring on and off her finger.

'And the investigation?'

'It's not good.'

'Do you want to tell me?'

'It's nothing – solid. Just – noise. Inside the walls.'

'Bloody hell, Loo.'

'It could be anything, you know that. Air in the water pipes or whatever.' She hopes she sounds more confident than she feels.

'But they don't think that.'

'God, no. They're delighted.'

So pleased with themselves, just like Michael and Simon before them.

'And it's not – you know – them?'

She takes a deep breath, then another, uncomfortably aware of the pressure building in her chest, the ache. 'I don't think so,' she says. 'I suggested spending the night at the Lion, but they won't have it.'

'Are you OK? You sound a bit – freaked out.'

'I didn't think – I wasn't really expecting it to be like this.'

To be so insistent, just like before.

'Ah, Loo.' Dan's voice softens. 'You don't have to stay, you

224

know, no matter what Cathy says. Leave them to it, see how far they get then.'

'I know,' Lucy says, pushing her car keys back into her pocket. 'Only – I think she's hoping for some answers, about Bee, if nothing else.'

'Sorry.' Hal appears in the doorway. 'I didn't mean to—' He gestures at her phone.

'That's OK.'

He looks pale, off-colour, shaken.

'I'll just—' He crosses the room and goes out into the garden.

'Loo?'

'Yes. I'm here.' She turns her attention back to her brother. 'Anyway I just – I'm not sure that I can. Go, I mean. What if something happened to them?'

'Like what?'

'I don't know. But what if it did?'

'They're not kids.'

'But they are, Dan, they are.'

18

Then

Olivia Farrell wasn't what Isobel had been expecting. When Simon had passed on the news that Michael was bringing in a medium to help, the first thought she'd had was of a dotty old lady, swathed in scarves and beads, speaking in hushed tones of the dear departed. The second had been of a younger model, a hippy given to talk of auras and levels of consciousness, a more carefree version of Cathy, perhaps. But Olivia was neither of these.

She was, Issy decided, businesslike. If you didn't know better, you might think she was a teacher, or an academic of some sort. She wore a simple linen dress and sandals, and her hair, dark but streaked with grey, was swept back in a ponytail. She had only one piece of luggage, a somewhat battered suitcase, which she carried out of Whitby's railway station to Simon's car herself, despite his protests, her leather handbag bouncing against her hip as she walked. Calm and friendly, not dotty at all.

Olivia chatted politely as Simon drove them out of town, up onto the moors and out towards Longdale. She'd never been to this part of the world before, she'd been quite impressed with their findings so far, she was glad of the opportunity to meet the girls, well, Loo really, she supposed. All this interspersed with the odd question about Simon's studies and did he intend going back, about Issy's career, what were her ambitions; little nuggets of information gleaned casually as they rode along past the dry stone walls and the pale green fields and the moors, always the moors, purple and red now and dry as tinder.

'Is it much further?' asked Olivia after a while.

'Fifteen minutes or so,' said Simon.

'I didn't realise it was so far. I've inconvenienced you, both of you.'

'Not at all,' said Simon. 'We're grateful you're able to help.'

'Well, I hope I can, but what I do isn't an exact science.'

'And what do you do, exactly?' asked Isobel.

'I'm a medium,' said Olivia.

'Yes. I know. I just meant – well, why are you here?'

'Michael asked me to come and take a look at the little girl, Loo, to give him my opinion.'

'He doesn't think Loo is – I don't know – at risk, somehow? Possessed?'

Olivia's laughter was unexpected. 'Good lord, no. Wherever did you get that? He thinks the little girl is a medium too.' Simon slowed the car to allow a couple of sheep to amble across the road. 'A remarkably powerful physical medium, were his actual words, which isn't really my thing at all, but he sounded so excited on the phone . . .'

'I'm sorry. What is your thing?' asked Isobel.

'I'm a mental medium.' Olivia turned to look at Issy properly, taking her in. 'Sorry, it sounds silly, I suppose, to be so specific, but broadly speaking there are two categories of medium. People like me who are . . . sensitive – who can hear spirits, or receive impressions, and who can pass them on, give a sort of running commentary. And then there are people who can produce phenomena – raps, knocks, even moving objects, in some cases.'

'Physical mediums.'

'Yes.' Olivia's smile was warm, reassuring.

'Like Loo,' said Simon.

'Well. That's what I'm here to assess,' said Olivia, keeping her gaze on Issy. She wore no makeup, Isobel noticed. Her skin was lightly tanned and a faint scar ran across one eyebrow, puckering the skin a little.

'And you've done this sort of thing before?'

'I work with Michael fairly frequently, and I've met one or two physical mediums before. We've agreed that I'll observe the little girl, Lucia, when you interview her, just to – well, offer a second opinion on her, I suppose.'

'What's it like?' asked Simon as he took the turn for Longdale. 'Being – sensitive?'

'Mostly it's just background noise,' said Olivia, turning to look at the road ahead.

'Isn't that, I don't know, a little distracting?'

'I've learned to tune it out, as if it was a radio playing in another room. I'd go mad otherwise. Usually it's just a jumble of odd impressions that don't make sense. But sometimes, sometimes I get a very clear image, or a voice, a voice just a little way behind me speaks and—'

The car rattled as Simon hit a pothole too quickly. 'Sorry. Still getting used to country roads,' he said. 'This is Longdale now. We'll pick the professor up at the pub and go straight on to the farm if that's OK with you.'

Olivia leant back in her seat, resting an elbow on the open window. 'Just as you like,' she said.

They had made themselves a nest from old blankets and the bedspread and some cushions from the living room. The sun beat into the dusty fabric and it was too hot to move, even though they could hear people walking around the side of the house.

'Hello,' said Michael, as he approached them. 'How are you both today?'

Bee wrinkled her nose. 'Bored,' she said, throwing her sketchpad to one side.

'Hello,' said Loo, sitting up and blinking in the bright sunshine.

'This is Miss Farrell. She's come to help us.'

The woman standing behind Michael looked old, older than Issy and Cathy, but then she smiled and she didn't look old at all. 'My name's Olivia,' she said, looking directly at Loo. 'You must be Lucia.'

'Loo,' said Bee. 'She's Loo and I'm Bee.'

'I see,' said Olivia. 'Well, it's very nice to meet you both.'

'Have you been drawing again, Bee? Can I see?' said Simon. He sat down on the bed spread and reached for the pad. When Michael and Isobel went into the kitchen in search of Cathy, Olivia stayed where she was, smiling down at Loo.

'Shall we go inside?' she said, and Loo stood up, ready to show her the way. 'Or,' said Olivia, as if the idea had only just occurred to her, 'would you rather go for a walk? You could show me the farm.'

Loo glanced at Bee; this wasn't what they'd expected at all. But Bee wasn't looking at her, she was looking at Simon, as he went through her sketches.

'I'm sure your mother won't mind,' said the woman.

'All right,' said Loo, being careful to not to speak too loudly, not wanting to catch Bee's attention. 'If you like.'

'It's not really our farm,' she said, once they were out in the lane. 'We just live in the house.'

'I see,' said Olivia, looking back at the small, slightly crooked house, its date of construction, 1885, baked into a brick set over the front door. 'Do you like it here?'

Loo didn't answer straightaway. 'It's all right,' she said, eventually.

The late afternoon sun bounced off the overheated tarmac as Olivia turned and walked up the hill and Loo fell into step next to her.

'Where shall we go?' asked Olivia.

'Do you want to see the barn?'

'Yes. If you like.'

'Oh.' Loo stopped, looking back at the house, blinking in the bright sunshine. 'We're not really allowed. I forgot. We could go up into the field, instead.'

'That might be nice.'

'You can look out over the valley. I'll show you Simon's tent too, if you want.'

They walked in silence for a while, Loo leading the way. 'Here.' A lopsided gate gave access through the dry stone wall into the rough and uneven field beyond. It took the two of them to lift and push it far enough to slip through and then to push it back into place. 'Sorry, usually we just climb over the wall.'

'We?'

'Me and Bee.'

'Do you spend a lot of time together?'

'We share a room.'

'What about school?'

'We don't go,' said Loo, 'and we don't care.' The dry grass scratched their bare legs as they made their way up the hill towards Simon's tent, bright orange and sagging a little underneath the late afternoon sun.

'Do you live in London?' Loo asked.

'Yes.'

'With Michael?'

'No.'

'Oh. Near him, then?'

'Not exactly.'

'Bee wants to live in London.'

'Does she? And what about you?'

Loo stopped and squinted up at Olivia, beads of sweat sticking strands of her uneven fringe to her face. Her frock hung limply on her thin frame. 'I don't know,' she said.

Back in the garden, Bee let Simon look through the sketchpad and smiled, pretending she hadn't noticed what they'd done, pretending she wasn't furious. He'd fooled her at first. She'd been so sure they'd take the woman to meet Cathy, she hadn't thought she'd just go off with Loo like that. And Loo shouldn't have gone.

'I like this one.' Simon was holding up a sketch she'd done of the valley, but it wasn't very good. She'd overworked it; sometimes she just drew in order to have something to do with her hands, to stop her scratching and nipping and pinching. And sometimes she didn't know when to stop.

'Thank you,' she said, and smiled. If she had thought he meant it, she'd have given it to him, but she didn't offer. He was sitting very close to her, which would have been a treat if Loo hadn't gone off like that, and if Issy wasn't hanging around, getting in the way. He smelt nice today: soap and suntan lotion and underneath that, very faintly, cigarettes.

He turned a page in the book. He was good-looking, Simon, almost like a pop star, or an actor, and she wondered if she'd ever dare ask him to sit still and let her draw him. She'd done a few sketches, from memory, hidden away, sketches even Loo didn't know about. Glimpses of him pottering around by the tent or sunbathing shirtless in the field. They were private.

They played a game sometimes, she and Loo, seeing how close they could get to him without him realising. Close enough to count his eyelashes, to see where he'd scraped himself shaving, close enough to wonder—

Loo was just a baby, really, and he was never going to notice her. But more and more Bee had begun to think that maybe one day, Simon would look at her the way she'd seen him look at Isobel; if she had nicer clothes, perhaps, and if Loo wasn't in the way all the time. But Loo wasn't there now and although Simon wasn't really interested in the drawings, he wasn't really interested in Bee either.

It wasn't fair.

They had made it as far as the tent, where they stopped and looked at the view. She seemed nice, this woman, and the odd tense sensation Loo had been carrying around all summer, especially when she and Bee were around the grown-ups, had begun to fade. She flopped down on the grass, pretending to feel more tired than she did.

'It's hot,' she said.

'Yes.' Olivia sat down next to her.

'Are you going to stay in the village? With Michael?'

'I'm going to stay at the pub for a few days, if that's all right with you.'

Loo stretched out her legs and wiggled her toes. 'I suppose so.'

'Did Michael tell you about me? About what I do?'

'Sort of.'

'Would you like me to show you?' Olivia wasn't looking at

her; she was gazing out over the valley. Loo tried to recall what it was that Michael had said, about mediums and contact and the 'survival of the spirit'.

'All right.'

'Right.' The woman sat upright and crossed her legs, resting her hands gently on her knees. She closed her eyes and breathed deeply.

'Your name is Lucia Corvino,' she said, making her voice a bit deeper. 'You have brown hair and brown eyes, you live on a farm and – and – you bite your nails.'

She opened her eyes. 'How am I doing?'

Loo smiled.

'Not impressed?'

'You're just saying stuff you can see.'

'Yes. Yes I am.' Olivia nodded as if Loo had been particularly clever. 'Because that's all I do, really. I just say what I see – well, in my case, what I hear. There are things in the world anyone can see, if they care to look, and the rest . . .' She reached out and took hold of Loo's hand. 'The rest only a few people can see.'

'Or hear.'

'Or hear. But it's there, all the same.'

Loo wanted to take her hand away. She felt a little flicker of unease and now she regretted coming with this stranger, or at least not bringing Bee along too. Olivia looked into her eyes for a few moments, still holding her hand lightly. It took a lot of effort not to look away.

'You went into the barn. You're not supposed to, are you? But you went in, you and Bee and—' She dropped Loo's hand. 'Is that what's bothering you?' she said softly. 'Is that it?'

Bee was lying on her bed, the top bunk, staring at the ceiling when Loo got back. The bedroom window was open and the

234

lace curtains framing it wilted in the late afternoon heat. Loo picked up a book and lay on her own bunk.

'What's she like, then?' Bee was pretending she didn't care.

'She's OK,' said Loo.

'She's old,' said Bee.

'Yes.'

Bee launched herself off the top bunk and landed with a thud, squatting down next to her sister, grabbing the book and throwing it across the room.

'Is she nice?'

This was a trick question.

'I don't know,' said Loo. 'I couldn't tell.'

Bee reached up and grabbed hold of the top of the bunk beds, testing them, trying to pull them away from the wall.

'Don't,' said Loo.

'Don't,' said Bee, in a little-girl voice, pulling harder, rattling the bed frame.

'Bee.'

'Bee.'

'Stop it.'

'Stop it.'

'She's a medium,' said Loo. 'She says she can sense things, she can receive messages.'

Bee let go of the bed and sat down on the floor with a thump. 'Can she?'

'I don't know.' Loo tried to think back to the conversation on the hill. Olivia had asked lots of questions and she'd listened carefully, but she'd told her stuff too. Private stuff about when she was a kid, before she met Michael, when she'd been able to hear voices that told her stuff she wasn't supposed to know, when she'd thought she was going mad. 'Maybe,' she said. 'She knew we'd been in the barn.'

'You told her.'

'No I didn't.' She was sure of that.

'Will she tell?'

'I don't think so.'

Bee ran her fingers through her hair, lifting it up and back from her face; she looked older momentarily, grown-up. 'What else did she say?'

'She said she'd like to talk to Tib,' Loo said.

'And did she?'

'No. It was just me and her. She's going to watch the next time Michael talks to us.'

'And?'

'That's all.'

'Hmm,' said Bee, turning away again, leaning her head against Loo's mattress and stretching out her long legs in front of her. 'That's not what he told Cathy.'

'What happened? What did he say?'

'Michael wants her to do a séance,' Bee said. 'They're going to sit us in the dark, around a table, and they're going to prod you and poke you until Tib comes along.'

They'd read all about séances in one of Simon's books one after-noon when they'd gone up to the tent, only to find he'd gone off with Issy somewhere. It had sounded a bit scary, really. Loo wanted to get out of bed, but Bee was in the way and she was trapped.

'And then when she does . . .' Bee let her voice trail away.

She doesn't know, Loo decided. She doesn't really know what they're planning. They wouldn't talk about it in front of her. They think she's a little kid, like me.

Michael escorted Olivia to her room in the Red Lion, or at least that's what it felt like. They had known each other for over twenty years now and still Olivia couldn't quite get past

236

the slightly formal, old-fashioned facade that Professor Michael Warren preferred to present to the world. She, usually so confident in reading people and situations, was never quite sure of him – it was one of the reasons she liked him so much.

'You're very quiet,' he said, as they reached her door.

'I have a lot to think about.'

'What did you make of her?'

'Loo? She's an odd little thing, isn't she?'

'Odd how?' That was the Michael she knew, always pressing for clarification, never giving his own thoughts away until he was quite sure of himself.

'Well, she appears to be very close to her sister.'

'Not unusual in such a remote situation, surely?'

'There's quite an age gap, though. I can't really see what they'd have in common.'

'Bee is very much the stronger personality, I'd say. She seems to need to dominate, to establish precedence.'

'So she needs Loo as a follower? But then . . .' Olivia smiled apologetically. 'As I said, there's a lot to think about. I'll unpack and we can catch up in a little while. We can discuss how you'd like to run things over dinner, perhaps.'

'Of course.' He turned to his room, fumbling in his jacket pocket for his key. 'I do appreciate it, you know,' he said as he unlocked his door, not looking at her, 'that you came such a long way with so little preparation.'

'I know,' she said, 'and I think you were right to call me. It's a very interesting situation.'

'Take as long as you need,' he said, opening his door. 'You know where I am when you're ready to talk.'

19

Now

Lucy doesn't sleep. She curls up in the armchair, wrapped in the sleeping bag she bought in town, and she even closes her eyes from time to time, but she doesn't sleep.

The other three settle into their routine, one occasionally leaving the room to deal with their cameras as the others make notes or read. After a while, they turn off the overhead light and the room is lit by the dull glow of the monitors and a couple of battery-powered lanterns.

Two, three hours pass and she can see them relaxing, lowering their guard, and gradually, all is silent. She, listens, waits. Then someone's alarm goes, a soft, insistent buzzing.

Nina sighs, finds her phone, silences it.

No one else moves.

'Lew? Lewis?' It's their turn to check the cameras, change the little memory cards, upload the still and silent images of the empty rooms. Lewis doesn't stir.

Lucy watches the young woman peel away her sleeping bag and pull on her boots.

Upstairs, directly above their heads, a door bangs shut.

'Shit.' Nina gets to her feet, listening. 'Lewis?'

Another dull thud shudders through the ceiling and Nina

doesn't hesitate. She grabs one of their little cameras and without bothering to wake anyone else, she's out of the door.

Lucy could leave her, of course. To face whatever it is all alone. It's noise, nothing more, air in the pipes, an old house creaking and settling, she'd like to believe that. But there is something sickeningly familiar about it, even after all these years. Something deliberate.

Careful not to wake the others, Lucy stands and makes her way to the door.

Nina follows the sound to the top of the house, to the attic. The stairs are bare and dusty and they lead to a small landing with only a single door. The door is open.

Did we do that? Did we come up here?

Nina knows that she didn't, but then one of the others might have. She didn't really keep track as they were setting up, that's more Lewis's area. Anyway, the door is open – perhaps someone did it earlier – but that doesn't explain the noise, the dull thudding she can feel in her bones – and it's cold up here, freezing.

They haven't much bothered with the top floor – it had been occupied by Dan Corvino and no phenomena had ever been reported there. Dan is a distant figure in the book, a teenager with a job that took him away from the house; he seems to have escaped the worst of the haunting. Which isn't to say that nothing had ever happened, of course.

The ceiling slopes and its beans are exposed. It feels cramped. She can smell . . . cigarettes. Cigarettes and dope. The room is empty.

'Hello?'

She has to do something, say something.

'I heard a knocking,' Nina says, lifting up the GoPro and sweeping it around the room, 'but there's nothing here.'

It's cold, though. Freezing.

She doesn't know much about Dan Corvino, although she'd tried to find him. When she started her research, she hadn't realised he'd left the country. She's pleased that Lucy and he are in touch though; that could be very helpful.

'There's no one here,' she says. She'll go back downstairs and deal with the SD cards and she'll wake Lewis up too, make him take his turn. 'Nothing.'

The room doesn't feel empty, though; it feels as though there's someone there, just out of sight. Her skin prickles in the cold. Goose bumps. She forces herself to stand still and just behind her, she could almost swear to it—

Breath.

Someone takes a breath.

Moves closer.

The hairs on the back of her neck lift.

This is it.

This is—

Her.

And then, something sharp, on the soft flesh inside her elbow, once, twice, three times. She flinches and rolls up her sweater sleeve. Blood is blossoming under the skin, forming little bruises.

'Nina?' Lucy's voice drifts upstairs. The landing light flicks on. 'Are you OK? Nina?'

She shivers, waits to see what will happen next, but the room is empty. She rubs at her arm, but the marks don't fade. 'Yeah,' she says, crossing to the door. 'I'm here.'

Lewis finds them both on the first floor landing. He looks sleepy, sleepy and cross. 'I woke up,' he says, 'and you were gone.

241

Did you hear it? The knocking? There was something knocking again, right?'

'Yes. I thought – I just wanted to check upstairs.'

'And?'

Nina rolls up her sweater sleeve. The bruises are still there, a constellation of them, scattered across her skin.

Lucy's arm tingles. She can feel them again, the pinching fingers that would wake her in the dark.

'I went up into the attic,' Nina says. 'I couldn't see anyone, but there was a – presence, you know? Just for a moment or two. And this . . . happened.'

'Are you all right?' asks Lucy, stepping closer, taking hold of Nina's hand, running her fingers gently over her skin.

'Yes, I mean . . .' Nina's expression changes; she looks uncertain for a moment. She pulls away from Lucy and pushes her sleeve down. 'We should take some photos – of my arm, I mean. And we should change the cards over. Did you bring them, Lew?'

Hal is awake too when they get back downstairs and Lucy lets Lewis fill him in as the two of them open one of the laptops and start uploading files. Nina goes into the living room and Lucy follows her.

'Would you?' Nina is holding out her phone.

'Sorry?'

'Photos? If you don't mind?'

'Oh. Yes.' Lucy takes the pictures as required, the camera flash bouncing off the girl's white skin. 'That's it?' she asks when she's done. 'You're not hurt anywhere else?'

Nina inspects her arm, rubbing gently at the bruises. 'I don't think so, no.'

'Well, here you are.' Lucy hands back the phone and sits

next to Nina on the sofa. Sleep seems impossible now and she wonders if this latest incident could be enough, if she could manage to persuade them all out of the house tomorrow. Maybe if she agreed to an interview, back at Blue Jacket House.

'Did you hear it too?' Nina asks. 'Just now? The knocking in the walls?'

'Yes. I heard it.'

Nina can't help herself. She leans forward. 'Was it the same? Like before? When you were a kid, I mean—'

But Lucy isn't listening. 'Wait.' She looks around the room, puzzled. 'Wait,' she says.

In the dining room Hal has taken the iPad to the table and is keeping an eye on Lucy and Nina as he deals with the memory cards. Lewis has been dispatched back upstairs with a torch and new cards and Hal tries to concentrate on the task in hand. His head aches; he'd been asleep and then he'd woken suddenly, the odd booming sound that had filled his dreams had turned out to be real. Someone – Lewis, he thinks – had turned on the overhead light and there were voices upstairs. It had taken him a moment or two to realise it was the others. By the time he'd caught up with them, it was all over. The knocking, whatever it was, had stopped.

The files are imported, ready to play. Before he clicks on the icon, he picks up the iPad again, just to check, just to be sure.

Lucy and Nina are sitting upright, rigid, looking around the room. Nina flinches, both women do, and Hal picks up the iPad and goes to the door.

He can hear it now, the sharp cracking sound coming from the living room, like hailstones hitting a window. The next crack is so loud he half-expects to see the screen in his hand break apart.

Nina has been counting aloud, for the record. She can't possibly know what it is she's counting, though. To her it's just an odd sound, a sharp crack, loud enough to make you jump; she hasn't made the connection. But Lucy has heard it before.

They're coming faster now.

The rapid spit and fire of marbles, flying through the air and smacking into wood and glass and tile, bouncing onto the carpet with dull thuds. It sounds just as it did then. If she closed her eyes, she'd be back there and if she reached out, instead of Nina, it would be her sister sitting there.

But she keeps her eyes open, even as the light in here gets brighter, fiercer. She can see the look on Nina's face – not fear or confusion, she's lit up, just like Bee always was, and Lucy is uncomfortably aware of the pressure building in her head. They stand, looking about the room trying to locate the source of the sound, and there they are, reflected in the window. The image begins to tremble, to vibrate as the window starts to shudder, twisting their limbs into impossible shapes.

It won't hold.

It can't hold.

It's worse this time.

Nina steps forward. 'It's outside,' she says. 'Is there someone—' Her voice fades as she places a hand against the pane, the glass thrumming against her skin. 'There's someone—' she tries again. But they can't see; neither of them can see beyond their mirror images.

Lucy feels what she should do next, rather than thinking it; she grabs Nina and pulls her away from the window. They

244

fall to the floor as the pane explodes, showering them with fragments of needle-sharp glass as the cold night air rushes in.

Lucy takes Nina into the kitchen, leads her to the sink and turns on the tap.

'Here.'

The water rushes icy cold over the younger woman's hands, running a rosy pink around the basin.

'Ow.' Nina tries to pull away.

'Hang on. Let the water run on it for a bit longer.' Lucy vanishes for a moment or two before reappearing with a small towel. 'Here.'

'It'll stain.'

'It doesn't matter.' She turns off the tap and examines Nina's fingers. 'It doesn't look too bad,' she says. 'Some fairly deep scratches, but you'll live. You were lucky.' She dries the cuts gently, blotting away the last of the water and the blood.

Hal sits on the bottom stair in the hall as Lewis bustles past with a broom and dustpan he's found somewhere. He lets them all get on with it, soothing themselves with practicalities. He leans against the wall and closes his eyes.

'We got it, right?'

He opens his eyes and Nina is standing over him, damp hair pushed back from her face, a thin red weal running from her temple to her ear, the towel wrapped around her right hand.

'We got it all on video?'

'Yes.'

'Did you check?'

He gets to his feet. The last thing he wants to do is go back into that room, to replay events, but he has no choice.

'We can look now,' he says.

245

20

Then

'You're late,' said Bee, as Isobel walked up the lane. They were in the front garden watching out for her, and Simon was sitting on the doorstep watching them.

'I do have a job, you know.'

'Where's your car?' Loo liked Issy's car. It was powder blue, a Beetle.

'At home. I've been working on a story with Liam Carter in Danby, he dropped me off on the way back.'

'Are you going to take our photo today?' asked Loo. Issy sat next to Simon and Loo sat cross-legged on the grass in front of her while Bee swung slowly on the wooden front gate.

'Maybe,' said Isobel. 'When I get my breath back. Aren't you fed up of having your picture taken?'

'We don't mind,' said Bee, concentrating on moving the gate inch by inch across the path, the rusting hinges complaining. 'We were in the newspapers again. Cathy thinks we don't know, but we do.'

'We saw the paper in the kitchen, but then she moved it,' said Loo.

'She thinks she's hidden it, but we know all her hiding places.' Bee jumped down and turned to face them. 'We're bored,' she said.

'Can't we do something?' said Loo. 'Can we go and get an ice cream?'

*

Bee and Loo took their time choosing as Simon looked around the village shop, which was to his eyes little more than a post office counter, a rack of newspapers and a few shelves crammed with tins and plastic-wrapped bread.

'Morning, Isobel,' said the woman behind the counter, not much older than Issy and wearing an apron over her cotton shirt and skirt. Her smile faded when she saw the girls. 'Not at work?'

'Not until this evening,' said Issy.

Bee leant over and whispered something in Loo's ear and Loo giggled.

'Have you two found what you want yet?' asked the woman.

'Not yet,' said Bee, leaning over the small freezer and making a show of rummaging around inside it.

'I'm covering a swimming gala over in Whitby later,' said Isobel.

'Well, they've got the weather for it.' The woman rearranged the folded papers on the counter, pushing them into line; her hands were stained with newsprint, her nails painted a sickly pink. 'You've been up the farm then?' she said.

'That's right.'

The woman looked over at the girls, her expression a combination of distrust and pity. 'I saw it,' she said, 'in the *Mirror*.'

'Have you ever heard of anything else happening at Iron Sike Farm?' Simon said.

The woman looked up at him. You could practically hear the questions floating around in her head. *Are you the dad then? Or someone to do with Isobel?* He smiled politely.

'No,' she said eventually. 'Never been a hint of trouble until they moved in.'

A faint stress on 'they'.

'I see.' Behind him the lid of the ice-cream freezer thudded shut.

'Here.' Bee put their ice creams, a Mivvi for her and a choc ice for Loo, on the newspaper display, ice particles soaking into the front pages as the woman snatched them up again. The two grown-ups chose orange ice lollies and, once Simon had paid for them, they crossed the road to the war memorial, a stubby stone cross surrounded by wooden benches, and sat to eat in comfort.

'I love ice cream,' said Loo, before biting into her choc ice and scattering shards of milk chocolate down her front.

Bee pulled the paper wrapper from her lolly and dropped it with exaggerated care into the bent wire bin. 'That shop's rubbish,' she said. 'They don't sell proper food at all. Everything's processed and overpriced.'

'You sound like your mother,' said Simon.

'Her,' said Bee. 'She doesn't know anything.'

They ate in silence for a moment or two.

'They don't like us here,' said Bee.

'What makes you think that?'

Bee took another bite of her lolly, her mouth already stained red, melting ice cream dribbling down her grubby fingers. 'We came down for a walk, when we moved in, back in March. And Cathy took us in the shop and she said hello and was polite and all of that, and she introduced us and bought some of her rubbishy food and a newspaper—'

'Bee,' said Loo, 'don't.'

'And she was there, that woman, and an old lady too and then, after she'd served us, they didn't even wait until we'd got out of the door.' Bee stopped for breath, took another bite of ice cream.

'What happened?' asked Simon, curious despite himself.

'I heard her – I heard one of them say we were gypsies, dirty gypsies.'

'Really?'

'I heard them too,' said Loo. 'They thought we wouldn't hear 'cos Anto was making a fuss.'

Simon looked at Isobel, ready to follow her lead, unsure whether he should offer sympathy or condemnation.

'Haven't you got any friends?' Issy asked. 'There are a few kids your age round here, aren't there?'

'They're all boring,' said Bee. She might have said more but Loo managed to collapse the last of her choc ice all over her frock and Simon and Issy started to fuss over her, as if she was a bloody baby.

'Can we go?' said Bee, standing up. She wanted to be well out of the way when the stupid cow in the post office found that her ice-cream freezer was unplugged.

'Can we go to Whitby?' said Bee as they idled their way back out of the village. 'We could go to the beach.' They hadn't been to the seaside since moving to Longdale, not once. There was no bus and the train service which snaked along the valley was slow and expensive, or so Cathy said.

Loo turned to Issy. 'We could go to your house,' she said. Issy had described her little flat, up in the roof of an old Georgian house, close by the harbour; it sounded perfect to Loo and she liked to pretend that she and Bee lived in a flat, too. She tidied their room every day and had taken to picking flowers from the garden which she kept in a grubby jam jar on the window ledge. 'Please, Issy.'

'Maybe another time,' said Isobel.

'We never go anywhere,' said Bee, 'and it's too hot. It's not fair.'

'We can't just vanish,' said Simon. 'What about the professor?'

'We could stay close by then,' said Loo. 'We could go to the Lido.'

'The what?'

'Down by the river,' said Isobel. 'People swim there sometimes. It's just a flat bit of river bank.'

'Please?' said Loo. 'Cathy won't let us go on our own.'

Simon and Issy looked at one another, until one of them, Loo wasn't sure who, gave in first.

'All right then,' said Simon.

'But not for long,' said Issy.

The path ran across one of Peter Eglon's fields and down to the Esk. They had to walk one by one in single file so as not to damage the crops. Bee, then Simon, then Loo, then Issy, all the way down to the river. The water was shady there, dark green, cool and quiet.

'Let's swim,' said Bee.

'You can't swim,' said Loo.

'Paddle, then,' said Bee, looking out across the glistening water. 'It's shallow enough.'

It was, and the river ran slowly here; it was low and clear enough to see the great stone slabs that lay on the river bed, rusty brown and shadowy.

'It's too cold for me,' said Issy, sitting on a fallen tree trunk and fiddling with her camera.

'You haven't even tried it,' said Simon.

'I don't need to. You go in if you want, but you'll be sorry.'

Loo was standing on the very edge of the river bank, peering in. Loo was right, the water was shallow here, and the light danced on it, dazzling her.

'Well, I'm going in,' said Bee.

'Fine.' Simon sat down and, after kicking off his shoes and socks, began to roll up his jeans. 'Me too.'

'Don't say I didn't warn you,' said Issy, raising her camera.

251

'Coward,' said Simon.

Bee kicked off her sandals and clambered carefully down the bank. 'Shit!'

'Is it cold?' asked Loo.

'No,' said Bee, walking into the river, up to her knees, up to her thighs.

'Bee. Your frock,' said Issy. Bee looked down; the skirt of her dress swirled and bloomed briefly against the river's lazy current before darkening and sinking.

'You'll get soaked,' said Loo, perching carefully on the bank and slipping off her flip-flops. Bee reached down and snatched at her dress, then, glancing over her shoulder at Simon who had just stepped into the river, she pulled it up and over her head.

'Catch!' The dress landed next to Loo. She placed her feet gently into the water. Bee was a liar; it was freezing. Simon staggered a little, from the cold perhaps, or maybe the pebbles on the river bank shifting.

'Jesus,' he said. 'Bee.'

Loo could feel the goose bumps rising on her legs. Her feet were watery pale in the river, numb. She stood and edged her way cautiously in, wobbling slightly as her feet made contact with the cool and slimy mud.

Behind her, Issy took her place on the river bank, kicking off her sandals and dipping her toes in the water. Bee, wearing only a pair of faded blue knickers and an off-white bra, waded further in.

'This is brilliant,' she said.

'Not too far, Bee,' said Issy.

'Brilliant!' She turned to face Simon, scooping up armfuls of water to splash him, making the air between them sparkle. 'Come on, Simon, come in,' she said, splashing the water again,

252

droplets catching in her hair and on her face. 'You know you want to.' As if they were quite alone, the two of them.

'It's cold,' said Loo and Simon turned to look at her. 'I don't like it.'

'Don't be daft,' he said, extending his hand. 'Come on, Lucia.'

She thought for a moment and then tucked the hem of her skirt into the leg of her knickers, and made her way carefully towards him, slow and determined.

'There. See?' he said, catching hold of her fingers. 'Well done you.'

And he stood there smiling at her as the sunlight bounced off the water and a cool breeze wrapped itself around them both.

'Come on,' said Bee. 'You have to come right in, Loo.' And she stepped back, the water rising to her hips.

'Bee . . .' Issy was knee-deep now, her camera abandoned on the bank.

'Come back,' she said.

Bee looked at Issy and smiled. She stepped back, once, twice more, until the water circled her waist, then she slipped under the water and out of sight.

None of them moved. The water closed over Bee's head and still none of them moved.

'Bee,' said Loo, 'don't.' And she let go of Simon, pushing forward, frantically propelling herself towards her sister.

'Christ.' Simon caught hold of her and pulled her into his arms. 'No, Loo, not you as well,' he said, hauling her back towards the river bank. 'It's all right, it's all right.' And Loo wrapped her arms and legs around him, burying her face in his neck, suddenly too afraid to look.

It was Issy who got to Bee, reaching her just as she resurfaced, coughing, gasping for air. She saw Issy and scowled.

Without speaking, Issy grabbed hold of Bee and dragged her roughly back to safety, the pair of them staggering against the water, leaving a foaming wake. Bee slipped on the muddy stones, falling forward and vanishing briefly under the water again, pulling Issy with her, before Issy forced her way back up, pushing Bee up onto the river bank.

Bee climbed slowly out of the river on her hands and knees and lay breathless on the ground, water streaming from her skin and hair, her underwear transparent. Blood ran freely down her leg from a scrape on her knee.

Issy sat down next to her. 'You stupid bloody girl,' she said. 'Can't – can't—'

Bee was lying on her back, gasping, struggling for air.

'What were you thinking?'

She rolled onto her side. 'Can't—' Her shoulders were heaving. 'Bee?'

'Asthma,' said Loo. 'She has asthma.'

Simon and Issy were both kneeling over her now.

'Does she have medicine, Loo? An inhaler?' asked Issy.

'It's at home. I think. She never bothers with it, she never—'

Bee took one last shuddering gasp of air, then lay motionless on the ground.

'Shit.' Simon leant over Bee, placed one hand tentatively on her shoulder. 'Bee, Bee, can you hear me?'

There was no response.

'Bee.'

He shook her and the girl rolled onto her back, her eyes closed, pale and still.

'Bee,' said Loo, 'Bee. Don't.'

There was a minute of agonised silence then Bee opened her

254

eyes and burst into laughter. 'Your faces,' she said. 'You should see your faces.'

Michael and Olivia were sitting in the kitchen, a newspaper spread out on the table in front of them.

'Good grief,' Michael said when he saw them all. 'What happened?'

'We went to the Lido,' said Bee, 'paddling. Is there anything to eat?' And she picked up the newspaper before he could stop her. The picture on the front page was the one Isobel had taken of the professor holding up the marble, the rest of the room slightly blurry behind him. The headline was one word. PROOF?

'Isn't there a picture of us in this one?' she said, flicking through the paper.

Cathy came in from the garden carrying a basket half filled with greens from the vegetable patch. 'What on earth have you two been up to?'

'I'm sorry,' said Simon. 'The girls wanted to go down to the river and—'

'We went paddling,' said Loo. 'Then Simon carried me back.'

'But look at the state of you,' said Cathy, dropping the basket on the table, grabbing a tea towel and setting about drying Bee's hair.

'It's just water,' said Bee, pushing her mother away.

From somewhere above the door came three sharp raps in succession.

'Bianca,' said Cathy.

'Don't fuss.'

Three more sharp raps.

'Come in,' said Bee, but of course no one did. In the front bedroom the baby began to wail.

255

'Bathroom now, both of you,' said Cathy. 'Get dried off and put some clean clothes on.'

'I'm hungry,' said Bee. 'What are we having for tea?'

'Now,' said Cathy.

'Bye, Simon,' Bee said, flicking her long hair back over her shoulder, pointedly ignoring the other grown-ups as she led the way upstairs. Cathy sat at the table, closing the newspaper, pushing it to one side.

'We were thinking,' Michael said, 'that today might be a good opportunity to involve Olivia in the conversation with Tib.'

This wasn't the first time, of course. Michael had been pushing for this ever since Olivia had arrived. Upstairs a door slammed and the baby's crying took on a frantic quality.

'The thing is, I don't have much time,' said Olivia. 'I'm expected back in London shortly. We neither of us mean to rush you, but I'm not able to stay for very long.'

'We're very fortunate,' said Michael, 'that Olivia is able to join us at all, that she is willing to help Lucia.'

'I understand that,' said Cathy. 'It's just, I'm not . . . sure.'

'Sure of what?' Michael asked.

'I'm not sure it helps,' Cathy said. 'Maybe all this attention, all this fuss, is just making things worse. I'm sorry,' she said to Olivia, 'I know you've come a long way, but maybe we should just call a halt to everything.' She stood. 'I'm sorry – the baby—'

'We were thinking that Olivia would conduct the next session,' said Michael. 'She would be able to assist Lucia, amplify Tib if you like, and—' The rest of his explanation was drowned out by the sound of feet rushing down the stairs, of garbled voices calling out.

Bee got to the door first, barging her way into the room.

'Upstairs,' she said. 'You have to come, Michael. You have to come and see.'

It was chaos.

The girls had divided the room in half: the walls on Bee's side were plastered with posters of American TV actors from the programmes she was no longer allowed to watch. Loo's walls were a jumble of bands and singers she'd already begun to outgrow. The grown-ups were crowded in the doorway, none of them willing to follow the girls in. The mattresses on both beds had been overturned and bedding lay draped over the rest of the room; pillows were sodden where one of Loo's jars of flowers had shattered; the contents of the dressing table had been swept onto the floor; and over the walls, plastered over the smooth shiny faces with their perfect smiles, were scraps of paper.

'We went and got dry,' Bee said, 'and then we came in here and – Jesus, what's that?' She'd stood in something, a dark damp patch on the carpet. 'God, that's disgusting.' She hopped clumsily to the window ledge, where she could perch and examine the sole of her foot, wet and sticky.

More paper was scattered over the room, over the mess and destruction, yellowing pages, closely printed, shivering in the soft breeze from the open window, as if they had only just come to rest.

'Someone's ripped up my books,' said Loo, her voice bright with tears. 'Why would anyone do that?'

Issy worked methodically, working with the available light, taking wide shots of every aspect of the room and then working her way around clockwise, taking close-ups of every possible detail. Focusing in on the torn scraps, the dust, the tacky yellowish substance that had dribbled over the bedding and the floor.

'You OK?' Simon asked.

'Fine.' It was glue, that was all, wallpaper paste. Someone had torn apart the books, paperbacks for the most part, and had glued them across the furniture and the walls. Occasionally a single word had been torn out, and several were plastered over the mirror. Michael was copying them into his notebook.

Heart
Maiden
Fear

But they made no sense.

The remnants of the books lay scattered across the girls' belongings. The most disturbing thing, Isobel decided, was the intensity of it all, the sheer energy it must have taken. The rage.

'Have you ever seen anything like this before?' she asked.

'Not first-hand,' said Simon.

'Borley Rectory,' said Olivia, standing in the doorway.

'Excuse me?'

'There were messages written on the wall at Borley Rectory, back in the 1930s.' Olivia stepped into the room, examining the walls carefully.

'"Get light, mass, prayers",' said Simon.

'Well remembered,' said Michael.

'What?'

'I was reading about it last week,' said Simon. 'There was a message scribbled on a wall, and others left on scraps of paper. The book's in my tent. You can borrow it if you want.'

'Did she do it?' Issy doesn't want to say the name out loud.

'I suppose so,' said Michael.

'And what are you going to do about it?'

'Issy,' Simon said.

'No, no,' said Michael. 'Isobel is quite right – we've let things go on far too long as it is. We need to – regroup.'

Downstairs Loo had fallen asleep on the sofa, clutching one of the dolls she'd temporarily reclaimed from the baby. Cathy was sitting by the empty fireplace, and Bee was curled up in Michael's armchair, watching her through half-closed eyes.

She was definitely thinner, her mother; the last of what she'd been calling the baby weight had melted away. But she seemed to be losing something else too; Bee couldn't quite work out what. Joe was still away, still in Glasgow teaching, or seeing someone about a commission – something, anyway. Glasgow or Edinburgh now. Cathy didn't seem too sure what he was up to, really. She said that she rang him when she could, from the phone box in the village, but none of them had spoken to him for ages, not even when the phone in the hall was still connected, Bee was almost certain of that. No one except Cathy.

She sat as still as she could, thinking about the mess upstairs. They'd have to throw all their stuff out now, they'd have to paint over the walls; maybe Cathy would let her choose the paint. Maybe they wouldn't be made to share again, maybe she could get Cathy and Joe to agree to give her the downstairs room after all. Maybe she could get Cathy to let her ring Joe and ask – she'd like that. She was considering how she might go about suggesting this when the door opened and Michael came in.

'Do you have a moment, Cathy?' he asked.

21

Now

They sit in Lucy's car, looking at the house. The morning is cold and damp, a fine mist is clinging to the garden and the path is riddled with fat black-green slugs.

She doesn't know about Hal, but Lucy feels exhausted, almost hungover. She had managed to sleep for a few hours in the end, but that sleep had been punctuated by Lewis and Nina's insistence that they stick to their schedule, checking the batteries in the cameras and changing over the SD cards, although Hal had at least persuaded them both to wait before looking through the rushes.

At around eight Lucy had volunteered to drive into the village to fetch some breakfast. Hal had offered to keep her company, but they hadn't spoken much.

Lucy's eyes are gritty and sore; the prospect of spending another day here fills her with something like dread and Hal seems to feel the same way. They'd spun it out as long as they could, the two of them wandering slowly through the village shop, picking out more pre-packaged sandwiches, biscuits, apples, a bag of oranges, cobbling together their change to use the automated coffee machine installed by the door, all under the uninterested gaze of a pale young girl at the counter, before setting off for the farm. Now they're here neither of them can quite manage to get out of the car.

'Come on then,' says Hal eventually.

She walks slowly towards the front door carrying their shopping and only at the last minute does she remember to turn and take the path round to the back of the house. She'd forgotten where she was for a moment; no, she'd forgotten when she was.

She steps into the kitchen and flicks on the light.

'Watch your step.' Hal's voice is mild, but closer than she expected, and it makes her jump. She looks down and sees more slugs, two of them tracing a lazy path across the kitchen floor.

'Thanks.' As Hal closes the door, the silence of the house seems to swallow them up. The kitchen light is bright, too bright, bouncing off the yellowing walls and boarded-up window. Lucy leads the way to the dining room. 'Morning,' she says. 'We're back.'

'This is great, thanks,' says Lewis, helping himself to a sandwich and a coffee.

'You're welcome,' says Lucy.

'Have we caught up with the SD cards?' Hal asks as he sits in front of a laptop, scrolling through the files on-screen.

'Mostly,' says Nina, looking at Lewis, her expression a mixture of guilt and excitement.

'The downstairs footage is all up to date,' says Lewis.

'But we've had a few problems with the girls' room,' says Nina.

'Problems?' Lucy is standing by the window.

'What happened?' asks Hal.

'Nothing's recorded there,' says Lewis. He sounds almost triumphant.

'We must have something,' says Hal.

'We don't. We have the files, but they won't play.'

'Well, you've made a mistake.'

262

'We didn't—'

'There's a card error of some sort, or the files are corrupted, empty.'

The camera from the girls' room lies discarded on the table. 'We've checked,' says Nina.

'And they're not empty,' says Lewis, 'they just won't play. Look.' He leans across Hal, clicks on the mouse pad and a message appears on the screen.

The document 'GBR5' could not be opened. QuickTime Player cannot open files in the 'data' format.

'It's the same on the other files,' says Nina, 'but only from the camera in the girls' room.'

Hal frowns at the screen, glad perhaps to have a simple problem to deal with, something technical, fixable. 'Let me have a look,' he says.

Nina sits down at the table, folding her arms. She looks pale this morning, fragile.

'Haven't you got enough now?' Lucy says. 'Shouldn't we think about leaving? Especially after—' She hardly knows how to go on. 'I mean, the window.'

'Absolutely not. We're here to investigate, aren't we? And anyway, it was . . . amazing – almost as if, as if it knows that we're here. As if it's trying to get through.' Nina takes a sip of coffee. 'Did it happen to you too?' she asks. 'The bruising?'

'I don't remember,' says Lucy. Nina's enthusiasm is exhausting and she needs time to think. 'I need to speak to my mother,' she says. 'I won't be long.'

It's cold and damp, but at least outside Lucy feels as though she can breathe. She pulls her phone from her pocket. She checks the time. Only a few more hours, she tells herself, and if she can get them away from the house before it gets dark again, so much the better.

She sits down on the kitchen step, gently placing her cardboard coffee cup on the damp stone next to her. The sky is low over the moor, a dark, slushy grey. Cathy answers straightaway.

'Mum.'

Lewis is on his second sandwich. Nina has taken herself off to use the bathroom and Hal has abandoned the computer and is slumped on the sofa. Now he's back in the house he really doesn't feel too well, although Nina and Lew seem fine. They're all a bit spaced out from lack of sleep, maybe, but it's obvious that whatever was going on last night hasn't put either of them off.

He closes his eyes, tilts his head back and sighs. It's happened before, this problem with the files, he's sure of it. Only he can't remember where or when. Maybe renaming them would help. The room smells of bacon and coffee – and cigarettes, even though they're not supposed to smoke in here. There's something else too. It's a comfortable smell, familiar, anyhow. Lewis says something, asks another question, and Hal mumbles a reply.

If the data is in the wrong format then—

The tape is going round and round, but all it's recording is the tick of the clock on the mantelpiece.

The question was

The question was

Where are you?

Here

It was a stupid question anyway. He clears his throat and moves in his chair. He always sits in the same chair, by the fire, and he always starts with the same questions.

Who are you? Where do you live?

Here.

Who else is there?

Mam.

What do you do there?

But he's not in the house any more; he's walking through a field, down a hill. He should have his boots on, but he can feel the sharp prickle of the grass under his feet.

What do you do there?

Work.

He's walking with great effortless strides, the way you do in a dream, towards—

Towards

How old are you?

I don't know.

The barn. Someone has left the door open. He reaches out and the hand that isn't his pulls at the door and

What's your name?

Tib.

Hal jerks awake so violently he almost falls onto the floor. Across the room Lewis is staring at him, the camera in his hand, his bacon sandwich on the table, forgotten.

'That was fucking awesome,' he says.

Nina finds them more or less where she'd left them: sitting side by side at the table, hunched over the laptop. She picks up the Sony. 'Is this good to go?' she asks. 'Can I take it back upstairs and try again?' But there's something wrong. Hal looks dreadful, as if he might collapse.

'You need to see this,' says Lewis. 'Go and get Lucy.'

It's infuriatingly brief. An image of the table, too close, swooping in and out of focus, swims onto the screen and then the camera moves on to Hal who is sitting on the sofa, his head tilted back, his eyes closed. The image is a little unsteady, but clear enough.

He seems to be talking in his sleep.

I don't know.

He seems to be listening to someone.

Tib.

Then there's a sharp exhalation as the camera slips momentarily and Hal wakes up.

'Is that all?' Nina is staring at the screen, as if she could will more video to appear.

'You're lucky I got that,' says Lewis. She didn't understand. He knew she wouldn't. The video doesn't quite capture it: one minute Hal was flaked out on the sofa and the next . . . It wasn't like he was talking in his sleep, it wasn't like he was talking at all. More like something was talking through him, and the voice – Jesus, the voice, whispery, hoarse. Lewis has heard the tapes, they're easy enough to find online, but he doubts Hal has.

Tib.

'I was dreaming. I thought it was a dream.' Hal rubs his hand over his face.

Nina is looking at him as if she's never seen him before. 'How did you do it?'

'I didn't do anything.' Hal stands. 'I didn't—' But he can't finish the sentence, and in his rush to get out of the room he knocks his chair to the floor.

They leave him alone for a moment or two, for which he's vaguely grateful as he throws up in the bushes underneath the kitchen window. Once he's vomited up his breakfast he wipes his mouth with the back of his hand and sits on the back step.

'Here.' Lucy appears, holding a bottle of water.

'Thanks.'

She sits down next to him as he drinks, careful not to touch him. 'If it's any comfort,' she says, 'I think everyone's feeling – something.'

'Right.' He takes another sip. 'And what about you? What are you feeling?'

'I feel it might be time to pack up and leave,' says Lucy.

'Hal?' Nina calls out as she walks through the kitchen.

He stands, wiping his hands on his jeans. Nina is standing in the doorway now, her leather satchel swinging from one hand.

'Hal,' she says, 'can we talk?'

22

Then

They travelled back to the village in silence. Simon drove with Olivia next to him, apparently absorbed in the landscape, Isobel and Michael side by side in the back seat. Simon and Issy had offered to help, but Cathy had insisted she would clean the girls' bedroom herself.

'Thanks for the lift,' Olivia said to Simon as she got out of the car in front of the Red Lion. 'I expect I'll see you tomorrow.'

'Why don't you drive Isobel back into town now?' Michael said to Simon, opening the passenger door. 'Take the evening off, enjoy yourselves for a little while.'

'Are you sure?' Simon was torn between the chance to spend time with Issy and the opportunity to plan the next session with Michael and Olivia. Cathy had finally agreed to a séance – the destruction in the girls' bedroom was an escalation they couldn't afford to ignore.

'Quite sure,' Michael said. 'Have a good evening, both of you.' He slammed the car door shut.

Isobel watched them as he and Olivia walked into the pub, neither looking back. 'We've been dismissed,' she said.

'Don't be ridiculous,' said Simon, but he looked younger, somehow, a little lost, and Isobel felt the need to cheer him up if she could, to at least make him smile, and to find herself some little distraction. Things were changing, and she wasn't sure that it was for the better.

'Come on then,' she said. 'Take me home and I'll cook you some proper food.'

'Shit.' Isobel looked up from the fridge. 'I don't really have very much in.' She'd forgotten that she barely had time to shop these days.

'It's OK.'

'No it isn't, I promised you dinner and now—'

'Don't worry about it.' Simon was standing a little too close, filling up the attic flat. She was wondering if he was going to make a move and what she should say if he did when his stomach growled, making both of them smile.

'I have eggs,' said Issy. 'We can have scrambled eggs.'

'Great.'

'And beer. Have a drink.' She handed him a bottle of lager, cool, not really cold enough but welcome nonetheless, and he sat at the table watching idly as she moved around the tiny kitchen.

'Do you think she'll be able to help?'

'Sorry?'

'Olivia. Will she be able to get rid of – it?'

Tib.

'I don't know,' said Simon. 'I suppose so. She's pretty famous.'

'Well, I've never heard of her.'

'In research circles.'

'Ah.' She set the cleanest of her saucepans on the oven, dropped a slice of butter in it and lit the gas ring.

'There's a lot of stuff about her in the archives, back in London.' Simon watched as Issy found a bowl and began to crack eggs into it. 'You're not really interested, are you?' he said. 'In this bit, in the Society?'

'I'm interested in this story,' she said, putting the bread under the grill and lighting that too before looking at Simon. 'So it follows that I'm interested in the Society, I suppose. But only as background. What I really want is some answers, a solution.'

'We want answers too.'

'No, Simon. You want proof.' She began to whisk the eggs with some milk, a little more briskly than necessary.

'Isn't that the same thing?'

'No, I don't think it is. In a way, you need Tib and all the fuss and chaos she seems to bring, because she proves your case. But what about Bee and Loo? Aren't they getting a little lost in all of this?'

'You make it sound as if we don't care about them at all.'

'That's not what I meant. But you saw that room. Surely the best thing for the girls now is that we – someone – put a stop to it.'

'You make it sound as though they're in danger.'

Issy looked at him. 'Well, are they?'

'No, of course not,' Simon said. 'And anyway, that's why Olivia's here, to help. Issy, come on, you know we're doing our best here.'

Issy opened a cupboard and took out some plates and placed them on the table. 'Go on, then,' she said. 'Tell me more about Olivia.'

'She was discovered by Michael about twenty years ago,' said Simon. 'When she was on the verge of being diagnosed as psychotic, more or less. She'd been hearing voices since she was in her teens and suffering odd waking dreams that meant she knew things, things about other people, that she shouldn't. She and her family were terrified.'

Issy added the eggs and milk to the pan and began to stir them.

'Apparently, she read an article in a newspaper that Michael had written, about famous mediums throughout history, and as she read it, she recognised her symptoms, or rather, what she'd been taught to think of as symptoms. She turned up at the Society's office the next day, begging them to help her.'

'How?'

'She still wanted to be cured at that point, just cured by the right people.'

'But they couldn't cure her. She's still a medium, right? She still hears the voices?'

'Oh yes. But they helped her accept it, her gift.'

'Did they not test her claims?'

'You think she's a fake?'

The defensive note in his voice made Issy smile. 'No. I just – it's a lot to take on trust, that's all, and didn't they want their proof?'

'Sorry. Yes, of course they tested her. In fact, her results pretty much set the standard for present-day testing. She's quite exceptional.'

'But it's a bit odd, don't you think? Using a medium in an investigation like this? I thought you were supposed to be objective.'

'But if we can communicate properly with Tib, if Olivia's able to make contact, then we can get more details about Tib, something solid, verifiable,' Simon said.

Isobel turned to face him, puzzled, not for the first time, by the rules and procedures he took for granted. 'But is that really how it works? I mean, shouldn't you be more . . . well . . . scientific?'

'This is science, it's just . . . experimental.'

'But the girls need – shit!' Issy snatched the saucepan up from the gas and began to stir it frantically. 'Sorry,' she said.

*

They ate at the table, the tiny dormer window above them propped open as wide as they could get it.

'This is great, thanks,' said Simon.

'Apart from the burnt bits.'

'It's fine, really.'

Isobel had put some music on: Joni Mitchell played softly in the background, occasionally challenged by the distant call of a seagull.

'When will you go back to London?' she asked.

'I don't know. A week or so, I think. It depends on what happens tomorrow.' It always did. One week more, just one week more, an endless refrain. Although it was obvious to Isobel that Cathy was losing patience, that she wanted her home back, her husband too.

'Not long, then.' Isobel put down her knife and fork, pushed her empty plate away. 'Why do you think they wanted to get rid of us?' she asked.

'They didn't.'

'If you say so.'

He almost blushed. 'They have the case to discuss. Or maybe they're, well, you know . . .' His voice trailed away.

'I'm having another beer,' Isobel said. 'Do you want one?'

They took their drinks into the living room and sat on the sofa. It was a comfortable space, crammed with books, the walls covered with large framed prints. They were mainly portraits, of an older couple, some children captured in a whirl of exuberance on a beach somewhere, and a young woman, her face half obscured by a veil of fine fair hair, her huge eyes reflecting a cloudy sky.

'That's good,' said Simon, pointing to the girl.

'Thanks.'

'Really. You're very good,' he said, as if he'd not quite realised before. 'Tell me what you think about Olivia.'

'You already asked me that.'

'Michael, then. Me.' He felt her sigh, felt her shift in her seat. She was always there, Isobel, watching: he'd got used to that, to her. What story would her photos tell if they took all of them, the pictures of the farm, the girls, Dan and Flor, Cathy, him, everyone, and pieced them together? Would that be the truth? Would they find their answers, their proof?

'I think you mean well.'

The thought tumbled away. 'Thanks.'

'But sometimes I wonder if that's quite enough.'

'How do you mean?'

'She's all on her own. Cathy. She's – vulnerable.'

'She has Joe.' The silence went on for so long, he wondered if she'd heard him. 'Issy?'

'He's not coming back, Simon.' She sounded disappointed.

'Of course he is—'

'If that was your family, your child, going through this, would you stay away?' she said. 'Cathy's putting a brave face on, for the kids, but it's obvious he doesn't want to be around.'

'He has commitments, he's teaching—'

'In August?'

He turned to face her, surprised by the venom in her tone.

'Jesus, Simon. Doesn't it ever occur to you to ask why?'

'I don't—'

'Why has Joe left them all at the farm? Why did the noises start when they did? Why did Cathy let the police in, the press? You? Me? Why did Tib – whatever that might be – turn up?'

'We're doing our best—'

'I know. I know you are. We all are. But why doesn't anyone – God, I don't know – why don't you challenge them? Why do you always just go along with them?'

274

'I'm sorry—'

'And stop being polite. For God's sake, stop being so bloody polite.'

He put his drink to one side and reached for her hands. He'd never seen her like this before, on the verge of tears, raging. 'Issy.' He looked into her pale green eyes, then leant close, drew her closer and kissed her. Her lips were soft and her breath was warm and sweet and for a moment it felt like everything was going to be fine. Isobel, his Isobel. Then, very gently, she pushed him away. 'No, Simon,' she said.

He'd got it wrong.

'Oh, God, Issy. I'm sorry. I shouldn't have done that. I'm an idiot and—' He backed away, scrambled to his feet.

'Shut up.'

He couldn't read her expression, dismay perhaps, embarrassment. 'I'll go,' he said.

She leant back on the sofa, weary, defeated. 'Oh, for God's sake. You don't have to go anywhere. Can't we just . . . it doesn't matter, Simon, it's forgotten. Really.' She picked up her drink, took a swig of beer and tried to smile up at him.

'You're sure?'

'We're friends, aren't we? Sit down, Simon, don't be so daft.'

He wasn't sure what to do next. When he'd thought about kissing Isobel, and he'd thought about it a lot recently in varying scenarios, it hadn't occurred to him that she wouldn't respond. That she just wouldn't be interested. That he would feel so foolish.

'I don't want you to go. I want to talk to you,' she said. 'I'm sorry. It just gets to me, sometimes, the way we've complicated it all, the way we've—' She took a breath. 'Tell me what will happen next. Tell me what a séance is like.'

He hesitated and found he couldn't quite bring himself to leave. 'OK, then,' he said.

Michael and Olivia went for a walk after dinner. Coming out of the pub, then – in silent agreement – turning right, away from the climb to the farm and following the road down through what passed for the centre of the village, towards the redbrick chapel and the wooden-framed village hall. The houses they passed had their windows open, light bleeding out onto their gardens and the road, the sound of TV audiences, laughing heartily in far distant studios, drifting out into the heavy night air.

They paused at the village hall. The road forked here, leading to the next village or down past the abandoned playing field to the tiny branch line that served the community. From the farm you could hear the trains, but never see them, Loo had told Olivia, and they weren't supposed to go down to the line, but they did. Sometimes.

'There's not much here, is there?' she said, pausing by the gate and looking into the field which had been set up as a rudimentary cricket pitch. It was an odd landscape, bare, forbidding. She wouldn't like to live here, so close, trapped underneath the swell of the moor top. And there was something odd about the farm too, something confined, hemmed in.

'That was the appeal of the place, or so I gather,' said Michael. 'Cathy thought it would be best for the children and Joe would have the space to work. Inspiration.'

'Have you met him?'

'No. He's away working and the phenomena didn't begin until, what, a week or two after he'd gone.' He caught her expression and smiled. 'I know how that looks,' he said.

276

'It's a reasonable assumption. The father – who Loo adores, by the way – takes off and the next thing you know, the furniture's flying around.'

'Do you think that's it? She's faking? They're both faking?'

Olivia knows him so well, the forced calm of his voice tells her that it's a possibility he must have considered.

'They don't fit in terribly well, do they? They don't seem to have any friends,' she said.

'Dan works for a local farmer.'

'Over in the next village.' Michael looked startled for a moment. 'Loo told me,' she said, leaning against the gate and smiling up at him. 'The poor child is starved of normal conversation. Once she started I thought she'd never stop. Hasn't it occurred to either of you to talk to her?'

'We talk every day.'

'Yes. I'm sure you do.'

Michael shoved his hands in his pockets, wishing he had something to occupy him.

'I saw Carol a few weeks ago,' said Olivia.

'Ah.'

'She's looking well. Considering what she might do after her graduation.'

Michael hasn't seen or spoken to his daughter for close to six months.

'She was with a young man. I didn't ask, of course, but he seemed to be quite attached to her.'

Michael placed his hands on the top of the fence. 'Yes, she mentioned . . . someone. I'll get in touch when we get back, once we have this case wrapped up.'

'Is it going to be that simple?' Olivia asked.

'Isn't it? We have everything recorded and witnessed, it's quite remarkable.'

Olivia stood back from the gate, regarding him seriously. 'I'm sure you've been very diligent,' she said. 'I wouldn't expect anything less.'

'So what do you think?' he said, taking her by the arm in a courtly, old-fashioned gesture as they turned back towards the village. 'Is she genuine?'

'Oh, yes,' said Olivia, without hesitation. 'I'm afraid she is, the poor little thing.'

They'd finished all the beer and moved on to a bottle of brandy left over from Christmas. Issy had found the latest bundle of contact sheets and now they sat on the floor, side by side, going over them.

Cathy in the kitchen.

Michael in the living room talking to the girls.

Dan standing in the doorway.

Florian's toys scattered over the kitchen floor.

Simon sitting in front of the tent.

And the girls, over and over again, the sisters with their wild hair and odd dressing-up-box clothes. Something about that still bothered Isobel. They hadn't always dressed like that, but she wasn't quite certain when the theatrical element, and it was theatrical, she was sure, had started to creep into the images. She could check, but that would mean going through all the files piled precariously on the little desk underneath the window, setting everything out in chronological order. And she just never had the time, these days.

She rubbed her face. She didn't really like brandy, and she couldn't understand why she was drinking it. She felt sticky and hot and vaguely sorry for Simon, who she liked, she really did. She shouldn't have lost her temper with him. She shouldn't have kissed him. If only they could be friends.

The first time she'd met the girls they'd come into the kitchen when she was talking with Cathy, trying to get permission to photograph them, on her second or third visit before she'd gone to the paper and they'd taken the story from her, sending Liam Carthy out to do the interviews.

They'd appeared in the doorway, hand in hand.

Barefoot, she'd noticed that, but Loo had been wearing shorts and a T-shirt, Bee a faded blue cotton dress. They had looked normal and a little bit subdued. She'd taken a few shots of them sitting side by side on the sofa. They hadn't smiled for the camera, which had suited her just fine.

When had they started dressing up, and what was so familiar about the effect?

Simon was looking at a series of pictures she'd taken in the garden, the baby sitting on a quilt under the tree, a podgy fist shoved into her mouth.

'It's late,' he said, dropping the contact sheet onto the pile, stifling a yawn. 'I should probably make a move.'

'OK. Yes.' She hauled herself to her feet, avoiding his eye; there was no point in making things worse for them both, not when they'd managed to create the illusion that nothing had really changed. She saw him to the door, carefully stepping back out of reach as they said their goodbyes.

'Take care.'

'Night, Issy.'

She closed the door behind him and stood still for a moment, trying to remember what she'd intended to do with the pictures. It would keep, she decided.

She'd tidied the photos away and was about to turn out the lights when there was a knock at the door. Light. Tentative. She could pretend she hadn't heard. She doubted he'd make a fuss. She opened the door and there he was, looking positively guilty.

279

'I'm sorry,' he said. 'I know this sounds . . . The car won't start.'

'Don't tell me you've run out of petrol,' she said, smiling despite herself.

'Issy . . .'

She stood back. He was in no state to drive anyway. 'Come in, just . . . come in,' she said.

By the time she walked back into the living room, clutching a pillow and a spare sheet, he was stretched out on the sofa, eyes closed, snoring gently. She put them on the floor where he'd see them if he woke.

She went into the bedroom and closed the door firmly behind her. She couldn't explain it, the way she felt, or rather, didn't feel – not to him, not to herself. She didn't know where to begin.

Bee lay on her side waiting for her sister to fall asleep. She lay very still, she was good at that, and steadied her breathing. She could hear Loo reading, the scratch of a page being turned – she was a fast reader, and Bee could, if she'd chosen, keep count of her progress – and then after a while the scratching slowed, before ceasing altogether.

Loo was supposed to blow the candle out once she was done, that was the deal for being allowed to use it at all, and Bee should do something about that, but she didn't want to wake her up. She shifted carefully to the edge of the bunk and looked down at the chest of drawers next to the bed. The candle, half gone, burned steadily, casting a soft golden light below her.

She closed her eyes and listened for a few moments more. Loo was definitely asleep.

The river, she decides, the two of them are walking by the

river and this time they are alone, she and Simon. They stop and without speaking, she takes him by the hand and leads the way along the bank, and they find a hidden place underneath a weeping willow. It's sheltered, shady, private there, the light a soft green and this time when she pulls off her dress, this time he . . .

The bed shuddered as Loo rolled over and Bee waited for her sister's breath to steady once more, counting in her head, one minute, two.

Bee kicked back the bed sheet and pushed up her nightdress. She moved her hand across her belly, light fingertips stroking her skin, moving lower, lower. She closed her eyes and this time when she took off her dress Simon didn't step away.

23

Now

'I'm sorry,' says Nina. 'I didn't mean for you to get so . . . involved.' They're sitting in Hal's car.

'You've got enough now, surely?' He's in the driver's seat, his skin a clammy grey; in shock, more than likely. It occurs to Nina that if he actually wants to leave, right now, one of them will have to take him home. There's no way he can drive himself.

'We've got hours of stuff to go through yet,' he says. 'More than enough material, right? And you have Lucy now. Even if she leaves, you can stay in touch, interview her, Cathy too.'

'I know.' But they can't go. She can't let him go. 'We have to clean up, though, sort out the living room, the window.'

'Yeah. Right. It wouldn't do to leave the place untidy.'

'And the thing is – me and Lewis have never worked with . . .' She's brought her bag with her, crammed with the folders her father had collated. Her notes scribbled over his, her questions too. She pulls it closer, hugging it. 'I mean. The original team, they were able to work with a medium.'

'What, holding hands in a circle and candles flickering and "Is there anybody there?"'

'Not exactly. But she was able to work with Loo, to help her make contact.'

'Jesus. I thought they were scientists.'

'They were. That was one of Michael Warren's things, the use of mediums in psychic investigation. He sort of pioneered it.'

'Well,' Hal says, 'I am not a medium.' He'll give it another couple of minutes and then he'll go. They'll sort something out about the cameras – maybe he'll come back tomorrow to pick them up, maybe he'll meet them at Blue Jacket House when they report back to Cathy; he'd like to see her again, to say goodbye.

'I'm sorry, Hal. But I need to ask – what was it like? Could you hear her? See her?'

'It was—' It's not that the experience is fading, more that he can't bear to recall it. 'I don't know—' It makes his head ache. 'I read the book,' he says. 'Some of it. Your dad's book.' Has he told her that already? He can't remember. He blinks. His eyes are sore: even the pale light reflected by the dull grey sky is too much for him as it bounces off the road, the bonnet of the car. He feels sick again. 'I probably just remembered . . . you know . . .' Tib. 'I probably just read about her, about them.' He has the book somewhere, stuffed into a camera bag, he knows he does.

'Look,' she says. 'Can't you just hang on for a while? There's some material, stuff my dad left behind – I haven't even shown Lewis yet. Only I'm – I think I need you to stay on, to help me.'

'I'm sorry, Nina, I really don't think I can.'

Nina takes this in for a moment, looking down at the satchel in her lap, then she appears to come to a decision. 'She wasn't interested in us, you know. Cathy. Not until she found out about Simon being my dad. I should have told her straightaway about me; it would have saved us a lot of time.'

'Why didn't you?'

'Oh, I don't know.' She rubs at her face. 'It got hard, you

know? Telling people he had died. Having to comfort them, pretend to be all right.' Her bag slips and the files slide out, one falling open, the contact sheets drifting into the footwell of the car. Nina bends down to retrieve them, placing them in order slowly.

'She's very keen on going through Issy's pictures, isn't she? Cathy, I mean.' She runs her fingers over the black and white images. She looks up at Hal and smiles sadly. 'And I think there's something there. Something to do with Bee. It's a bit confusing, but as far as I can tell, the pictures of the girls are—' Then her expression changes. She's looking beyond him, past the house, at the familiar figure making her way across the dull green field towards the barn.

'Oh, shit,' she says, leaning forward. 'What now?'

24

Then

Bee woke up early, for once. She slipped carefully from the top bunk, landing lightly on her toes next to Loo's bed. Loo could have pretended to be asleep, but she knew that wouldn't work.

'Get dressed,' said Bee softly, her sour morning breath tickling Loo's ear. 'And don't make a noise.'

The house was still as they sneaked out of their room, closing the door carefully behind them. This was the tricky bit: Cathy might be up early, especially if the baby was grizzling, and the two of them stood motionless on the landing for a moment, straining to hear her moving around.

Silence.

The stairs and hall were carpeted and they were able to get to the back door without being found out.

'Where are we going?' Loo asked, following Bee down the garden, past the apple tree.

'To see Simon,' said Bee, scrambling over the dry stone wall.

Usually they would creep up to the tent, going round by the road, or crawling up the ditch that ran the length of the field, arriving there as if by magic, giving Simon no time to plan an escape. But today Bee strode up in full view of the world, Loo half a pace behind her. They were wearing new clothes from the dressing-up box, carefully selected the night before: Loo's clothes were too big, and there had been no time to alter them. They'd had to find safety pins to take the skirt in at the waist and the hem trailed across the long grass, but she quite liked the effect.

The tent was still.

'We can't wake him up,' said Loo.

'Well, shut up, then.' Bee dropped to her knees and slowly pulled the flap carefully to one side. 'Shit!' The tent was empty.

Loo looked around, half-expecting Simon to pop up out of thin air. 'Maybe he's in the barn,' she said.

Bee gave her one of those you-are-so-stupid looks.

'He might be,' said Loo.

'Fine. You keep an eye out for him then,' said Bee, ducking inside.

'You can't go in there.'

'Don't be such a baby.'

It was cramped in the tent and, hampered by her long skirt as she crawled around, Bee knocked over a pile of books and papers stacked on the empty sleeping bag.

'Shit!'

'What?'

Loo sounded terrified.

'Nothing. Hang on.' Bee sat down on the bag – his bed, really – and began to rifle through the papers.

'What is it?' Loo stuck her head inside.

'Nothing. Keep watching.' Loo did as she was told and Bee was left alone with Simon's notes. She wasn't quite sure what she was looking for, but she did take a sad sort of pleasure in seeing her name written in his hand. Did he think of her when he wrote it? Did he see her face as he formed the letters? She wished he knew her as Bianca. Bee was a kid's name.

Bianca Corvino.

Bianca Leigh.

She was so intent on looking for her name, it took a second or two for the sentences she was reading to make sense.

M. W. called a halt to the session as it was obvious that Bee was becoming agitated, jealous, I suppose, of the attention Loo is receiving.

'Bee—'

'Shut up.'

After all, it's Loo we need in order to make contact with Tib. There's not much point in including—

'Bee.' Loo had poked her head inside the tent again.

'What?'

'There's a car.'

I almost feel sorry for her.

'Bee.'

M. W. is certain that the phenomena have been centred around Loo all along, and we will probably get the best results in the séance with O. F. if we separate the girls—

Bee dropped the sheaf of notes on the sleeping bag. If he noticed they were out of place, they could always blame Tib.

'Bee.'

But then, she didn't care if he noticed. She grabbed a handful of notes and began to tear them up, dragging them into long strips and scattering them over the groundsheet and bedding. She tried to pull one of the books apart, but the hardback cover defeated her; she settled instead for the Ordnance Survey map Simon had folded open to the area around the farm.

'Bee. We have to go.' Loo was still there, crouched in front of the tent, one hand gripping the sweaty orange fabric. 'Bee.' She sounded as though she might cry.

Bee's hands were shaking. 'Yes, all right,' she said. She crawled back out and got to her feet. There it was in the distance, Issy's car, the stupid blue Beetle.

'Come on,' said Bee, grabbing her sister's hand and dragging her down the field, the two of them running as fast as they could, their white skirts flapping behind them like sails, like wings.

He might not be in the car, she supposed, she might be wrong, but she didn't think so. He hadn't spent the night in the tent, and where else could he have gone? Who else did he know? Bee ran down the incline, tilted herself at the stone wall at the bottom, vaguely aware that she was barely in control now, skimming over the ground, her limbs jagged, her head thrown back.

They reached the wall and scrambled back over it, Loo following silently as Bee led the way, crouching as her sister did when they crept across the front lawn, overgrown and neglected, sliding themselves against the cool dark stones of the garden wall. They could hear the car turning at the end of the lane.

'What are we doing?' said Loo, trying to get her breath back.

Bee reached out and pinched her, hard, on the soft paler flesh of her inner arm. There was some satisfaction in seeing her sister flinch and in seeing Loo's tears, satisfaction too in her silence.

'Shut up.'

The car stopped and she waited. Her legs were cramping and she was beginning to think that she had been mistaken after all, when she heard Isobel's voice, shockingly close.

'Here we are, home sweet home.'

'Well, it's not much, but the view is terrific.'

Simon. Almost close enough to touch.

Crouched there with Loo, Bee forced her head against the

290

dry stones and closed her eyes, digging her fingers into the cracks in the wall. Stupid bloody Isobel. She thought about when she'd knocked her camera out of her hands, the expression on Issy's face as the film spooled out, clouded and ruined. She should have done worse – she should have stamped on the lens until it shattered, she should have given her something to cry about.

The stone smelt rotten, old and dead. Next to her, she felt Loo moving, cautiously raising her head above the edge of the wall, unable to resist the temptation to look at him. She wanted to see too. She had to look. Just to be sure.

'Thanks for the lift, Issy.'

'You're welcome.' They were leaning against the car, side by side, looking up at the house. Issy was wearing a printed cotton dress and her hair, so vivid, so bright, was hanging loose. She looked happy, smug; Bee could have slapped her.

'Are we OK?' said Simon, glancing down at Isobel. 'You know, after . . .'

Isobel nudged him gently with her elbow. 'Of course we are.'

'Good.'

'I'd better be off.'

'Right.'

'I'll see you this afternoon.'

'Sure.'

They didn't notice the girls; they were too wrapped up in each other. Isobel smiled up at him, then got back into the car. Simon watched as she drove away.

He turned and let himself in through the front gate. The girls crouched back down in the shadow of the wall. All he had to do was look down to his left and they would have been discovered, but – his head full of Issy, no doubt – he didn't look, and vanished around the back of the house.

Bee realised that she'd clamped her hands against her mouth. She could taste her own sweat and the grime and dirt from the wall; her heart was pounding. Slowly, she unclasped her fingers; she felt sick. He thought she was a kid. It wasn't fair.

Next to her, Loo was silent.

'See?' said Bee, leaning in close to her sister, still keeping her voice low. 'He doesn't care about you; he doesn't even like you. You're a stupid little girl and all this time he's been shagging Isobel.'

Loo began to cry quietly.

When he got back, tired, hungover and wishing for nothing more than a hot shower and a proper breakfast, Simon found the tent in disarray. He should make a note of it all, he supposed, and get Issy to photograph it, but she'd gone off to work. She wouldn't be back until the afternoon and he could hardly leave everything in this state until then. Besides, there was something small-scale, something human about the mess.

He decided he wouldn't mention this incident to anyone.

He began to tidy the books and papers aware he'd need to keep them safe in order to rewrite his notes, and wondering when he would find the time. His thoughts drifted to the inconvenience of his car breaking down as he tried to decide whether Michael or the Society might contribute to the cost of the repairs. It had been sweet of Issy to bring him back though, especially after he'd made such an arse of himself.

When he was done he stretched out on the sleeping bag and closed his eyes. Just a couple more days and they'd be done here. There was the séance to get through, but after that . . . This time next week he'd be home. A lazy breeze tugged at the tent and he slept.

*

Olivia and Michael arrived at the farm just after lunch time. They found Cathy sitting in the kitchen, watching a mug of tea cool, dirty laundry piled on the floor by the sink.

Michael rapped gently at the open door. 'Good afternoon, Cathy.'

She stood, forcing a smile onto her face. 'Come in,' she said, looking around the kitchen. 'Sit down, please. I'll make some fresh tea.'

'Please don't worry,' said Michael. 'It's probably best that we make a start, don't you think?'

'If that's all right with you,' said Olivia. 'It's very important that you feel confident about what we're going to do this afternoon.'

'Yes. Right. And what exactly are you going to do?' Cathy asked, leaning back against the sink and folding her arms.

'Nothing for the moment. I'd like to spend some time alone in the living room first, preparing myself.'

'Of course,' Michael said. 'Is there anything you need?'

'No. Just to be left alone for a while. An hour or so, shall we say?' She turned to Cathy. 'Is Loo close by?'

'She's upstairs, with Bee. Is that all right?'

'Of course it is.' Olivia smiled at Cathy, her expression kind, confident and reassuring. 'I'll let you know when you can bring her in.'

Strictly speaking, the girls weren't in their room, they were sitting on the top landing, listening. They had spent the morning in the garden, being conspicuously good, reading and drawing but above all listening, trying to find out what a séance – *this* séance – might actually involve. But they hadn't got very far.

Now they watched as the woman, Olivia, went into the front room. Just as she got to the door she paused, and stood very still. Loo had a feeling that she knew they were there, that she might turn and look right up at them, but the moment passed and she went into the room instead, closing the door quietly behind her.

'What are we going to do?' said Loo. She'd been trying not to think about it too much. 'Bee?'

Bee yawned. 'The same as we always do. They'll ask their questions and Tib will turn up and answer them,' she said. She stood up. 'I'm going to get something to eat. I'm starving.' She thumped her way down the stairs, smacking her hand across the wooden spindles as she went, leaving her little sister behind.

Loo edged herself to the top step. She was hungry too, but she didn't want to follow Bee. She wanted to see Simon; he wouldn't be around for much longer, she knew that, and she'd like to talk to him, but she couldn't think what she might say. Besides, he would have seen the mess in the tent by now, and there was a bit of her that was worried he might have guessed who'd done it, that he might be cross with them. So she stayed where she was, trying to imagine that Tib was there too, Tib who would know what to say, what to do. About Simon. About the séance. About Bee.

She leant back against the wall, closed her eyes and tried to picture her, sitting on the landing next to her.

Tib was pretty in the pale blonde way people seemed to like so much, tall and thin, older than Loo, older than Bee. Her dress was made of some dark, coarse material, and her fine golden hair was pulled back in a single plait. Her hands were red and rough. Loo had found that as the days passed, she could picture Tib more clearly, more easily, although she could never quite look at her directly. She'd never seen her face, and that bothered her, but she could always tell how Tib was feeling.

Usually she was hungry, sometimes she was in a temper, and often she wanted to make fun of people – Michael, for example. She could have answered his questions if she'd wanted to, but she never did. It was more fun to watch him creep around her, afraid that he might scare her away – as if she was scared of anything.

25

Now

They need something to patch up the window. That's what Lucy tells herself as she slips out of the back door, across the garden and up into the field. There'll be something they can use in the barn. She'll just take a quick look around and be back before they've realised she's gone.

Better to do this on her own, she thinks.

The door hangs open, the rusting bolt dragged back.

'Hello?' There won't be anyone there, there have been no passers-by, no one calling at the house to check up on them, but she calls out anyway. Lucy wonders if anyone in the village realises they are there and, if they do, whether anyone cares.

She steps inside, lets her eyes adjust to the gloom, and looks around. The air is damp, chilly. She finds herself unwilling to stray too far inside, away from fresh air and daylight, and considers briefly pulling the second door open too, just to be sure.

She can still hear Cathy's voice. *You're not to go bothering your father.*

And her father's too, distant now, harder to conjure, to get the tone right. *You'll feel the back of my hand.*

But they're not here. No one is here.

She steps inside. It's not too dark – the shutters on the ground floor have been replaced at some point with small windows; the panes are grimy and the light is greenish and dull, but she can see well enough.

The barn has become a dumping ground for unwanted tools and scraps of wood, tiles and bags of cement, left over from work on the house over the years, she supposes, and the floor is a patchwork of worn stone, broken slates and rusting wire. She glances up at the hayloft. The joists and planks look secure enough but even if there was a ladder she doubts she'd risk the climb. Woodworm and dry rot, she thinks, remembering her father's warnings. The scary stories her brother Dan would tell.

Such a baby.

If she turned around she might catch her, Bee, laughing at her; Bee was never afraid of anything.

Larger shapes lurk at the back of the building, collapsing hunks of machinery, cannibalised and forgotten, some covered with dusty tarpaulins, some layered with rust. There had been some old-fashioned tools too, she recalled, a sickle and a scythe, long blades curving like claws. Her father must have liked them.

She begins to pick through the junk. She moves some sacking and old garden tools, and uncovers some plastic pipes and bags of gravel. She makes an effort to concentrate, to shut out anything that might be lurking, looking for a way in.

Gradually she's able to focus on the task she's set herself. There are some offcuts of hardboard, but they are too small and anyway she doubts she could find the tools to fix them in place. What they really need is something flexible – sheeting of some kind. They need to show willing, at least, and not leave the place exposed to the elements.

Dust drifts down from the ceiling, from the hayloft, settling on her like a fine scattering of snow.

Lucy looks up. 'Hello?' She stands slowly, wiping her grubby hands on her jeans. Above her a floorboard creaks softly. There's an open trapdoor in the ceiling where they used to prop the ladder; she moves under it, craning her neck, listening.

'Lucy?' Nina is standing in the doorway, slightly out of breath. 'Sorry,' she says. 'Only we're not supposed to come in here. It's one of the conditions we had to agree to. We have to stay away from the barn and any machinery on the premises.'

'Oh. I see.' Lucy moves away from the trapdoor, forces out a smile. 'I was – I thought I might find something to cover over the broken window. To patch it up.'

'OK,' says Nina, stepping into the gloom, clearly unable to resist the temptation to trespass, just a little. 'If you put it that way . . .'

'Well, if we're quick, then?' Lucy says. 'And just watch where you step.'

'Sure.'

'Here,' Nina says. She's found it half wedged behind the door, some black plastic sheeting, the kind they use these days for baling hay. 'What about this?' They drag it out between the two of them. It looks like discarded offcuts, one piece ragged and mud-stained, but the rest might do. 'Good enough, do you think?'

'If you can find some gaffer tape.'

'Hal, perhaps?'

'Yes, I suppose so.' Lucy grabs an armful of plastic. 'Right, then,' she says.

Further back, in the gloom, a window rattles. The breeze catches at it and it opens, swinging back and forth. 'We should probably see to that, don't you think?' Nina moves past Lucy without waiting for a reply. It can hardly matter, Lucy wants to point out. Someone has decided to let this place rot; once the roof finally goes that'll be that, and closing a window now will make no difference at all.

The window isn't too high and, neatly avoiding the stacks of roof tiles someone has left piled against the wall, Nina reaches ups and pulls it shut, forcing the rusty latch back down into place. It's hardly worth it, the grey glass bears a tracery of fine cracks and the next strong wind will push clean through it, but she smiles at Lucy anyway. Pleased.

'There.'

Old bits of timber lean unsteadily against discarded sacks of gravel, breeze blocks and tiles are stacked in the corner, there's even a couple of old doors and a blackened sink. A cement sack has split and dust has leaked out onto the floor.

It takes a moment for them to realise what they're looking at.

Footprints.

Bare feet.

They don't move.

'Not me,' says Lucy, gesturing to her boots, still laced and clumped and clotted with mud.

'Me neither,' says Nina.

They could have been there for days, months even, but there is something about the prints, something fresh in the negative image in the dust and in the pale floury trail that disappears into the dark, that gives the overwhelming impression that someone else is there. Just out of sight. Playing a game. The wind gusts and far above them loose tiles on the roof lift and settle, the planks overhead straining and releasing as if someone is walking there.

'Hello?' says Nina, stepping forward.

'No.' Lucy grabs her by the hand. There's something wrong. The more she looks at the prints, the more she's reminded of – what? Bait. Bait in a trap, bait to pull them in, to make them look the wrong way. The footprints lead to the far corner, inky black there, and as she stands, her fingers wrapped around Nina's wrist, she's sure she can hear something scrabbling in the shadows. Something frantic.

'We're going now,' she says, loud enough for it to hear. But Nina doesn't want to leave. Lucy can feel the tension in the young woman's muscles, the pull towards the dark.

'Hang on . . .' Nina fumbles in her pocket and pulls out her phone. 'We just need to get some pictures.'

'Now,' says Lucy. 'Please.'

Above them the window Nina had closed so carefully snaps open again and the air that swirls through the barn smears the fine-powdered footprints across the floor. But Nina doesn't stop. Lucy can hear the fake shutter sound these things emit as she carries on taking her pictures. In a far corner, something heavy, metallic – a scythe, perhaps – slides slowly to the floor, scraping the old stone as it falls.

'Please, Nina.'

'Yes. All right,' Nina says, shoving her camera into her pocket.

Lucy takes the shortcut, without even thinking about it, across the old flagstone yard, mossy green and overgrown now, averting her eyes, fearful of what she might see if she glances back, leading the way straight down the field to the garden wall, waist- height, grey, damp. They throw the rolls of plastic sheeting over and onto the wet grass.

'We should go back,' says Nina.

'No.'

'We might have missed something.'

'You said yourself, we're not supposed to be there. It's not safe.' This is to the part of the wall they always used to scramble over, the bit where the top two layers were missing, creating a gap just wide enough for a person to squeeze through. Left that way on purpose, she now realises, after all these years – a quick getaway, should anyone need it. She climbs over first and the pair of them are back in the garden, partially hidden from the house by the apple tree, catching their breath.

'But there was something, wasn't there?' says Nina. 'Don't you think?'

'No,' says Lucy. The expression in the younger woman's eyes, eager, fascinated, reckless, is almost more than she can bear. 'Let's go and sort this window out.'

'Does this mean you're staying?' asks Hal. He is holding the thin black sheeting in place as Lucy tapes it to the window frame. It's a bodged job, plastic patched together to make a piece large enough to reach, fixed in place with gaffer tape. Nina has said she'll ring the letting agents and let them know, although how she'll explain it away is anyone's guess.

'I'm not sure,' Lucy says, 'what about you?'

'I don't know. Probably. If we both go, then they're stuck here, aren't they? Not just them, all the AnSoc gear too.'

'If we both go, they'd have to come with us.'

'I suppose.'

Nina has shared the pictures from the barn, and there has been a heated argument about whether or not they should go back and film there. Hal can't imagine for one second he'd get either Lewis or Nina to leave now.

'Why did you stay?' he asks. 'When you were a kid, I mean. Why didn't you all just pack up and go?'

'Go where? Cathy and Joe and five kids?'

'But weren't you scared?' Hal asks.

Lucy concentrates on smoothing the tape into place, sealing them in. 'It wasn't that bad. Not at first. It was . . . like playing

302

a game. And I was never on my own, you know? There was Simon, and the others, and Bee, there was always Bee. We thought it was fun. At first. Looking back, it was Cathy who suffered the most.'

'She doesn't strike me as someone who is easily spooked.'

'Well, it was a long time ago and she was very young.' Lucy pulls a chair into place, climbs onto it and begins to work at the top of the window. 'And all she wanted was to protect us. We didn't really understand that. And then, of course, in the end, she couldn't.' She smooths another strip of tape into place.

'Does it happen to you now?' He pulls the plastic taut, watching her work. 'The – dreaming – thing? The voices?'

'No. Michael used to talk about people having a gift, people like Olivia. But I didn't – don't – pursue it.'

'You can do that? Just shut it out?' He sounds doubtful.

She stops and looks down at him. 'Yes,' she says, 'of course I can. I grew up, and I moved on. What happened earlier, with you, just because it happened, you don't have to do anything else, you know, no matter what Nina or Lewis say. They have no right to – use you.'

'Isn't that a bit harsh?'

'No. It's self-preservation. Some people get a glimpse of what might be the truth, their truth anyhow, and they think they can find a way into – into something not meant for them. And it never ends well. Never. People lose perspective.'

'But you have to try, surely? If you get the chance.'

'But it never leads anywhere. Questions answered with questions, that's all they ever got from Tib. That's all anyone ever gets, as far as I can tell. And maybe it's best not to know. What good does it do anyone, living or dead—'

The phone in Lucy's pocket rings, the sound cutting through the room.

'Sorry,' she says, stepping down from the chair and pulling her phone out. 'Can you carry on in here? I just need to . . .'

'Sure,' says Hal. 'No problem.'

'Mum?'

'Well, who else?'

'Sorry. Are you all right?'

'I'm fine. I'm—' Cathy hesitates. 'Quite alone.'

'Sorry?'

Cathy sighs and Lucy can see her, sitting by the window in her room.

'Mum?'

'I'm perfectly all right. I've been looking through the photographs Nina sent again.'

'And?'

'There's nothing there. Nothing useful.'

'Mum?'

'What?'

'If you get anxious, or anything, get someone. Get Sarah to sit with you.'

'There's no need for that.'

Lucy follows the path around the house into the front garden. She takes a breath, bracing herself. 'Things have been happening, Mum.'

'What things?'

'More noises, like they had on their tape. And a broken window.'

She can't bring herself to mention the footprints in the barn.

'Oh, Lucia.' Her mother's voice is soft. 'Is it happening again?'

She reaches the front gate. She can see that, for some reason, Hal has forgotten to lock the car door. It hangs open, lazy, abandoned. 'I don't know,' she says.

She bends down, leans in.

She's about to close the driver's door when she notices it. Something pale has slipped down the side of the seat, and despite herself – it's best not to know, it's best not to look – she picks it up. It's one of Issy's contact sheets, come adrift from one of Simon's files.

'I want you to take care, Lucia. Do you understand?'

There they are: two girls silhouetted at the far end of a long room.

The barn.

The hayloft.

The thumbnail images playing out like an old film, the girls shifting position, and there, at the edge of the frame, a shadow.

'Yes. I have to go,' Lucy says. 'I'll call you back later, OK?'

She finds them in the kitchen. Hal is dealing with one of the cameras, removing the tiny memory card and replacing it with a new one. Nina and Lewis are by the blanked-in window, she with her hands shoved down deep into her pockets, hunched, tense, and he clutching a clipboard. They are talking softly, but they might be arguing.

'How's Cathy?' asks Hal.

'Oh.' Lucy has folded the single sheet carefully and put it in her coat pocket. Maybe Nina won't notice it's missing. Maybe she has more. 'She's fine.'

'When we're done here,' says Nina, 'do you think she'd agree to an interview?'

'Jesus, Nina, take a breath,' says Hal, turning the camera over in his hands. He opens out the viewfinder; he's looking like his old self again. Nina manages a half-smile.

'I don't know,' says Lucy. 'Possibly, I suppose.'

'Great,' says Lewis. 'That's great.'

'Did you finish in the living room?' Lucy asks Hal.

'Yeah, all done,' he says. 'It's not perfect, but it'll hold for a while.'

'And Hal's definitely staying on. Well, for a bit longer anyway,' says Nina. 'We're hoping you will too.'

It's dim in the kitchen with the only natural light seeping in from the open door and the hallway, and Nina's expression is hard to read, but all Lucy can think of is the two little girls, playing in the barn, the black and white images crumpled up in her coat pocket. 'I see. Yes,' she says.

'Yes, you'll stay?' Nina sounds surprised.

'Yes. If you like,' says Lucy.

'Good,' Nina glances at Lewis, 'that's settled then.'

26

Then

Simon was in the garden.

'When will we start?' he asked as Michael walked out into the blazing sunshine, the heat rising up to meet him.

'As soon as Olivia is ready.'

'And what does she need, exactly?'

'What do you think, Simon? A darkened room? Bell, book and candle?' The professor was actually making a joke; at least Simon thought it was a joke.

'I'm sorry, I didn't mean – I don't really know what to expect,' he said. 'This is all new to me.'

'Ah, well, in that case, I apologise; all she really needs is a quiet room, and a supportive atmosphere.'

'Supportive?'

'Calm, open-minded, no one shouting the odds at the wrong moment. There's room for debate, for healthy scepticism when she's done, but during a sitting, we follow her rules.'

'Our rules, surely?'

Michael smiled. 'We must learn to defer to an expert, where needs be.'

The thought of Michael, so quietly self-assured, deferring to anyone didn't quite make sense to Simon. 'But surely, there are protocols, checks we should set in place,' he said.

'I've worked with Olivia on many occasions, I value her

abilities and I trust her. She is not under investigation here.'
The professor's tone was mild, but Simon still had the sense
he'd been rebuked.

'I see.' Simon looked up at the house. 'But we can still record
the séance, yes?'

'Of course.' Michael smiled again, and then took himself off
to investigate the little apple tree by the wall, his hands clasped
behind his back, every inch the affable academic, relaxed, confident, in control.

Olivia could hear the yelling from the front room. Bee and
Cathy, in the kitchen. The tone was clear enough even though
the words were muffled. She wasn't surprised. Volatile spirits
frequently attached themselves to volatile situations, and
between the three of them, she was sure Bee and Loo and
Cathy could generate enough energy for a dozen poltergeists.
She was more or less done, anyway, and far too experienced to
let a teenage girl knock her off balance.

She turned her attention back to the mantelpiece and picked
up a framed snapshot of Joe and Cathy. They looked terribly
young, smiling bravely up at the camera. The background looked
familiar, a swarm of tourists in front of an elaborate church,
pale marble columns and bronze horses . . .

'What are you doing?' Isobel was standing in the doorway.

Olivia hadn't heard her come in. She probably had Bee to
thank for that, what with the racket she was making.

'Trying to get to know everyone,' she said. 'I find it helps.'
She put the picture back in place, and gathered up the letters
she'd found, bills mainly, wedging them neatly behind the clock.
She smiled at Isobel and crossed over to the window.

'I see.' Issy was unable to drag her eyes away from the bundle
of letters. Olivia could see her trying to make sense of the scene,

308

noting where the letters had been placed, taking in the other keepsakes on the mantelpiece, the little clues the family had left scattered there.

'Can I help you?' Olivia asked.

'Does Michael know . . .?' The younger woman caught her breath, started again. 'I'm sorry. Do you know where Simon is?'

That was not what she'd intended to say, Olivia was almost certain.

'In the kitchen, perhaps.'

Remain in control.

Olivia placed her hand against the wall, wondering if she might sense Tib, hovering close by, but all she could feel was Bee, raging.

'Oh. Thanks.'

It seemed to Olivia that Issy might say something else, might step into the room and close the door quietly, but the moment, if it was there at all, passed. She concentrated on stilling the trembling in her fingers, counting her heartbeat, until Issy shut the door and left her alone.

Isobel sat in the garden underneath the apple tree watching Simon and Michael moving about in the kitchen. She wished she'd asked Simon more about Olivia Farrell, how long she'd known Michael, the other cases she'd worked on. How close they might be. He was a widower, after all, and the age gap wasn't so very much, and she was attractive. Beautiful.

The trouble was, she couldn't be sure. She couldn't be sure what she'd seen. She leant her head back against the tree trunk and went through it all again. Olivia had been standing by the mantelpiece with the bundle of letters in her hand.

She closed her eyes, tried again. Olivia was curious about the family, that was all, and it wasn't as if she'd actually caught her reading the letters. Brown envelopes, bills and circulars and a bundle of postcards. How long had she been there? Picking through the family's past? Issy pushed the thought away and replayed their conversation – not the words, but the expression in the medium's eyes, the curve of her mouth. The heat of the summer's day washed through her limbs and she could barely move. She should go inside, into the cool of the house, but that didn't appeal. She'd rather stay here and think a little more about Olivia, imagine what she might say to her, the next time they were alone.

Bee slammed the kitchen door behind her and dragged herself slowly upstairs. It wasn't fair.

They didn't want her to be in the séance.

Well, she was going to fix that. She'd wait for Loo and make sure she knew what to say.

Back in the bedroom she picked up a paperback, one of Loo's, and climbed up onto her bunk. She'd left the door open and she lay there, listening. At first, she didn't even bother with the book, but when she heard footsteps on the stairs, she opened it and held it up in front of her. The footsteps turned out to be her mother; Bee could feel her standing there at the top of the landing, looking at her, but she didn't say anything. After a while, a long while, her mother had moved on to the bathroom, and when she was done, she'd walked back downstairs without hesitating.

The words on the page in front of her made her eyes ache. They seemed to blur and flicker and the paperback book, old with browny-orange pages and a buckled black cover, smelt of cigarette smoke. Loo had probably borrowed it from Dan. She read a lot: in bed, when she was eating, on the toilet, picking up books from around the house then leaving them all over the place, face down, their spines cracking, their pages curling, reading two or three at once, sometimes more, and Cathy – pleased to see her daughter so studious – never really bothered to check the titles Loo had chosen.

Bee looked at the front cover. The words danced and flickered still, but the picture, a young woman in a flimsy white night-gown cowering in front of a blood-stained altar, told her all she needed to know.

Silly little girl.

Bored, she abandoned the book and went to the window, looking out over the garden, which was empty except for Isobel, who was dozing under the tree.

It wasn't fair, the way Simon looked at Issy, the way she laughed at him, as if she didn't care; the way he looked at her as if he couldn't see anyone else.

She leant her head against the drawn-up window frame. In the attic above, the regular thud of Dan's music seemed to soak through the ceiling like a heartbeat.

'The candles blew then disappeared.'

She let the song wash over her as she closed her eyes and imagined what it might be like if Isobel was out of the way, for once.

27

Now

It seems to Lucy that now she has agreed to stay, no one is in much of a rush to do anything. They check their readings, they make their notes, and then they eat, each helping themselves to their dwindling supply of sandwiches and crisps. Lewis takes his lunch into the living room and Nina follows, shutting the door behind them.

Hal works at his laptop for a while, still trying to solve the riddle of the files they can't open. When he finds he can't, he goes outside. He sits on the back step, rationing out his cigarettes, looking up at the moor. Lucy keeps him company for a while: she enjoys his silence and his second-hand smoke.

She's still sitting there when Nina comes out, followed by Lewis. Lucy gets to her feet. 'Right,' she says, 'are you ready?'

The sooner they start, the sooner they're done.

'Yes. Well, not exactly,' Nina says.

'We were just talking about that,' says Lewis. 'And we were wondering—' He looks at Nina. 'We've been thinking,' he says.

'About?'

'The original investigation,' says Nina. 'Olivia Farrell.'

'What we've got so far is great,' says Lewis. 'The video's good, you know? And the audio. But it could still be—'

'Open to interpretation,' says Nina.

'We need more,' says Lewis. 'We need something conclusive. Ideally, we need to reproduce what happened to Hal.'

'Yeah, good luck with that,' says Hal softly.

'Contact,' says Lucy. 'That was what Michael used to talk about. Communication.'

'Yes. That's what – Nina thinks we should try again. To talk to it. Her. Tib.' Lewis looks embarrassed.

'Yes,' says Lucy. 'I see.' She's barely surprised. Looking back, this is where they have been heading all along.

'And we wondered,' Lewis says, his words coming out in a rush, 'would you? Would you be willing to try?' He turns to Hal. 'Both of you?

'No way,' says Hal, standing, throwing down his cigarette onto the damp path. 'You have plenty of material. Just run the observations like you planned and—'

'The obs are no good if there's someone there trying to make contact and we just ignore her,' says Nina.

'There's no one there.'

'You said you'd help.'

'With the cameras,' Hal says. 'Not with . . . this is different.' He turns to Lucy. 'You can't possibly think this is a good idea.'

'I'm not a medium,' says Lucy.

'That's not what Michael thought,' says Nina. 'My dad either. They thought you were – gifted.'

'Olivia knew what she was doing.'

'But you were there,' says Lewis. 'I mean – you remember what it was like, right?'

And she does remember, of course she does.

'I know it's a lot to ask,' Nina begins.

Lucy puts her hand in her pocket, feeling for the marble she's kept on her ever since she found it in the garden at Blue Jacket House. She can't be sure, that's the problem. Now she's seen the contact sheet, she doesn't know what else Nina has kept back from them, what else she might have in mind. She's tempted to leave, to let them get on with it, but she finds she daren't take the risk. She'd like to believe that if she left nothing would happen, but she's not sure, and if she stays, then at least she might regain a little control. 'If I agreed,' she says slowly, 'there would have to be conditions, rules. I would be in charge.'

'Sure,' says Lewis. 'Anything.'

'And if we do try, then we try once, and once only. Just like Olivia did, and then we pack everything up and we go.'

28

Then

When Isobel pushed the living-room door open, she tried to be quiet, not that it mattered. Everyone was looking at the two girls in the centre of the room, barefoot in their white chemises and their billowing petticoats. Still. Solemn.

'I'm scared,' said Loo.

Bee was gripping her sister's hand and Issy was reminded of the fingerprint bruises she'd seen before, dabbed up the inside of Loo's arm, along her leg, vanishing up her skirt.

'There's nothing to be afraid of,' said Michael.

'I don't want her to go. You can't make her go. I want Bee.' Loo sounded as if she might cry. For a moment Michael looked uncertain and Isobel wondered if he might postpone the sitting. If he did call it off, then maybe she could talk to Simon, tell him about Olivia, the way she'd been – not snooping, exactly, but something close to it. Find a way of asking him if that was normal, acceptable.

'Very well,' said Michael. 'If you think that would help.'

Olivia with the photo in one hand and the letters in the other. None of this quite making sense any more. Issy bumped awkwardly against the door. 'Sorry.'

'That's quite all right, Isobel. If you could take your place and then I think we can begin,' Michael said.

Olivia with her fine dark hair and knowing smile, so cool, so calm.

'Issy?'

'Yes. Sorry.' She took up her place and checked her camera.

They used the hard upright chairs, brought in from the kitchen. They set them in a rough circle: Michael, Simon, Cathy, Bee and Loo next to each other, and Olivia.

Issy stayed by the window. One camera in her hand and another, a smaller Olympus Trip, in her lap. Dan was outside with Florian, the silence in the room broken intermittently by the thump of a football against a wall and by Florian's voice, high-pitched, questioning.

Simon was holding a tape recorder: a second larger model was placed on the floor, a microphone propped up on a pile of books, pointing at the girls, at Loo. Olivia sat still, upright, with her hands folded loosely in her lap.

'We're just going to sit quietly for a while. You may close your eyes if you wish, and we're simply going to allow ourselves to breathe, gently, steadily . . .'

Loo closed her eyes obediently and Olivia went on.

'. . . allowing our minds to clear as we breathe gently, steadily, deeper now. With each breath we are calmer, more receptive, more alert.'

The late afternoon light cast a lazy golden glow around the room, dust motes swirled slowly in the air, the room seemed to gather itself in.

'Our minds clear as we hear the world around us, but we remain silent, focused.'

A loud thump echoed above their heads, followed by a cascade of knocks. Bee bit her lip and shifted in her seat.

'Quietly breathing in and out, waiting—'

The second wave of knocking was louder, almost drowning out Olivia's voice entirely. Loo opened her eyes and looked around the circle as the noise built to a climax. 'Don't,' she said, and the noise stopped abruptly.

'Who's there?' said Olivia. There was no answer, of course; the question wasn't a genuine enquiry, more a way of asserting her presence.

I am here and you will speak to me.

It was warm in the little front room. The unnaturally hot weather had gone on for too long. Like most people she knew, Olivia wished it would break. She wasn't made for this permanent, endless summer; it wasn't natural. Isobel was a distraction, her camera too. She was finding it hard to concentrate.

Michael looked relaxed enough; he didn't seem to doubt that she'd speak to them.

Tib.

Simon looked anxious, though; this was his first séance, he didn't quite know what to expect and was probably worried he wouldn't record everything, and Cathy, she looked uneasy too. Loo seemed the most worried, strained to breaking point, unable to calm her breathing, barely managing to sit still. If she carried on like this, Olivia might have to call a halt to things. She needed Loo to be at ease, relaxed.

Bee sat next to her sister, ramrod straight, alert, buzzing with energy.

Loo's hands were clammy. She was too hot and she wished now that she had gone down to the kitchen and had something to eat or drink after all. The noise from upstairs had made her jump. She'd felt herself beginning to drift away and then the thumping had started and now she could feel it still inside her chest and the soft, sleepy feeling had vanished. She

319

wondered how long they'd been sitting there. No one seemed in a rush.

Carefully, she opened her eyes. The first person she saw was Isobel, perched on a chair by the window, staring at her. Issy smiled encouragingly and rather than smile back – that would feel wrong, not serious – Loo nodded her head. The exchange made Simon look away from the circle, towards Issy, and Loo remembered that morning all over again.

Simon and Isobel. She felt hot and sweaty and a bit sick. She could feel Bee next to her, though she didn't dare look. She could feel her willing her to do something.

Get on with it.

Loo let her head drop forward, the way she always did when Tib wanted to talk, and she waited for someone to ask a question. Her eyes fluttered shut and she thought she could hear footsteps, a light pattering up and down the stairs. They seemed to go on forever, up and down, up and down, until they stopped outside the door, and Loo waited for it to fly open, for someone to come in.

She felt herself begin to float away, and the thudding of her heart eased.

'Who's there?' said Olivia.

She waited for a while. Maybe if she didn't answer it would all stop, and they could go down to the shop, buy some ice cream.

'Who's there?' said Olivia again.

'*Tib.*'

'Where are you?'

'*Here.*'

The same stupid questions. Her head felt heavy; she could almost fall forward off the chair. She had the feeling that if she did, she'd sink slowly through the carpet and into the floorboards, that she'd carry on falling forever.

'How old are you?'

'Don't know.'

She didn't need to open her eyes to know that Simon was checking the recorder, that Issy had lifted her camera and was waiting for the right moment to press the shutter release, that Michael was leaning slightly forward, hardly daring to breathe, all of them watching her.

'Where do you live?'

'I. Don't.'

'Where did you live?'

'Farm.'

'What did you do there?'

'Helped.'

'Helped who?'

'Mam.'

'What did she do?'

'Cooked. Cleaned.'

'Was it her farm?'

'No.'

'Whose farm was it?'

'I . . .'

'Whose farm?'

'I . . .'

'Who was the master here?'

The stone hit the window with a sharp crack and was followed immediately by a cascade of smaller pebbles.

'I . . .'

Silence.

Loo was listening too, wondering what Tib might say next.

'Who is he?'

'Mustn't.'

'Why not?'

321

Her throat ached and sweat prickled along the back of her neck.

'Are you afraid of him?'

Loo waited.

'No.'

'The master of the house?'

She could hear her own breathing, shallow, ragged.

'Are you afraid, Tib?'

'Yes.'

'Who do you fear?'

'Her.'

'Not him?'

'Her.'

She could feel Olivia thinking, deciding what to say next.

'I have a very strong sense of him,' she said and Loo could imagine Michael nodding and making notes. 'A powerful man, with a strong connection to the land, this farm, a family connection. But there is another presence too, a female energy. She's . . .' Olivia hesitated. 'There's a feeling of . . . anger, rage.'

Loo could almost see them herself.

'Who is he, Tib?'

'No.'

'What about your mother, then? What's her name?'

'No.' A chair moved, Cathy's chair.

Olivia cleared her throat. 'Tell me about her, tell me about your mother.'

'She . . . she . . .'

'I can sense her, in the kitchen,' said Olivia.

'Yes.'

The scullery, Loo thought.

'Baking.'

'Bread.'

322

'And you helped, didn't you, Tib?'

'*Yes.*'

'She's close.' Olivia's voice was low, urgent, speaking for the tape machine, speaking so Michael could take notes. 'Very close. There's a barrier . . . a barrier of some sort between her and Tib . . .'

'I want you to stop,' said Cathy, but Olivia ignored her.

'Tell me more about your mother.'

'*Blood.*'

'What?'

'*Blood*—'

'Where?'

'*I . . .*'

'Where?'

'*Stones . . .*'

'Where?'

'*The barn. I saw.*'

'What happened there? Can you tell me what happened there?'

'*I saw her,*' she said.

For a second no one moved, then Loo's head jerked back as she reached out for Bee, only Bee, Issy's camera whirring as Loo flung herself at her sister.

'*I saw her. I saw her. I saw what she did.*'

She fell into Bee's arms, burying her face against her neck and shutting her eyes, and Bee pulled her close, her fingers pressing hard into her skin, hard enough to bruise.

29

Now

They sit cross-legged on the living-room floor.

'Do we hold hands, or what?' says Hal.

'No. We just . . . sit. The point is to be open, receptive,' says Lucy.

He can't quite believe he's doing this, filming himself doing this, no less. He looks at Nina and Lewis, who have already settled themselves into attitudes of solemn expectation; it's ridiculous really, a joke.

'Think about the state you were in before, on the sofa, listening but not trying to listen,' says Nina.

'To be honest, I was just trying to tune Lewis out.'

'Cheers.'

'Sorry.'

'Well, this time, try to tune us all out,' says Nina.

At first Lewis is bored.

Then he's cold.

Then he's cold and bored.

He had begun by closing his eyes, breathing deeply, listening, but had quickly found that sitting cross-legged was uncomfortable and felt slightly ludicrous.

He opens his eyes. Nina is to his left, chin up, eyes closed, still. To his right sits Lucy. She's shrugged off her coat and is

325

sitting quietly, her head dropped forward, loose strands of hair sweeping down over her face.

Opposite Hal is watching him. He looks . . . sceptical.

Lewis shifts his weight cautiously. He can't honestly say that he feels the atmosphere is especially charged, but he doesn't want to be the first person to break the mood. It's getting dark in here, even though it's only early afternoon. But there's no natural light, after all, just the black plastic sheeting stretched over the empty window pane. He doesn't like that, the lack of light. He finds himself hoping they'll stop soon, that they won't be sitting there for too long in the dark.

Lucy can't be sure she's hearing anything at all, not at first.

Footsteps pattering up and down the staircase.

'Who's there?' she says and the sound stops.

From where she sits Lucy can see into the empty hall – they were careful to leave the door open, to leave all the doors in the house open. A stair creaks. Silence.

The trick is to tune everything out, to let go. Only she can't. She won't. She's painfully aware of the sofa against her back and the damp air surrounding them, of their inexperience, their innocence. It's just a story in a book to the rest of them.

She'll put on a show, she'll go through the motions and when they don't make contact, then they'll pack up and leave, and this time she won't come back. It's not much of a plan, but it's the best she's got. All she has to do is concentrate on keeping it out, keeping her out, whoever she is.

Hal decides he'll give it five more minutes, then they can all get up and pack away their gear and they'll be done. Now he's thought about it, he's pretty sure that's what Lucy is hoping for. This comforts him.

326

He has got past being embarrassed, being uncomfortable; it's actually helped, sitting here like this, waiting. Whatever is going on, whatever is here – and he's willing now to admit that perhaps not everything can be explained or be reasoned away – it's still not something they can talk to, or interact with. It's not something they can make sense of.

The business earlier on the sofa, that was just a dream, a particularly vivid dream. Tib, whoever she was, doesn't care about them. Hal stretches his neck and lets his head hang forward. Tib's not going to talk to them, and the other stuff – as if on cue, the knocking in the girls' bedroom starts up – it's just so much window-dressing.

Party tricks.

Did he say that out loud?

Maybe they should go upstairs, see what all that noise is about. He opens his eyes.

The others have vanished.

Hal should be afraid, but he's not. He stands and brushes the dust off his jeans.

He's

He's

He'll go and find them and then they can get out of here. He opens the living-room door and steps out into the darkened hallway. He must have been sitting there for much longer than he realised.

'Hey!' It's an effort to shout. He clears his throat and tries again. 'Hey!'

This time there's an answer.

'Hal?' Lucy. She must be in her room. Her old room.

He takes the stairs slowly. He's alone, but he has the feeling he's being followed. He even stops once, turning to look behind him, but there's no one there, just the carpeted stairs falling away into the shadows.

'Hal, where are you?'

Here.

He goes into the bedroom. It's dark in here too. The door knocks back against the girls' bunk beds. There's a figure there, huddled on the bottom mattress, underneath the blankets, crying.

The poor little cow.

The curtains by the window stir lazily, and he can see someone standing there, someone else.

'Where are you?'

I'm here.

'What's your name?'

Hal.

Behind him, the figure on the bed sniffs. She's crying.

'Oh, shut up.'

He can't tell who said that. He steps closer and the room seems to stretch out in front of him, dusty bare boards give way underfoot and the window is bigger somehow, taking up the whole wall.

'It's all your fault,' says the girl and now there are two of them, hand in hand. The taller girl reaches up and pulls the curtains open and the sun, the blazing sun, fills the room, dazzling him.

'Your stupid bloody game.'

It's the unshaded light bulb, of course, although why it should be burning so very brightly puzzles him for a moment.

He's lying on the floor.

Shit.

Lucy is leaning over him, her hand wrapped around his. He shuts his eyes and the buzzing in his head recedes a little.

'Can you sit up?'

'Sure.' He's pretty certain this is a lie, but he gives it a go anyway. Nina and Lewis are staring at him. The Sony, he notices, is no longer on the tripod under the window; someone has placed it on the floor, next to him.

'Switch it off,' he says.

But no one moves.

'What happened?' he says.

Lucy slowly releases his fingers. 'Can't you remember?' she says. It's a trick question, she's testing him.

'I had a dream. It felt like a dream.'

Another one.

It's darker now and a sudden gust of wind strikes the plastic sheeting at the window which bulges then shrinks, a black lung, sucking, wheezing. Hal leans across and switches off the camera.

'We got it on video,' says Nina, 'if you want to see.'

On the screen it's Lucy who speaks first.

'Hal. Hal, can you hear me?'

He doesn't answer; he just shakes his head absently.

'Shit,' says Lewis and he and the others scramble across the floor to him.

'Hal?' Lucy reaches towards him as a door upstairs slams shut.

Nina gets to her feet and for a moment she is all Hal can see as she approaches the camera, then the room tilts and sways as she vanishes, picking the camera up and turning it on the three of them.

'What do we do now?' she asks, out of shot.

Hal finds that the best way to view the footage is professionally, looking at the framing, the quality of the image and the sound.

'What do we do now?' asks Nina again. She keeps them both in frame, just him and Lucy. He doesn't answer when Lucy says his name, not at first, but after a while . . .

'Can't you get it any louder?' he says, tapping on the mouse pad.

'No.'

He can't make it out. He's speaking, mumbling; Lucy is listening intently.

'What am I saying?'

'Something about a game?' says Lewis.

On-screen the mumbling stops and the four of them are still again. Lucy is leaning over to speak to him.

It doesn't make sense.

The image wavers briefly as Nina steps in closer.

As Lucy reaches out and takes Hal's hand there's a sharp crack off camera, and Lewis glances over to his right. Hal falls back, limp, and the two of them catch him and lay him down on the floor. Nina finally places the camera there too, close to Hal, too close.

His face fills the screen.

'Hal? Hal?' Nina's voice, they're leaning over him; then something changes, he lies still and the room is quiet again.

She's gone. Just looking at the screen he can tell that she's gone.

'How long was I . . .?' His voice trails away.

'Three minutes? Four?'

'It felt . . . longer. I was dreaming. I was upstairs and she was there.' He looks at Lucy. 'I thought it was you at first.' She looks terrible, her face drained of all colour.

Back on the screen he sits up and moves out of shot. Lucy sits back against the sofa, wrapping her arms around herself.

'Who was there?' asks Nina.

'I can't remember.'

Lucy stands up.

'Sorry,' she says, 'I just need to . . .'

And she walks out of the room.

Hal watches himself reaching out towards the lens then the screen goes blank.

The bathroom hasn't changed much. Someone has replaced the fittings: the bath tub now stands on claw feet and the taps are bulbous things carefully marked hot and cold, but the room itself remains dark and cramped, and the mirror over the sink is still too high and too narrow.

Lucy sits on the edge of the bathtub. She pulls her phone out of her pocket, noting the slight tremor in her hands, and stares at it.

She should ring . . . someone.

She can hear them all downstairs, watching their video, their proof. She feels cold, shivery, as if she's coming down with something. Maybe they have enough now, despite her best efforts.

Maybe they will pack up and go away and the past couple of days will become a postscript in Simon's book and nothing more. She'll agree to an interview, anything they want, if only they'll leave. Surely that will be enough.

She closes her eyes and plays the scene again; she doesn't need Hal's camera and anyway, it's the voice she's trying to conjure up, the feeling that she recognised it.

Recognised her.

Impossible.

'I'll give you everything you want,' says Lucy. 'Interviews, family photos – such as they are, access to Cathy, introductions to my brothers and my sister. Whatever you need to complete your work here.'

They are sitting at the dining table, which is covered with laptops, cables, Nina's notebooks and Lewis' clipboards.

'That's very generous of you,' says Nina. 'Very kind.'

'But we have to go. And we have to go now.' Lucy glances up at the window. The sky is darkening and even if they did as she asked, straightaway with no comment or dispute, she doubts they'd be ready to leave before darkness has fully fallen. It doesn't matter, she tells herself – as long as they get away, as long as they get out of the house.

'No.' Nina's voice is flat, determined.

'Hang on,' says Lewis. 'We need to talk about this.'

'No, we don't, it's a bribe, pure and simple.'

'But we could go, do the interviews,' Lewis smiles encouragingly at Lucy, as if Nina's tone might cause her to withdraw the offer, 'and then come back to do follow-up observations here. It's a terrific opportunity, Nina.'

He might agree at least, Lewis might go along with her, and Hal too, judging by the state of him – it's taken a toll this time, his waking dream, and it's clearly not an experience he wishes to repeat.

'Lucy's not asking us to drop the investigation,' says Lewis.

'Of course not,' says Lucy. 'I'm offering you my help.'

'Then why can't we stay?'

'Because it's – because that's what we agreed, one sitting just like the first time – and – and, and I'm sorry – you're just a group of . . . students.'

'We know what we're doing.' Nina's getting defensive now, and that won't help at all, but Lucy can't work out how to turn the conversation around.

'Well, I certainly don't. It was irresponsible of me to agree to let things get this far.'

'We don't need your permission to be here.'

'I realise that. But if things are getting out of control . . .'

'If things are getting out of control, then maybe that's what we need. If things get out of control then maybe we'll actually get some answers and the last thing we want to do is run away from that.'

Lucy folds her hands in her lap. The urge she feels to hit Nina, to slap some sense into her, appals her and she takes a breath, once, twice. She can do this; she can get them away.

They have been here too long already. She has no choice. 'What if I gave you your answers?' she says. 'What if I told you – everything? Would you leave, with me, right now?'

'I don't understand,' says Lewis.

'New information,' says Lucy. 'Things that Simon didn't write about, couldn't write about. If I told you, would you leave?'

There is a long pause. It seems to Lucy that the house is getting colder. Distantly, at the top of the house a door thuds shut, and she could almost fool herself that Bee will come downstairs to see what's going on, what all the fuss is about.

'Sure,' Nina says. 'If your information is . . . relevant.'

Lucy stands up and goes to the window. She looks out across the village, the valley, the houses picked out by their tiny bright yellow lights. It's getting dark and they still have to get away. She doubts Nina will keep her word, but still she has to try.

'It was a game,' she says. 'It was our game.'

30

Then

It was ages before the grown-ups left them alone. First Michael was hovering around them, asking questions and taking notes, then Olivia crouched down by the sofa and spoke to Loo in her soft voice, reassuring her, telling her how brave she'd been. Last of all Cathy had appeared with a glass of lemon barley water, cloudy and sour, and through it all Loo lay on the sofa. It was like being ill, the way everyone fussed over her; everyone except Bee.

But at last the grown-ups decided they needed to have a talk about what to do next, and because no one had thought to ask her what she wanted to do, they'd left Loo behind in the living room.

'Bee can keep an eye on you, can't you, Bee?' said Simon. Bee had pretended to be fed up, and Simon had smiled and teased her and, in the end, she'd agreed and he'd gone off with the others looking pleased with himself.

He closed the door carefully, so as not to disturb Loo, and the two of them listened until they were sure everyone was in the kitchen.

'God,' said Bee, pushing Loo's legs out of the way and flopping down onto the sofa, 'you messed that up, didn't you?'

'Shut up . . . they'll hear you.'

'You shut up.' Bee's bony fingers found a soft spot on Loo's arm and she nipped her, hard. 'Shut up, shut up, shut up, shut up.'

'Don't!'

'What was all that rubbish about the barn for?'

'It wasn't rubbish. Dan said make something up, so I did.'

'About the house, stupid, about poor old Tib and her wicked mother.'

Loo stood up and went to the open window, sticking her head out cautiously. There was no sign of Dan or Flor. 'Do you think she'll stay now?' she asked. 'Do you think she'll try again?'

'Olivia?'

'Yeah.'

'Dunno.'

Loo would have liked to go outside, sit in the garden, or go for a walk, but she didn't think Bee would let her. 'I'm hungry,' she said, sliding down the wall and closing her eyes.

Bee didn't answer and for a while Loo just sat still, thinking about the stuff Olivia had said, about relaxing and opening her mind, but mostly she just listened to the sounds of the garden, the road, and the valley beyond. They would all go soon, she realised, Olivia, Michael, Simon, even Issy, and she had that sad, back-to-school feeling she used to get.

'The barn,' said Bee again, as if she couldn't quite believe it. 'You're bloody useless, you are.'

Cathy was leaning back against the sink, her arms crossed, frowning, as Michael continued to speak in a low, determined voice about breakthroughs and scientific method, and the best course of action. Simon was standing to one side, still holding the recorder; he would have liked to play the tape back, check that he'd got it all – he didn't even want to think about the consequences of messing that session up – but it was best perhaps to wait until Michael and Cathy were done. He watched the boy, Flor, push his way into the circle of grown-ups.

'Mum.'

'Not now, Florian.' Cathy placed a hand on his head absently, barely noticing when he shrugged her off and made his way to the table, grabbing at the bread she had left out.

'Here, I'll do that.' Simon put the tape recorder on the table, picked up a knife and cut inexpertly at the slightly stale loaf. The resulting slice was uneven, but at least the boy hadn't lost a finger getting his tea. He retrieved the butter from the fridge, it was too hard, it caught at the soft bread and tore holes in it, but Florian didn't seem to mind. He snatched it up and began to eat, scattering crumbs over the table.

'You're welcome,' said Simon.

'I don't understand, I don't understand where she's getting all of this from. Has it been here all along? In the house?' said Cathy.

'It would seem so,' said Olivia.

'It's got worse, you've all made it worse—'

'Not at all,' said Michael. 'What's been happening here, it's a kind of miracle.'

Cathy's laugh, short, harsh, bitter, stopped him in his tracks. 'You said you would help her.'

'Lucia is clearly very sensitive, very gifted,' said Olivia, 'and it would be irresponsible of us to go now and to leave her to try to cope with this on her own.'

'No,' said Cathy. 'If you really wanted to help, you'd make it stop. But you don't, because you need it. All the noise and the confusion and the fuss.'

'Nobody likes seeing you or the girls upset,' said Michael.

'But you don't really mind it either, do you?' said Cathy. 'It's all research to you. All material for the book.'

'That's not true.'

'I honestly think you need to let us try again to contact Tib, to see if we can bring this to a natural conclusion,' said Olivia, stepping forward, taking control. 'It doesn't do to ignore these things, Cathy, and to be honest, once I leave Longdale, I'm not entirely sure when I'll be able to come back.'

There was a silence, broken only by Florian kicking softly at his chair as he ate his bread and butter.

'No,' said Cathy. 'I've had enough. I want you to go.'

'I really don't think that's the answer,' Michael said.

'I don't care what you think.' Cathy went to the door. 'I want you to leave. Right now.'

Isobel lit the gas under the kettle.

'They have to go, don't they?' said Cathy. 'They have to respect my wishes.'

The others had left the house, at least, and were gathered under the shade of the apple tree in the garden. Michael, Olivia and Simon.

'Of course they do,' said Issy. Although, of course, none of them were going anywhere, not until Cathy had calmed down a bit, or not until they were sure she was OK, that's how they'd put it. They had agreed to wait outside while Cathy discussed things with the family, with Issy too.

It wouldn't do, the professor had said, to rush such an important decision.

Cathy had called the girls in from the living room and they sat at the table, a plate of bread and butter in front of each. Dan was leaning on the scullery door, watching his mother.

'Cathy,' said Isobel.

'Don't.' Cathy placed a bowl of apples on the table, turned back to the sink and began filling glasses with water. 'Just don't.'

'Cathy,' Dan said. 'Sit down for a minute.'

'I just have to—' She turned to the table, water slopping over her hands and onto the floor as she stopped suddenly, as if she had forgotten where she was and what she was doing. Dan pushed himself away from the door. 'Here,' he said, taking the glasses from her. 'Do as you're told.'

Between them, he and Issy got Cathy to sit, they cut more bread and butter for Flor and Loo and refilled their glasses, they made a pot of tea; even Bee helped, fetching milk from the fridge and clean mugs from the draining board.

'Can we take some tea outside,' Loo asked, 'for Michael and Simon?'

'No,' said Cathy. 'Not right now.'

Loo looked out of the open door; they were still sitting under the tree, talking quietly. She couldn't see Olivia anywhere. She must have gone for another walk.

'They have no idea what it's been like,' said Cathy. 'Not really. None of you do. I'm sorry, Issy, but you don't.'

'No, I know.'

'They said they could help, but they haven't – they've made it worse.' Cathy looked around the room, at the children. 'We can't carry on like this. They say they want to help and you think they're listening and then they just – they just do what they want.'

'I know.' Isobel picked up the teapot and began to pour. 'I understand.'

Outside, they played the tape while they were waiting. The second time Michael had Simon pause it occasionally so he could make notes. Olivia had wandered off to explore the garden, such as it was, which was a pity as Michael would have liked more of her opinion on the voice, on the exact nature of this contact: was it a warning or an echo? He made a note of the question in his book, underlining it carefully.

'Are they OK, do you think?' Simon asked, looking up at the house.

'I'm sure they're fine,' said Michael. 'I'm sure Isobel will be able to smooth things over.'

'I don't want them to go,' said Loo. 'I like them.'

'They're OK,' said Bee, 'I suppose.'

'Dante?'

Cathy had told them they could help decide. They didn't have a vote, she wasn't daft, but they could say what they thought.

'I don't know,' said Dan slowly. 'But if they reckon they can help, make it all stop, and if Bee and Loo want to keep going, then I suppose it's OK.'

'We're finished,' said Bee, pushing her plate to one side.

'Can we go out to play?' said Loo.

'No,' said Cathy. 'I don't want you out of my sight.'

'They'll be all right, you know,' said Issy, 'if they stay in the back garden.'

Cathy looked out of the window. They were still there, Michael and Simon. 'I don't think so,' she said.

'We could talk, then,' said Issy. 'You know? Properly?'

Cathy considered this. 'Only if you take Florian too, and you stay where I can see you,' she said as the two girls stood, scraping their chairs back across the floor. 'And Dan's in charge.'

'No,' said Dan. 'I want to stay here with you, hear what Issy has to say.'

'It doesn't matter what she says, I won't change my mind.'

'I'm not going to try to change your mind,' said Isobel. 'But maybe you should think about the book.'

Cathy snorted. 'I've heard enough about the blasted book, thank you very much.'

'Bloody hell, Cathy.' Issy put down her cup. 'He's going to get paid for it, at some point, you know. I mean, hasn't it occurred to you that maybe you should get something too?'

'I'm not sure. I mean – we asked him to help. I don't think I could ask him for money too, could I?'

'Well, I'm going to.'

'But that's different. This is your job.'

'And the newspapers paid, didn't they?'

'A bit. Not much.'

'Well, then.'

'We should get paid too,' said Bee.

'Get rid of them if you want, Cathy,' Issy went on. 'But you should come to some sort of financial arrangement, while you can. You should settle that with Michael and the Society now, before they leave.' She raised her cup, drinking back the dregs of her tea as Flor climbed down from his chair, knocking his way past her.

'Ow.' Issy jerked forward, spitting her tea back into her cup and over the table.

'Florian,' Cathy said. 'Mind Isobel. Say sorry.'

'Sorry.'

Issy didn't seem to hear. She pushed her chair back and ran to the sink, her hand cupped under her mouth; she leant over coughing and spitting.

'What's wrong?' Cathy stood too. 'Did it go down the wrong way?'

Issy shook her head, her lips suddenly darker now, her fingers

341

and chin too, smeared with red spittle. Cathy looked down into the sink. 'Dan,' she said. 'Go and get Michael. Go and get him now.'

'What's wrong?' Loo asked. Issy started to cough again, she looked like she might be sick. Loo peered into the sink and saw that in the bottom of the cracked ceramic, by the plug, lay two narrow slivers of sharpened glass, gleaming scarlet in the sunlight.

'It's from a light bulb, I think,' said Simon. He had retrieved the glass and laid it out on the draining board.

'How did it get there, though, into Isobel's cup?' Cathy looked as though she might faint.

'We've discussed this,' said Michael, 'the removal and appearance of small objects in poltergeist activity.'

'Apport,' said Loo. 'That's the word.'

'Shut up, Loo,' said Dan, softly.

Issy was sitting by the kitchen table, a towel pressed against her mouth. There had been a lot of blood, but she'd been lucky, just a cut lip and a scratch inside her cheek.

'But it's never actually hurt anyone before,' said Cathy. 'I mean, not like this.'

'Well, it's entirely possible Tib doesn't understand that her actions have consequences,' said the professor. 'That despite this unfortunate incident, she still means you no harm.'

'Or maybe she does,' said Bee, smiling at Issy.

'If we made contact, of course,' said Michael, 'we would know for sure.'

Cathy went to the sink, turned on the tap and rinsed it out again, even though it was clean, even though she told the kids off all the time for wasting water. Her hands were shaking and they were all waiting for her to decide. 'I need to talk to Joe,' she said.

342

'Of course,' Olivia said. 'You go and ring him and talk it over. We can wait while you do that.'

Cathy seemed surprised by this response, as if she'd been expecting a fight. She dried her hands and noticed a spray of fine red spots on the tea towel. She'd have to soak it. 'I need my purse,' she said, running her hand through her hair.

'Here.' Olivia picked up the bag Cathy always kept hanging on the back of the door. 'Would you like me to walk down into the village with you? I'd be happy to talk to Joe as well, if you think that might help.'

'I could give you a lift,' said Simon.

'No. I'm fine, I'll walk,' said Cathy, looking around again, as if she was a stranger, seeing it all for the first time. 'Would you just – keep an eye on the children? I won't be long.'

Florian wasn't supposed to walk into the village on his own, but he reasoned that with his mother in front of him, he wasn't really alone. And he'd keep an eye out for cars. He wasn't stupid.

Anyway, if she looked back, he'd just run up to her and ask if he could go with her. She wouldn't send him home. He could probably do that anyway, run up to her now and grab her hand and she might be cross but she wouldn't take him back. But Flor decided to stick with following. It was more exciting that way.

'You're going undercover, Flor,' Dan had said, taking him out into the garden once Cathy had set off, making a pretence of babysitting him. 'You're a man on a mission.' He had sounded funny, sort of serious and sort of like he was taking the piss.

The grown-ups thought he was a baby, a bloody baby, and if he was tugging at Cathy's skirt and asking for a drink of water while they were all in the kitchen having one of their meetings

343

they thought he didn't understand what they were saying. But he was nearly seven. He knew what was going on.

Cathy walked past a couple of women in the village, standing in the street, but Flor couldn't hear what she said to them. She kept on walking anyway and didn't look back. He smiled at the women and hung around by the shop, as if he was looking in the window at the display of sweets and biscuits and packets of tea, but really he was watching Cathy reflected there, pulling at the door of the phone box.

'Are you all right, pet?' said one woman. He didn't answer, just nodded and gave her the blank stare that worked so well with the grown-ups at the farm. She went off, whispering something to her friend that made them both look back at him, but he didn't mind, he was trying to see what Cathy was up to. He decided to risk getting a bit closer and he crossed the road to the War Memorial.

He could see her from there. She was inside the kiosk, but she wasn't talking to anyone. Instead she was standing with both hands clasped on top of the phone, her head down, crying.

31

Now/Then

'Liar,' says Nina. 'You're a fucking liar.'

'Yes,' says Lucy.

'You'd say anything to stop us, wouldn't you? Anything to get us to leave. This is all such bullshit.'

'You couldn't have,' says Lewis. 'You couldn't have fooled them for all that time. You were just a couple of kids.'

'But we did,' says Lucy. 'I'm sorry, but we did and it wasn't even that difficult.'

Lewis stands up. He's still holding the camera, but absently, without bothering to focus it on Lucy or anyone else in the room.

'It was Dan's idea, really, I think. Dan and Bee's anyway,' says Lucy. 'He had a book. We had so many books, they were the only things we had too many of, looking back. Anyway, he had one about famous cases – mediums, and ghosts, and it gave a sort of history of the supernatural. We read about the Fox sisters, about the spirit rappings and them being mediums, fake mediums, and the way they fooled everyone. Dan thought it sounded like fun.'

It'll be a laugh, Loo, don't be a spoilsport.

'Dan?' says Nina.

'Yes.'

The room is getting darker now, Lucy notices, and as if he's heard her, Hal stands and switches on the light. She had known it would be difficult to tell the truth, or at least part of it, the part they needed to hear, after all these years. What she hadn't reckoned on was their disbelief.

'Before we moved up here, in our old house, Bee and I had our own rooms. She and Dan were much closer in age, they were both in their teens, they went to the same school for a bit. It was always the two of them together and they always had this – attitude. They were cool, I suppose.'

As thick as thieves.

'Well, that's how it seemed to me. They liked the same books, the same bands. And they used to like winding Cathy up. They hated that we'd moved away from their friends and Bee hated having to share with me. She hated being lumped in as one of the girls.'

She's starting to babble now, but she wants to get to the end of her confession, to get it over and done with.

'But they let me join in with them for this, for the game. They needed me, and we found it worked for us, in the end. No one ever questioned the age gap. We had a dressing-up box and we found all these old clothes in the scullery.'

She hasn't thought about that in a long time, the way they looked then, the way the clothes felt.

'We started dressing in matching outfits. We'd seen those old photos, the ones of Alice Liddell and her sister – you know, *Alice in Wonderland* – and the more people looked at us, just the two of us, the less attention they paid to the boys.'

'Florian as well?' asks Lewis.

'Yes.'

He had been so keen, delighting in spying on the grown-ups, in being allowed to join in for once; Cathy hadn't stood a chance.

346

Nina is standing by the fireplace, silent, bereft.

'Anyway, the police officer came and then Isobel turned up,' Lucy says.

'You can't have faked it all,' says Lewis. 'What about the thing with the marbles?'

She should have realised, they won't take her story on trust; they're going to want details, too many details when there isn't enough time.

'The boys, Florian and Dan, were outside the window. It was always the boys, throwing things, moving things. They had catapults, heavy-duty ones that could fire stones and pebbles.'

Or marbles.

'And that summer, we always had the windows open.'

'What about the police officer?' says Nina. 'He saw the chair move. What about that first night?'

'Please,' says Lucy. 'We don't have time for this.' She needs them to pack everything up and get as far away from the farm as they can.

'No,' says Nina. 'You tell me. You tell me what you did.'

Loo was sitting at the kitchen table eating a piece of toast and reading. The back door was open and Cathy was outside collecting the laundry, unpegging it, folding it into rough quarters and dropping it into a blue plastic laundry basket. It was supposed to be Bee's job, but she had vanished not long after tea. Cathy drew back suddenly, inhaling sharply, rubbing at her arm, and Loo tried to concentrate on the print on the page in front of her.

Bee was upstairs in the bedroom then, crouched down under the window ledge most likely, just in case Cathy thought to look up. Ever since Joe had left, both girls had become adept at flicking tiny pebbles and bits of gravel at unsuspecting targets

347

in the garden below; it had to be someone's fault, after all, that he had gone. Someone had to pay. The hardest bit was ducking out of sight, giving up the chance to see your victim inspecting their skin, looking round the garden, puzzled, wondering what might have stung them.

Loo closed her book and got herself a glass of water, trying not to look as though she was checking up on Cathy. She downed it all in one go; the water made her throat ache, left her breathless. Her mother kept an old shaving mirror on the ledge behind the sink and next to it she had left a lipstick. Cathy wasn't one for makeup as a rule; the tiny gold cylinder looked out of place as it glowed in the late evening sun. Loo rinsed her glass and put it gently on the draining board. Still keeping a careful eye on her mother she picked up the lipstick and left the room.

The plan was to wait until Cathy had put Flor to bed and Flor was under strict instructions not to complain or whine.

'Just ask for a story and listen like a good little boy,' Bee had said. 'Keep Cathy busy until Dan gets back.'

'But I won't know when he gets back.'

Flor was being thick on purpose, he had a clock in his room, he could tell the time.

'Till half past seven, then. All right?'

'All right.'

Misdirection, Dan had called it. They were going to get Cathy to look the wrong way. It would be a laugh.

Serve her right, Bee had said, for what she'd done.

The game involved a lot of rules. One was if you were out of the way, on your own, knock on the walls or the banister. If you were upstairs you could bang on the floor, but that was hard, because of the carpets, not as effective, Dan said.

348

You could slam the doors too; the hard bit there was getting away quickly then making it look as if you were as puzzled as everyone else. Cathy had been irritated at first – she'd thought they were messing about, but she couldn't prove it. But as they'd gone on with the game, and neither Bee nor Dan seemed to be getting tired of it, the irritation had been replaced by something else.

She had a lot of books, did Cathy. Art books mostly, but a lot about what she liked to call the spiritual life, too. What Dan called hippy bollocks, which made Bee laugh. And they did a good job of being visibly afraid, all of them; even Bee, now and then, managed to cling to her mother, burying her face in her neck, seeking comfort. And gradually, Cathy had become afraid too.

The plan was for a grand finale.

Dan would come in at his usual time, he'd go upstairs and start playing his music, and if there was music playing, then it followed that he must be in his room listening, right? The girls would go to bed as usual, and once Flor was settled for the night the three of them would start the knocking.

'I don't like it,' Loo said, curled up in the corner of her bed, so far back Cathy had to kneel down to reach in to her. And that bit was true: she didn't like it. Even though she knew it was only Flor or Dan knocking on the walls, it still scared her. Besides, there would be such trouble when Joe got back.

Downstairs the living-room door slammed shut, making her jump.

'There's nothing to be frightened of, sweetheart.' Cathy was practically crawling into bed with her, on her hands and knees, her back to the door, while above her, on the top bunk, Bee raised herself slowly and silently onto her knees, her hands filled with marbles, and once she was sure her mother was fully distracted she let them fly.

They hadn't expected the policeman, but still, they stuck to their plan.

The phone was still working then, at the beginning of the summer, and they had huddled in the living room, Loo and Bee, as Cathy had stood in the hall, clutching the receiver, insisting that someone come out to the farm. Immediately. She'd shouted up to Dan to come and help too and when he'd appeared in the hall, barefoot, pretending to be annoyed, she'd told him to put some shoes on, to go and take a look around outside.

'What for?' he'd asked, making a bit of an argument about it.

'Just do as I say, please.'

And he'd pulled on his work boots and gone out of the back door.

'I don't want to,' Loo had said to Bee, hanging back by the door as Cathy paced up and down the hall, glancing up at the ceiling, waiting for goodness knows what to happen next. She'd never seen her mother like this before, it didn't feel right.

'Don't be daft,' Bee said softly, glancing into the living room. 'Don't be so bloody wet.'

'Oh, God.' Cathy was standing by the stairs. 'Florian, Antonella.'

'I'll check on them,' said Bee, pushing past her mother. 'I'll be quick.'

'I'm thirsty,' said Loo, just as they'd planned, and she took her mother by the hand and led her into the kitchen.

They had seen PC Thorpe once or twice in the village. The first time he'd thought they were truanting and had walked them back to the house, making dark threats about parents and head teachers and the law. Cathy had refused to let him in, and it had only been when Joe had appeared behind her, filling up the hall, that the copper had accepted her assertion that her children were being home schooled.

She practically dragged him inside this time, and Loo was scared now, properly scared, because she was sure once the policeman found out what they'd been doing they'd really be in trouble.

She wanted to hold her mum's hand. She wanted to cry.

Bee and Loo followed the adults upstairs.

'It's just the four of you then?' the policeman asked. 'You, your – husband and the two girls.'

'My husband's away,' said Cathy.

'Flor and Anto are asleep,' said Bee. 'I looked.'

'My son Dante is here,' said Cathy. 'He's checking outside.'

Dan had been busy, before Cathy called him downstairs. In the girls' room the wardrobe doors hung open, the drawers were pulled out and their clothes, pretty much all they had, were draped around the room and scattered on the floor.

The window was wide open and the net curtain flapped lazily in the breeze.

Loo couldn't help it. It all looked so – scary. She grabbed hold of her mother's hand.

'It wasn't like this,' said Cathy. 'It wasn't. My God, who did this?'

He made them wait downstairs while he searched the house. That was the worst bit. Loo was sure that he'd find some sort of clue Dan had left behind, or see that the shape in Flor's bed was a bolster covered by a sheet. The idea, pinched from a book,

351

that she'd thought so clever now seemed obvious and childish, but Dan – who had kept just out of sight in the garden – told them later that the policeman wasn't much of a detective, he'd barely searched the house at all. They'd spooked him good and proper, him and Cathy both.

'There's no one here, you're quite safe.' The policeman hadn't spotted anything, and now she was sure of that Loo felt much better.

'No.' Cathy stood in the centre of the room, her back to the fireplace. 'You don't understand. There's something here, there's a – presence.'

'Well.' The policeman was starting to look uncomfortable. That'll teach him, Loo thought suddenly, that'll teach him to go on at us about the truant officer, the kid-catcher. 'Well, that may be, but it's not something I can do anything about. Have you thought of the vicar, perhaps?'

Behind Cathy the chair shuddered, and began to shift a little across the carpet.

'Look.' Loo pointed at the chair, just as they'd rehearsed, giving Flor his signal. 'Look at that.'

'He saw it move,' says Lucy. 'Flor was squashed underneath it and he could make it shake, could make it slide a little way over the carpet – and after that people couldn't help themselves, they told stories, they embellished . . .'

This is not what they want to hear.

'. . . and the reporter they sent, not Issy, this bloke from the *Gazette* once they'd got interested – I don't think he ever believed us at all, I think he just wanted a good story so he elaborated too, I suppose. And that was the version everyone read, you see, everyone seems to forget that, and it coloured everything that came after. We were going to stop, but after the policeman came, after Isobel turned up, then Michael, Simon . . . Whatever we did seemed to fit in with that story and the ones that followed. No one was really interested in verifying what had happened. They just wanted a headline.'

'My father wanted more than that,' says Nina.

'He was very kind,' says Lucy. 'He was, truly. But you have to remember it was Michael Warren who was in charge, and he set the tone, I suppose. And it was so much easier to fool someone who wanted to believe.'

'And all the time it was Dan and his brother shoving the furniture around while everyone kept an eye on you,' says Hal.

'Yes, largely. We didn't always know what someone might do. We didn't always plan it. If we saw a chance, any of us, we took it.'

Messing up the house, the bedroom.

Tearing up her books and scattering them across the carpet; she'd never been sure who had done that.

Everything in pieces, beyond repair.

'It was our job – mine and Bee's – to make sure no one ever looked the wrong way: to keep their attention on us. We stole stuff, we switched things around, we eavesdropped on the grown-ups,' says Lucy. 'Sometimes Dan was out at work, but sometimes we just said he was. No one ever checked up on that. And when it seemed we might run out of ideas, we could look in Simon's books – he just left them lying around in the tent. We could work out what they wanted, him and Michael, how a haunting was supposed to go.'

And everyone was so willing for it to be true, that was the real trick to it, it wasn't hard at all, and once you know the method, as with most illusions, it is disappointingly obvious.

Here it is, the great secret of her life, and now it's out in the open it's a poor pathetic thing.

'And you fooled them all,' says Lewis.

'Yes.'

'Even Simon?'

Lucy glances up at Nina. 'Yes. I think he believed us. I'm not sure about Issy; she used to get this look on her face some-times, towards – towards the end – when Bee was being particularly dramatic, or – or when I did Tib's voice.'

'No,' says Nina.

'That was you?' asks Lewis.

'Yes,' says Lucy, her mouth dry, wishing she'd never begun this, wishing she could get to the end of it. 'We read about mediums producing ectoplasm and we knew we'd never get away with that, but there were some who could channel spirit voices . . . We all tried it, ventriloquism. Dan was pretty good, but he wanted to stay – behind the scenes. Bee was dreadful, I was better . . . which isn't really saying very much. I always leant forward and let my hair fall over my face. Sometimes I even covered my hand with my mouth, especially if I was nervous.'

'Where did you get the name from?' Nina asks.

'I don't know.' Lucy feels as though she may cry now. 'It just – came out one day. I must have got it from a book.'

'Did Cathy know?' asks Lewis.

'God, no. That was the whole point. She hadn't a clue.'

It had been funny at first. Losing your marbles, Dan had said, when they were planning it all, making Bee laugh until she could barely breathe, until she went scarlet in the face, sucking greedily at her inhaler, swearing at Dan for setting her off.

Lucy can't bear to look at them any longer. She goes to the

window; she can see the road, and their cars parked in front of the house, but the valley is fading into the dark.

'So.' Nina's voice is low, but steady. 'You go along with us for the whole weekend just so you can, what? Make sure we don't get anywhere? Keep us from the truth? And then when we do make a breakthrough, when it turns out we don't need you any more, when it turns out there is something here after all—'

'Nina,' says Lewis.

'Because there is, isn't there? You may be a fucking liar, but we're . . . The stuff we've got, on video, on tape – that's not us. And it's not you either, is it?'

Lucy doesn't reply.

'Is it?'

'Come on,' says Hal. 'Please.'

'It won't work,' says Nina. 'We're not going anywhere.'

'Why?' says Lucy. 'What is so very important that you need to stay? I'm offering to tell the truth.'

'But you're not,' says Nina. 'You're lying. You're still lying. Even now.'

The photos, Lucy thinks, too late.

'Because that's not the whole story, is it?'

'My dad was planning to retire,' says Nina, going through her father's folders, sifting through the black and white prints and the contact sheets, and her father's typewritten notes, spilling them onto the table, arranging and rearranging them. 'He wanted to donate his work, all the cases, to the Society's archive. So, he was going through it all. And he was doing that, and—'

Nina pushes her fingers into her hair and looks at them all, refusing to cry. 'It was very sudden,' she says, 'and things were a bit – difficult for a while. Anyway, after the funeral, I was sorting out his files, and I found Isobel's pictures – all these pictures – and I could see that it didn't make sense.'

She spreads out the contact sheets, picking through them. 'There's so much material, that's the problem. You see – here, that's the séance in the living room, just before it, anyway.' She picks up a sheet and examines it before discarding it and picking up another. 'There's stuff taken in all the sessions they ran, loads of random stuff, just of the family.'

'Nina.' Hal stands, places one hand over hers. 'It's OK. We get it.'

'There's too much,' she says, pausing to gather her thoughts. She steps back from the table, from Hal, folding her arms. 'It's in his notes. It's all bits and pieces, stuff that looks like he might have started transcribing tapes, interspersed with a sort of journal he kept, but that was mostly times and dates of the interviews with the girls – and there are Issy's photos. Not many, but it's there.'

She looks at Lucy, straightening her back, raising her voice and aiming for a confidence she doesn't yet feel. 'It's all bits and pieces, really, but there's enough to put you there in the barn, you and Bee, Michael, my dad. Everyone.'

'But that doesn't make sense,' says Lewis, 'the haunting was centred on the house. All the evidence—'

'The haunting was centred on the girls,' says Hal, 'on Bee, and on Loo.'

'I think you ran a second séance but not in the house – up in the barn. And that's when everything went wrong.'

Nina falls silent, and they stand there, the three of them, waiting. The room is cold, and it seems to Lucy that it's darker too, that the light bulb is dimming slowly, and the faint buzz of it is working its way inside her head.

'It that true?' Hal is looking at Lucy. 'They did it again? Another séance?'

356

'No,' says Lucy softly.

They have to go, she thinks. They have to get away while they can.

'Cathy didn't want to,' she says eventually, 'not really, but yes. They did.'

'In the barn, because you said something had happened there.'

'Yes.'

'Why did you say that?' asks Lewis.

'Oh, God, I don't know, I was just . . . Look, can't we just leave? If we pack up now we can go through all of this later. I promise I'll—'

'Why did you say it?' Nina's eyes are bright with tears.

'I don't know, I was just a kid, I was just . . .'

Caught up in it all.

32

Then

Isobel listened as Cathy went through her conditions with Michael and Simon, the latter making notes and managing to give the impression they were setting down some kind of binding agreement.

Every 'yes' and 'I see' seemed to calm Cathy a little more. They could use the barn, the studio, but only once, only this evening, and that was to be the end of it.

Her priority was the wellbeing of their daughters.

They were to talk to Tib with the aim of laying her to rest.

This was no longer an investigation; they were going to rid her daughter of this . . . presence.

Round and round they went, the same fears being voiced, the same responses, edging closer to an understanding.

Olivia was in the garden. Issy could see her through the open door, sitting underneath the tree, her head tilted back, her eyes shut, sunning herself, or meditating, it was hard to say. Her long legs were stretched out, crossed at the ankles, and her skirt had ridden up a little. Issy raised her camera.

As the shutter clicked, Olivia opened her eyes and looked right at her.

'When do you want to start?' asked Cathy.

'As soon as we can, Cathy, don't you think?' said Michael.

*

Loo had given them the slip. She could hear them, thumping up and down the stairs calling her name, and someone, Issy, she thought, had walked right past where she was hiding and through the kitchen into the garden. She had the hazy idea that if they couldn't find her, they wouldn't be able to try again and then maybe Olivia would leave and it would all stop.

'Loo . . . Lucia . . .'

It was cooler in the scullery. She'd tried to reach the jars of jam her mother still kept on the top shelf, but after a couple of half-hearted attempts – kneeling on the lowest shelf and then pulling herself up by her fingertips – she'd given up.

She'd found the newspapers though. They were spread around her on the floor and her fingers were stained grey with newsprint. She liked the photos. She and Bee looked different, as if they might be in a film or on the telly. She wasn't impressed with the stories though – they'd written things she couldn't remember Cathy saying, and things she was certain she would never say in a million years. So there they were, themselves and not themselves, printed onto the paper.

She was just considering another attempt at the high shelf when the door began to move. The latch lifted and as she watched she almost expected to see Tib appear, in her long dark frock and with her sad-angry face. In the newspapers Tib was just as real as Loo and Bee. Sometimes it felt as if Tib wasn't just inside her head; she was outside too, getting stronger, wanting to play her own game now.

The figure at the door looked at her and Loo could feel her heart beating.

'Hello,' said Olivia.

She closed the door behind her and leant against it.

'I was hungry,' said Loo.

360

'I see.' She looked at the papers on the floor. 'Here.' Olivia moved closer, reaching up over Loo's head to produce not only jam, apple and bramble, but a packet of digestive biscuits.

'Thank you.' Loo opened the biscuits and offered them to Olivia. They were a bit stale but they still tasted OK, especially when dipped in the jam.

'We've been looking for you,' said Olivia.

'Are we going to do it again? The séance?'

'Yes. But this time we're going to go into the barn to talk to Tib.'

'Why?'

'Because I think Tib is unhappy and I think the barn is important to her. Is that OK?'

Loo thought about this, about the way Olivia had joined in when Tib was speaking, almost as if she was part of the game too. She nodded. 'Does Michael want to know what happened to her?' she asked.

'Yes, he does.' Olivia took another biscuit and snapped it in two. 'And we'll ask her all about that. But this time, when I talk to Tib, I'm going to help her go away, and when she goes, she won't ever come back.'

'Really?'

'Yes. Would that be all right too? Would you like that?'

'Yes.' Loo didn't even have to think about this question. She dipped a bit of biscuit into the jar, scooping out the clear purple jam. 'Yes, please,' she said.

Michael undid the padlock, and he and Simon pulled both barn doors open. Everyone stood still for a moment, beneath the bright sun, peering into the dark. Issy coughed, cleared her throat, raised her camera.

'Come on, then.' Bee slipped past her and led the way in.

They worked quickly to clear a space by pulling the trestle tables to one side and by stacking, at Cathy's insistence, a dozen or so half-finished canvases by the door, covering them carefully with torn and stained oilcloth.

Issy took a few shots: dusty brushes left propped up in grimy jam jars, a couple of pheasant's feathers wedged in the window pane, a handful of flints left on the sill. Still life.

'Can we go upstairs?' asked Bee, one foot on the ladder that led up to the hayloft, with Loo right behind her.

'No,' said her mother.

Bee pulled herself up onto the first rung, ready to ignore Cathy, filled with a blazing energy that seemed to cut through the gloom, the muscles in her neck and outstretched arm tensed. Ready for a fight.

'We need you here,' said Olivia, and Bee hesitated before stepping down, kicking the ladder hard enough to make it rattle before turning away.

'All right, then,' she said. 'Where do you want us?'

Olivia turned to Loo. 'I'm getting a very strong sense . . . Tib said there was blood on the stones. Did she mean here?'

'I don't know. I think so.' Loo looked at the rough stone floor, the brick remnants of the animal byres. For a moment she could hear it – the double doors above rattling, scraping over the floorboards, a silence, then something crumpling; she could see the blood. Outside, she thinks, the words fluttering away before she can speak, outside on the overgrown flagstones.

'Loo?'

'Yes.'

'Is that right?'

They should go.

They should go.

362

Go now.

'Loo?'

'Yes.'

'Good. Now, I'll tell you again what's going to happen. We are going to talk to Tib, you and I, and we are going to help her understand what happened to her and we're going to help her move on.'

Move on where? Lucy wanted to ask, but Olivia was squeezing her hand so tightly. 'Look at me, Loo. I need you to look at me, I need you to concentrate.'

Where would Tib go?

Dust fell from above as a floorboard settled and Loo wanted to call out to everyone, 'We have to go now', but Olivia's grip was strong and behind her Bee was glaring as if she'd messed it up already. It occurred to Loo that if she did this one thing then maybe Olivia would keep her word and maybe Tib would move on. Even if she didn't want to, maybe Tib would leave her alone. She'd like that.

'Can you do that, Loo? Can you help me?'

'Yes.'

'Good.'

Olivia let go and the blood in Loo's fingers tingled.

'We need to make a circle here,' Olivia said. 'Hold hands and step back and make a circle.'

And as the light grew dim and the shadows lengthened, they did as they were told.

Olivia stood to her right, Bee to her left, then Simon, Cathy and Michael. Bee stretched out a hand and wrapped her fingers around Simon's.

'No, wait,' said Olivia. 'You too, Isobel.' Issy was by the door, her camera, as ever, in her hand.

'Oh, no. Not me.'

'Yes,' said Olivia. 'Please.'

Loo could feel her pulse thumping as Issy decided what to do next. It was coming back, the light floaty feeling from earlier on; she didn't even need to close her eyes this time. Her heart pounded in her chest and she thought that if she let go of Olivia and Bee she might begin to float up above the floor, to rise up above the dusty stones.

Very slowly Issy put the camera down on one of the tables and walked towards the circle. She didn't want to, Loo could tell, but she couldn't find a way to say no. Loo felt sorry for Issy now, sorry for all the times she'd giggled when Bee had said something rude about her behind her back. She could feel the words swelling up inside her, punched out by the rhythm of her heartbeat.

Go now

Go now

Go now

Simon pulled his hand away from Bee and stepped back, making space for Isobel between them. He took her hand and after a moment she stepped into place and held hands with Bee.

The feeling grew stronger and her heart filled her up.

Now

Now

Now

Olivia's voice was softer this time, further away. 'We listen to our breath, to the rise and fall of it, and each breath brings clarity, brings peace, and we can hear you, we can hear you, Tib.'

Loo let her head fall; she licked her lips and to her left Bee

364

squeezed her fingers a little. *Get on with it, stupid.* To her right, Olivia spoke. 'I can see her,' she said.

'Where?' said Michael.

'She's here, she's inside the circle, walking around, looking at us.'

'What does she look like?'

'She's Bee's age, a little older perhaps. She's wearing a long dark dress, but with the sleeves pushed up. She has long blonde hair. She won't stay still, I can't quite . . . She must be cold. She's looking for, for . . .'

A way in, thought Loo.

'A way in.'

'Out, surely? A way out of the circle,' said Michael.

'No. Not that, a way in . . . to speak. Is that it, Tib? Do you want to speak?'

Bee squeezed her fingers again, and Loo let her head fall forward and got herself ready, but the voice, when it came, wasn't hers.

'*Yes.*'

'Tib, is that you?'

'*Yes.*'

Bee was gripping her hand so tightly now, Loo could barely stand it; hot sparks of energy seemed to be pulsing through her fingers, burning her.

Bee to her left, Olivia to her right.

They probably didn't even need to hold hands now, she thought. If they let go, there'd be little lightning strikes crackling between them, like sparklers on Bonfire Night. Olivia could feel it too. Loo was sure she could.

'Can you see her?' Michael's voice was urgent.

'No . . . I . . .' Olivia was breathing heavily; it must have been the effort of holding on to Loo, holding her down. You can let go, Loo thought, it's all right.

It's not me.

'Yes,' said Olivia. 'She's . . . there and not there . . .'

'Tib,' said Michael. 'Where are you?'

'*Here.*'

Her voice was firmer, stronger, nearer. Loo raised her head, half-expecting to see her dancing around in front of her.

It wasn't dark in the barn, not properly dark, and they were all standing holding hands; opposite her she could see Simon and Cathy, and they were looking at Olivia. Olivia looked ill: her eyes were wide, panic-stricken, and her skin was beaded with sweat.

'Do you want to talk to us?' asked Michael.

'*Yes.*'

'She's there,' said Olivia. 'She's . . . she won't stay still.'

'What happened to you, Tib?'

'*I saw. I saw her.*'

'What did you see?'

'*Her.*'

'Who?'

'*Her.*'

'What happened?'

'*With her knife. Sliced. Slashed. I saw.*'

She can feel their excitement, Simon and Michael. This is why they're here, this is what they wanted. She can feel the way it makes Tib stronger.

'Who? Who did she hurt? Why did she do it?' asked Michael.

'*I saw.*'

'Stop it,' said Cathy. 'Stop this now.'

'*I saw her,*' said Tib. '*Bitch. I saw her with her knife.*' She began to laugh. '*I know what you did.*'

'Jesus, no!' Isobel pulled away from the circle. 'For God's sake, Michael, you can't let this go on, she's just a kid.'

'Come back to the circle, Issy,' said Simon, holding out his hand.

'No! It's not right. Why can't you see that it's not right?'

'*Come back to the circle, Issy.*' Tib was making fun of them.

Loo didn't think she could hold on much longer. Her arms ached and her fingers were burning and anyway Isobel had broken the circle and that meant there was a way out now, or a way in.

Tib didn't need her any more.

She pulled her hands free and watched for the sparks to jump from Olivia, to her, to Bee.

Come back

Come back

Come back

Her sister stood with her arms outstretched, grinning, daring Isobel to raise her camera, to capture her image now. She's not herself, thought Loo, a phrase she'd heard her mother use, but never properly understood until now.

'*Come back to the circle, Issy,*' said Bee.

33

Now

'Was there even going to be a new edition of the book?' asks Lewis, looking around the room at their gear, the cameras and the monitors and the laptops.

'No,' says Nina. 'Sorry, Lew. No, there wasn't. He was planning on coming back, that bit was true. I just wasn't sure why.'

'So, you came to the farm instead,' says Lucy.

'Once or twice, yes. I couldn't get into the house, but I had a look around the village.'

'We're supposed to be a team, Nina,' says Lewis. 'You can't just use people.'

'I was going to tell you, I was. But then if we got here and nothing happened . . . And it's – complicated.'

'Oh, of course it is.' He sits down in the armchair, weary suddenly. 'Fuck's sake, Nina,' he says.

'So,' Hal says slowly, 'the question now is, what did Simon Leigh see in all of this that he hadn't seen before?'

'What?' says Nina.

'You said it yourself, you didn't know why he was planning on coming back.' Hal picks up a contact sheet. 'But he knew about the second séance all along, and he'd kept quiet about it for years. He had no reason to come back, unless . . .' He puts the sheet down, picks up another.

'He must have seen something new,' says Lewis.

They clear everything from the table and begin to work methodically, setting everything out in rows, photographs, contact sheets, negatives, trying as best they can to put it all in chronological order.

Nina sees it first. 'Here.'

It's a snapshot of the girls standing by the front gate.

'There's nothing there,' says Lewis. 'Well, there's you guys, obviously,' he glances at Lucy, 'but apart from that, I don't see . . .'

'There's this,' Hal says, pointing to the house. 'This shadow here.' He looks at Nina. 'Is that it?' he asks uncertainly. 'But isn't that Simon? I mean, it could be him.'

Someone caught going out, or going in.

They each pick up the next sheet in the sequence, examining every image frame by frame.

'Bloody hell,' says Hal. 'Here.' He holds out the sheet. The girls are still in the front garden, looking out over the valley. Loo is in the foreground, Bee is behind her and further back . . .

'It could be a trick of the light,' says Lucy. 'The door's open, the hall is in shadow.' She takes hold of the paper. 'It could be Cathy, or Dan, even.'

'Could be,' says Nina.

Lewis finds one too, a smeary shadow looming behind Flor who is crawling across the mat in front of the Aga, absorbed in some private game.

There are more with a shadow that doesn't fit, that flickers in and out of the sequences of images, there and not there.

Taken alone, each photo could be a mistake – poor framing, a miscalculated exposure. But it is always the same mistake, the same shape and angle, as if something is trying to get through. They set them out, then stand back, trying to take it all in.

'Tib,' says Lewis. 'Right? He thought they had managed to photograph Tib, and not realised it. That was why he was going to come back.'

'Jesus.' Hal drops the photos he's been looking at onto the table.

'You said she wasn't real,' says Lewis.

'She wasn't. Not the one you've heard on the tapes, not the one Simon wrote about,' says Lucy. 'That was all me, us.'

'But Simon didn't know that, did he?' says Hal. 'He thought she was real all along, and when he found these photos, he thought he had his proof. Is that it?'

'I don't know,' says Nina. She picks up one of the negatives and holds it up to the light before holding it out silently to Lucy.

She can remember the day these pictures were taken. They had walked up to the tent, and Isobel had taken two or three shots in quick succession of them standing looking back down towards the house. In the negatives their dark hair appears white, their pale clothes heavy and dark. It's the last shot, and she's in the distance, looking away from the camera, towards the two girls. She is quite distinct. Reversed in the negative, a young woman in a white frock, with thick dark hair.

The girl on the video.

She hands the negative to Hal.

He looks at it closely before passing it along to Lewis. Simon's proof, bundled away by Isobel all those years ago. Hal doesn't say anything; he looks sick.

'I don't understand,' says Lewis. 'If you faked her . . .'

'We did,' says Lucy. 'We had made it up, all of it. Only gradually, that summer, things got . . . confused . . . and that last time, it was – different. It had always been me doing the voice, but sometimes . . . once or twice, towards the end, I didn't really feel in control and then, that day in the barn, it wasn't me Tib spoke through. It was Bee. I thought she was cross with me at first. I thought she was messing around.'

34

Then

It was Cathy who spoke first, stretching out a hand to Bee, her voice soft, hesitant. 'Bianca, sweetheart . . .'

'No.' Bee stepped back, out of reach.

'Who are you?' asked Simon.

'I'm Tib.'

She felt them draw back from her, all of them, and it didn't matter that the circle was broken, it had filled her up, let her through and now they'd see, all of them would see. She wanted to dance. She wanted to fly up to the rafters. Maybe she would.

'Who hurt you, Tib?' said Olivia.

'He did. She did.'

Simon was squatting over his tape recorder, making sure that they were getting it, their proof. Isobel picked up her camera, but she wasn't using it; she was clutching it like a little girl with her favourite teddy, as if it might keep her safe.

And Cathy, Cathy was crying.

Serve her right.

'I don't understand, Tib.'

'Go on, go. If you've had enough, go. But don't think I'll take you back.'

'Who said that?

'That . . . bitch and her – her knife . . .'

The barn door, which Simon had so very carefully pushed

back against the wall, slammed shut. Up in the loft space the noise began, a steady pulsing rhythm, a leaden mockery of a heartbeat.

She really could take flight now, and she knew it. She was laughing as Cathy shrank back from her touch; she was unstoppable, invincible.

'Stop it,' said Cathy, looking first at Michael, then at Olivia. 'You said you could stop it.'

She didn't look like Bee any more. She looked . . . more than herself. Not a girl any more. She seemed taller, stronger, fiercer.

'Bee,' Loo said, although she didn't know what to say next. They were going to let Tib go, that's what Olivia had said; but this Tib didn't want to go anywhere.

Her sister stopped and turned slowly. Loo wiped her sweaty hands on her skirt.

'Don't,' she said.

'*Don't*,' said Bee.

Up above them in between the rafters, the thudding went on, louder, faster, enough to shake the floorboards, to rain dust and grime down through the cracks. Loo wanted to tell them to stop, Dan and Flor, but if she did, then they'd be found out and that was still something to fear. She couldn't imagine what they thought they were doing. Surely they'd heard Bee, surely they'd realised something had gone wrong?

'What do you want?' said Michael, raising his voice, conscious they were being recorded, still thinking he was in control.

'*I . . . I . . .*' Uncertainty flickered across Bee's face and the knocking from the attic floor stopped.

The silence that followed held for a moment as they switched places, Bee and Tib, on and off, in and out, and you could only spot the difference if you really looked, if you really knew her, but Loo could tell easily enough. It was all going to be all right, she tried to hold on to that thought, it was just a game, their game.

The click of the shutter snapped the silence, a flash – and Issy never used a flash – blinding them as, shrieking, Bee hauled herself up the ladder and out of sight.

They were all looking at Isobel now. who was looking at the camera in her hand as if it had a life of its own; so there was no one to stop her when Loo climbed up the ladder too.

There were no windows in the loft. It was darker up there and for a second or two Loo was afraid that Bee might have vanished entirely. She stood still, her heart pounding, trying to work out what they were going to do next. Dan should be up here, Flor too; they'd be able to find a way out of this. Behind her the ladder rattled as if someone was testing it, trying to climb up it quietly, trying to catch them out. She ducked down and pushed, not daring to look back as the ladder clattered to the stone floor below and someone, Simon perhaps, swore softly. She hoped he was all right.

'Oh, well done, Loo. How are we supposed to get down now?' Bee's voice drifted from the far end of the loft, where the air was thick and dark.

'They'll put it back,' said Loo. 'Someone will come and fetch us.'

Bee sighed. 'And what will we do then?' she said.

'I don't know.' Loo tried to creep quietly, lightly, across the floorboards. If they thought she was still near the edge, maybe they wouldn't try again, not for a while, and if they stayed downstairs for a bit, then maybe Bee would stop the game of her own accord.

'Where's Dan?'

'Dunno. Don't care. He said he didn't want to play any more. Because of the glass. Bloody Isobel.'

Loo looked around, hoping Bee was wrong. Dan was always able to get Bee to calm down, but there was no sign of him. There were no places to hide; there were a few blankets in a corner, a couple of empty bottles, but that was all, no sign of the boys.

They had made this loft their den this summer, Dan and Bee: they had taken to sneaking away from the house in the evenings, without Loo and Flor. Which was so unfair. Anyway, when he came back Joe would give the pair of them a good hiding and serve them right.

If he came back.

Joe, the father who was there and not there. Bee had told her stories, things she'd seen, things she'd heard, when they thought they were alone. But she was making that up, Loo was almost sure. Didn't Joe always say she was an awful bloody liar? The look on her sister's face when they broke in through the window.

'God, Loo. You are so thick sometimes.'

'Where did you get all that stuff from?' Loo asked.

'What?'

'The story about Tib's mum – that thing about the knife.'

Bee looked at her blankly for a moment or two. 'Nowhere,' she said. 'The same place you got the story about blood on the stones.'

'I made it up,' said Loo. 'It just – came into my head.'

'Yeah, well. Me too.' Bee tapped her skull. 'It just popped up in here.'

But the bit about the knife still bothered Loo.

It had bothered Cathy too.

'What about Cathy and Joe?' Loo asked.

'I told you,' said Bee, sighing, weary. 'I saw her here, down-stairs. I saw both of them, I could hear them too. He said he was going and all she had to do was – be nice to him.' Bee slumped against the double wooden doors at the side of the barn.

Something rapped sharply against one of the wooden beams.

One.

Two.

Three.

'Flor?' said Loo, but there was no answer.

'There's no one here, Loo.'

'Dan?'

'Shut up, stupid. You'll give it away.' Bee looked ill, hot and clammy, strands of her long dark hair clinging to her face.

'What's wrong, Bee?' She felt sorry for her, she looked so . . . lost.

'They were yelling at each other and she picked up a knife.' Bee smiled at her sister, not kindly. 'There was blood everywhere, Loo. You should have seen it.'

'Don't.' She was lying, she knew her sister was lying about the blood, but she wished she'd shut up all the same. 'Please, Bee.'

'Don't call me that. It's not my name.'

'What is your name, then?'

Bee rubbed at her face. Her hands were dusty, and she left long grey grimy streaks across her skin.

'As I was walking on the stair, I met a girl who wasn't there. She wasn't there again today . . .'

'Bee, don't—'

'. . . I wish, I wish she'd go away.'

Loo could hear voices below them, deciding what to do, who to send up the ladder.

'Where are they?'

Dan and Flor should be there, banging on the floor, joining in, just like before. 'Not here.' Bee's answer was punctuated by a sharp crack above their heads as something struck one of the rafters. 'Not here,' she said again and she began to laugh. 'Dan said he didn't want to play any more. He's been a good boy and taken Anto off for a walk. Wanker. Anyway, we don't need them, do we?'

'Bee, don't, let's go back. We'll go down to the village and get some ice cream.'

'What with?'

'We'll ask Simon. He'll pay.'

Bee snorted. 'Him,' she said.

Loo could hear the grown-ups downstairs, her mother's voice, insistent.

Do something.

'Bee.'

'I told you, that's not my name.' As Bee's voice rose the ones below paused. They were listening.

'Who are you, then?' Loo couldn't help herself; they'd played the game for so long this summer, she didn't know how to stop. Bee pushed her hair back off her face, and she stood, a jagged figure in her white dress, pressed against the peeling paint of the wooden door.

'I'm Tib,' she said. 'Poor dead Tibby.'

'You're not dead.'

'Not yet,' said Bee and she turned to the doors and began to lift the heavy wooden latch that held them shut.

'What are you doing?' Loo hoped they could hear her below, she hoped that was the sound of them pulling the ladder upright, banging it back into place. Bee dragged one of the doors open. It moved surprisingly smoothly on its old hinges and somehow the fresh air and light only made the barn seem worse, dark and stifling. Loo backed away from the edge. She didn't like the way the ground lurched away from the walls, the way the bright light tried to fool you into coming closer.

'Poor Tib. No one loved her,' Bee said.

'But we made her up.'

'I made her up.'

'She's not real.'

'She is now,' said Bee, pulling the second door open.

Loo wished Dan was here. He always knew when to make fun of Bee, how to make her laugh and bring her back again when she got like this. All doomy.

'Loo? Are you there? Are you all right?' Simon's voice carried across the loft, low and serious and kind. He was there, at the top of the ladder.

Bee's face darkened.

Not herself.

'He doesn't like you, you know,' she said. 'He thinks you're a little girl.'

'Loo?' said Simon. 'Are you OK?'

Bee grabbed hold of her sister, her bony fingers wrapped around both her arms, and the two of them stood face to face, Bee leaning down, her voice soft and vicious.

'This is all your fault.'

They were close to the edge now, and Bee, taller, stronger, more determined, pulled her sister round, so Loo had her back to the open doors and the dizzying drop beyond. Bee's nails dug into Loo's skin.

Bee shook her, pushing her back a little. It's not such a long drop, Loo told herself, and anyway she doesn't mean it. It's just a game. She remembered another game they used to play, a long time ago, taking it in turns to fall back into each other's arms, letting go and trusting that the other would always be there. The way Bee would wait until the last moment to catch Loo, the fear and exhilaration that she might not. She doesn't mean it.

Simon was closer now. Loo could see him out of the corner of her eye, but she didn't dare turn her head.

Bee would never let her fall.

'Bee,' said Loo. 'Tib.' She felt her sister's muscles tense. Bee was very strong, strong enough to lift her, strong enough to—

'Bee!'

She could hear the panic in Simon's voice as he ran towards them, only a few paces away now, almost close enough to touch, and for a moment, a second, Bee looked unsure and she let go, and he was reaching out now, and Loo could tell it was all going to be all right.

Then she fell.

35

Now

Nina starts to tidy away the pictures. She pauses and looks down at her hands as if she can't control them, as if she doesn't know what she is doing.

'I'm sorry,' she says, and the sheets fall away, tumbling lazily onto the floor. 'I just have to . . .' and she leaves the room.

She doesn't know where she's going. She doesn't even know if she is going. She gets to the front gate and has to decide, turn left and go back down to the village, right and up to the moor. She's still trying to decide when Hal catches up with her.

'You OK?'

'No.' She doesn't go anywhere in the end, she simply leans against his car and crosses her arms, hugging herself as she looks up at the house. 'Fuck's sake, Hal. What am I supposed to do with all of this?'

'I don't know, Nina. I'm sorry, I don't.'

'It was faked. His whole career – his life – based on . . . fraud.'

'But he didn't know that, did he? He thought it was the real thing, that it was some sort of breakthrough.' says Hal. 'And anyway,' he goes on, uncertainly, 'it wasn't all faked, was it? Not if those pictures are right.'

'I don't know,' says Nina. 'I just don't . . .'

He pulls her close. 'It's all right,' he says. 'It's OK.' He can feel the sobs rising inside her and the next thing she says is muffled, indistinct. He releases her a little.

'What did he do?' she says. 'What did he do?'

'I'd give them a minute, if I were you,' says Lucy and Lewis turns away from the window, from the dark figures in the gathering shadows.

'Yes. OK.' He goes back to the table and begins to gather up the sheets, careful to keep everything in chronological order, stacking the folders to one side, glad of something simple to do.

'I think I need to speak to my mother again,' says Lucy, and she slips out of the room.

'Lucia? Are you coming back now?'

Lucy sits on the bottom stair, leans her head against the wall. She could go. She could get into the car and drive to Blue Jacket House now and they could finish this conversation face to face. 'No. I – in a little while,' she says. 'I think there's something we need to do here first.' But when she does leave, she is never coming back. 'There are photos, of the barn – Olivia, us—'

The séance.

'I see.'

'She knows, Mum. They know.'

Up on the first floor something moves across the landing and pauses, looking down at Lucy, waiting. She forces herself to look up, but there's no one there.

'What will they do now, do you think?' asks Cathy.

'I'm not sure. I'm trying to get them to pack up, but they seem pretty determined.' She's almost certain there's no one

382

there. 'But when we're done, we'll be able to talk – you know – properly, about Bee.'

'What are you going to do? Lucia?'

'I think they'll want to go up to the barn, like we did. They'll want to see for themselves.'

'Oh.' Cathy's voice is soft. 'Yes. Of course.'

Lucy hesitates. 'I'm not sure,' she says, 'but I think I should probably stay here, just to – keep an eye on them.'

'Lucia—'

'It's fine, Mum. I don't want you to worry.'

'It never seemed – right,' Cathy says. 'That it all ended so quickly – so carelessly, as if she didn't matter at all. I want you to take care, do you—' She stops speaking abruptly. Someone must have walked in, and Lucy listens to the distant voices, the routine of her mother's life playing out.

'Who's that?'

'It's . . . Sarah.'

'Can you put her on? I'd like a quick word.'

'In a minute. But you have to remember, you have to . . .' Cathy hesitates. Sarah must be close by.

'I know, Mum.' She can think of nothing else to say. 'I'll be careful. Now put Sarah on. I love you.'

There's no response, only dead air, and then Sarah's voice, young and a little uncertain. 'Hello? Mrs Frankland?'

'They were looking out for themselves,' says Nina. 'That's all they cared about in the end, not Loo, not Bee.' She sounds sad, resigned. 'They kept quiet about the séance, about being in the barn, and they left Cathy Corvino to deal with everything that came after all on her own.'

'Surely not. I mean . . . didn't anyone check?'

'Why would they?' she says. 'As far as the police and

ambulance were concerned it was just Cathy and the kids here that day. My dad even put it in his book. He wrote that they had finished their investigation, that and Michael and Olivia were long gone by the time the girls sneaked into the barn to play, and what happened next was an accident, an afterword. That was the official version of events, and no one ever questioned it.'

'Until now.'

'Yes, until now.'

They stand in silence for a while, until the drizzle turns to rain.

'I'm sorry,' Nina says. 'Hal, I'm so sorry.'

'What for, exactly?' Hal could get used to this, the way she fits against him, the frantic thudding of her heart. She moves away from him, turns towards the house

'I think I need to ask another favour,' she says.

When she's finished speaking to Sarah, Lucy stands and makes her way carefully up the stairs, placing her weight deliberately on each tread. She has retrieved the marble from her pocket and is clutching it, as if it will help, as if it will give her courage. It seems to her that someone is moving around inside the bedroom, pacing quietly back and forth. Waiting. After a long moment she reaches out, pressing her fingertips against the wood, pushing gently. The door swings open: an invitation.

She could go back downstairs.

She could walk out of the house, get into her car and leave.

She steps inside, holding her breath, almost hoping it has been restored and that she'll see the room the way it was, one last time. But everything has gone now, everything she remembers, anyway, and the room is empty. The window is boarded up and the walls – she runs a finger over the wallpaper – even

384

the walls are different. She turns and looks at the mantelpiece; above it someone has begun to peel back the layers of paper on the chimney breast, revealing ragged ends, stripes below blue, then flowers, and below this, green. She steps closer, pulling at a loose edge. It curls up and away from the wall, revealing a pale scar of paper underneath.

She lets the scrap of wallpaper fall to the floor. She's on the verge of speaking aloud when she remembers the camera set up in the corner, and anyway, she can hear the others downstairs now, the kitchen door crashing shut; Lewis and Nina and Hal, voices raised, urgent. She can't hear what they're saying, but she thinks she knows what is coming next.

36

Now/Then

It's getting dark by the time they get to the barn. It only takes one trip; they can carry all the gear they need between them. Lewis drags the door open as wide as he can.

Lucy watches as Hal sets up the camera and Nina and Lewis place the smaller ones, the GoPros, on the window sills, forming a rough square to work in. They have their torches and the light on the Sony, but that's all; they move slowly, carefully, trusting that the batteries will last and that their lights won't fail. The footprints are still there, still smeared, as if someone has tried, and failed, to sweep them away.

Someone has found a ladder somewhere and dragged it through the barn, placing it against the lip of the loft space, and Lucy places a hand on one rung. It could have been Nina, or one of the boys, any one of them could have wandered off alone at some point and decided to explore. Lucy decides she won't ask. She'd rather not know.

There's a trickle of dust as above something steps lightly over the bare floorboards, carrying the faintest of vibrations through the rotting wood of the ladder.

'Right. Are we all set?' asks Nina. 'Hal?'

'I suppose so.'

'Lucy?'

'Yes.'

She is standing where she stood all those years ago, her back to the ladder, facing the door which opens out onto the inky darkness. Hal to her left, Lewis to her right and opposite her, Nina. They are holding hands and her fingers are cold.

Nothing is happening.

Maybe she's not enough, even with Hal, even though this time she wants it to work. Maybe they need Olivia, or someone like her.

It must have been exhausting for Olivia, trying to live up to Michael's expectations, to the ideals of the Society. So tempting too, to take shortcuts, to do a little research, to learn a few techniques – cold reading, they called it. Lucy remembers Olivia sitting in the field telling her all about herself, telling her things anyone could see if they only bothered to look. Hiding in plain sight.

It seems to Lucy now that Olivia's gift had been a fragile thing, delicate, unreliable, human, not enough on its own for Professor Warren and his theories; no wonder she'd worked out ways to give herself the advantage, a bit of an edge. It had taken her years to realise that Olivia at least had tried to help, had been offering a way out, a way to release Loo from her burden. She had understood that Loo had been afraid and tired and had needed for Tib to be taken away. It was too late by then, of course, but at least she'd meant well.

Maybe Lucy has got it wrong, Simon too, and Tib was only their invention, after all. Maybe there's nothing to fear.

A dull thud echoes through the loft.

From where he stands, Lewis can see the small red light on the GoPro on the window sill and he finds it oddly comforting.

Not that he's afraid. It's no worse here than the house, he tells himself, just a bit colder, more draughty. He tries to clear his mind, to tune it out, everything he knows about the farm, the house, here. He concentrates instead on Nina. Her hand, smooth and cold, gripping his.

Nina keeps glancing up at the ladder and the loft space beyond. She should be concentrating on the circle, on Tib. But she can't still her thoughts; now they are finally here, she finds she can't focus, can't steady the juddering in her heart. It's almost as if she's afraid.

Hal can't quite believe that they are here, that Lucy has agreed to try to contact Tib again, not after last time, back in the house, not after . . . He wishes that Nina would be still, he can feel it bouncing off her, the grief, the confusion, the tension. He's reminded of a phrase her father used in his book, the little he's read of it.

'The farm was possessed by a volatile spirit.'

Well, he'd got that right, in the end, by all accounts.

Maybe Lucy knows something he doesn't. Maybe this is a way to draw a line under everything, for Cathy and her, for Nina. Because there's something else going on, something she hasn't told either Lewis or him yet; he's sure of that.

This isn't helping.

He closes his eyes.

Let them be there but not there; stop thinking, stop trying. He can feel Lucy's hand in his.

Lucy

Lucia

Loo

*

389

It's cold. Lucy watches their breath frosting, curling up into the beams above them.

Light and shade, but mostly shade.

Then something – changes. The shadows deepen.

'Hal?' says Lucy.

'Yes.'

He feels it too, then.

The air lifts and falls as something moves around the circle. Looking for a way out, looking for a way in.

The skin on the back of Lucy's neck prickles. She remembers standing in the dark in her mother's room at Blue Jacket House, listening to the soft footfall, back and forth, back and forth.

It's behind them now, Nina and Lewis. No. Between them. Blinking in and out, like a faulty light bulb. It's staying longer each time, fraction building on fraction.

It.

She.

The shadowy folds of her gown, a long pale braid of hair falling loose over her shoulder. The girl in the sketchbook, in the few frames of video.

Lucy can't see her face.

She is barefoot.

Lewis swears softly under his breath and Hal is clutching Nina's hand as if he's afraid she might break free.

They can see her too, then, all of them.

The girl flickers into existence inside the circle. She's there for whole seconds at a time now.

She lifts her head, opens her mouth as if she might speak.

'Shit!' Hal jerks back, breaking free of the circle, shaking his hand. The sensation, not unlike a sharp surge of static electricity, stings, and Lucy lets go of Lewis too. Something, someone, brushes past her in the shadows.

'Did you see that?' Nina sounds shockingly young, uncertain. 'Did you see her?'

'Yes.' Lucy can hear the soft rustle of heavy skirts brushing over stone, someone creeping around the edges of the room, a hushed, breathless giggle in the dark.

They have their torches, she reminds herself, the door is open and the moon has risen, breaking weakly through the cloud. Something brushes against the back of her neck. It's cold. She flinches as something, someone, nips the skin on the inside of her wrist.

Hal picks up the camera, releasing it from the tripod, frowning slightly as he lifts it into position. 'Who's there?' says Lucy.

The answer is a sharp rap, a knocking in the joists above their heads.

'Shit!' Lewis jumps back, stumbling on the uneven floor.

'Where are you?' asks Nina.

Hal sweeps the camera slowly from left to right, as far as he can extend, his eyes fixed on the screen. Lucy thinks she can see him shake his head.

'Where?'

'What do you want?' says Lewis, his voice surprisingly steady.

The only response is a thunderous beating at the ceiling above.

Isobel was the last out of the barn, reluctant to look, to find out how the story ended this time.

The bright sunlight dazzled her for a moment or two, but then she could see. Olivia had caught hold of Cathy and was pulling her back, even as she struggled against her, lashing out, desperate to reach her girl, her darling. Olivia held on as Cathy's legs buckled and gave way, as she realised it was too late.

Michael was on his knees, bending over the figure on the ground, one hand resting lightly on her neck.

'No. No. No.' Cathy's voice rose into a wail, cracking, splintering.

She was a broken thing, white and still, leaking black-red blood onto the bleached grass and cracked flagstones of the old farmyard, only a little blood but enough; Bee was still, and silent.

Issy moved closer. The girl was lying on her back, her hair spread out, looking up at the clear blue sky, her big dark eyes open, fixed. Gone.

'Oh, Bee,' she said, her camera, her stupid camera, still in her hand. She looked up to the open barn doors above where Simon held Loo, or she held him, gripping fiercely, her thin frame heaving with sobs, her face hidden as he looked down at them all, pale and blank.

No one moves as the noise builds. It's definitely above them, something heavy beating down on the floor of the loft, shaking the beams, disturbing the years' accumulation of dust that scatters gently on them.

'We should go up,' says Nina.

'No,' says Hal.

'No,' says Lucy.

The knocking stops and they can all feel it then, Lucy is sure, the way the atmosphere charges, the way the air seems to crackle, ready to ignite.

It charges and then . . .

The lights fade – their torches, the camera, everything.

'Shit,' Nina says. 'We got it, right? Is the camera still working?'

There's enough light from the open door to make them out, the three of them, Hal with his camera, Nina and Lewis side by side.

'I think so,' says Hal. 'I think—'

Behind them the barn door slams shut and they are plunged into darkness.

It won't open.

They all take turns pushing at it, but the barn door, neither door, will shift.

'Shit.' Hal steps back and considers his options.

It's not too bad, the darkness, once you get used to it. Lucy's eyes have adjusted a little, and Hal has replaced the batteries in the camera light, working by the flickering flame of his lighter. They have used it to scan the room, to make sure everyone is OK, to check that they are still alone.

There's no one there.

But still, Lucy would like to get the door open.

'It's no good,' says Lewis, 'we're trapped.'

'Hang on,' says Hal. 'Let's just stop and think.'

Lucy leans back against the door and considers her options. If there were some tools left behind, perhaps they could find something to use on the hinges.

'Maybe if we can find something to force it,' says Nina, tugging at the handle.

'Wait.' Lucy picks up a torch from the nearest window ledge, shakes it and flicks the switch. A frail beam of light cuts through the gloom. 'Try the other ones,' she says.

Lewis's torch doesn't work, but the other two come back to life, after a fashion, casting a sickly glow through the interior of the barn. It's not ideal, but it's better than nothing. Lewis uses an app on his phone instead, following as Nina leads the way across the uneven floor. Lucy and Hal are slower, she sweeping her torch up and across the walls, he adjusting his camera.

Nina has reached the back wall of the building. It's dark and the stone is soaked through with damp. She's hoping to find some tools they could use but all she can see are a few rusting tractor parts. They need a hammer, an axe, or a blade perhaps.

They all hear it then, the long cold scrape of a blade across stone.

Lucy can remember how it was, in her dad's day; the sickle and the scythe, propped up behind one of the tables. Another reason to keep out. They weren't to touch them, Joe had said; even a blunt edge can cut.

'What's that?' says Lucy.

'I . . .' says Lewis. 'I don't . . .' and Lucy's not sure what happens next.

Nina moves towards Lewis, she takes one step, two, and then she's there, behind her, the girl – or maybe it's just her shadow – and Lewis staggers and falls forward. 'No,' he says, dropping his phone. Does he cry out? Lucy thinks he cries out, and in the sudden darkness as Lewis folds and crumples, it seems to her that something flexes and coils, something reaches out and knocks him against the wall.

'Jesus! Did you see that?'

Hal doesn't want to think about the tone in Nina's voice.

Wary of tripping and falling in the dark, he makes his way carefully over to Lewis. He's slumped against the wall, one leg twisted underneath him at an impossible angle. Hal puts the camera down, then lifts Lewis's head gently; there's a rapid pulse fluttering under his fingers and his eyes are open, even if they are glassy, confused.

'Lewis, Lew, can you hear me?'

A cut runs from just below his eye to his chin, not too deep, he thinks, he hopes. Behind him someone breathes softly on his neck.

He won't look. He won't.

'We need to call an ambulance,' he says.

'How will they get in?' asks Nina.

'I don't bloody know, but we have to call them.'

Nina goes through her pockets, slowly, too slowly, and Hal wishes he had something he could put against Lewis's face, something to stem the bleeding.

'I've lost my phone,' Nina says and for the first time her voice is tinged with panic.

Lucy tries hers, but there's no signal. 'Nothing,' she says.

'Jesus.'

Hal leans down over Lewis. 'Lew? Lewis? It's all right. We're going to get you out of here, OK? We'll find a way out.'

Lucy retreats to the door under the pretext of trying her phone again. She stumbles over the uneven floor, bits of stone and rubble shifting under her feet, tears stinging her eyes.

She doesn't know how this is all possible, she can't reason it out. The girl she thought she'd conjured up a lifetime ago is here – is present – once more. Lucy is eleven years old again, caught up in a game she can no longer control, almost breathless with fear. She's forced her way through again, and this time . . .

She's allowed them to be locked in.

Locked in with her.

Stupid, stupid, stupid.

She tries the phone again, but she can't make her hands work, stabbing at the lock screen once, twice before she sees the emergency icon, presses that, and puts the phone to her ear. She feels sick. The urge to drop the phone, to curl up on the floor, eyes tight shut, is near-overwhelming.

She wants her mother.

Nina is sweeping her torch slowly across the wall. 'What about these windows?' she says. 'Have we tried any of these yet?'

There's no reply.

Lucy's phone is useless. She shuts it off, waits, tries to steady her breathing, tries to think

Nina tries again, raising her voice. 'I said—'

The pounding on the floorboards above them drowns her out.

One.

Two.

Three.

Then silence.

The ladder rattles against the loft.

Lucy has to do something.

'OK,' she says, trying to sound confident, as though she has a plan. 'I want you two to stay here with Lewis. Try your phone please, Hal, try mine again,' she hands it over, 'and get the door open if you can.' She's shaking, she hopes they don't notice, she hopes they'll listen and do as they're told.

'Why? Where are you going?' says Nina. Lucy glances up towards the hayloft.

'No,' says Hal. 'No way.'

'You can't,' says Nina.

Lucy takes off her coat, long, heavy, expensive, and drapes it gently over Lewis. 'Keep him warm and try to keep him conscious. Get out and ring for an ambulance. Walk down to the village if you have to. Do not come after me.'

'No,' says Hal again, grabbing her wrist.

'I'll be fine,' says Lucy. 'I promise.'

'What are you going to do?' asks Nina.

'I don't know. Try to talk to her, I suppose, make contact,

396

anyway. That's what she wants, isn't it? That's what all this has been about.' She pulls herself free and goes to the ladder; she places one hand on a rung and tries not to think of woodworm or dry rot. She can feel the wood vibrating under her hand, humming with life. She begins to climb.

Simon set off for the phone box in the village even though he knew there was no point, it would make no difference, Bee was beyond help.

Between them Olivia and Isobel were able to get Cathy away from the body, not back to the house, she wouldn't do that, but back inside the barn at least, in the shade, out of sight. Issy held her and let her cry for a while, murmuring nonsense, making comforting sounds, even though there was no comfort to be had.

Michael vanished, returning after a few minutes with a sheet from the laundry basket, which he shook out clumsily. Olivia stood in the doorway and watched the white sheet unfurl in his hands, watched it billow and fall gently on the girl on the ground. Then he stood for a moment, head bowed, almost in prayer; unwilling, she suspected, to leave the dead alone.

He turned and made his way back to the barn.

'Cathy? Cathy, can you hear me?'

Cathy's sobs had subsided a little; she sat quietly on the ground, clutching at Isobel, her tears falling silently, helplessly. Her expression was blank. It was as if grief had suddenly removed her from the world, as if she might never find her way back.

'Cathy?' The professor knelt down in front of the two women. 'This is important. We need to think about what happens next. The police are coming, Cathy. We need to be clear on what you will tell them.' When Cathy didn't reply, he reached out and took her hand. 'You need to think about the others, Cathy. Cathy, can you hear me?'

'What?'

Cathy looked bewildered, the way people do when you wake them suddenly. She looked young and afraid, and Issy could feel her shivering despite the heat of the day. It's the shock, she thought, she needs a doctor.

'If you tell them about us, if you tell them what we were doing . . .'

'You said it would help. You said you would help.' Cathy looked past him, looked at Olivia. She wanted to go outside again, Issy could feel her body straining. If she moved, if she decided to go to her daughter, Issy didn't think she'd be able to hold her back. 'I – you said it would be all right . . .'

'It would look bad for you, Cathy, if it got out that you'd allowed the children to participate in a séance.'

'What?'

'We don't have very much time. You need to decide quickly.'

'I don't—'

'An investigation, a scientific investigation is one thing. But a séance – they won't understand that. They will look for someone to blame.'

'It was your idea—'

'You're her mother. They will blame you, do you understand? They will punish you. They'll take the children away, put them in care.'

'No—'

'You can't be sure of that,' said Isobel. 'We can explain it was an accident. We were here, we're witnesses.'

'Well,' said the professor, 'we could try. But I didn't see what happened, did you?'

'No. I – no.' It had all been too quick. She'd followed Simon up the ladder, she'd raised the camera and hit the shutter release, it was second nature these days, a reflex, but she hadn't really seen anything.

'And the stories in the papers won't help. For every believer there is a sceptic. Some people might choose to believe you are unstable, Cathy, unfit to be a mother.'

'No,' said Cathy, 'no, no, no.' She began to cry properly again, deep, heavy sobs. Issy pulled her close. This is unbearable, she thought, impossible.

'Listen to me,' the professor went on. 'If you listen to me, I think we can help.'

'Stop,' said Isobel. 'You have to stop. She can't possibly . . . The best thing to do is tell the truth. Michael? Olivia?'

Finally, Olivia moved away from the door. She stepped into the shadowy barn, smiled sadly at Issy, at Cathy. 'I think Michael is right,' she said.

Upstairs Loo lay as still as she could, curled up on the floorboards, the dust tickling her nose, making her wheezy, a bit like – she tried not to think about her sister.

'What happened?' Simon had asked. 'Tell me what happened, Loo.'

But she couldn't say, she wasn't sure.

Tib, it was Tib. She wasn't real, but she'd done it anyway.

Did she say that?

'No. I don't know. I can't—'

There were so many lies, she couldn't see straight. They'd lied about the knocking in the walls, the marbles flying through the air. Bee had lied about Cathy and Joe, she'd enjoyed that – frightening Loo with her stories about the knife. Telling her Cathy had hurt him, sent him away – worse. They'd lied about

Tib too, only in the end Tib had seemed the most real thing of all, the only real thing, the most – dangerous.

She remembered Simon climbing up into the loft, the look on Bee's face.

And then . . .

'Wait here,' Simon had said afterwards, as he'd disappeared back down the ladder and Loo had sat quietly for a while, waiting, not looking to see where Bee had landed, how very still she was now, before deciding she'd like to lie down, maybe go to sleep.

She kept her eyes closed, and a careful ear out for Tib, but she was quite alone.

They hadn't really forgotten her, she knew that. She could have called down, for Olivia, for her mum, but she didn't know what she should say to them.

Better to stay here for a bit then.

Perhaps when she woke up, it would all be better.

She could hear the grown-ups' voices buzzing through the floorboards; they were talking to Cathy. It was a bit like being back in her bedroom, when you could half hear people chatting in the kitchen. Her mother wasn't saying much. Michael was doing most of the talking, his voice deep, serious. Occasionally Olivia said something, Issy too.

Issy sounded cross.

If she lay still, Loo could almost imagine she was back in bed. With her eyes closed she could almost imagine Bee was safe, asleep in the bunk above her. She cried for a little bit then, as quietly as she could.

It was Isobel, in the end, who came up and found her, who helped her to her feet and back down the ladder. When Cathy saw her, she let out a terrible moan, and pulled her close, holding on so fiercely, Loo thought she might never let go.

By the time Loo could struggle free, they had all gone, Michael and Olivia, Simon and Isobel. Dan was there, with Flor – too shocked to cry for once – and with Anto, who was slumped in his arms, still half asleep. No one asked again what had happened, and anyway, by then she couldn't remember.

'Listen,' Cathy said. 'I need you all to listen to me.'

Isobel found Simon packing up his belongings. It was still warm, but if you looked towards the horizon, you could see the faintest sketch of cloud, a thin charcoal line that promised rain; summer was finally going to break. Simon paused, his hands full of clothes, grubby T-shirts and worn jeans.

'You look awful,' he said.

'Thanks. So do you.' She sat on the grass in front of the tent, collapsed and waiting to be packed away, and looked down over the farm. The emergency vehicles were long gone and Cathy and her children were somewhere in town, awaiting the arrival of Cathy's parents. Simon had never seen anyone die before, he couldn't really take it in – the sudden, shocking, permanent absence of her, Bee.

'What do you think will happen to them?' he asked, sitting next to her.

'Depends on the police findings, I suppose.' Isobel wasn't really convinced that their plan, their shoddy and shameful scheme to save face, would work. She found herself half-hoping it wouldn't.

'But it was an accident, Issy. That part's true.'

'Yes.'

They hadn't had much time, once Cathy had agreed, and Issy had been the last person to leave, to follow the others along the shortcut to the farm. 'I'm so sorry, Cathy,' she'd said.

Cathy was clutching at Loo, holding on so tight the poor

kid could hardly breathe. Dan stood to one side, cradling the baby in one arm, keeping a firm grip on the little boy, Florian, with his free hand. Half a family now, incomplete.

'Go,' Cathy had said. 'Go now.'

Issy had driven them away, Olivia and Michael, passing the ambulance as it rattled along the moors road, its siren howling, useless. They had left them behind: Cathy barely there, lost, adrift, all the fight gone out of her, surrounded by her children.

'Do you want to tell me what happened?' Isobel said.

'I don't know, I can't . . .' Simon looked down at his hands, afraid suddenly that he might cry. 'I can't – remember . . .'

Issy crossed her legs, shading her eyes as she gazed down towards the farm, the barn, the sun lowering in the sky. She could still feel Cathy in her arms, sobbing, trembling, bereft. 'It doesn't matter,' she said.

'I can't untangle it,' he said. 'I – shit.' He rubbed at his eyes, cleared his throat. 'I asked Loo, she was closer – but she – she's just a kid, Issy.'

'I know,' said Isobel, 'and anyway, it was an accident.' She was quiet for a time, until she was sure he'd be able to speak again. 'Here,' she said, pulling several bulging manila folders out of her bag. 'I want to give you these.'

He opened one and out slid pages of proofs and bundles of negatives held together with elastic bands.

'And these.' She held out three black plastic cylinders, film canisters. 'Today's stuff too. That's all of it, I think.'

'Are you sure?'

'Yeah. I mean – there'll still be a book?' It was a terrible thing to ask, but she had to know.

'I suppose so.'

He didn't like to admit it, but he was fairly certain the professor would carry on. As they were walking back to the farm he had said something about protecting the integrity of their research. It had sounded logical at the time.

'Right. Well. You'll let me know what you want to use?' He could hear the effort Isobel was making to sound professional. 'Then we'll go on from there. You know, payment, copyright, acknowledgements. I don't want them back, not any of them.'

'Of course. Yes. All right.' He ran his fingers over the bundles of pictures, dropped the canisters onto his pile of clothes; there wasn't much else to be packed.

'What will you do now?' she asked.

'I'm not sure. I'm heading back to London once my car's fixed and we'll probably come back for, well, if there's an inquest.'

'Yeah.'

'Then, I don't know. Try university again, perhaps.'

'Something safe, with lots of books.'

'I suppose so. What about you?'

'I'll go back to work: golden weddings and cricket matches. Small-town stuff.'

They would all leave in a little while. Once Simon was ready, they'd collect Olivia from the pub, drive her and the professor to Whitby, and Issy would say her goodbyes. The paper would cover this story, no doubt, reusing her old shots, perhaps, and she would do her best to stay out of the way, if she could, while she looked for another job.

'We could catch up, when I come back, if you like,' Simon said.

'Yes, I'd like that,' said Issy, knowing that if she was still here when he returned she would be busy.

'Good.' Simon put the folder carefully to one side and they sat quietly for a while, not speaking as they looked across the valley, watching the clouds roll in across the darkening sky, waiting for the rain to fall.

37

Now/Then

They listen to the radio for a while, a station Sarah's not that fond of, to tell the truth, but she's sort of got used to it in the time she's worked at Blue Jacket House.

'I like your ring,' says Cathy and Sarah looks down at her hand. The engagement ring has been there just long enough for her to get used to it, but not so long that she doesn't still feel a secret rush of joy when it catches her eye.

'Thanks,' she says. She's pretty sure she showed Cathy when she first got engaged, she's fairly certain she showed everyone at work, staff and residents alike. But she's used to her being a little forgetful.

'I wish you every happiness,' says Cathy, looking down at her own hands. 'It can be so wonderful, being in love.'

'Like you were with Joe?'

'At first,' says Cathy. 'For a little while, anyway.'

Sarah hopes she's not going to try to warn her off marriage. 'Then what happened?' she asks.

Cathy closes her eyes. 'He couldn't stand it, after a while, me, the children, me, all of us. He couldn't settle, couldn't work. So he took a job. I told them he was teaching, painting – he wasn't of course, he was labouring on a building site, like he used to do when we were students. We needed the money, that's what he said. But that's when it all started, all the –

trouble. We had parted badly, there was an argument – in his studio – and I did, said, some foolish things. I picked up a knife, threatened to damage a painting. I was being childish. But we'd quarrelled before, I'd said worse, done worse, and so had he; I thought we would make it up. I thought there would be time.'

She's very still and Sarah wonders if she should suggest getting ready for bed.

'I should have been – kinder – I think. He was a wonderful painter, you know,' says Cathy. 'And he came back, when we lost Bee, he came back for a while.' Her eyes fill with tears and she brushes them away, impatient. 'We divorced when Lucia was about thirteen. He died ten years ago.'

'I'm sorry,' says Sarah, and she wonders if she should ring Lucy Frankland.

I think my mother will need some company tonight. I don't want her to be alone.

'Have you ever seen her?' Cathy asks, abruptly. 'The girl in the garden?'

'I'm not sure,' Sarah says, hoping Cathy won't ask any more questions about the barefoot girl. Mrs Wyn Jones would not be happy about that conversation. 'I don't think anyone's seen her, since, you know, your accident – but I'm not sure.'

'No, nor am I.'

The loft is smaller than Lucy remembers, of course. The roof is lower, and is pitched more steeply into the darkened corners. At the far end the double doors have been pulled open, revealing a view of the distant valley and the cloudy night sky.

She takes a single, careful step away from the ladder and a floorboard gives a little under her weight. Dry rot, Dan had always insisted. 'It's not safe,' he'd say in his mock-serious voice, conjuring images of bony ankles snapping and splintering like twigs. 'You'd be better off back at the house.'

As far as she can tell, the loft is empty.

'Hello?' She makes her way towards the open doors, moving cautiously, not so much from a fear of falling, but because there's a part of her that's no longer sure she'd be able to resist the temptation to jump.

She puts her hand on the bolt, grips it firmly and risks a look to the ground below, but it's too dark to see anything. She steps back again. She sits down carefully, pressing her back against the wood, and then she can feel it – the energy, the charge as she has come to think of it, humming inside the wood, building again. She closes her eyes and waits.

There are voices below, a thump as Hal or Nina smacks something against the door, the rattle of the hinges floating up into the loft.

A car slowing to pass through the village.

There's a chill in the air and an insistent buzzing starts to fill her head. She feels dizzy still, sick.

'Lewis, can you hear me?'

''Course.'

Hal kneels down next to Lewis. He should check his pulse again or something, for all the good it will do; he's not used to feeling helpless. Lewis is alarmingly pale and he has a distant look in his eyes as if he wants to go elsewhere. 'We're going to find a way out and then we'll get you to hospital,' Hal says.

'Yeah, right.' Lewis glances down at his leg, the wrongness of it bulging under Lucy's coat, and looks hastily away.

'Look at me, Lew,' says Hal. The last thing he wants is for the poor bloke to throw up or, worse, pass out.

'I'm fine,' says Lewis. 'Go and help Nina.'

407

Hal breathes. 'Yeah,' he says, getting to his feet. 'Just, stay awake, all right?'

They've had to give up on the door for the moment. If he didn't know better, he'd think the bloody thing had been locked on them. But there are windows running either side of the building; they're small, but he's pretty sure one of them could get through. He can hear Nina at the back of the building, shifting stuff out of the way. He picks up his torch, flicks the switch off and on again and it comes back to life, casting a pale beam through the dark. He can't rely on it of course, but it's better than nothing.

'Nina?'

'Here.'

He finds her creating clouds of dust as she drags an old cement bag across the floor.

'Up there, I think,' she says. He turns his torch on the window, set at about head height. Like all the others it's shut, but the latch hangs loose and the panes of glass are rattling in their frames. Nina drops the bag on the floor, sending up more dust. 'It was open this afternoon. If I can just get up . . .' She unwraps her scarf and undoes her coat, fumbling in her jeans pocket for a tissue to cough into. 'There's another bag in the corner.'

'You OK?'

'Yeah, it's the dust, that's all.'

'And Lucy?' He looks up at the loft. 'Do you think she's OK?'

'I hope so.'

She pulls her coat off and throws it into the corner. 'Give us a hand, will you?'

They drop the second bag on top of the first and it's just high enough for Nina to boost herself onto the deep window ledge.

'Fuck.'

'You all right?'

'There's no fucking room.' She's balancing on her knees and he can hear her pulling at the window latch. She fills up the whole space and even if she can open the window, he doubts that she can pull it back and manoeuvre her way through.

'Let me try,' he says.

'You won't fit . . . oh . . .' Without warning she pushes herself backwards. 'Fuck it, the bloody thing's stuck,' she says as she lands clumsily on the cement bags. 'We'll have to smash it open.'

Lucy can feel someone moving across the floor and she tries to let her in, her soft tread, back and forth, back and forth. Her bare feet pressing down on the dusty boards, and her face – she'd never been able to give Tib a face. She slows her breathing, tries to control the rising nausea, tries to call the girl out of the shadows.

With a final kick, Hal forces himself through the window. He has to go headfirst in the end, once they smash it with an old broom they find. It isn't that bad, his jeans and sweater have protected him from the worst of it, although his hands are scratched. Falling into the dark, he manages to wind himself and he lies on the grass for a moment, profoundly grateful to be out of that place.

'Hal?' Nina's voice is muffled by the thick stone walls.

'Yes. I'm here.' He stands, fumbling in his pocket for his phone. The moon is bright enough to see by, and he makes his way along the side of the barn to the front. He treads carefully; it wouldn't do to fall now. There's still no signal. He could drive into the village for help, he supposes; it would only take a few minutes and it would get him further away from the barn, which is a very appealing idea, but he should check the door first. Just in case.

Nina can hear him on the other side.

'. . . stuck . . . the bolt's loose, but I can't . . .'

'Ambulance, Hal, just get a signal and ring an ambulance. Hal?'

He doesn't answer, but the silence that follows convinces her that he's gone away to do exactly that. She hopes so. All she can do is go back to Lewis, who is trembling under Lucy's coat. Shock, she supposes. 'Not long now,' she says.

'No. Not long,' says Lewis. 'Poor old Loo.'

'Lewis?'

His head falls forward, and she reaches out to steady him.

'Lew? Can you hear me?'

His hand shoots out from under the coat, gripping Nina's arm fiercely. 'No,' he says. 'Don't go.'

'I'm sorry, Lew. I have to.'

'Why?'

She doesn't know what to say.

'You can tell me, you know,' says Lewis. 'You can trust me.'

But it's beyond her, there's too much to say.

'Oh God, Lew.'

I'm so sorry.

'Don't go.'

Above them the floorboards creak and bulge, dust trickling down onto the two of them before settling again, silent.

'I think I have to,' she says. 'Lewis?'

But his eyes have closed. Nina gently frees herself from his hand and once she's sure she can detect faint but regular breathing, she covers him with Lucy's coat again and heads towards the ladder.

*

Hal can't understand why the door is stuck. He's put his back into it, lifting and pulling, his feet slipping in the mud. He can see the grooves the door has worn in the ground through the years, curving parallel lines scored into the long grass, and he's tried its twin, the left-hand door, the one no one seems to use, but he can't move it. What he needs is something to force it.

He runs back to his car, avoiding the shortcut through the garden, around the house, heading instead across the field to the road. He has a vague idea that he might flag down a passing car, fetch help that way.

He gets to the car, opens the boot, and begins to rummage through the random tools that have collected there over the years. Eventually he finds a crowbar – God knows why it's there in the first place, but it should do the job.

He stops and checks his phone again; he could ring and wait for an ambulance here.

He doesn't have to go back at all, not really. He could get in the car and drive away. Get to the pub and ring from there. He's standing with his hand on the door, car keys in his hand. Every instinct telling him to run.

It had been awkward, clambering up the ladder without dropping the camera, trying not to make a noise and Nina felt a bit bad about Lewis. But she wasn't doing him any good holding his hand downstairs.

She'd had to place the Sony on the floor when she got to the top, climbing carefully up onto the rough floorboards, then picking it up again, trusting that it could cope with the light levels and the shaking in her hands.

She moves quietly, lifting the camera and framing the scene as well as she can.

Lucy is sitting with her back to the door, her head drooping slightly, her eyes closed.

The buzzing has filled her head, settling to a dull throb, and Lucy has the feeling that if she could only focus, she might break through, adjust to it somehow, and this noise, this flat pressure, would resolve itself. She might make contact, after all.

She hears something take a step towards her, real enough to place pressure on the wooden floor. Lucy opens her eyes. It's Nina, the camera in her hands, the light cutting through the dark. 'No,' Lucy says. 'I told you to stay with Lewis.'

'I want to see—'

'No.'

'But she's here? There's something here, right?' She lifts the camera and scans the loft.

'I don't know,' says Lucy, 'but you should go back down and—'

One, two, three.

The thuds force their way through the wooden floor, vibrating through their feet, up their spines.

Something skitters across the floorboards and Nina turns, sweeping the camera in front of her again, trying to catch whatever it is in her viewfinder. Rats, Dan and Bee used to tell Lucy, rats as big as cats, Loo.

It seems to Lucy that the air in the room is thicker now, heavier, pressing in against her skull once more. It makes her head ache. She wonders if Nina can feel it too. 'Please,' she says, scrambling to her feet. 'Don't.'

'Is it her?' Nina says. 'Is she here?'

One, two, three.

Then, silence.

*

412

At first Hal thinks he's too late.

Lewis is lying motionless on the floor, his head drooping onto his chest. Blood is beginning to seep through Lucy's expensive coat.

'Lewis. Lewis.'

His eyes flutter open. 'Here. I'm here,' he says. 'Phone?'

'Yes. I had to go back to the car, but yeah, I got a signal.'

Hal looks behind him to check that the door is still open. He's forced it back as far as it will go, dug the crowbar into the ground to hold it in position.

'We're going to have to move you, get you outside.'

'No. No.'

'Yeah, I know, it'll hurt. But best not to stay in here, don't you think? There's an ambulance coming, it won't be too bad.'

He and Nina should be able to lift Lewis between the two of them. They'll worry about explaining why they moved him later.

'No,' says Lewis again. 'Nina.'

A breeze wafts in through the window. It makes Lucy's skin pucker, chills her to the bone. Whatever this is, they have given it a focus, they've given it a form and they've let it in.

'Lucy?' Nina takes a step closer.

Hal glances back at Lewis, still slumped against the wall, and at the barn door, still wedged open. He doesn't want to leave him alone, not really. He particularly doesn't want to leave the comforting sight of the open door. But he needs to get Lucy and Nina down. Between them they can take Lewis outside. 'OK,' he says, as if Lewis can still hear him, 'it'll be OK. Not long, Lew. Not long.'

He shoves his torch into his pocket and climbs the ladder carefully. He tries to not think about falling, about the way

413

Lewis's leg has twisted and fractured, about what happened to Bee Corvino, the crushing impact of skull against stone.

Nina is standing with her back to Hal, holding his camera. Lucy is beyond her, too close to the sudden drop into the dark for Hal's liking.

'Hello?' he says, stepping off the ladder, and the moonlight brightens, there's a buzz in the air, in his head. 'I got the door open,' he says. 'We should go. I'll need some help with Lewis.'

Reluctantly he steps closer, not quite convinced the ladder will stay in place, that they won't all end up trapped here. 'Seriously, both of you. You need to come and help.' He looks past Nina at Lucy and there's a jolt of something, recognition perhaps – a thickening of the atmosphere as a shadow in the corner of his vision shakes itself free, solidifies and then fades away. 'Lucy?'

Something cracks in the rafters, splintering the silence.

He can feel it again, the buildup of pressure. They don't have much time. 'Nina,' he says, 'time to go.'

Nina turns to face him, swinging the camera round on him, when she's there between them, caught in a patch of moonlight. Tall, pale, white-blonde hair, her muddy brown dress torn at the hem, her bare feet grimy and bruised. Flickering. There and not there.

The moon disappears behind a cloud and the girl vanishes.

'Jesus.' Nina saw her, it, too. 'Do it again,' she says, looking at Hal, then at Lucy. 'Bring her back.'

'I can't,' says Hal. 'I don't know how.' That's not quite true; he can feel her there still, just out of sight, it's as if all he has to do is adjust his focus and – but he's not sure he wants to, he's not sure that would be wise. It's the same for Lucy, too, he's almost certain.

She looks dreadful though, as if she may collapse at any moment, and he wishes she'd come away from the open doors. 'We need to move Lewis.'

Neither Nina nor Lucy answer. The chill evening air seems to crackle with energy. The silence stretches until . . .

Three sharp raps in the far wall.

Three in the doors behind.

Then in quick succession, three above them, dancing down each oak beam, and below them, beneath their feet, thudding along the floorboards.

Surrounding them.

Angry.

Lucy makes a visible effort to pull herself together. 'Stop it,' she says, and the noise dies away. 'Right. Enough. There's nothing here but conjuring tricks. Hal's right. It's time to go.' She looks puzzled, coughs, tries to clear her throat, then – covering her mouth – she coughs again.

Her hand comes away smeared with ink.

Not ink, she realises. Blood.

She can't breathe.

Lucy doubles over, falling onto her hands and knees, coughing, spitting, scattering a fine spray of dark droplets over the floorboards, her whole body shaking.

'No,' she says, when at last she can speak. 'No, no, no.'

She can feel herself drifting away. The urge to give up, to let go, is near-overwhelming. She can taste the blood in her mouth, warm and salt.

'Lucy,' says Nina, shaking her arm gently. 'Lucy. Do you think you can stand up?' She is lying on the dusty floor and they are hovering anxiously over her. She's not sure what happened – did she faint? She licks her lips, remembering, leans over to spit, then wipes her mouth again, not looking at the dark stains on her fingers.

The pounding in her chest slows and she sits up. 'I – yes. They were going to leave, did you know that?' Lucy says, clinging on to the words. 'Cathy had finally had enough and she'd told them to go.'

'Right,' says Hal, glancing back, checking the ladder is still in place.

'Only she put some glass in Isobel's tea, and Issy nearly swallowed it. Bits of broken-up light bulb.'

Issy spitting blood into the clean white sink.

Lucy lets them help her to her feet. They haven't worked it out yet, she realises, they don't see. 'And that changed everything,' she says. 'That really scared Cathy. She made them promise to stop it all, to get rid of Tib.'

'Because she was here all along,' says Nina. 'And that's what my dad saw, he realised—'

'No,' says Lucy. 'I told you – it wasn't Tib. It was Bee who put the glass in Issy's drink.' She wipes her mouth and her fingers come away bloody. 'It was Bee.'

Dan had been furious.

'Are you mad? Are you actually fucking mad, Bee? You could have killed her.'

Bee shrugging, making out that it was no big deal, a bit of a laugh. 'But I didn't,' she said, and then she'd said something about Dan fancying Issy and wasn't that a bit pathetic.

They'd argued it back and forth for a bit, in hushed voices out in the garden, worrying that the grown-ups might hear.

Back when the worst they could imagine was being found out.

*

Nina lets go of Lucy and looks at the patch of dusty floorboard where she'd seen her, the pale girl. 'But that doesn't make sense,' she says uncertainly. 'That's not Bee. She doesn't look right. She doesn't look like her.'

'I know,' Lucy says, more certain of herself now the dizzy sensation has begun to recede. 'But it feels like her. It feels like . . .' She tries to recall the girl in her mother's drawing and the girl on their video. She remembers the feeling someone was in the house, watching her; she remembers standing in the bedroom, drawing her fingers across the damp wall, the old layers of paper; one concealing another. 'Sometimes it feels like Tib, the way she was that last time, and sometimes – it feels like Bee.'

One story on top of another.

A palimpsest.

'We should go,' says Hal, and she can tell he feels it too: Tib, Bee, so many girls pressing to get through, closer now.

It's the only thing that makes sense. Not one girl, but many.

'I think it is Bee, trapped here, with Tib, with all of them.' Lucy says.

'All of them?' says Nina.

'Yes. I think so. Yes.'

'Right. But even so,' Hal says, looking towards the ladder again, 'we can work this out later, yeah?'

'You don't understand,' says Lucy. 'Bee's here and I can't leave her.'

Lucy stands in the centre of the room. She can do this; she imagined Tib once before, maybe now all she has to do is imagine her sister.

She places them all there, in the loft, Nina and Hal and

herself, and in her imagination, they look at a patch of floor, washed in moonlight, and they wait. Time passes: minutes, seconds, heartbeats.

Lucy closes her eyes.

The girl who might be her sister is standing by the door, looking out over the valley. She's too tall, too fair, too different, she is all wrong. She flickers in and out of existence, there and not there. Silent.

Something clatters against the roof and the sharp crack echoes through the room, then Lucy can feel it, the way she used to feel it when she was a little girl and she woke up in the middle of the night, afraid. 'Bee?' she asks.

The floorboards vibrate as something heavy strikes them.

One knock for yes.

'Bee, is that you?'

That's not my name.

She's not sure she hears the answer, maybe she just feels it.

'Bee?' She tries again. The moon goes behind a cloud and the girl vanishes.

There's a dull thudding in the walls in the far corner and it comes back to Lucy so clearly, the way she felt sometimes, towards the end of that summer, the sensation that the thoughts she had were not her own.

She tries again, calling the girl back, placing her inside the circle, the way she did before.

Something moves in the far corner. A rustling, shivering.

'Bee?'

She can see her out of the corner of her eye. A hunched figure, hungry, her long skirts sweeping against the floorboards, her hair held in a loose plait; she moves in and out of the shadows. Her face – Lucy still can't make it out, anyway this isn't Bee, this is . . .

418

'Tib,' says Nina. 'Is that you?'

She stretches up, out, she is formed now of muscle and bone, rough hands reaching out; she steps out of the shadow. And at last Lucy can see her face.

'No,' says Hal.

And there are so many of them. So angry.

No, the girl says, her voice pressing inside Lucy's head, no, no, no, no. And she rushes forward, pale, screaming.

Lucy braces herself for what is coming, she waits for the blow to land, but nothing happens. The girl has vanished and she is safe, still on her feet, unmarked. Maybe there really is nothing here after all, just noise and rage and no real danger. It's only as Hal cries out that she realises it's Nina who has been struck, Nina who is falling forward onto her hands and knees, as the air is knocked out of her.

She drops the camera and curls up on the floor, choking, gasping. And Lucy can almost see them, the girls, circling her.

'No,' she calls out. 'No. You have to stop.'

She feels the answer forcing its way into her head.

No.

No.

Lucy kneels down next to Nina, Simon's girl, rolling her onto her back, and her breath is shallow now, coming in ragged gasps, her eyes are open and her lips are tinged with blue and she's not breathing – dear God, she's not breathing – and there are so many voices in her head now, she doesn't think she can bear it, the noise, the rage.

'Bee,' she says, looking up, 'I want Bee.'

And the knocking builds up in the walls again, in the walls, the ceiling, the floor; thunderous, enraged.

*

419

Bee grabs hold of her sister, her bony fingers wrapped around her arms. The two of them stand face to face, Bee leaning down, her voice soft and vicious.

'This is all your fault,' says Bee. 'You and your stupid bloody game. I saw them. I heard them.'

They are close to the edge now, and Bee, taller, stronger, more determined, pulls Loo round so she has her back to the open doors, her nails digging into Loo's skin.

'That wasn't me, that was Cathy. You said it was Cathy.'

'Pissing about when Joe was trying to paint, knocking at the shutters.'

'It was – a joke.'

They had both done it, once or twice, hoping to draw him out, hiding from him, half-hoping he'd find them anyway, even if it did mean a telling-off.

Bee shakes her, edging her closer to the drop. 'You made him go away, it was all your fault.'

'I didn't,' says Loo. 'I didn't.'

'And now he's going too.'

Simon, of course, always Simon.

'I didn't. I don't . . .' Loo is crying now, heavy snotty tears. She's breathless and confused. Bee has got them all mixed up, Joe and Simon, Tib and Loo.

'Why,' Bee shakes her again, pushes her a little further towards the edge, 'why do you do it? Why do you make them go away?'

The great empty space is behind her now. It's not such a long drop, she tells herself, and anyway Bee doesn't mean it. There's another game they used to play, taking it in turns to fall back into each other's arms, letting go and trusting that the other would always be there. The way she'd buckle under Bee's weight, the way Bee could wait until the last moment to catch her.

Behind Bee a shadow moves.

Simon, she thinks. It's Simon.

He's there now; Loo can see him out of the corner of her eye.

'Bee,' she says. 'Bee.'

She feels her sister's muscles tense; she is strong, strong enough to lift her, strong enough to—

'Bee!'

She can hear the panic in Simon's voice as he moves quickly towards them, only a few paces away now, almost close enough to touch, and for a moment, a second, Bee looks unsure and she lets go of her. Simon is reaching out and Loo can tell it's all going to be all right.

He's come to save her.

She steps forward and as she goes to move past, she knocks Bee off balance, just a little, to get to him.

Maybe Simon loves her. Not the way he loves Issy, but a little bit, all the same.

'Bloody useless,' said Bee. 'It's me he wants, not you.'

'No.'

'Poor old Loo. He just feels sorry for you.' And Lucia twists, bringing up both hands, grabbing hold of her sister's dress. All at once she's sick of her, sick of them, Bee and Tib, the pair of them in her head, going on at her until she can't think straight.

She can see them both now, Bee in front and Tib in the shadows, stretching out slowly, familiar, as if she has been there all along, and somehow Loo finds a way to switch off, to step aside from herself, and to let Tib in.

At the very last moment Bee understands what is coming. Loo can see it in her face, and it makes her happy.

She takes a breath and pushes as hard as she can.

'Please.'

The moon breaks through the hazy patchwork of clouds and

there she is. The knocking in the walls dulls into a faint tapping, as if the girls, whoever they are, have receded too. Tib has vanished and underneath all the rage and the grime there is just Bee, her sister, playing dress-up all along. 'I'm sorry,' Lucy says. 'I didn't know. I didn't mean to, Bee. I didn't mean any of it.'

Nina stretches, tilting her head back, exposing her throat, and takes in a long agonised breath. Hal leans over her, trying to lift her as she takes another gasp of air and begins to cough, her chest heaving.

Lucy is framed by the open doors, by the torn sky scattered with stars.

Nina can see the tremor in Lucy's hands as she reaches out to Bee, who seems in the moonlight to be perfectly solid, perfectly real at last. She wants to ask Hal if he can see her too, but she can't speak. She can feel his arms around her, holding her close, comforting, safe.

Sarah is sitting in the chair by Cathy's bed, the radio her only company as Cathy sleeps. She's missed her last bus anyway, and although she's sure Jean would let her use one of the guest rooms, she's decided that she'll stay with Cathy.

I don't think she should be alone.

And the thing is, even if some relatives fussed too much, especially the ones who never visited, when you worked with the elderly and the frail, if someone asked you to stay close, to take extra care, you started to pay attention. She hadn't always felt that way, but then she'd seen the girl, and she'd started to wonder. You saw odd things being so close to death, sometimes.

Cathy stirs in her sleep, her eyes opening briefly, and then something changes, something in the set of her features and in the rasping quality of her breathing. Sarah has seen this before. It's as if she's no longer here.

'Cathy? Mrs Corvino?' She shakes her gently. She is still calling her name as she hits the call button as hard as she can, over and over again.

It's Bee as Lucy last saw her, hot and grubby and bad-tempered.

'Bloody hell, Loo.' She looks confused, as if she can't quite remember how she got here.

Slowly, Lucy stands up, she reaches out and takes Bee's hand and for once, her sister doesn't pull away. Her hand is clammy, her fingernails broken and bitten; this is her sister, perfect in every detail.

'It was my fault,' says Lucy, loud enough for Hal and Nina to hear, loud enough for the camera lying on the floor. She edges towards the open doors. 'All my fault. It was terrible, that summer, you know. We were all so unhappy. All we wanted was Joe to come back, and all we had was each other. And I couldn't think of a way to make it stop, to say no.'

'Cathy,' says Bee, and she sounds sleepy, like a fretful child. 'Where's Cathy?'

Loo tugs at her sister's fingers; she needs her to concentrate. 'Listen to me,' she says. 'It's all right now. You can go.'

'No,' says Nina.

'You can't make me,' Bee says and the pressure starts to build again. Lucy can feel it, the sickening buzzing inside her head.

'I want – I want . . .' Bee looks directly at Hal and Nina. Hal feels his skin prickling. 'The girls,' she says. 'I want—'

They're coming back, he thinks, all of them.

'You don't belong with Tib,' says Lucy, pulling the blue-green marble out of her pocket, holding it tight. 'You should be here, with me. We can go together now.'

'No,' Hal says.

'I miss you, Bee,' says Lucy. 'I love you.' It's her last great secret and it's the truth.

'Don't,' says Nina.

'Here we go,' says Lucy softly. She is still holding Bee's hand and it's the easiest thing in the world to let go, to step back and finally let go, to fall through the open doors onto the freezing ground below.

In the barn, Lewis is woken by the sound of Lucy's phone. He pulls it clumsily from her coat pocket and stares at the caller ID on-screen.

Blue Jacket House.

38

Now

The voices are muffled and someone, Nina, she thinks, is holding her hand. She can feel that, Nina's cold fingers wrapped around hers.

She sees her, suddenly, briefly, her face mottled with tears.

Simon is there too, Lucy can hear him.

'. . . be all right . . . Lucy . . . Lucy . . .'

She looks up at the stars, scattered across the inky sky. The biggest sky she's ever seen, blue-black, velvety soft. Her vision blurs, she must be crying and she wishes she could wipe away the tears, see properly.

'Keep still.'

'I am.'

Did she say that?

Bee is lying next to her, her petticoat skirts spread out, one arm flung back over her head; they are still holding hands.

She can hear the siren and understands what is being said to her.

Ambulance

Lewis

Then Hal lowers his voice.

Cathy

The siren gets louder, then cuts out.

Hal walks away, she feels that, but Nina is still there, still holding on. Fierce. 'It's all right, it's going to be all right,' she says.

The stars glitter, too many to count.

She wonders where Bee has gone.

39

Now

Cathy's instructions had been quite clear. She wanted a secular service, and had chosen the music and the readings. The crematorium is a low modern building set in rolling green hills on the outskirts of the town, and a herd of cows continue to graze indifferently in the field beyond the memorial garden as Lucy, Dan and Florian stand outside after the short service, shaking hands and embracing Cathy's friends who have come to say their goodbyes.

Jean is there, professional, calm, Sarah too, teary and clutching a hankie – she was with Cathy when it happened. Lucy must find the time to speak with her properly, thank her, reassure her. There are people Dan seems to know, and Flor makes the best of the situation, meeting all these strangers with a firm handshake and murmured thanks.

There are more people there than she expected and Lucy's grateful for that, happy at least that her mother hadn't been lonely at the end of her life, that she'd been held in some regard by those who knew her.

The line of mourners progresses slowly, and they wait until last, Hal, Nina and, left leg encased in plaster up to his hip, slightly unsteady on his crutches, Lewis.

Lucy hugs them in turn. 'You'll come back to the house, won't you?' she says.

*

Lucy doesn't know if this is usual, a final courtesy extended by Jean, or a special arrangement, organised in advance by Cathy, but a funeral tea has been laid on at Blue Jacket House. They use the dining room, a buffet has been set up in one corner, and members of staff, those unable to attend the service, seek out Lucy and her brothers to offer their condolences.

Her younger sister Antonella hasn't been able to make it; her job, her family, her other commitments. There's talk of her coming over from America in a couple of months' time, when they, the family, will scatter Cathy's ashes in a private ceremony.

They sit by the window, Hal, Nina and Lewis, and after a while Dan joins them while his wife, Julie, helps Lucy see to their guests, exchanging pleasantries, venturing stories, memories of happier times.

Gradually people leave and Sarah and Jean begin to tidy up. Flor and his wife decide their two boys have had enough, and make arrangements to meet Dan and Lucy for lunch the next day. Flor knows perfectly well who Hal, Nina and Lewis are, and about their connection to the farm, but he makes no mention of it. Lucy hugs her younger brother too; she can feel his surprise at this. She resolves to be kinder to him in the future.

Julie announces she's going to go upstairs, get on with packing up Cathy's things. She kisses Dan on the cheek, takes Lucy's hand and squeezes it gently then leaves, shepherding her daughters out in front of her.

Lucy walks over to the table by the window, suggests they move into the living room, out of the way.

'Issy sent flowers,' she says, as they settle themselves in the sofas once again. Dan finds an armchair for Lewis and drags it into place, and the younger man sits down with a slight thump. He

428

looks pale, as if the pain medication he's been given isn't quite up to the job.

'That was kind,' says Nina. 'Have you spoken to her?'

'Not yet,' says Lucy. 'I'd like to but – you know, I'll see how she feels. Have you?'

'Yes.' Nina looks embarrassed. 'I'm sorry. I just – there were things she needed to know,' she says.

'I see.'

'Things?' Dan smiles politely.

'To do with her photos. To do with my dad.'

'Ah.'

'And you,' says Hal, 'how are you?'

A dislocated shoulder, cuts and bruises, concussion.

A miracle.

'I'm fine,' says Lucy.

They had suspected a fractured skull and Lucy had spent an inordinate amount of time under observation at the hospital. Two consultants had examined her notes and her person, almost irritated, it seemed to her, that she hadn't suffered more serious injuries, but she had been discharged eventually.

Everything hurts, of course, everything is tender, she looks dreadful, and she wonders if she'll ever feel comfortable in her skin again, but she is to all intents and purposes quite well.

'Thank you for coming,' says Dan, although he's probably said it before.

'We wanted to,' says Lewis. 'We liked Cathy. We wanted to pay our respects.'

'We wanted,' says Nina, 'to reassure you.'

There won't be a book, no new version of events of the haunting of Iron Sike Farm, not even with all the evidence they have.

'Are you sure?' Dan looks as if he can't quite believe them.

'Quite sure,' says Hal, glancing at Lewis.

'I mean there never really was one in the first place,' says Nina. 'But now – well, it wouldn't be fair.'

Lucy is afraid she might cry.

'I wanted to thank you,' says Nina.

Hal reaches out and takes her hand in his.

'Oh,' says Lucy, because it's so obvious now. 'You thought it was him, you thought it was Simon.'

'No. No.' Nina shakes her head. 'But I was . . . afraid – you know? It was always at the back of my mind. That he might have been involved in her death, somehow. I mean – why did he keep quiet about Bee? He was there, he must have seen what happened. And Issy couldn't get a straight answer out of him either. She told me so in her email, she didn't really think he'd done anything wrong, but – she knew he was keeping something back.'

And things happened like that, didn't they? They had happened all the time, or so it seemed, men who had seemed so kind, so genuine – all the charming and respectable men who got away with it.

'He was,' says Lucy, 'he saw – I think he saw me. He asked me, I think, what I'd seen, what had happened. But I was—'

'When he found the pictures of Tib, perhaps he realised there was something everyone had missed at the time,' says Lewis.

'I think he thought that if he could prove it was Tib, well, then. That might be – better, for you and for Cathy,' says Nina.

'And she wanted to know too,' says Lucy. 'Once she started seeing . . . her, the girl in the garden, that's why she was so keen on you, and all your photographs. She wanted her proof too.'

'There's no point now,' says Dan, 'in dragging this all up again. It was an accident.'

430

He has been very insistent on that, despite what Lucy has told him in private.

It wasn't your fault, Loo. You weren't yourself.

'And we won't,' says Lewis, 'truly, we won't. But there is something you need to see.'

Nina has brought her satchel with her and today, inside, there is only one folder. It's bent at the corners, the typewritten label has faded and someone has written over it in blue ink: 'Parish records and notes, census details Iron Sike Farm'.

'It says in my dad's notes,' says Nina, 'that just after the voice identified herself as Tib, Michael Warren asked him to find her in the parish records.'

Proof.

'But he couldn't,' says Dan. 'She didn't exist.'

'There was nothing,' says Nina, 'in Longdale church, so Dad wrote to the *Gazette*, Issy's paper, and he chased up the census records at the turn of the century too. But then Bee died, and everything changed, and they packed up, and this was – I think – handed on to Michael Warren. Then eventually handed back to my dad.'

'And they missed it, both of them,' says Lewis. 'As far as we can tell.'

Nina opens the folder.

The first document is a photocopy of a census return for the year 1891.

'Here.' Nina leans forward and points it out.

The address given is Iron Sike Farm, Longdale. The family name is Chadwick, which means nothing to Lucy, but the family are not the only occupants of the house.

Tabitha Bone, servant, aged seventeen.

'It's not the same name,' she says.

But it's close.

The second document is a photograph.

'It's a scanned image, so it's not too brilliant, sorry,' says Nina.

The family are standing in front of the house, Iron Sike Farm. A couple Lucy takes to be husband and wife are standing in the front garden, their children – six, no, seven of them – ranged on either side.

Behind them on the front step stands another, older couple, and a little to one side, half hidden in the doorway, is a young woman in a plain dark frock. She is tall and thin, her fair hair pulled back in a thick plait.

The photograph bears no names, but there is a date.

1891.

'We're trying to find a birth certificate,' says Lewis, 'and a death certificate, for Tabitha.'

It might be her imagination, but Lucy thinks she can see a shadow behind the girl in the photo, something jagged, trying to push its way through. Not one girl, but many, she thinks.

They stay a while longer, talking things through. Dan has warmed to them a little and after a while he starts to answer their questions about that time at the farm. Reminiscing, even though there will be no book.

'Can I ask you something?' Hal is leaning forward, trying to keep his voice low. 'It might sound a bit daft.'

'Sure.' Lucy stands. 'Let's go outside.'

They walk across the grass to the bench, Hal fumbling in his pockets. They sit down and he lights a cigarette.

'Sorry,' he says. 'I expect this is against the rules.'

'If we get caught,' says Lucy mildly, 'they'll never let us back in.'

Hal smiles and they sit in silence for a while.

'The thing is,' Hal says, 'I wanted to ask. You could feel it too, couldn't you? That house. It wasn't – right. Was it?'

'No.' Lucy has been thinking about this, about that first summer as well as the last weekend. 'No, I don't think it ever was. I always felt there was something wrong – I'm not sure what. And they think they can untangle it, don't they? Nina and Lewis, they think Tib was Tabitha. They think Tib pushed Bee; all of it so very neat.'

'And did she?'

Lucy doesn't know what to say; she finds she can't quite look Hal in the eye. She's discussed this with Dan, confessed. And the other sense she had, that Tib was larger than one person, that Bee had been held in something older, something more complex than they had imagined, it's hard to put into words.

'I don't know,' she says eventually. 'For the longest time I couldn't remember, and then when I did – when it came back in bits and pieces – it was as if I could see what happened, but I couldn't feel it, I wasn't connected to it. It was almost as if it had all happened to someone else. Until we went back to the farm.'

'And,' Hal goes on, 'do you feel – different, now?'

'Different?'

'Yeah. Since the house, since Bee. Different here.' He taps the side of his head. 'Like you can see things . . .' His voice fades.

'Like something inside has clicked into place,' says Lucy, 'and you can't reset it, no matter how much you'd like to? Different like that?'

'Oh, fuck,' says Hal. 'I hoped I was imagining things.'

'I'm sorry,' Lucy says, and she is.

'Yeah,' says Hal. 'Me too.'

433

He stubs out his cigarette and leans back, folding his arms. 'What was she like, Bee?' he asks.

'Irritating,' Lucy says, after a moment. 'Loud and restless and irritating. Selfish, too. And it was as if – as if everything she felt was too much, too bright, too big.'

'That must have been difficult, coping with that.'

'Yes.'

'And maybe that wasn't the only thing you were dealing with, either of you.'

'Maybe not,' says Lucy. 'Everyone was consumed with the mystery of our poltergeist, Tib. But for us, the biggest mystery was Joe. We didn't know where he was, or when he would come back. We only knew that it was Cathy's fault he had gone.'

'And was it?'

'Oh, I don't know. She told us he was teaching – off being an artist somewhere – but it turned out he was labouring, working on building sites, and sending back money whenever he could. Bee had overheard them, though, in the barn – there had been an argument and Cathy . . .' She hesitates. 'It sounds so stupid,' she says softly. 'I knew Bee was making stuff up, but still, I half believed her. She made me think Cathy had done something, hurt him – Joe. We were both so angry with her.'

'You were just a child,' says Hal.

Lucy looks at Blue Jacket House. Someone stands and comes to the window, a girl caught in silhouette against the warm lights of the living room. She raises a hand to the latch and opens the door.

Nina.

She calls out to Hal to come back in, and he and Lucy stand. It's time to go, to say their goodbyes.

They walk slowly across the lawn to the open windows. Lucy has tried occasionally, since she got out of the hospital, to see

434

if she can sense her still, her sister, Bee, walking a little way behind her, perhaps, waiting. She tries again now, as they reach the door and Hal steps inside; she turns and looks back across the garden, hoping to see her again, scowling, untidy, impatient.

But she's not there.

Acknowledgements

To my agent, Julia Silk, who read an early draft of this novel and gave me the most perfect piece of advice at exactly the right moment.

To Sophie Orme, who has had faith in this book, and in me, from the very beginning, and whose passion and insight have helped shape it. She and the whole team at Zaffre have been wonderful.

To Sophie Coulombeau, who encouraged me to think about the kind of writer I wanted to be; her support and example have been an inspiration.

To Rob Redman of *The Fiction Desk*, who has an admirable policy of finding and publishing new writers.

To Paul Richardson, filmmaker, who answered my many questions about cameras, and software, and filming in general with endless patience and generosity. Any mistakes or omissions are, of course, mine, not his.

To Bidi Iredale, who shared her experience of caring for a parent living with dementia, and who allowed me to steal her childhood home and do terrible things to it.

To Wendy Havelock, author of the finest text message ever sent – the one that insisted I go along to that creative writing class I was dithering about. She believed I was a writer long before I did, and I doubt any of this would have happened without her.

To my sister and brother, because only children don't really get it.

To my brilliant Mum, and to all of the above, my love and thanks.

Reading Group Questions

1. Loo and Bee's relationship is always difficult, and Loo struggles with her brothers, too. How does this novel explore sibling relationships?
2. In what ways is Lucy haunted by her past? How are different kinds of hauntings explored in this book?
3. How does *The Wayward Girls* examine memory?
4. How do you think Joe and Cathy's unusual lifestyle affects their children?
5. Why do you think Loo pushes Bee? Is it Loo, or Tib, who does it?
6. What connects Tib, Bee and Loo?
7. Whose fault are the events of that summer? Joe's, Bee's, Loo's – or someone else's entirely?
8. Who was your favourite character in the novel?
9. How would Loo and Bee's childhoods have been different if they were growing up today, not in the 1970s?
10. The 1976 strand of the book is set in a long, hot summer. How does the heat and the weather affect the story and the atmosphere?
11. In what ways do the adults in this novel fail the children around them?
12. Did you change your view on how genuine the haunting was during the course of the novel?

Hello!

Thank you for reading *The Wayward Girls*, my debut novel. Publication has been a long and frankly thrilling process, and I can't quite believe that we've got to the point where I'm sitting at my desk writing a letter for the paperback edition, trying to explain to you what it is I love about gothic fiction, ghost stories, and the uncanny, and why I wrote this novel.

I wanted to write the sort of book I would have wanted to read when I was Bee's age; specifically, I wanted to write the sort of book I wanted to be *in* when I was Bee's age, the kind of book you could lose yourself in during a long, hot, endless summer.

Adolescence is bad enough. That sense you have that you're coming into all your power, but of course as far as the outside world is concerned, you're still a kid. I wanted to explore the combination of that power – all that potential – and inertia. The feeling you can get in a long, hot summer of being trapped, being bored out of your mind, and as consequence, ripe for mischief. Going through all of that, whilst being stuck in a tiny bedroom with your sister, just seemed to me to be filled with possibilities. The enforced intimacy that engenders, the general assumption that because you're sisters, then naturally you're going to get along, the smaller more everyday power plays, but then the way siblings will instinctively close ranks against outsiders.

But since I was, like Bee, a teenager in the 70s, there was always going to be something a bit darker in the mix too, a touch of the supernatural. When I look back, I remember the 70s as an era of folk horror, urban legends, Uri Geller and spoon-bending, news reports about poltergeists, and those terrifying pubic service information films that had the Grim Reaper lurking around electricity pylons and riverbanks, ready to drag unwary children to a grim and early death.

Put down on paper in black and white, it all looks faintly terrifying, but of course it wasn't – it was fun. Especially in contrast to real life, which was safe and unremarkable, with absolutely no chance of moving objects with the power of the mind, or contacting the spirit world via a home-made Ouija board. Not that I tried. Much.

So, that was my starting point: two teenage girls and a haunting, and the aftermath of that. I didn't expect was that I'd have to fact check my own memories, though. I never thought of the 1976 section of the book as a period piece, but even so, there were so many details I assumed were true that I did indeed need to verify. Small things like the brands of popular ice-creams, makes of car, what music was in the charts, all the details and moments that seemed so vivid had to be researched. It was quite sobering to discover through the process of writing a novel that deals with the way we can be haunted by the past, that we are *all* highly unreliable narrators.

My next novel, *The Hiding Place*, will be published next year. It's set on the north-east coast, and if *The Wayward Girls* is about sisters, then this novel is about mothers and daughters. It's also about superstition, folklore and the rough magic of superstition, private rituals and hidden things. The kind of magic where – because there are no written rules or explanations – actions and objects become deeply ambiguous.

The starting point for *The Hiding Place* is the practice of placing objects in a building – usually a home – to protect it. These concealed objects are frequently, but not exclusively, shoes, and the act of hiding them seems to take power from the secrecy of the act; shoes can remain undisturbed for centuries.

What would happen, I wondered, if someone hid a shoe in a house? Why would they do that? What were they trying to keep out?

What would happen if someone found it? A chapter follows on from this letter – I hope you enjoy it.

If you would like to hear more about my books, you can visit **www.bit.ly/AmandaMason** where you can become part of my Readers' Club. It only takes a few moments to sign up, there are no catches or costs.

Bonnier Books UK will keep your data private and confidential, and it will never be passed on to a third party. I won't spam you with loads of emails, I'll just get in touch now and again with news about my books, links to the odd short story and maybe even a deleted scene or two. And of course, you can unsubscribe whenever you want.

And if you would like to get involved in a wider conversation about my books, please do review *The Wayward Girls* on Amazon, on Goodreads, on any other e-store, on your own blog and social media accounts, it really makes a huge difference to authors when readers share their thoughts, and it's such a lovely thing to read people's responses. I can be found on Twitter as **@amandajanemason** and on Instagram as **@amandajmason**.

Thank you again for picking up *The Wayward Girls*, I hope you loved reading it as much as I loved writing it.

Best wishes,
Amanda Mason

Read on for an extract from
Amanda Mason's next novel

The Hiding Place

There was no signal. Of course there wasn't; there never was here. The house was too close to the cliff, overshadowed by it. But still she gripped the phone tightly, staring at the screen, willing the little bars at the top to fill up, trying to think.

The kitchen was a mess, and she was sitting on the floor, backed up against the cupboard under the sink, her legs splayed out – not very elegant, not very ladylike – and she could smell blood.

No. That was just her stupid imagination.

Get a grip, she thought, her fingers aching as she clutched the phone in both hands. *Get a grip, get up and* – she paused, lifted her head, listened.

It was faint, too faint to be sure, but wasn't that . . . ? She strained to hear. Couldn't she hear someone upstairs, moving slowly, deliberately along the first-floor landing?

Now, she thought, her heart hammering. *Get up now.*

She'd put it back, hadn't she? She found herself wishing that alone would be enough. She could still feel it, her talisman, her little piece of luck, warm in the palm of her hand, soft and yielding. The way it seemed to – fit. That had been the hardest part, giving it up, even after everything went wrong. Even though she knew it was the right thing to do, the only thing to do; even when she'd wanted to keep it close.

She grabbed the edge of the sink, slowly pulling herself to her feet, then straightened up, trying to ignore the dull ache deep in her belly. She'd given up so much already.

Don't lose your nerve.

She shifted the phone from one hand to the other, flexed her fingers, listened. She could definitely hear footsteps. They were not so much moving across the landing as resonating deep inside the fabric of the building, inside her. The sound was comforting, in its way.

At least she wasn't alone.

The front door scraped open and – there was no mistaking it this time – someone stood hesitating on the threshold. Upstairs the footsteps stopped.

'Hello?'

It was him.

She'd made it clear he needed to keep this to himself, their arrangement. And later when they asked, she would say that she had come back to the house to retrieve her phone.

Her heart pounding, she moved silently to the corner of the room, to the fuse box.

Maybe he'll go away.

She could hear the door rattling softly on its hinges as he pushed it further back. It was dark in the hall, she knew, gloomy.

There was a shuffling as he tried to make up his mind. It wouldn't be long, a few seconds at most before he stepped inside.

She would say she had come back to the house to retrieve her phone and – and . . .

She had found him there, and no, she'd had no idea – there was no reason for him to be in the house, no reason at all.

And there had been nothing she could do.

An accident, she thought as she reached up, opening the cupboard door.

She had been too late.

'Hello?' His voice soft, uncertain.

The floorboards shifting as he stepped inside. The noise upstairs started again, bolder now, insistent.

She placed her hand on the switch, closed her eyes, and pushed.

1

Nell looked up at the gate; its slender fleurs-de-lys curves at odds with the worn sandstone buildings either side of it. It was new, wrought iron, unpainted, unfinished, the pale pewter grey standing in stark contrast with the rest of the long cobbled street and its mismatched Georgian shop fronts, the low doors and the sagging bow windows.

'Unbelievable.' She shook her head.

'What now?' said Chris.

'These yards aren't private. They've no right to block it.'

'Well, it's not blocked, is it?' said Maude. She reached past Nell and pushed; the bolt was hanging loose, and the gate opened easily enough, clattering against the enamelled sign that had been set into the wall, BISHOPS YARD. 'See?'

'It's out of place,' said Nell. 'And it's ugly.'

'Yes, well, grab a bag, would you?' Chris opened the car boot. 'Best not hang around.'

The journey had taken longer than they'd expected, a combination of motorway delays and too many stops to accommodate Maude's alleged travel sickness. Then they'd been late collecting the keys from the letting agency up on the West Cliff.

'I'll go over with you,' the woman had said, 'get you settled in,' but there'd been no mistaking the relief in her eyes when

Chris had declined her offer. The shop was empty, the sign flipped to CLOSED and Nell had the impression that the rest of the staff had left for the day.

'We'll manage,' Chris said. 'My wife's a local girl.'

'Really?'

'We've kept you waiting long enough, and I'm sure you need to get home.'

The woman picked up a folder and two sets of keys, glancing at Nell, most likely trying, and failing, to place her. 'Well, if you're sure.'

'We'll be fine,' Chris said. 'Thanks.'

But Nell had forgotten about the one-way system, or maybe it was new, and once they'd left the agency, they'd had to follow the road up onto the cliff, and down onto the seafront, before driving up the harbour to cross the little swing bridge into the east side of town. Over the river, they'd turned onto the cobbled street, slowing the car as they checked the names of the yards. Chris had parked as close as he could, up on the pavement, more or less.

'It's a gate, it doesn't have to be pretty,' said Maude, picking up her rucksack and leading the way.

'Well, thank you for your insight, sweetheart,' said Chris, 'I'll be sure to—'

Nell nudged him and shook her head.

Maude counted off the numbers on the houses as they walked up the yard. There was a narrow gutter running the length of it, not quite central, not quite straight, carving its way through the worn cobbles. 'One, two, three,' to their right, 'five, six, four,' to the left. She came to a halt at the bottom of a flight of stone steps, steeply pitched, shallow and uneven. 'That doesn't make sense.' She looked up at Nell, frowning. 'Why is it like that?'

'Oh, I don't know.' Nell considered the question; most of the houses were low sandstone cottages with neat pantile roofs; one or two had well-tended planters by their doors. Numbers five and six were no less orderly, but were built of red brick, and were set further back. All the houses were silent, their windows blank and grey, and it was impossible to tell if they were occupied or not. Nell wondered if the three of them might be the only inhabitants of the whole yard.

'I think,' she said, 'it depends how you look at it.'

Maude followed her gaze, 'Yeah?' she said.

'Do we have to do this now?' asked Chris, squeezing past, 'Can't the history lesson wait?'

Maude chose not to take her father's side, for a change. 'Those look new,' she said, 'so, the houses are numbered in the order they were built?'

'Not our place and maybe not the cottages, but yes – anything that came after them.'

Maude absorbed this. 'Right,' she said, then she pointed to the next house, which was about halfway up the steps. 'Is that us, then?'

'No.' SPINNAKER COTTAGE was engraved on a brass plate fixed to the bright blue door. 'We're right up at the top.' Nell couldn't be sure, but there seemed to be movement at one of the windows, someone watching them perhaps as they gawped at the yard like a bunch of tourists. They had shown Maude the pictures, of course, when they'd booked it, but she'd barely acknowledged them, dismissing her father's enthusiasm for the house, the town, the whole trip with a single word: *whatever.* Twelve going on twenty-one, as Chris had taken to saying.

It wasn't so easy to dismiss in real life. Elder House stood at the top of the steps, stiff, formal, imposing, looking down on the rest of the yard. It was rigidly symmetrical, solid, with stone mullioned windows and diamond shaped lead lights. The roof was slate, and there was a grey-greenish tinge to the dressed stone; it was old – but unlike its neighbours – there was something untouched about it.

Dark, Nell thought, the way the house backed up against the cliff like that, she doubted it ever got much direct sunlight, even at midday. And it didn't look like a holiday let, there was nothing quirky or inviting about it. She turned and looked down the yard. The way it veered ever so slightly to one side meant it was impossible to see the street from here; the effect was oddly isolating.

Chris paused and called down to them, 'Are you two coming, then?'

Maude rolled her eyes, 'Yes. Right. Fine.' Nell took her time following her.

The steps led up to the left side of the house, and to the narrow flagged path that ran around it. There was a sheer drop of ten or twelve feet between it and their nearest neighbour, Spinnaker Cottage, and Nell had to resist the urge to warn Maude to stay away from the edge. She was a sensible kid, as a rule.

Chris was waiting for them by the front door. He found the right key, inserted it into the lock, struggling with it as it seemed to stick, shudder, then give. The door opened into a hall, a gleaming parquet floor dominated by a wide, wooden staircase. It was silent and the air was still; the house smelt faintly of beeswax polish and lavender, and underneath that, something else, something . . . Nell couldn't place it. They stood there for a moment, the three of them, waiting.

'Are we going in, then?' Maude pushed past her father and dropped her things at the foot of the stairs.

Nell followed her, flicking on the hall light, hoping to dispel the gloom. A sharp prickle of static electricity took her unawares, and she caught her breath; Maude turned away, not quite masking a smirk.

There was a door to the left, and Nell opened it, revealing a long room that ran right through the house – the kitchen-diner. At the far end, on the counter, next to the Aga, there was a welcome pack, a cellophane-wrapped hamper filled with someone's idea of essential groceries and finished off with a shiny blue bow.

They had done a decent job of knocking through a wall; the shift from polished floorboards to worn flagstones was all that indicated there had once been two rooms where now there was one. The leaded windowpanes lent the room a slightly greenish cast.

Without thinking, Nell crossed the kitchen, squatted and lay her hand against the stone floor. It felt cool beneath her palm, and – this must have been imagination – slightly damp.

She stood up. There was a smell here too, although this was easier to place; it put her in mind of wet soil and rotting vegetables. It might have been the rag rug in front of the Aga, but it seemed new enough, the regular, clipped tongues of fabric springing up from the sacking base. Maybe they were the first visitors of the summer season, that would explain the damp, unused air of it all.

She didn't like it.

More than that: she didn't want to stay. The thought took her by surprise, and she tried to ignore it. It wasn't as if she had a choice.

It took a couple of trips to get everything out of the car, and by the time they were done, Chris's mood was beginning to sour. 'Next time,' he said, 'we choose somewhere with parking.'

'You were the one who wanted to stay in a yard,' said Nell.

'You're the one with the big old family party to go to.'

It wasn't really her fault, of course, the house, the trip. Nell had glanced at the invitation when it had come, more than a month ago, then put it to one side, intending to send a polite refusal, but never quite getting around to it.

Chris had picked it up from her desk one day, when they'd been discussing Maude, and the long summer that was suddenly stretching out in front of them. 'There's always this,' he said, opening the card before handing it to her.

There was an email address and a phone number printed inside, with the time and the date underneath the announcement: *David and Jennifer Galilee, Silver Wedding Anniversary.* There was a handwritten message too, although the writing was unfamiliar.

It would be great to see you, if you could find the time.
   Love, Jenny and Dave x

'We won't know anyone.'

Chris raised a sceptical eyebrow.

'You know what I mean,' Nell said. 'You won't know anyone. And I'll – it'll be awkward.' She couldn't remember the last time she'd spoken to her cousin, her dad's funeral, probably.

'It's up to you,' Chris said, 'but you never know, it could be fun. It might be nice to get away for a bit. Get Maude away from – everything.'

'It's a long way to go, just for one party.'

'Then we make it worth the effort. Stay on for a bit, show her the sights.'

'There are no sights.' She stood the card on her desk. The photo on the front showed a yacht sailing out of the harbour on a clear summer's day. 'Do you think she'd like it?'

'I don't see why not. It's the seaside, isn't it? Everyone likes the seaside.'

They hadn't been back since Maude was small, six or seven years ago, when an ice cream had been a treat, paddling in the sea an adventure. Before the arguments and the sulking, before everything had become so complicated and Maude's easy affection had been replaced by something more guarded, more unpredictable. The rush of nostalgia took Nell by surprise. 'Go on then,' she said, before she could change her mind, 'but don't blame me if she gets bored.'

She had pretty much left everything up to him after that. 'I don't mind where we stay,' she'd said, 'as long as we're together.'

She hadn't imagined he'd settle on somewhere so big, so uncompromising.

'Can I choose my room?' Maude was already halfway up the stairs.

'Sure,' said Chris. 'Go and have a look around. Don't mind me. I'll be having my heart attack in the kitchen, out of the way.'

Maude didn't look back.

Nell leant back against the banister. 'Well,' she said, 'here we are.'

'Hmm.' Chris pulled her into a gentle hug, resting his chin on her head as he looked around the hall, taking it all in.

'This is all very – showy,' Nell said. 'Very posh.'

'But . . .'

'There's a weird' – she hesitated – 'smell. Don't you think?'

'A smell?' He held her at arm's length. 'Seriously?'

'Well, yes. Haven't you noticed it?'

'No.'

'It's not so bad here, but in the kitchen it . . .' She didn't much like the way he was looking at her, as if he found her amusing, and ever so slightly foolish. 'Forget it,' she said. 'It's just . . . it's not very us, is it?'

'Isn't it?'

Chris had shown her the posting on the website, and she remembered flicking through images of a fitted kitchen with an electric Aga, cosy sofas and a log burning stove in the living room, exposed beams and leaded windows. She hadn't really taken it in. Her mind had been on other things.

She tried again. 'It feels . . .'

'What?' That same expression. Amused. Superior.

Wrong. It felt wrong.

'I like it,' said Chris. 'It's solid. Classy. There's a bit on the website about its history, former occupants and all that. You should—'

'Dad! Da-ad!' Maude's voice echoed down the stairs.

'What?'

'Come and see.'

'No.'

'You said I could choose.'

'But not this, obviously.'

'Why not?'

It was pretty impressive, Nell had to admit. The master bedroom: oak panelled, with an open fireplace, and dominated by a big brass bedstead. The ceiling was a little low perhaps, and its exposed beams seemed to dip slightly, but the room had an air of understated, if impersonal, comfort. There was a pitcher and ewer perched on a table underneath one set of windows, and a chest of drawers beneath the other. There was no wardrobe, but there were cupboards built into the wall either side of the tiled chimney breast, their tiny brass latches fitting flush against the painted wood.

Maude didn't mean it, of course – Nell could see that, she had no more intention of claiming this room than she did of letting either of them forget she was here on sufferance; the brief truce her interest in the yard had signalled was clearly over.

She fixed Nell with an accusing stare. 'He said.'

'You know perfectly well what your father meant.' Nell walked to one of the windows. Below them, to the left, the door to Spinnaker Cottage opened and a woman came out. She was blonde, wearing jeans and a waterproof jacket. As she walked down the yard, her scarf, a monochrome geometric design, fluttered in the breeze.

'Any other room,' Chris said, 'but not this one.'

'It's not fair.'

'We need the double bed,' said Chris, certain, surely, of the reaction this would provoke.

'God,' said Maude, after a horrified pause. 'You two are gross.' She turned and strode out of the room.

'What?' asked Chris, meeting Nell's gaze. 'What have I done now?'

'Nothing,' said Nell, turning her attention back to the window, 'but you can tell she's just spoiling for a fight, can't you?'

'Well, what am I supposed to do when she's being such a – brat?'

Just take a breath, Nell thought, just listen to her. 'Oh,' she said, the blonde woman had reappeared and was walking up the steps, a determined expression on her face as she headed straight for Elder House. 'I think we have a visitor.'

She could hear them, talking by the door downstairs. She'd sent Chris to deal with the woman, and now she sat on the bed, listening to the rise and fall of their voices, running her hand over the soft blue and white quilt. Her limbs were heavy, she was tempted to kick off her shoes and lie down, curl up and close her eyes, to leave the house to Chris and Maude as she slept.

Maybe it wouldn't be so bad, once they settled in.

The woman's voice was rapid and determined, Chris's responses, deeper, more considered, and gradually his voice came to dominate the exchange. After a while they said their good-byes and Nell heard the door close.

She stood up and went to the window again, just in time to catch a final glimpse of the woman walking down the yard, upright, brisk.

'Nell!' Chris called up the stairs. 'I just need to move the car.'

'OK.'

She heard him go into the kitchen, then emerge again. As he left the house, he slammed the front door behind him.

The floorboards on the landing shifted and sighed.

'Maude?'

But there was no answer, evidently she was yet to be forgiven. She thought again about the online posting for the house. There had been no reviews, she remembered. No user comments. The owners must be new to the holiday-let business. Maybe that was why the place felt so . . .

Expectant.

Maude passed along the landing again; her footfalls muted by the carpet but still managing somehow to signal her discontent. Maybe she should have a word.

She had assumed that Maude would take the back bedroom, but when she opened the door, it was empty. 'Maude? Hello?' She waited for an answer, as if Maude might be hiding some-where. It was only when she went back onto the landing that she noticed the steps, the wooden ladder that seemed to be fixed permanently in place, leading up to a hatch-door and the attic.

'I thought I'd lost you,' Nell said, climbing the last few rungs.

'I'm exploring,' Maude said, 'I mean, if that's all right.' She'd retrieved her bags from the hall and was bent over her rucksack, fiddling with the straps. Nell wasn't sure, but she thought she might have been crying.

'Of course it's all right.' Nell straightened up cautiously and looked around. Sleeps ten, the online ad had said, which had struck her as optimistic, even given the size of the place, but she had forgotten the attic. The beds here were no more than bunks, really, thin mattresses on wooden frames, two set at each side of the room, underneath the sharply pitched eaves, and separated by a narrow red rug. On the far wall, an old brick chimney snaked up to the ceiling, clinging to the whitewash. 'Do you like it?' she asked, keeping her tone carefully neutral. 'Up here, I mean?'

Maude abandoned the bag on the rug and turned to look at Nell, stepping back a little, out of reach. 'It's OK.' She looked hot and grubby, her hair coming loose from its ponytail; a little rounder in the face these days, a little taller too.

'There's a bedroom downstairs, next to the living room, you know.'

'That's for kids.'

'Or the one next to the bathroom. That's practically en-suite, if you think about it.'

'I like it up here.'

'It isn't too – gloomy?' The air was stale, still. She would be much better off downstairs, surely, closer to Nell and her father.

Maude didn't bother to answer, she went to one of the dormer windows, and after struggling with the catch for a moment, opened it as far as she could. 'I can see the roof,' she said, stretching up on tip-toe.

'Can you?' Nell stood behind her. Here, on this side, the back of the house, there was no view to speak of, just the dull grey slates and the looming cliff. Nell lay her hand on Maude's shoulder and squeezed reassuringly. 'Well. You don't have to decide right now, if you don't want to.'

Maude didn't answer. She turned and wriggled free, working her way around the room, opening the rest of the windows one by one, before facing Nell once again. 'It's OK,' she said, 'This will do.'

There was another pause. 'Are you—?' Nell began, but downstairs, the front door opened and closed, and distantly she could hear Chris calling out. Maude picked up her suitcase and set it on one of the beds, unzipping it. 'Go on,' she said, without looking up.

'Right,' said Nell, 'don't forget to ring your mum, once you're sorted.'

Maude pulled a book from the suitcase and set it carefully to one side. 'I won't,' she said.

Behind her, one of the windows shuddered, rattling in its frame as a breeze caught it; the room seemed to shift, to expand and settle again.